Bello
hidden talent rediscovered

Bello is a digital-only imprint of Pan Macmillan,
established to breathe new life into previously published,
classic books.

At Bello we believe in the timeless power of the imagination,
of a good story, narrative and entertainment, and we want to
use digital technology to ensure that many more readers
can enjoy these books into the future.

We publish in ebook and print-on-demand formats
to bring these wonderful books to new audiences.

www.panmacmillan.com/imprint-publishers/bello

Richmal Crompton

Richmal Crompton (1890–1969) is best known for her thirty-eight books featuring William Brown, which were published between 1922 and 1970. Born in Lancashire, Crompton won a scholarship to Royal Holloway in London, where she trained as a schoolteacher, graduating in 1914, before turning to writing full-time. Alongside the William novels, Crompton wrote forty-one novels for adults, as well as nine collections of short stories.

Richmal Crompton

QUARTET

First published in 1935 by Macmillan & Co.

This edition published 2017 by Bello
an imprint of Pan Macmillan
20 New Wharf Road, London N1 9RR
Associated companies throughout the world

www.panmacmillan.com/imprint-publishers/bello

ISBN 978-1-5098-5949-8 EPUB
ISBN 978-1-5098-5947-4 HB
ISBN 978-1-5098-5948-1 PB

Typeset by Ellipsis Digital Limited, Glasgow

Visit **www.panmacmillan.com** to read more about all our books
and to buy them. You will also find features, author interviews and
news of any author events, and you can sign up for e-newsletters
so that you're always first to hear about our new releases.

Contents

PART I

1900

Chapter One

They were having tea at the dining-room table. Lorna and Jenifer wore clean starched pinafores over their gingham frocks, Laurence a holland smock that covered his blouse and most of his short serge knickers, and Adrian a white sailor suit complete with cord, whistle, and long, bell-bottom trousers. Adrian was nine and emancipated from pinafores and smocks. Jenifer, who was only six and the youngest, wore a feeder as well as a pinafore. It was a very old feeder, with the word "BABY" embroidered in washed-out colours across the hem. Jenifer disliked it, and when she wore it pulled it down as far as she could so that "BABY" was hidden by the edge of the table.

She had pulled it down as soon as she took her seat, and now she wasn't thinking about it, but was surrendering herself to the enjoyment of having tea at Grandma's. She always loved coming to Grandma's. She loved the spacious, high-ceilinged rooms, with their polished floors and pieces of old furniture standing by themselves so that you could see how beautiful they were, not all crowded together as most people's furniture was.

Once Jenifer had heard Mother say that the rooms looked "bare," but Grandma had laughed and replied, "My dear, you know I've always hated crowds."

It was Grandma's birthday today, and they had each taken sixpence out of their money boxes and gone into Leaveston this morning to buy her a present. They had visited shop after shop and stayed in each so long without being able to make up their minds that Miss Marchant had lost patience.

"Now this is to be the *last*," she said, jerking Jenifer sharply by the arm.

Miss Marchant never became openly angry. Her irritation found outlet instead in little tweaks and pulls and pushes. When the children annoyed her she would punish them indirectly by dragging the comb mercilessly through the tangles when she did their hair, or letting the soap get into their eyes when she washed their faces, or snapping the elastic beneath their chins when she put on their hats. She would also often vent her irritation with the elder ones upon the younger ones, as being less likely to resist or retaliate. She always left Adrian alone, because Adrian, though he was nine years old, had a disconcerting way of bursting into tears when his feelings were hurt. Lorna was Miss Marchant's favourite, not only because of her flower-like prettiness, but because she alone of the four children seemed to have some real affection for the mother's help. Laurence and Jenifer, therefore, came in for more than their fair share of the tweaks and pulls and pushes, which they bore with philosophical indifference. They felt glad, however, that they always came to Grandma's on Miss Marchant's free afternoon. It would have spoilt Grandma's, somehow, if Miss Marchant had been there . . .

Grandma had been very much pleased with the present they had finally bought for her—a china jug that the man let them have for one and six instead of three shillings, because it had a little crack in it.

Jenifer hadn't wanted to buy it.

"Oh no, Lorna," she had protested, "not that. Not for *Grandma*."

"But why ever not?" Lorna had said rather crossly. "It's just an ornament. The crack won't matter at all."

And Jenifer somehow couldn't explain why it seemed terrible to give Grandma—Grandma who was so perfect—a jug that had a crack in it, even a very tiny crack.

"Darlings, how sweet of you!" Grandma had said. "We'll have the milk in it for tea today."

And then Lorna, with that air of sweet dignity that made her appear so much older than her ten years, had explained that the jug had a tiny, tiny crack in it.

"You see," she said, "it's a so much better one than we could have afforded if it *hadn't* had the tiny crack, and we thought if you'd just use it as an ornament——"

"Of course, darling," said Grandma, and she laughed as she kissed them—the gay happy laugh that was so like Mother's.

She sat now at the head of the table, straight and slender, and looking like a queen, thought Jenifer, with her white hair and blue eyes and soft pink cheeks and faint secret smile. You never saw Grandma cross or upset or unhappy. She was always kind, always interested in you, and yet part of her seemed to be far away where you couldn't reach it however hard you tried. Everything about her was lovely, even her name, Caroline Silver. Jenifer often used to say it aloud to herself because it sounded like music.

Aunt Lena sat at the other end of the table. She was tall and thin and angular, with faded hair that was taken straight back from her forehead and done in a tight bun behind her head. She always wore white shirt blouses with stiff linen collars, navy-blue serge skirts, and a leather belt into which her watch, at the end of its long gold chain, was neatly tucked away. Her pince-nez, too, had a gold chain, but a very thin one, that attached them to a little pin on her blouse.

Aunt Lena was always very busy "seeing to" something or other. She kept house for Grandma, and had a District, for which she made soups and jellies and shapeless underclothes of coarse grey calico.

"Sit up straight, my dear," she was saying to Jenifer.

Jenifer sat up straight, pulling the feeder down so that "BABY" still didn't show.

"And your mouth is too full, Laurence dear," went on Aunt Lena.

Aunt Lena always kept up a stream of little admonitions and reproofs. Even when she read to them, she kept stopping to say, "Don't fidget, Adrian," or "Don't loll like that, Lorna," or "Are you listening, Jenifer dear?"

Jenifer noticed that Aunt Lena and Grandma never seemed to have much to say to each other, though Grandma and Mother always talked and laughed a lot when they were together.

Aunt Lena had given Grandma a beautiful cushion for her birthday present. It was blue satin with red poppies embroidered all over it. She had made it herself, sitting up late at night to work at it so that it should be a surprise for Grandma. "It's beautifully done," Mother had said, when Grandma showed it to her, and Aunt Lena had flushed slightly and jerked her head back as if she were annoyed.

"Why didn't you have candles on your cake, Grandma?" said Lorna, looking at the iced cake in the middle of the table.

"Darling," smiled Grandma, "it would take us all the rest of the year to get through the cake if I had candles."

"When do people stop having candles?" said Laurence.

"It's nearly time I stopped," said Adrian in the high-pitched voice that he used when he was excited (it took very little to excite Adrian. He'd been excited all day just because it was Grandma's birthday). "I shall be ten next year and——"

He broke off. The sweeping gesture he had made with his hand had upset his mug of milk. It spread slowly and relentlessly over the embroidered table-cloth.

"Oh, Adrian!" said Aunt Lena.

There was an unusual note of sharpness in her voice because it was the best cloth, which she always washed and ironed herself, and she'd hesitated about putting it on today with the children coming.

"How careless of you!" she went on, the note of sharpness accentuated as she saw that the milk was making its way through the lace insertion on to the bare mahogany.

Adrian stared in speechless horror at the destruction he had wrought. He'd spoilt Grandma's beautiful tea-cloth. Everyone in the world hated him. No one would ever forget it or forgive him as long as he lived. He couldn't bear to go on living . . . The big dark eyes in the pale oval face seemed to grow bigger, darker . . . the wistful mouth began to quiver. Immediately the spell of dismay that held the table was broken. Adrian was going to cry. He must be stopped at all costs. At once. Before he began. It was too late once he had begun.

Aunt Lena hastily put out a hand and patted his shoulder. She remembered that his crying fits often ended in his being actually sick, and really that, on top of the milk, would be too much.

"It's all right, Adrian," she said, trying hard to sound as if she didn't mind about the cloth. "We know it was only an accident."

Lorna slipped from her chair and went to Adrian, putting her arms round his neck. "It's all right, Adrian darling. Aunt Lena says it's all right. You didn't mean to . . ."

Jenifer watched them dispassionately, her mouth full of bread and honey above the degrading feeder. Adrian never got into trouble. It didn't matter what he did, he'd only to look like that, and everyone began to fuss round him and try to stop him crying. Of course, it was terrible when he *did* cry. Jenifer knew that he couldn't help it, that even the tragic gaze and quivering lip, which gave people a last chance of averting the catastrophe of his tears, was quite genuine. Still, it seemed to give him an unfair advantage over the others. Jenifer herself had tried the same tactics, but without success.

"We'll all help Aunt Lena clean it up," Lorna was saying, smiling at Adrian and stroking his dark curls.

He looked at her with tear-brimmed eyes, gulping. The crisis was over. He wasn't going to cry . . . Jenifer's clear hazel eyes were fixed on Lorna. Lorna was always nicer to Adrian than she was to the other two. Adrian admired her and did what she wanted, and Lorna was proud of her influence over him.

Watching her now as she stood smiling down at him, Jenifer thought: She's thinking about herself really, not Adrian. She's thinking how sweet she's being to him. She's showing off to herself.

Jenifer's eyes turned to Laurence. Laurence was wholly unmoved by the little scene, had indeed barely noticed it. Someone had upset a mug of milk, but then someone was always upsetting mugs of milk. Laurence sat, as usual, lost in his day-dreams. There was nothing poetic or fanciful in Laurence's day-dreams. He was generally thinking about insects. He loved small things like insects and birds and even mice. He kept collections of insects in wooden boxes with glass tops, and spent hours watching them. He would sit in the garden motionless for whole afternoons, watching a spider spin its web or a colony of ants at work. He was a solid silent child, and Miss Marchant often said that she was afraid he was going to turn out stupid. Though there was no hostility between the two couples, he was Jenifer's ally as Adrian was Lorna's.

"It'll be all right if you put it in water straight away," Mother was saying.

"Of course I'll do that," said Aunt Lena.

She spoke rather stiffly. Really, Marcia needn't talk as if she were an authority on household matters, when everyone knew that she left simply everything at home to that poor Miss Marchant, and that she, Lena, supervised the smallest detail of her household most conscientiously.

"I suppose it ought to come off," said Grandma. "The children can take their pieces of birthday cake into the garden."

"I'm *terribly* sorry," said Adrian again.

The nightmare feeling of desperation and misery was, however, leaving him. It was a dreadful thing to have done, of course, but he no longer felt that he couldn't bear to go on living. He quite definitely could bear to go on living. He could even enjoy a piece of Grandma's birthday cake in the garden.

Grandma cut the cake, and the children each took a slice out into the garden, where they sat down to eat it under the copper beech at the end of the lawn. Then Lorna went to old Croft, the gardener, who was digging in the vegetable garden. Adrian followed her, and Laurence, lying on his stomach, began to watch the little red spiders that ran in and out of the moss. Jenifer remained seated tailor-fashion beneath the copper beech. Now that her feeder had been taken off, the starched frills of her pinafore tickled her neck. She kept putting up a hand to smooth them down, but they always stood up and began to tickle her neck again. She wished that she had brought one of her dolls with her. Lorna said that it was babyish to play with dolls, but Jenifer loved her battered family of six with an unchildlike brooding tenderness. The more battered and featureless they were, the more she loved them. If she had had them with her now she could have made up stories for them. It never seemed worth while making up stories just for oneself. Laurence didn't care for stories except about insects. "Is it about an insect?" he would say when she offered to tell him a story, and she didn't like making up stories about insects. She would rather make up stories about fairies, but, of course, Laurence didn't believe in fairies. "If ever I *saw* one I'd believe in them," he said with an air of great reasonableness. Even when Jenifer tried to make up a story about insects for him, he was always interrupting and saying, "But it *couldn't* have done that, Jenifer. They don't." And when Jenifer explained that it was a magic insect he lost all interest in it.

She thought with a warm happy feeling of her six children waiting for her at home. She would put them to bed and go on with the story of the magic windmill that she had begun to tell them last night. She hoped that when she was grown up she would have heaps and heaps and heaps of children . . .

She could see Lorna talking to the gardener, the sun shining on her golden ringlets. The gardener was smiling down at her. Lorna was his favourite, as indeed she was most people's favourite. She laughed suddenly—a clear rippling little laugh that jarred vaguely on Jenifer, because she knew that Lorna was trying to make it sound like Mother's. Lorna's own laugh was quite different, but lately she had been doing the new laugh whenever she remembered.

Peter, Aunt Lena's cat, walked slowly across the lawn. Jenifer called "Peter," but he took no notice. He was rather a disagreeable cat and scratched you when you tried to play with him. He didn't even like being stroked. He used to spend hours sitting on the morning-room hearthrug and gazing up at Aunt Lena's canary that hung in a cage in the window. Aunt Lena said that they loved each other, but she never let the canary out when Peter was there. She said that Peter might be rough with it without meaning to hurt it.

Suddenly Jenifer remembered the red and white ivory chessmen, which stood in the cabinet in the drawing-room. Perhaps, as it was her birthday, Grandma would let her take them out and play with them. And there was the beautiful new cushion. She did want to look at the beautiful new cushion again . . .

She went into the drawing-room, where Grandma and Mother and Aunt Lena were sitting in the big bay window recess, talking.

"May I have the chessmen out, please, Grandma?" she said, standing in the doorway and smoothing down her pinafore frill, which was tickling her neck again.

"Yes, my dear," said Grandma, smiling at her.

Anyone but Grandma would have added "Be very careful with them," but Grandma knew that, when you loved anything as much as Jenifer loved the little chessmen, of course you'd be very careful with them . . .

She sat down by the china cabinet and took out the figures—white and red, exquisitely carved—arranging them in a little procession on the polished floor. Mother, Grandma, and Aunt Lena went on talking in the window recess in lowered voices that she couldn't hear . . .

"And how's Flossie?" the old lady was saying.

Lena stiffened. She always disliked the way in which Mother and Marcia spoke of Miss Marchant, referring to her as Flossie behind her back (her name was Flora) and sneering at her plainness and general unattractiveness. It wasn't kind or Christian, especially when you considered what a good woman Miss Marchant was, going regularly to church on her free Sunday evening (when she happened to get it, that is, because Marcia was simply conscienceless about asking her to give it up), and working so hard in the house and looking after the children so well.

"Oh, she's as dreadfully worthy as ever," laughed Marcia. "I wish I could afford to do without her, but I can't. I could never manage with only one maid if it weren't for her. She's nurse and governess and cook and lady's-maid and heaven knows what else. I can't think why she stays."

"She's in love with Frank, my dear," said the old lady, calmly.

Marcia laughed again, and Lena's pale cheeks flushed. Really, it was dreadful the things Mother said. And for Marcia just to laugh as if it were funny! Whereas, if it were true, it was wicked, and, if it weren't true, it was a very unkind thing to say. In any case, it wasn't a subject to joke about.

"Do you think so?" Marcia was saying. "I'd flattered myself it was partly my *beaux yeux*. She seems quite devoted to me."

"No doubt she thinks she is. She's probably completely unaware that she's in love with Frank. She has to be. If she weren't, her conscience would make her leave the scene of her temptation. Her only way of cheating her conscience is not to know anything about it."

Lena interrupted in her clear precise voice. She really must put a stop to this dreadful conversation. Anyone as old and as, presumably, near the grave as Mother ought to be thinking and talking about very different things.

"Mr Markson was telling me today," she said, "that there were more people at Matins last Sunday than there'd been for the last four months."

"Who's Mr Markson, dear?" said her mother.

"He's the curate at St. Matthew's," said Lena shortly, because, of course, Mother knew perfectly well who Mr Markson was.

"That's very interesting," said the old lady, and the faint note of irony in her voice made Lena compress her thin lips. Mother was always worse when Marcia was there. They seemed to combine to try to make her seem priggish and uninteresting and—oh, all the things she really wasn't. Their conversation consisted chiefly of gossip, and Aunt Letty had always taught Lena that a gentlewoman never gossips. A gentlewoman, Aunt Letty had said, should talk about subjects of general interest. Mother and Marcia never seemed to be interested in subjects of general interest. It was of general interest that there had been more people at Matins at St. Matthew's last Sunday than there had been for the last four months. It was of far more general interest, anyway, than making horrible insinuations against Miss Marchant's moral character . . .

To Jenifer the grown-up conversation was only a vague murmur in the distance. She had arranged the chessmen in a procession and had even taken down the four little ivory elephants from the other shelf, because if Grandma didn't mind about the chessmen she surely wouldn't mind about the elephants. Two elephants led the procession and the other two brought up the rear. The polished floor was the desert, and they were marching across it, keeping a look-out on all sides for wild beasts and enemies. One chair leg was a date tree, and another a well of water. The elephants would put their trunks in and drink deeply. Then, after weeks and weeks of marching, they'd reach the carpet, and that was the sea; then they'd have to get into a ship and sail away till they reached the hearthrug, and that was a terrible storm and— She went rigid as a sharp pang shot through her gum. And another. And another. Then a dull ache that grew sharper . . . sharper . . . Toothache. She'd try not to think about it. She'd—she clapped her hand to her cheek and crouched down, a small silent huddle of agony. A little moan escaped her.

"Oh, darling," said Mother. "Is it toothache?"

Jenifer nodded. All the forces of her being were absorbed in wrestling with the pain. There were none left for speech.

"Oh, dear!" said Mother. "She had it last night. Miss Marchant put witch hazel on it, but it hasn't really cured it."

"Of course it wouldn't," said Grandma.

Jenifer rocked to and fro on the floor, making involuntary little bleats of pain. Aunt Lena swept across the room to her and gathered her tenderly into her arms.

"Poor little thing . . . There! There!"

Panic invaded Jenifer. She hated a fuss more than anything else in the world. She pushed away Aunt Lena's arms.

"It's all right, it's all *right*," she said breathlessly. "Don't talk about it."

"But, darling, I'm so *sorry* about the naughty pain. Naughty, naughty pain."

"It's all *right*," said Jenifer again. "Leave me alone."

She knew that it was rude to speak like that to Aunt Lena, but it was so hard to be polite when you had toothache.

"Leave her alone, Lena," said Mother. "It'll probably go. It was the birthday cake."

Lena returned to her seat, feeling hurt and annoyed. What an odd child Jenifer was! Any normal child would have clung to her, grateful for her sympathy, not pushed her away like that.

Jenifer still crouched on the floor, flushed and dishevelled, her small face distorted, her eyes darting round the room as if seeking escape from her misery. Suddenly she saw the blue satin cushion embroidered with poppies. The smoothness and brightness of it seemed fraught with mysterious comfort.

"Please may I put my face on it, Grandma?" she said in a high unsteady voice. The nerve gave another sharp stab as she spoke.

"Of course, my pet," said Grandma.

Jenifer went to it and laid her face against it. Its coolness was grateful to her flushed cheek. The softness and bright colour seemed to ease the pain at once, as she had known they would.

"That better?" said Grandma.

She nodded.

Lena's lips were compressed. Really, Mother needn't have let the child put her sticky little face (she hadn't washed it since tea, and it was sure to be covered with honey, not to speak of birthday-cake icing) on the cushion that she'd taken weeks and *weeks* embroidering for her birthday. It was the cushion that had made Lena feel hurt and aggrieved all day. She'd taken endless trouble over it, sitting up to embroider it sometimes right into the early morning, and Mother hadn't been half so pleased about it as Lena had expected her to be. She had thanked her and said what a lot of trouble she must have taken over it, but she had never once said that it was pretty, or that she liked it. And it was *beautiful*—much nicer than any other cushion in the drawing-room. And when she'd shown it to Marcia there had been a certain reserve in Marcia's manner, too.

"What a lot of work," Marcia had said. "Lena, darling, it's beautifully done."

And she had examined the cushion very hard and for a long time, as if she didn't want to meet either Lena's eye or Mother's.

And now, though she'd only had it for a few hours, Mother was risking its being *ruined*—the work of months—by Jenifer's hot sticky little face.

"How is it, darling?" said Marcia.

"It's not quite as worse as it was," came Jenifer's muffled voice from the cushion.

(Her mouth's *right* on the biggest poppy of all, thought Lena aggrievedly, the one that took a whole fortnight.)

Lorna entered and stood in the doorway.

"Poor little Jenifer's got toothache again," said Marcia.

Jenifer raised her head, and Lena took advantage of the movement to rescue the cushion, examine it with ostentatious anxiety, and place it out of reach.

Jenifer got up and stood at bay, her hand to her flushed cheek, her eyes bright and hard with pain, her breath coming in quick little sobbing gasps.

"I'd better take her to the dentist now," said Marcia, rising. "She can't go on like this. Come along, darling."

"I'll order the carriage," said Grandma. "You'll be there quite soon . . ."

Jenifer's eyes wandered again to the brightly coloured square that seemed endowed with such mysterious comfort.

"Grandma, may I take it in the carriage? Just to put my face on it. I'll be very careful."

Before Grandma could say anything, Lena interposed, speaking quickly and sharply.

"No, darling, of *course* you can't have the cushion. Aunt Lena's taken a lot of time and trouble making it for Grandma's birthday, and Grandma likes it very much and doesn't want it spoilt the first day."

"I like it very much, too. I won't spoil it."

"You won't mean to, darling, but of *course* it will spoil it to put your face on it."

"It makes my toothache better."

"Nonsense, darling. That's just imagination. Anyway, you mustn't

14

have Grandma's beautiful new cushion, so don't worry her any more."

Lena tried not to see the glance that Mother and Marcia exchanged, a quick amused glance of complete understanding. She went upstairs to her bedroom and brought down one of her bedroom cushions—a cushion of pink sateen piped with red. Jenifer was sitting upright in the carriage. Her small face was tense. Her lips were set in a rigid line.

"Here you are, darling," said Lena. "You can have this cushion as a *great* treat. It's a very beautiful one."

Jenifer looked at it.

"I don't like it. I don't want it, thank you."

"Very well," said Lena, trying to keep the irritation out of her voice. (Really, the *contrariness* of children!)

Marcia bundled the other children into the carriage, then took her seat next to Jenifer.

"Thank you so much for letting us have the carriage, Mother," she said. She drew Jenifer's face against the cool silk of her dress. "Try that, sweet." Jenifer's face rested there. It was comforting, but not so comforting as the cushion had been. The nerve still stabbed—just a second's rest in which she hoped that it had stopped altogether, then another sharp stab. She gave a little quivering sigh that was half a whimper and compressed her lips firmly. The carriage started off down the drive.

Lena turned from the front door.

"Well, I'll go and change, Mother," she said.

She spoke distantly. She was still feeling aggrieved about the cushion.

Chapter Two

It was too early to change, so Lena began to tidy the drawers in her bedroom. When she was feeling hurt or annoyed she always tidied the drawers in her bedroom, taking the things out and putting them back in neat little piles. Even when they were in neat little piles to start with, she still took them out and put them back again. The process, for some obscure reason, never failed to soothe and console her. She arranged the little piles today with quick, jerky, exasperated movements. It wasn't only the cushion. It was—everything. Ever since Mother came to settle in England she'd devoted her whole life to her, sacrificing her time and energy without stint or complaint, and Mother didn't even pretend to appreciate it. She hurt her constantly by ignoring her advice and preferring the company of Marcia, who was selfish and frivolous and had never sacrificed anything for anybody in all her life. One wouldn't mind being unselfish if only the people one was unselfish for appreciated it. She wished vaguely that Mother were more like the sort of old lady one had in mind when one thought of an old lady in general terms—a little deaf, a little blind, and more than a little helpless. Mother simply refused to be helpless. She would never take Lena's arm, she would never even wear a shawl or be read aloud to in the evenings. Lena's thoughts went back to the time when she had first come to live with Mother and Marcia. She had been full of such high hopes and intentions. Now—well, she didn't actually disapprove of Mother, because that would be wrong, but she couldn't help being glad that she had been brought up by Aunt Letty.

She had been only three years old when Father got his

appointment in India, and Mother went out there, leaving her with Aunt Letty, so, of course, she didn't remember them at all as they were then. Marcia was born when they had been in India for five years, and then they moved to Spain. At first they had wanted Lena to join them there, but Aunt Letty was so reluctant to give her up that gradually the matter was dropped. Dear Aunt Letty! Though Lena tried not to compare her with Mother she could never be grateful enough for the careful training that Aunt Letty had given her. When Father died Marcia was at a finishing school in Paris, and Mother took an apartment near the Champs-Élysées, but by that time Lena was looked upon as belonging entirely to Aunt Letty, and Mother made no further move to claim her. Then Marcia left her finishing school, and she and Mother travelled about Europe, staying in Vienna and Budapest and Paris and London and Berlin. And all the time Lena lived with Aunt Letty in her dear little cottage in a picturesque Cotswold village. It had been a quiet happy life—walks with Aunt Letty, lessons with Aunt Letty, long earnest talks with Aunt Letty . . . Aunt Letty reading *Victories of the Saints* or *Mrs Gatty's Parables from Nature* to her on Sunday evenings, teaching her needlework, taking her to visit the Poor. Then Aunt Letty died, and Mother and Marcia came to live in England, and Lena joined them. From the beginning she had disapproved of Marcia, and from the beginning there had been an odd secret bitterness at the heart of her disapproval. For Marcia was Fast. Lena, acting on Aunt Letty's constant exhortation to Believe the Best of everyone (Aunt Letty had always sprinkled her letters with capitals, and so Lena had got into the way of sprinkling her thoughts with them), had tried for a long time not to think that Marcia was Fast, but really there wasn't any other word for it. Even when she thought of her as Flighty, because it sounded kinder, it came to the same thing.

And Aunt Letty had brought Lena up so carefully. Lena always remembered how, when she was about ten years old, she went to tea to a neighbour's house where there was a large family of boys, and how she had romped with them in the orchard, playing Catch and Hide-and-Seek and Blind-Man's-Buff, and how Aunt Letty, coming to fetch her, had been shocked and had talked to her that evening very seriously and told her that it was fast to run about with boys like that, and how ever afterwards she had avoided boys, feeling self-conscious and embarrassed whenever she met one, and thinking of them with a secret shame that she did not understand. Then, later, when she was about seventeen, a young man, staying at a friend's house, had asked her to go for a walk with him, and she had been pleased and excited, for she liked the young man and felt a strange fluttering of the pulses whenever she thought of him, but Aunt Letty again had talked to her very seriously and told her that she had Better Not. A girl, said Aunt Letty, could not possibly be Too Careful. She was so easily Compromised, and the slightest Breath of Scandal was Ruin to her Reputation. Her Good Name should be her most Precious Possession, and she should never go a Step out of her Way for any man. She should certainly never, in any circumstances, Go for a Country Walk with him Alone. Again that vague panic had invaded Lena's gentle soul. The whole subject seemed to be fraught with horror and mystery. Aunt Letty's attitude implied that women walked blindfold on a tightrope above a sort of quagmire, and the quagmire was Men. One's only possible safety lay in having nothing whatever to do with them, and that was the plan that Lena thereafter adopted.

Yet deep down in her heart she always longed for some vaguely, impossibly perfect lover who should take her by storm, breaking down her defences and overcoming her reluctance. But he never came, and such men as were attracted at first by her girlish prettiness were subsequently repelled by the ungraciousness that masked her frightened shrinking from them.

For sex, in Lena's mind, was like some foul, veiled figure, at which her panic-stricken little soul dared not even glance.

And today, though she was over forty, she was still almost as ignorant as the little girl of ten who had promised with bitter remorse never to be "fast" again, still so much ashamed of every suggestion of sex that it gave her a feeling of revulsion to enter the bedroom that Marcia shared with her husband, and that the sight of a pair of his trousers flung untidily across the bed sent the blood flaming into her thin cheeks.

She took out her box of hairpins and straightened the pins so that they lay in ordered rows, then picked out one or two from which the bronze colour had worn away, leaving the bare metal, and put them carefully into the waste-paper basket.

Her mind went back over the years she had spent here with Mother, and again that feeling of resentment swept over her. She worked so hard, she gave up every minute of her time, and she got nothing—not even love—in return. She sat motionless, holding a neat little pile of fringe nets, staring dreamily in front of her. A desire for escape surged over her. She was in prison, and she wanted to get out. Strange uncomprehended powers and longings stirred within her. She imagined herself free . . . She would travel, do wonderful things, meet wonderful people . . . She saw herself living a full rich life away from all the petty domestic duties that now hemmed her in on every side. Perhaps she would meet the man of whom her romantic soul had dreamed so long in secret. Anyway, she would escape. After all, release must come to her sooner or later. She'd stay and look after Mother while she lived, of course, but Mother wouldn't live for ever . . . She caught herself up. That was wicked. Almost like wishing for Mother's death. She set her lips in grim self-condemnation and determinedly fixed her thoughts upon tomorrow's menu. The lentil soup warmed up for lunch, then chops and a *soufflé*. The maids could finish the cold lamb. And for dinner . . .

Downstairs a tall, thin, elegantly dressed man, with a golden pointed beard, was handing an armful of American Beauties to Mrs Silver in the drawing-room.

"But how nice of you to remember my birthday, André," she was saying.

He smiled down at her.

"Have I ever forgotten your birthday since I knew you?" he said.

19

"No," she replied, "I don't believe you have. You're very faithful, André. The most faithful of all my friends."

"Don't call it faithful," he said. "The word faithfulness implies something dogged and determined, and what I feel for you is very different from that."

"I know, my dear," she said. "You're very sweet."

"Why would not you let me take you out? We could have had a very happy day. There was a time, you know, when we always spent your birthday together."

"I'm growing old, André, and becoming domesticated, at long last. I had my grandchildren to tea instead."

"And did you enjoy it?"

Her clear blue eyes laughed at him.

"They're darlings, but I'm afraid I've never been a child-lover. Have you ever had tea with children when one didn't upset a mug of milk and another have toothache?"

"I have never had tea with children," he said simply. She laughed again.

"Well, come into the garden. It's a lovely evening."

"It is always beautiful weather on your birthday . . . Do you remember . . .?"

They passed through the French windows out into the fragrant garden, where the setting sun threw long shadows over the lawn.

"Will you not be cold?" he said.

She shook her head.

"Have you come all this way to be with me on my birthday, André?"

"Yes."

"I won't call you faithful again if you don't like it, but I'm a very old woman now, and I appreciate your friendship. I used to take it all for granted because I was young and beautiful, but now all that is gone, and your friendship touches me deeply."

"But it is not gone," he protested. "All I loved in you is still here."

"Not youth, André."

"Youth of body was never the part that mattered most to me," he said. "To me there has only been one woman of perfect charm and perfect beauty in all the world. Sometimes I feel sad to think that she is mortal like the rest of us. The thought of the death of perfect beauty is a sad one. Forgive me if I seem morbid."

"No. I know what you mean. And now I'm old it's all so impersonal. But beauty doesn't die, André. I shall die—perhaps very soon—but beauty goes on. Marcia is what I was when I was her age. And one of her daughters—Lorna, I think—will be beautiful when Marcia is dead."

He shook his head.

"No, Marcia is not what you were. She is beautiful, but something that was fine and shining in you is faintly blurred in her. One feels it, though one does not quite know what it is. There will never be another woman like you as long as the world lasts."

"Oh, André!" she sighed, her blue eyes soft and dreamy with memories.

Lena came down to the drawing-room and stood at the French windows, looking out into the garden. She had changed into a dress of black silk with discreetly high neck and elbow sleeves edged with black lace. Its boned bodice made her breast look very flat, and the black velvet ribbon round her neck emphasised the sagging muscles and yellowing skin.

It was that Frenchman. Really, it wasn't quite nice the way he always came to see Mother on her birthday. Though one tried hard not to, one couldn't help thinking that perhaps there'd once been Something In It. He was twenty years younger than Mother, of course, but Marcia had told her that he had fallen passionately in love with her when he was twenty and Mother forty. She'd told her before Lena, pursing her thin lips and saying, "I don't want to hear anything about it, thank you, Marcia," had time to stop her. Because one hardly liked to think of Mother's past. She seemed to have known so many men, and, well—surely it wasn't quite the Thing for a married woman to have men friends to that extent. Really nice married women, of course, didn't have men friends at all, because of what People might Say. But Mother's men friends were always writing to her and coming to see her and behaving to her as if she were still young and beautiful, which was absurd. Lena resented the fact that men treated Mother, who was an old woman, as if she were still young and beautiful. This Frenchman, for instance . . . Mother's hand was on his arm as they walked, and he was bending over her . . . Lena stood watching them, that strange feeling of bitterness deepening at her heart.

Chapter Three

Miss Marchant was plain and thin and sallow, with a mole on her cheek from the middle of which grew several long black hairs.

She invariably wore navy-blue serge dresses that smelt slightly musty, and people could never believe that she was only twenty-four, because everything about her, even her voice and the way she walked, was middle-aged. Her dress and her lank greasy hair were always immaculately neat.

She was looking out of the drawing-room window when the carriage appeared and had opened the front door before it drew up.

Marcia got out first.

"We left Mother's quite early," she explained. "Jenifer had toothache, poor lamb, so Mother let us have the carriage, and we've all been to the dentist. He's taken it out. She was so good."

"*Brave* little girl!" said Miss Marchant, and Jenifer, sensing another Fuss, froze into frigid immobility.

Miss Marchant swung her down from the carriage.

"Our little heroine!" she said, kissing her. "Sorry, my pet," as Jenifer flinched away from her. "I forgot your poor sore tooth."

It hadn't been the sore tooth, of course, that made Jenifer flinch. It had been that one of the little hairs from the mole had touched her cheek. Jenifer always thought of the mole as having a strange independent life of its own. Often when Miss Marchant looked quite kind and happy Jenifer imagined that the mole looked cross, and often it seemed to be watching her when Miss Marchant was looking in quite the opposite direction. Once she had had a nightmare in which she met it creeping downstairs all by itself. She always hated its touching her . . .

Adrian got down after Jenifer.

There was a strained look on his face, and he was very pale. It had been dreadful sitting in the waiting-room while Jenifer had her tooth pulled out. He'd felt all the time as if his own tooth were being pulled out. Every tooth in his head still ached, and he wanted to cry. Miss Marchant noticed his pallor and the look in his eyes that meant that tears were not far away.

"Poor little Adrian!" she said. "He's so tender-hearted. You're sorry for Jenifer, aren't you, darling?"

Next to Lorna, Adrian was her favourite, because in his passions of grief he would often cling to her for comfort, hardly realising who she was in his distress, and that gave her a warm pleasant feeling of being loved and wanted.

Adrian smiled—a faint unsteady smile. He couldn't explain that it wasn't pity for Jenifer that had upset him, but a horrible feeling that it was his tooth and not Jenifer's that had been pulled out. He ran his tongue round his mouth and was surprised to find all his teeth still there . . .

"When my first teeth were loose," said Lorna, "I always used to pull them out myself."

She was feeling rather irritated. It was ridiculous for people to behave as if Jenifer had done something wonderful, when she'd only had a tooth pulled out.

Jarvis, Grandma's coachman, was putting out his hand to help her down. She smiled at him prettily.

"Thank you so much, Jarvis," she said, and had the satisfaction of seeing his weather-beaten face relax into an answering smile of affectionate admiration.

"That's all right, missie," he said.

She stood for a moment by the carriage.

"How's your little girl, Jarvis?"

"She's well enough, missie, but a proper little terror, she is. I often says to her, 'Pity you've not got some of Miss Lorna's ways,' I says."

24

Lorna laughed—the new laugh—and shook back her bright ringlets.

"Oh *no!*" she said, modestly disclaiming the implied compliment. "But you said she had a cold last week, didn't you?"

"Fancy you remembering that, missie! Yes, she's all right now."

He touched his hat, said "Good-day, missie," mounted the box, and drove off.

Lorna went up the steps to the front door. She felt excited. He was only a coachman, but he'd looked at her in the way people looked at Mother, as if he were thinking how pretty and charming she was. It gave her a strange new sense of power . . .

The others had all gone into the morning room, where a pile of household mending, folded and completed, stood upon the round table in the middle of the room.

"But, Miss Marchant," Mother was saying, "you shouldn't have done this. It was your free afternoon. Why didn't you go out?"

"I'd nowhere particular to go, and—well, I like mending, you know."

"But it's so *good* of you."

A faint colour invaded Miss Marchant's sallow cheeks. Marcia's gratitude brought to her again that warm pleasant feeling of being loved and wanted.

A little imp in Marcia was laughing mischievously. The hated household mending was done. She'd deliberately left it in the middle of the morning-room table, so that it should catch Miss Marchant's eye. The household mending was supposed to be done by Marcia, but she never even attempted it. She either left it about till finally Miss Marchant did it, or took it to Brightmet House and asked Lena to do it. The best of patently pious people like Lena was that their principles wouldn't let them refuse to help you, however much they might want to. Lena might set her lips grimly and show quite plainly by her manner that she thought Marcia was shirking her obvious duty by bringing the mending for her to do, but her conscience wouldn't let her refuse to do it. It amused Marcia to make use of Lena's self-righteousness, just as it amused her to make use of Miss Marchant's weakness for being fussed over. And one part of her stood aloof from it all, laughing at herself as well as at the others.

"I've lit the fire in the drawing-room," Miss Marchant was saying. "It's been quite warm this afternoon, of course, but it does get a little chilly in the evenings."

"How sweet of you!" said Marcia. "Frank loves a fire. Come in and sit down and be comfortable. You deserve a rest after doing that wretched mending."

The drawing-room, overcrowded and devoid of taste according to more modern standards, had nevertheless a pleasant, cosy, homelike air in the year 1900. Small pieces of silver littered the "occasional tables" that were dotted about the room. The suite of green plush sofa and chairs matched the green roses in the highly decorative carpet, while green draperies, edged with little "bobbles," hung in artfully arranged festoons from the mantelpiece, and covered the door and piano back. Photographs in silver frames and flowers in silver vases stood here, there, and everywhere, and the mantelpiece was covered by innumerable pieces of the fashionable Goss china. The wallpaper, a silver trellis with large pink roses, was almost hidden by serried ranks of water colours—good, bad, and indifferent —and the interstices filled with little oriental fans and hand-painted plaques.

The fire that Miss Marchant had lighted was shining brightly on to the polished brass fender and white bearskin hearthrug. Lorna loved this room. It was the scene of most of those secret dramas that had lately begun to enact themselves in her mind— dramas in which she moved, mysteriously beautiful, mysteriously charming, against a background of vague but devoted admirers.

"Now, children," said Marcia, "go upstairs and take off your things. You'll see to them, won't you, Lorna? I want Miss Marchant to rest. Put everything away carefully and wash your hands and faces."

Across Miss Marchant's mind flashed the thought that, after all, it *was* her free afternoon, and Mrs Gainsborough needn't speak as if she were doing her a favour in asking Lorna to see to the children instead of her. Still—it was lovely to be drawn into the warm intimate circle of the family like this . . . Mrs Gainsborough drawing up a chair for her, shaking a cushion to put behind her head, moving up a footstool.

"No, really, Mrs Gainsborough, you shouldn't," she protested. "You really shouldn't."

How very kind Mrs Gainsborough was! Miss Marchant felt quite ashamed of the times when she'd thought her selfish and lazy and unworthy of the wonderful goodness of Mr Gainsborough. Marcia racked her brains for something to say.

"How's your aunt going on?" she said at last.

Miss Marchant's aunt suffered from a complication of diseases that Miss Marchant never tired of describing. Her sallow expressionless face became almost animated as she launched once more into the sea of her aunt's internal troubles.

"You see, what's good for one complaint isn't good for another," she said earnestly, "which makes it so difficult. She's been to four different specialists in one month."

There was a modest pride in Miss Marchant's voice. After all, it wasn't everyone who could say that their aunt had been to four different specialists in one month . . .

The children clattered noisily upstairs. The two girls shared one bedroom, the two boys another. They were both cheerful little rooms, with white painted bedsteads, chests of drawers, and dressing tables, to which Miss Marchant gave a new coat of white paint each Spring. Sateen curtains—blue in the boys' room, pink in the girls'—hung at the windows. Between the two bedrooms was the old nursery, now called the playroom. It contained a large table, its scored and battered surface covered by a red patterned cloth, a big deal cupboard—the bottom part devoted to the children's toys, and the upper part to the nursery crockery—some upright chairs, and an ancient basket chair that the children declared to be haunted, as it gave forth loud creaks even when no one was near it. On the window-sill, where Jenifer loved to curl up, stood Laurence's boxes of insects with their glass lids. The carpet was threadbare, and Marcia was always saying that she was going to buy a new one when she could afford it.

The children were scrambling into the bathroom to wash.

"Let me wash first," ordered Lorna in what the others called her "bossy voice," "because I'm the eldest, and, anyway, it's Ladies First."

She washed quickly and neatly, taking off several imaginary rings and slipping them on again with much elegant play of her fingers.

"Here, stop messing about like that," said Laurence. "I want to wash."

"It's not your turn next. It's Jenifer's. Ladies First."

"She's not a lady. She's only a silly kid."

Jenifer began to scuffle with him, and Adrian joined in, Laurence trying to put the soap down Adrian's neck, while Jenifer turned on the bath taps and splashed water at them both.

"Stop behaving like that," said Lorna sternly.

"Oh, shut up bossing," said Laurence.

"I shall tell Mother," said Lorna, and went out of the room.

"She won't," said Laurence, and added: "She's getting too bossy. She thinks she's everyone."

"Here, give me that soap," said Adrian.

There was the high-pitched note in his voice that showed he was growing over-excited. The others stopped playing and looked at him rather apprehensively.

"Your turn to wash, Jen," said Laurence. "Try and wash a few freckles off."

Giggling, Jenifer scrubbed at her golden freckled skin with a loofah. The frills of her pinafore and her short reddish curls became soaked. Laurence dragged her back from the wash basin.

"Go on, Adrian. Your turn!"

He began to dry Jenifer's face, and they scrambled about like a couple of puppies, ducking, wrestling, struggling for possession of the towel.

It was all right now that Adrian was out of it, scrubbing his nails with frowning concentration. You never knew with Adrian.

He'd be good fun one minute, and the next he'd suddenly start crying, and you never knew what it was that had upset him.

They finished washing and, damp and dishevelled about the hair and cuffs, went into the playroom. Laurence, suddenly sober and businesslike, took his stamp albums and catalogues from the cupboard and sat down at a table with them, turning over the pages one by one, occasionally moving a stamp, consulting his catalogue, taking out or putting back a "swop." He would sit like that for hours, absorbed by his stamps or insects, completely lost to everything that went on around him. Adrian got down his paints and sat at the table opposite Laurence. Adrian painted bold, queer, original designs of flowers and trees and landscapes. He was always very touchy about his paintings and apt to be offended if the others did not like them. He arranged his things with jerky fidgety movements, occasionally speaking to Laurence, but Laurence, absorbed in his album, did not even hear him.

Jenifer had taken the *Blue Fairy Book* down from the shelves and had curled up in the basket chair with it. She could not read all the words, but she knew the stories by heart and loved to go over them, picking out the familiar words with her fingers and reading the story to herself in a whisper.

Lorna entered the drawing-room where Miss Marchant was enlarging on her aunt's more delicate complications in a discreetly lowered voice. When she saw Lorna she coughed and said, "Well, dear," then added, "Which reminds me. I wrote a letter to my aunt this afternoon. I must run out and post it. A letter means so much to an invalid."

"I'll post it for you, Miss Marchant," said Lorna.

She had decided not to tell Mother that the children had been splashing water in the bathroom. She always enjoyed threatening to tell Mother about their misdemeanours, because it made her feel a member of the grown-up camp, but often, when she actually did tell her, Mother just said "Don't tell tales," which made her feel like a snubbed little girl.

"How kind of you, my dear," said Miss Marchant effusively,

and Lorna ran upstairs to put on her hat again. She felt pleased at the prospect of taking Miss Marchant's letter to the post. She wished she dared put on her Sunday hat—a shady, broad-brimmed leghorn with a wreath of daisies and buttercups—because she looked much nicer in it than in the sunbonnet that she wore every day, but of course she daren't. It would be dreadful to wear a Sunday hat on a weekday. She took off her pinafore and put on the sunbonnet, then stood looking at her reflection with a thoughtful frown. She'd often heard people say how like she was to Mother, and she'd often heard people say that Mother was a "perfect du Maurier," which meant that she was like the pretty ladies in the bound volumes of *Punch* that stood behind the glass doors of the dining-room bookcase. Laurence was rather like Mother, too, of course, but Jenifer wasn't a bit like her. Jenifer was pale and freckled and had a funny little crooked nose and a funny little crooked mouth. Lorna was obscurely glad that Jenifer wasn't pretty.

She drew forward two shining ringlets to hang over her shoulders, then ran downstairs and set off along the dusty lane to the village. She was pretending that she was grown up and that, instead of the short gingham frock and long bare brown legs, was a silk flounced dress that rustled and swayed about her feet as she walked. She even put a hand behind as if to hold it up. The new game of pretending to be grown up was terribly exciting. She'd only just begun to play it, and, of course, she hadn't told anyone about it, because they'd only make fun of it . . .

She had reached the post-office now, and stopped to slip the letter into the wide hole of the pillar-box. When she was quite little, she and Jenifer used to pretend that the pillar box was really a dragon under a spell, who ate letters, and they used to pull their hands away quickly from the opening in case the sharp hungry teeth closed on them. Jenifer used to listen and say that she could hear them crunching up the letters inside. Since she'd begun the new game of being grown up, however, Lorna had stopped playing silly games like that with Jenifer.

"Hello, Lorna."

It was Mark Burdett—a boy of about thirteen, whose family

lived on the other side of the common. He had been away to school, so she hadn't seen him for some time. His obvious admiration of her thrilled her. She saw herself through his eyes, just as if she were looking at herself in the mirror—golden ringlets, blue eyes, and soft flushed cheeks in the shadow of the pink sunbonnet.

She smiled at him.

"Hello, Mark. When did you come home?"

"I came home yesterday."

He looked awkward and sheepish. Her self-confidence increased.

"How long holidays have you?"

"About six weeks. I say . . ." he gulped.

"Yes?"

"Will you——? If my mother asks your mother, will you come to tea?"

She laughed—remembering in time to do the new one.

"I expect so."

"Are—are you going to be at home all the holidays?"

"We shall be going to the sea, of course."

"How long will you be away for?"

His face was red, and he was grinning self-consciously.

Again that strange new sense of power surged over her, and she began to tease him.

"Perhaps all the holidays."

His face fell in ludicrous disappointment.

"Oh, I say . . . I—I *did* want to see something of you——"

"Perhaps you will," she laughed, tossing the long ringlets back with a small sunburnt hand. "I must hurry home now. Goodbye."

"But, look here——"

She turned and walked away down the road—cool and poised and dainty.

The feeling of power and exhilaration still upheld her. It would be lovely to be grown up. Grown up like Mother, of course. Not like Aunt Lena or Miss Marchant. And then, when she was very old, she'd be like Grandma, and lots of people who had known her when she was young would write to her and come to see her, and everyone would say that she was "wonderful." She put her

31

hand into the pocket of her frock for her handkerchief and felt the little leather purse that held her money. There was last week's Saturday penny in it, not yet spent. She wished that she had bought a pennyworth of pear-drops at the post-office. Then she decided that it would have spoilt the whole adventure to have bought a pennyworth of pear-drops . . . She walked sedately up the steps to the front door and into the hall. Mother and Miss Marchant were still talking in the drawing-room. Through the half-open door came the sound of Miss Marchant's harsh earnest voice.

"My mother suffered from rheumatism, but I've never had it. I often have neuralgia, of course, but that's a different thing altogether."

Lorna went upstairs. The playroom was quite silent, but, looking through the crack in the door as she passed, she saw Laurence and Adrian sitting at the table and Jenifer curled up in an armchair with a book.

She went on to her bedroom, took off her sunbonnet, threw it into a drawer, then paused as she caught sight of her nails. They were terribly grubby. She hoped that Mark hadn't noticed. His were probably worse, anyway. Boys' always were. But grubby nails didn't go with her mental picture of herself at all. She went to the bathroom and began to scrub them. Suddenly she heard the sound of the key in the lock and the opening of the front door. That was Father coming home. She threw down the nail brush, dried her hands quickly, and ran from the room. The others were just coming out of the playroom, scrambling for the first place, pushing each other aside excitedly. They tumbled downstairs like a lot of puppies . . . Father stood just inside the front door, smiling and holding out his arms. Ever since they could remember they had raced to welcome him like that when he came home from work, and he had stood there smiling, waiting for them.

Lorna won the race, flinging herself upon him and being lifted up into the air by his strong arms.

"What a big girl!" he said, laughing as he put her down.

And suddenly Lorna didn't want to be a big girl. She didn't even want to be grown up. His bigness and gentleness gave her a feeling of being sheltered and cared for and protected, and she wanted to go on being a little girl.

"And here's Baby!" he said, catching hold of Jenifer, and swinging her up in her turn. He still called Jenifer Baby, though the others had stopped doing so years ago. Then he went into the drawing-room, carrying Jenifer in his arms, the others clinging about him. Inside the drawing-room he put Jenifer down and kissed Mother, holding her for a minute by the shoulders and smiling down at her. He always did that, even if people were there, when he came home. There was a sort of ceremony, almost of ritual, about his home-coming. No day had ever ended without it. No day ever could end without it. When Jenifer thought of God, she always thought of someone very tall and dressed in white robes, but with Father's face—a kindly omnipotent presence, a guarantee that all was well with the world, that nothing really dreadful would ever be allowed to happen to any of them.

Chapter Four

Frank Gainsborough lowered his tall figure into the green plush armchair by the fireplace. He had shaken off the children while he kissed his wife, but now they scrambled over him again, Jenifer and Lorna sitting on his knees, the boys on the arms of his chair.

Frank Gainsborough was a man of limited ideas and interests. It was, indeed, something starkly simple, starkly dependable, about him that had first attracted his more complicated and irresponsible wife. He worked hard, struggling to extract from a none-too-flourishing business sufficient profit to keep the family he idolised in comfort, and to shield them, as far as he could, from the shifts and restraints of poverty. Essentially a home-loving man, he looked forward throughout the day to this moment of home-coming. The thought of it ran like a golden thread through its most exacting tasks, its most harassing worries.

As he fixed his eyes now on his wife it seemed to him as if the sight of her were already washing away from his soul the grime and stain of the day's toil.

"Tired, darling?" she said. "What's it been like in Town?"

"It seemed very hot in the middle of the day, but it's quite cool now, isn't it? It's nice to see the fire."

"Miss Marchant lit it. She remembered that you like a fire on these half-and-half evenings."

"A fire's so homelike," he said, and added, "Thank you, Miss Marchant. It was kind of you."

"She's too kind," said Marcia, to whom it had occurred that, properly managed, Miss Marchant might offer to put the children to bed in spite of its being her free afternoon. "I don't know what we should do without her."

She smiled at Miss Marchant as she spoke, and Miss Marchant glowed and bridled with pleasure, feeling herself once more drawn into the heart of the family, enwrapped in its warm happy confidence and affection.

Frank was pulling Jenifer's curls.

"What's Baby been doing today?" he said.

They all began to talk to him at once, telling him about Grandma's birthday party, and the china jug they had bought for her, and the cushion that Aunt Lena had made for her, and Jenifer's toothache, and how brave she'd been. They remembered not to mention Adrian's upsetting his mug of milk, because, if they had done, Adrian might have been overcome by shame and horror at the memory, and the catastrophe so narrowly averted at tea-time might have taken place.

"Let's have a little music, Mother," said Frank at last.

Although, as he often said, he "didn't know one tune from another," he always liked "a little music" in the evening. So unmusical, indeed, was he that the performance of anyone but his wife, however perfect, merely bored him. His wife's singing and playing gave him pleasure because they seemed to be an integral part of her, interwoven in his mind with his deep and enduring love for her. She had been seated at the piano, singing "Cherry Ripe," when first he saw her . . .

She took her seat now at the piano, and the children slipped from his knee and crowded round her.

"Sing 'Buy a Broom,'" pleaded Laurence.

"No! 'The Mistletoe Bough,'" said Jenifer.

"No, no! It's too sad. Adrian doesn't like it," objected Lorna. "Let's have 'The Bailiff's Daughter of Islington.' It's got a happy ending."

"No! 'A Fox went out.'"

"No! 'Madam, will you Walk.'"

Marcia laughed.

"If you can't agree, I'll choose. We'll sing 'Come Lasses and Lads.'"

She struck the opening chords and began the song in her clear sweet voice.

The children joined in heartily, untunefully:

"Come lasses and lads, get leave of your dads,
And away to the maypole hie,
For every fair has a sweetheart there
And the fiddler's standing by.
For Willy shall dance with Jane
And Johnny has got his Joan,
So trip it, trip it, trip it, trip it, trip it up and down."

Marcia glanced at Miss Marchant, sitting stiff and aloof on the edge of the sofa.

"Come and join in, Miss Marchant," she called.

Miss Marchant gave her prim little smile and, crossing the room, took her place at the back of the group. She was short-sighted and had to bend over Marcia's shoulder to read the words. Marcia made a laughing grimace at the keys. She had loved to feel the children pressing close to her, though they hampered her movements and pushed their little heads between her and the music, but somehow Miss Marchant completely spoilt it, leaning heavily over her shoulder, breathing down her neck, singing loudly in a harsh shrill voice. The elusive fragrance of clean healthy childhood that had hung about the group was conquered by the faintly musty smell of the blue serge dress.

They sang "A Fox went out," "Buy a Broom," "The Tin Gee-Gee," and "The Owl and the Pussy Cat," and finally Frank, as usual, insisted on "Cherry Ripe."

After that Marcia struck a resounding finale of chords.

"Bedtime," she said, swinging round on the piano stool. "I'll go up and get the things ready."

"Let me see to that," offered Miss Marchant eagerly.

"Oh *no*, Miss Marchant," protested Marcia with demurely dancing eyes. "It's your free evening."

"I insist," said Miss Marchant. "No, don't say another word. I *insist*. I'm going up to get things ready at once. Come when I call you, children. Now shoo out of my way. Shoo! Shoo!"

She scurried out of the door with her high unmusical laugh. The arch bright manner was as unbecoming to her heavy personality as was the hot flush to the sallow skin. Jenifer felt something curl up inside her as she listened. Marcia was too much pleased by the success of her manoeuvre to feel any irritation. She rose from the piano and came across to the hearthrug, her lips curved into their faint mischievous smile. Then quite suddenly it struck her that it would really have been less trouble to put the children to bed herself than to have endured the boredom of Miss Marchant through the whole evening, as she had done, and the thought made her laugh aloud.

"What are you laughing at?" said Frank.

"Myself," she replied.

He took her hand and pulled her down on to his knee.

"How nice you look tonight!" he said.

"Don't I always?" she teased. "Do you know you're growing bald at the temples? Here and here." She traced the tide of his receding hair. "What shall I do with a bald husband?"

The children were struggling for possession of the piano stool, swinging round and round on it till the seat was as high as it would go, then swinging round in the opposite direction till it was as low as it would go.

Adrian came across to Marcia and leant against her shyly, touching the lace at her neck.

"Play something, darling," he pleaded.

He had adored Marcia from babyhood, worshipping unconsciously at the shrine of her beauty. He loved to fetch and carry for her, pretending that she was a queen and he her page, loved to touch her dress or satin-soft skin with gentle sensitive fingers.

"You won't cry if I do?" said Marcia, getting up.

Music often made Adrian cry for no reason at all.

"No, I won't. I promise, I won't."

"Very well. Just for a few minutes. But you must go the second Miss Marchant calls you . . ."

They moved away from the piano—Jenifer to sit on Frank's knee, Lorna on the arm of his chair, Laurence to lie full length on the bear-skin rug, while Adrian sat cross-legged on the floor at Marcia's feet, gazing up at her.

She played one of Chopin's Nocturnes. She had a quick facility in all things artistic. She played just a little better than the average amateur player. She sang just a little better than the average amateur singer. As a girl she had painted just a little better than the average amateur painter. But she did none of them as well as she might have done. There was a strain of indolence in her that had always shirked the discipline of application. Her beauty had made it so easy for her to slip through life without effort . . .

Jenifer looked dreamily at the friendly tendril of climbing honeysuckle that had found its way, as usual, through the open window into the room. She often made up stories about it, pretending that it was a fairy protecting them from the spells and enchantment of an invisible wizard. The fairy's name was Metaphelia and the wizard's Pollorodo . . .

Lorna watched the graceful figure seated upright on the piano stool, the silk skirts billowing out from the small waist . . . and again the longing to be grown-up swept over her. She saw herself sitting at a piano like that—white hands flashing over the keys, graceful golden head bent to the music, silk skirts billowing out from a slender waist, but, instead of just Father and the children, the room, which had suddenly become immense, contained hosts of shadowy figures, spellbound, adoring . . .

Laurence listened gravely, rather guardedly, feeling the spell, but holding himself aloof. He always felt like that when he listened to music. He didn't quite understand the effect it had on him, and he distrusted everything that he didn't quite understand . . .

Adrian was already fighting back his tears, terrified of breaking his promise and disgracing himself publicly for the second time in one day. Music was to him a kind of warmth to which he had to draw nearer and nearer till suddenly he was in the middle of it and it was burning him. And then he had to cry. Jenifer, seeing his bright eyes and quivering lips, was conscious of a faint hostility. The same things that made Adrian cry often made her want to cry. But with her sensitiveness went a quick fierce pride that hid all traces of it. She hated the part of her that wanted to cry, and Adrian seemed to typify it, so that often, when he cried in public, she felt as ashamed as if it had been herself.

"Ready, children!" called Miss Marchant from upstairs.

Marcia played a final chord and sprang to her feet.

"Off you go!" she called. She snatched up Jenifer from Frank's knee, set her on the piano stool, and spun her round, Jenifer shouting with delight.

"Now, off you go!" she said again, shooing them out of the room.

"You'll soon have that seat broken, my dear, if you keep doing that," expostulated her husband mildly.

"I know," she said, seating herself upon it and swinging round, "but they love it. I did, too, when I was a little girl. I was forbidden to go into the drawing-room at all, but I used to creep into it just to spin up and down on the piano stool. Once I did it in the middle of the night . . ."

He laughed, seeing her as a little girl in her white nightdress, spinning up and down on the piano stool in the middle of the night. He had not much imagination, but what he had was called into play by his wife alone.

"Come into the garden," he said. "Shall I get you a wrap?"

"No, thanks."

She took his arm and they walked out of the French window into the garden. It was a long narrow garden, bounded by a tumble-down fence. In the middle of the lawn, worn bare by the children's feet, lay a broken wheelbarrow and an overturned engine. At the bottom of the garden was a sand-heap, with spades and buckets scattered around. A swing hung from the chestnut tree that gave the house its name (just as a solitary fir tree gave its name to the next house), and near it was a roughly fashioned see-saw. By the bottom fence grew a small colony of laurel bushes, which frequently played the part of jungle or forest in the children's games and as a result were battered and misshapen. The back garden had always been regarded as the children's playground, while in front of the house symmetrically rounded beds contained the conventional displays of geraniums, calceolarias, and lobelias.

They strolled arm-in-arm round the garden, and Marcia threw interested glances up at the next house, where curtains of a crude shade of pink hung at the windows.

"Mr Frewin's really moved into The Firs at last," she said. "The removing-vans were there all this morning. I suppose we ought to call when he's settled. I believe he's dreadful."

"He must be rolling in money," said Frank. "He's opening another branch."

Marcia made a little grimace.

"A grocer! And he serves in his own shop! I did so hope that it would be someone nice."

"Well, my dear, trade's an honourable pursuit. I'm in it myself."

"Oh, darling, but not *retail*. Retail's so *dreadful*. Still—his things are quite good. I get everything there, you know."

"Well, now you'll be able to complain over the back fence if his butter isn't up to standard."

"I do hope he won't be a nuisance about the children—object to their making a noise and not throw their balls back and that sort of thing."

"He'll be kept pretty busy if he's going to throw their balls back."

They entered the drawing-room again, and Frank closed the French windows.

"Lena gave Mother the most *dreadful* cushion for her birthday," said Marcia, as she went to the piano and began to tidy the litter of music. "Very bright blue embroidered in red. It screams at you from miles away. Poor Mother! It's ruined her drawing-room. I expect she'll quietly dispose of it in a few days, and Lena will go about wearing her martyred look and thinking that no one loves her but her District. I get so sick of her District."

"How was your mother?"

"Splendid. She always is. André was going there this evening . . . What time is it? I'll go and see that Emma's got the dinner on."

At that moment Emma entered.

"Mr Frewin to see you, ma'am."

Mr Frewin himself followed close on her heels—short and stout, with a very red face, a protuberant paunch, spanned by a gold watch-chain, a check suit, and a colourful tie, set off by a large diamond pin. His sleek black hair gleamed with grease.

"My name's Frewin an' I've come to live next door," he announced with a smile that did full justice to several conspicuous gold teeth. "I dunno if it's the right thing for me to come round to see you like this as soon as I've got fixed up, but I thought it'd be sort of neighbourly."

The familiar imps of amusement danced behind the demureness in Marcia's eyes.

"How kind of you, Mr Frewin!" she said. "Do sit down. We shall be delighted to have you as a neighbour, shan't we, Frank?"

"Quite," said Frank Gainsborough, realising with some relief that the visitor was too imperceptive to read the amusement in Marcia's eyes. It wouldn't have been the first time she'd offended people by laughing at them . . .

Mr Frewin sank into one of the chairs.

"My sister'll be looking after me, an' she'll be coming along to pay her respects when she's got settled. There's a bit of trouble at present about some linoleum that doesn't fit. Not to speak of two of the vases gettin' broke in the move. She swears it was the one that smells of drink that's done it and that he's done it on purpose. She's a T.T., you see, and she always puts everything down to the one that smells of it . . . You've got kiddies, ain't you, Mrs Gainsborough?"

"Four," said Marcia.

"I've only got one. Gell. Ruby, her name is. She's staying with a friend till we're settled."

"How old is she?"

"Nine."

"The same age as Adrian. Ours are six, seven, nine, and ten. I hope you won't find them a nuisance."

"Nuisance? 'Course not. I like kiddies. An' my Ruby'll be glad to have someone to play with. Her mother died two years since, you know."

Marcia made an indeterminate murmur of sympathy, and he went on with increased cheerfulness.

"Well, I don't know why I'm chattin' on and on like this, wasting your time. What I really came in about was the fence. It belongs to you by rights, I believe, an' what I want to ask is, would you object to me having a bit of trellis put along the top, like, for growing roses?"

"Of *course* not," said Marcia. "Are you a gardener, Mr Frewin?"

Mr Frewin uncrossed one leg and crossed the other, fingered his watch-chain, and smiled his large gold smile again.

"No, but I like a good show for my money," he said. "I'm having it done by a slap-up firm, and this trellis was their idea. What I say is, if you've got a garden at all, you might as well have a swell one—plenty of flowers and such like in it. I don't know anything about flowers myself, but this firm's supposed to, an' if there's not a good show for my money I'll know the reason why. That's right, isn't it, Mr Gainsborough?"

Frank said "Quite" again.

Marcia rose.

"Won't you come and see our garden, Mr Frewin? There's nothing in it, but you can tell me how yours is going to be planned . . . Don't bother to come out, Frank. I know you're tired."

Beneath her amusement her mind was working shrewdly. She hadn't paid her last month's account at Frewin's. Frank had given her the money for it, but she'd spent it on a new blouse. However much she schemed and planned, her dress allowance never seemed enough. There was really very little vanity in her composition, but her beauty was like some ravenous animal that had to be fed continually. It had to have silks and laces, furs and feathers, large fashionable hats and flounced petticoats that made a gentle rustle as she walked. She had recognised the admiration in Mr Frewin's eyes, had even guessed that he had seen and admired her before he paid his call. If she were nice to him, he wouldn't worry her about last month's account, or this month's, or next month's . . . She'd be able to buy the new feather boa she'd set her heart on.

"We haven't many flowers, you see," she said. "We had quite a lot when we first came here, but only a very few seem to have survived."

"I'll send my man in with some," he offered promptly, twirling the small black moustache. "I'll send him tomorrow."

"I'm afraid it's the wrong time of the year," she smiled, "but perhaps in the autumn——"

"Autumn? Yes. I'll tell my man. I'll tell him to stock the whole place for you."

"Oh no, you mustn't do that, but just a few would be lovely. This is the children's sand-heap. I'm afraid it's rather black and soily now. We've not had it renewed for some time."

"I've still got the builders in my place. I'll send along another load. Now, don't say a word. They shall clear the old lot out and put a new one in. I'd like to. Little present for the kiddies from me, like."

"How kind you are!"

"Not at all. I'm fond of kiddies, I am."

"Ours are rather noisy, I'm afraid."

"I don't mind noise. . ."

"Your little girl must come over and play with them."

"She'd like to . . . I know you by sight, of course, Mrs Gainsborough, and I'm proud to think I'm going to be your neighbour."

His admiration of her was very obvious. Amused as much by herself as him, she was still devising ways in which it might be turned to account . . .

Frank Gainsborough watched from the drawing-room. He saw

43

the visitor's admiration of his wife, but he would have felt no jealousy even had the man been young and handsome. Obtuse enough as he was generally, his love for his wife quickened his perceptions. He knew that she exploited her charm shamelessly, that she shifted her duties and responsibilities on to others whenever she possibly could, but he knew also the bedrock of self-respect and fastidiousness that underlay her laughing indolence. She had learnt the knack of keeping her admirers at arm's length before she was out of her teens. When she couldn't shift her duties on to anyone else, she buckled to and performed them herself cheerfully and thoroughly. And he had never seen her discontented or ill-humoured. There was about her always this radiant laughing serenity.

When they came in, Mr Frewin was insisting on repairing the fence and buying the children a new wheelbarrow, as well as renewing the sand-heap and stocking the garden. He took his leave with much display of the gold teeth. He certainly wouldn't send an "account rendered" for the overdue grocery bill, thought Marcia, as she returned slowly to the drawing-room, but illogically, having gained her end, she decided to pay it next month, even if it meant going without the feather boa. Or—she needn't pay for the feather boa just yet. She'd manage, somehow. Often Mother came to her rescue when she was in a tight corner, slipping a five-pound note into her hand quite casually as she was saying goodbye after a visit. Mother liked one to look nice. She found Lena's tweeds and shirt blouses depressing.

Jenifer, as the youngest, had to go to bed at once, but Miss Marchant allowed the others to stay in the playroom for half an hour after they came up stairs. Lorna read *The Heir of Redclyffe,* and Adrian and Laurence went on with their painting and stamps. Laurence, closing his catalogue and reaching out for his packet of "swops," caught sight of Adrian's painting for the first time. He didn't know what it was meant to be, but the bold splashes of colour pleased him.

"Oh, I say, that's jolly!" he said.

Adrian's heart soared ecstatically at the praise. The blood flamed into his cheeks, and a lump in his throat prevented him from speaking. By the time the power of speech returned to him, Laurence was again lost in his stamps and didn't even hear his thanks.

The front door bell rang, and Lorna, going out of the room to the landing, peeped cautiously over the balusters. She could see Emma in her neat black dress, with the white cap whose streamers hung down to her waist and the long white apron that covered her skirt and came down to her ankles, ushering the visitor into the drawing-room. She returned to the playroom.

"It's a dreadful man in a check suit," she said. "Emma said Mr Frewin."

"It's the man who's come to live next door," said Adrian.

"Oh, that awful man," she said.

Hearing voices outside, she went to the window and hoisted herself up on to the broad window-seat.

"He's in the garden with Mother. His suit's *dreadful*."

Laurence raised his head from his stamps.

"He may be quite nice in spite of his suit."

"He can't be, Laurence. He's a tradesman."

There was something so final in Lorna's tone that Laurence returned to his stamps without further argument.

Jenifer was kneeling by her bed saying her prayers. She was saying them quickly, because she wanted to get them over before Miss Marchant came in. When Miss Marchant was in a good temper, as she was tonight, she would sometimes want you to say your prayers at her knee, which was horrible. If ever Jenifer had to do that, she would screw up her eyes tightly and gabble her prayers as fast as she could, seeing all the time, in spite of her closed eyes, the black hairy mole on Miss Marchant's cheek. The Lord's Prayer first. When she said the Lord's Prayer, Jenifer always wondered what was the word left out between "Thy" and "will be done." It seemed funny not to say what would be done. But she'd never asked. She hated asking and being explained to. Either your question turned out to be funny, and people laughed at you, or else they took it seriously and went on and on and on, explaining and explaining and explaining, till you wished you'd never asked them at all. Miss Marchant did that. Jenifer would much rather not know anything than have it explained to her by Miss Marchant. And Mother often just made fun of it and gave you a ridiculous answer that you knew wasn't true. She teased you, and you loved being teased by her, but it made you not want to ask her things. And it was, after all, much more exciting to find out things for yourself than have them explained to you by a grown-up. Jenifer used to put all the things she wanted to know in a certain corner of her mind, and then often a chance word or a sentence in a book would explain them, and that was far more thrilling than just being told.

"Bless Mother and Father and Lorna and Adrian and Laurence and Grandma and Aunt Lena and make me a good girl for Jesus Christ's sake, Amen."

As soon as she was in bed, Lorna came in and told her about Mr Frewin and his awful suit and that he was a tradesman, and for quite a long time after that Jenifer thought that a tradesman was a sort of criminal and was puzzled when she found that it was just the same as shopkeeper. Then Lorna told her as much as she could remember of *The Heir of Redclyffe,* which Jenifer found terribly exciting, but she kept interrupting to ask questions about parts of the story that didn't come into the book, till Lorna suddenly got annoyed and said, "I'm going to say my prayers," though she was only half undressed and obviously not ready to say her prayers yet. She slipped her red flannel dressing-gown on and flopped down on the floor by her bed. She took a long time saying her prayers, and Jenifer had an uncomfortable feeling that she was telling God how irritating she, Jenifer, had been about *The Heir of Redclyffe.* Then she got up and began to finish her undressing, but she was still aloof and grown up and didn't answer Jenifer when Jenifer spoke.

When Miss Marchant came to see that they were in bed, it was clear that her good temper was dispersed. She was frowning and tight-lipped. She had gone downstairs and found the atmosphere quite changed. Mr and Mrs Gainsborough no longer seemed to welcome her, no longer seemed to want to draw her into the heart of their family affection. She had, in fact, a horrible suspicion that Mrs Gainsborough had only been nice to her because she wanted her to put the children to bed. It had happened before, she remembered, more than once, but each time it happened she was so pleased by her kindness that she forgot to be on her guard. Mr Gainsborough had hardly looked at her when she went into the drawing-room. She wished that Mr Gainsborough could see her as she really was. She was never at her best with him. Of course, she couldn't afford to dress as well as Mrs Gainsborough did, and it was a well-known fact that men cared for nothing but looks; still, he might show a little gratitude for all she did in the house. Just a little gratitude and appreciation. She didn't ask for much . . . Miss Marchant felt irritated and aggrieved. She entered the girls' room and looked around for something to find fault with. She saw a drawer half open and closed it with a bang.

"It's very untidy to leave drawers open like this," she said severely.

"It was hardly open at all," said Lorna.

"Silence!" shouted Miss Marchant. She had a habit of shouting "Silence!" at them when she was annoyed that always made them giggle.

She went out, closing the door sharply.

The episode had dispelled Lorna's hauteur, making her a little girl again.

"Isn't she *silly!*" she laughed. "Let's play 'He never smiled again.'"

It was a game they had invented, founded on the story of Henry I. Their history-book stated that after being told of his son's death the King never smiled again. One of them pretended to be King Henry, and the other tried to make him laugh.

"You be the King first."

"All right."

"How are you today, Your Majesty?"

"Very well, thank you."

"*Silence!*"

They both giggled. They played it again and it ended in the same way. Gradually they grew sleepy.

47

"I'm sorry if I was beastly to you," said Lorna non-committally.

"It's all right. I'm sorry I was silly."

"It's all right. Good-night."

"Good-night."

The boys, too, were in bed, and Adrian was talking excitedly. Laurence's casual words of praise were still like fumes of wine in his head. He talked about anything and everything. Laurence made short monosyllabic rejoinders. At last Adrian's exuberance gave way to sleepiness, and he snuggled down in his pillow with much creaking of the bedstead. Laurence turned sharply to listen. Was Adrian crying? Often he cried just because you'd said something, or not said something, and you didn't know how it could possibly have upset him. When that happened Laurence would ignore it, even going to sleep before Adrian's muffled sobs had died away. He didn't dislike Adrian, but Adrian was inclined to be a baby and mustn't be encouraged. Tonight it was evidently all right, however. There came the sound of deep regular breathing from the next bed.

Downstairs Frank Gainsborough had heaved a sigh of relief as the door shut on Miss Marchant.

"Good Lord! I thought the woman was going to settle here for the evening."

"You weren't very welcoming, darling. And I'm afraid I wasn't either. But it's all right. She's gone to the playroom. She won't be coming back."

He knocked out his pipe against the fireplace.

"You've made a conquest of our next-door neighbour," he said.

"Yes. I thought it would be so useful when I wanted to buy a new hat instead of paying the grocery bills."

He was silent for a few moments, then said: "I wish I could give you every single darn thing you want."

She laughed.

"I'm glad you can't, darling. It would make life terribly dull."

Chapter Five

The next day there arrived a note from Mrs Burdett, asking if Lorna and Jenifer might come to a picnic that they were having that afternoon and stay the night at the cottage in the valley that the Burdetts used as a summer overflow house.

"Would you like to go?" said Marcia.

"Yes, let's," said Lorna. "I think it would be fun."

Jenifer was surprised, because Lorna generally adopted the grown-up attitude of disapproval towards the Burdetts.

"Do you think it would be wise to let them go?" said Miss Marchant anxiously to Marcia. She had been cold and detached in her manner all morning, but the invitation from Mrs Burdett made her forget that she was unappreciated and misunderstood. "You know what they *are*," she went on, sinking her voice to a sinister note.

"Mark's quite nice," said Lorna casually.

"Mark, yes," said Miss Marchant. "Mark's godmother pays for his education, and he goes to a school where he's taught to be a little gentleman—but the *others!* They're *savages.*"

"Oh, they won't do them any harm," said Marcia, irritated as usual by Miss Marchant's officiousness. "They can wear their old holland frocks, and it won't matter how much they get pulled about."

The Burdetts lived in a large tumble-down house at the end of the village and provided the local tea parties with unending material for gossip. People loved to describe to each other the state of the Burdetts' house—stucco peeling off, woodwork bare of paint, windows broken, both front and back gardens mere expanses of trodden earth. "And the inside, my dear!" they would always end, on a note of morbid relish. "It's even *worse*. And how they all get into it, is a mystery."

No one ever seemed to know exactly how many Burdett children there were, because Mr Burdett had adopted a large orphan family of his brother's, about the same age as his own family, and the two together formed a herd of young savages who never stood still long enough to be counted. They grew up anyhow, were clothed and fed anyhow, and, as if in defiance of every law of hygiene, were sturdy, rosy-cheeked children who seemed immune from all the ordinary ailments of childhood.

Mrs Burdett was well fitted to be the mother of such a brood. She was a massive woman, built on heroic lines, who would have been strikingly handsome had her mouth been smaller and her hair less untidy. She was, as a rule, sublimely unperturbed by the chaos in which she lived and the young savages who surrounded her. Passers-by who came to the house in a state of consternation to inform her that her children were out on the roof in their night clothes, and that one of them was sitting on a chimney with her feet on another, would receive the careless reply, "Oh, they'll be all right." That careless "Oh, they'll be all right" seemed to be a sort of amulet, protecting them from every danger. They got soaked to the skin and never caught cold. They fell from enormous heights and never broke their limbs. They played with children sickening for all sorts of infectious diseases and never caught anything.

There were times, however, when Mrs Burdett's placidity deserted her, and she would stride amongst her flock, purple with wrath, dealing blows right and left with her large muscular arms. Then the young Burdetts would flee before her in a panic-stricken crowd, scrambling out of her reach on to trees, roofs, fences, or balconies. Mrs Burdett's rages never lasted long, and, if they could keep out of the way of those large hands for two or three minutes (and they generally could), all would be well, and her placidity would return as suddenly as it had departed. Sometimes her usual slovenliness, too, would vanish and the soiled overall that formed her ordinary wear be replaced by an elaborate toilet, consisting of a silk flounced dress, an immense boa, and a large feathered hat. In this costume Mrs Burdett sallied forth to pay her social calls, and with it she could assume an air that would have done credit to a stage duchess. Indeed, even in her overall, with her hair coming down, there was something regal about her.

Like all her neighbours, Mrs Burdett had an At Home day, and then the drawing-room, which was kept locked for the rest of the month, was thrown open, and Mrs Burdett, majestic in her silk dress, sat behind a lace-covered tea table and poured out tea from a silver urn. There was something almost hypnotic about her magnificence on those occasions. She would refer to her "cook" and "housemaid," she would order an intruding child to go to "your nurse," and the knowledge that all these offices were combined in the person of an under-sized "general," somehow detracted not at all from the impressiveness of the atmosphere. She would even refer to the small third sitting-room, whose furniture consisted solely of prams, go-carts, bicycles, and broken coal buckets, as the "library," and carry off the situation.

Her husband was one of those insignificant little men whom such women generally marry. He fussed continually and ineffectively, and no one ever took the slightest notice of him. Among his noisy exuberant children he looked like a small hunted animal. He had an unfortunate stammer that he could only overcome by singing the words he wanted to say in a high treble voice. If he had to say something, he would struggle conscientiously with his stammer for some moments, then suddenly and unexpectedly burst into song. If he could get anyone to listen to him, he enjoyed discussing the news of the day, and would chant long dissertations on the shocking fashion in which the war was being allowed to drag on indecisively in South Africa and the general disloyalty of the Liberal party. In the distance it sounded like an anthem. He was secretary for some society, but no one, not even his wife, seemed quite sure what it was.

Early in the afternoon Mark arrived to escort Lorna and Jenifer. A godmother paid Mark's school fees and bought his clothes, and on his return from school at the end of the term the others ignored him completely till his veneer of public-school manners wore off and he became a young savage like themselves. The process generally took about a week. He had now been at home three days, and he was still watching his brothers and sisters with pained disapproval.

Marcia had said that the girls should wear their holland frocks, but when the day came she could not resist putting on the new sailor suits of white piqué with kilted skirts that she and Miss Marchant had just finished making. She stood at the door to watch them out of sight, torn between pride in the new sailor suits, which fitted beautifully, and apprehension as to their probable state on their return. Miss Marchant stood by her, tight-lipped and disapproving.

"Those suits will be *ruined*," she said, "and there's no knowing what they'll catch from those dreadful children."

"Oh, Mark will look after them," said Marcia, but without much real conviction, and already regretting the gesture of the white sailor suits.

Mark walked between them, carrying the Gladstone bag that held their night things.

"Are you all going on the picnic?" Lorna was saying.

"Yes," said Mark, "we're having the wagonette."

Mrs Burdett was a woman of inexhaustible vitality, and during the children's holidays she would arrange "expeditions" several times a week, engaging a ramshackle wagonette from a neighbouring farmer, which was drawn by a lumbering cart horse and driven by an ancient labourer called Noah. In this the Burdetts would visit distant fairs or circuses, or go off for a day's picnic. Generally several children were missing when they returned from these expeditions, but Mrs Burdett would shrug her shoulders and say, "Oh, they'll turn up all right," and they always did.

The wagonette was already at the Burdetts' gate when Mark and Lorna and Jenifer reached it. Little Burdetts swarmed everywhere—on the horse, on the shafts, on the garden gate, the garden fence, and the top of the drawing-room bay window.

Mrs Burdett stood at the gate, wearing a large mushroom hat

and a shapeless immemorial "dust coat" of shantung. She greeted Jenifer and Lorna affably, assuming something of her majestic air as she did so.

"There you are, my dears. So glad you could come. I hope your mother's quite well. Get into the conveyance and I'll call the children. It's quite time we started."

She took a whistle from her pocket and blew it, whereupon children scrambled down from roof, trees, and fences, and crowded into the wagonette. Noah climbed slowly into his seat, cracked his whip, and slowly, lumberingly, the wagonette started on its way.

It was not a peaceful journey. The young Burdetts scuffled and wrestled with each other, fought for possession of the seat next the driver, and tried to push each other out on to the road—all in perfect good-humour. The wagonette had to stop twice to pick up forgotten Burdetts, who came panting and shouting down the road behind it.

Jenifer sat wedged tightly between a boy called James, who carried a cricket-bat and a fishing-rod, and a girl called Petronella, who carried a cat dressed up in doll's clothes. (Mrs Burdett gave the boys plain names but let her fancy run riot in the girls'.) The cricket-bat stuck into her ribs and the fishing-rod into her eye whenever she moved, and the cat, who seemed to labour under the delusion that she was responsible for the outrage perpetrated upon it, occasionally shot out a paw and scratched her hand or arm.

Lorna sat on the end of the seat with Mark next to her. He was doing his best to shield her from the scuffling of the others, and from a white rat, which Luke, the boy opposite, was training to run up and down his arm.

Mrs Burdett sat by the door, nursing the baby. Her large handsome face wore a look of radiant content, and she was so inured by custom to the uproar around her that she did not even notice it. She was enjoying the rest, the motion, the fresh air, and the sense of holiday that these expeditions always gave her.

The wagonette lumbered slowly along the sunny road. It lumbered indeed so slowly that it was quite easy to leap down, retrieve a fallen ball, and climb back again without stopping it. The overhanging branches brushed their heads and the backs of their necks. Dust rose in a cloud behind them.

Sir Gerald and Lady Carfax of the Hall, coming down the road from the opposite direction, stood still to wave to them as they went by, then continued their interrupted constitutional. Jenifer watched the two thin upright figures, moving slowly, jerkily, like little marionettes, till they passed out of sight. They always fascinated her. They ought to have looked old, because they were both over eighty, but they looked quite young. Or, rather, they looked young in an old way, which was somehow horrible. She was glad that Grandma looked old in an old way. Still, she liked them, and she liked going to tea to the Hall, though she was secretly a little afraid of the stuffed heads with formidable branching horns that hung everywhere, because she could never help thinking how dreadful it would be if they suddenly came alive again and began to toss people. But there was a thrilling cupboard in the library that hid a hand basin with hot and cold water taps, and there was a musical box that played "Blue Bells of Scotland," and a little tin man who drew pictures on pieces of paper when you wound him up—real pictures of a horse and a ship and a sunflower that you could take home with you.

There was a sudden commotion in the wagonette as Luke discovered that one of his white rats was missing, and everyone began to take up the cushions and crawl about the floor, looking for it.

Sir Gerald and Lady Carfax walked on slowly with careful tottering steps.

"The little Burdetts, wasn't it?" said Sir Gerald, who was very short-sighted but wouldn't wear glasses.

"Yes. Dear children, but so noisy. And the two little Gainsborough girls were with them."

"Nice little girls."

"So pretty, the elder one. Like her mother."

"Yes. Good-looking woman."

Their voices were thin and ghostlike.

"Are you tired, my dear?"

"N-no, but we'll turn back at the end of the lane, shall we? Though we always used to get as far as the village."

"It's the heat, my dear."

"Yes. So tiring."

They looked a curious couple in the bright sunshine. His chest and shoulders were padded. His waist was pinched. His luxuriant black hair was obviously a wig, his moustache was dyed. A rather over-bright colour filmed the yellow-grey of his cheeks. She was his counterpart, with the tiniest of tiny waists, swelling hips and bosom, enamelled neck and face, bright golden wig. The enamel mask could not hide the old eyes that looked out of it. They had begun to defy the inroads of time in their middle age, and they had continued the process almost automatically. Their appearance was now grotesque, yet often some glance or movement would raise the ghost of their vanished good looks, and one saw them as they must have been in their youth, when they were the handsomest couple in the county. They lived a secluded life of unchanging routine in their barracks of a Victorian house, never emerging from their bedrooms till lunch time (though no one but his valet and her maid knew how long it took them to perform their elaborate toilets), going for a short walk in the afternoon, resting after tea before they dressed formally for dinner, going to bed always at half-past nine. The stiff, old-fashioned courtesy which they always showed to each other masked an affection that had stood the test of time. Each watched tenderly and with hidden desperate anxiety over the other's health.

The wagonette lumbered on down the road into the valley and finally drew up outside the Burdetts' cottage. It was a pleasant, if somewhat dilapidated, building that had originally been two labourers' cottages, separated from the road (a cart-track that ended at a neighbouring farm) by a wide stream, spanned by a plank. It was characteristic of Mrs Burdett that she had chosen the cottage because she thought that the stream would be "nice for the children." The "furniture" of the cottage consisted of articles that had been turned out of the Burdetts' house as past repair. Few of the chairs could be sat on, and a table with three legs looked strikingly intact among its neighbours.

The children poured down from the wagonette to the stream, splashing and shouting and pushing each other about. Michael, a sturdy child of two, was howling loudly. He had, indeed, seldom stopped howling since the expedition began. Howling seemed, with him, to take the place of breathing. He howled automatically, even when there was nothing to howl about, which, to do him justice, was not often. As the youngest (except, of course, for the baby) he was always being pushed over and trodden on and having his things taken from him.

"Well, leave them alone," his mother would say to him. "Keep out of their way." But he couldn't keep out of their way. He never felt really happy unless he was in the middle of them, being pushed over and trodden on and howling . . .

Mark drew Jenifer and Lorna away from the crowd and conducted them ceremoniously to the cottage. At the door stood Miss Burdett, a thin, worried-looking woman of about thirty, who was a distant cousin of Mr Burdett's. Mrs Burdett had asked her to spend her summer holiday at the cottage, and to Miss Burdett, whose home life was absorbed by an invalid mother, the invitation had seemed heaven-sent. She knew nothing of the Burdetts, and had accepted it with gratitude and delight. She had not, of course, realised then that it meant presiding over such of the young Burdetts as happened to be staying there. She had been at the cottage for a week now and had aged ten years since her arrival.

Mrs Burdett came slowly across the plank and up to the cottage door with the baby in her arms, smiling radiantly.

"Well, Hessie," she said, "isn't it a lovely spot!"

All that morning Hessie had been rehearsing the words that she was going to say to Mrs Burdett immediately on her arrival: "I'm sorry, Lilia, but I simply can't stay here. I mean, it was kind of you to ask me, but—well, it's too much for me. I can't stand another minute of it. I'm going home by the ten-thirty tomorrow morning."

She opened her lips and drew in her breath to say the words, but somehow they didn't come. Mrs. Burdett's childish pleasure in the outing, her magnificent assumption that she had given Hessie a real treat by inviting her to the cottage, were somehow disarming. She simply hadn't the heart to wipe that serene happy smile from Lilia's large countenance. Not now, anyway, when she'd only just arrived. She'd tell her later. After tea, perhaps. Whatever happened, she was going home by the ten-thirty tomorrow morning. She couldn't stand another day of it. It was like living with Red Indians or in the Zoo. She glanced down at the stream, and her thin anxious face froze into horror.

"*Look!*" she said. "They've pushed him right in. He's *soaking*."

Mrs Burdett looked at the figure of Michael, emerging dripping and howling from the stream, but the serenity of her smile remained undiminished.

"It doesn't matter," she said. "He'll dry in the sun." Her gaze travelled on to the other soaked splashing figures, and she added placidly, "They'll all dry in the sun."

"Shall I take the baby?" said the cousin, and Mrs Burdett, handing her the warm sleeping bundle, sank down with a sigh of content upon the wooden seat outside the cottage door.

"It really is *perfect!*" she said with another sigh. "I've been so excited about it that I hardly slept at all last night. I was terrified early this morning that it was going to rain."

Miss Burdett sat down by her on the seat with the baby on her lap. She was gazing with fascinated horror at the children who were still splashing about in the stream.

"Will—will they all be having tea here?" she faltered.

"Oh yes. We've brought the bread and jam. I suppose you've got enough milk?"

"They've sent some up from the farm."

The baby stirred and began to cry. Miss Burdett rocked it gently to and fro. Its cries increased in volume. Mrs Burdett took it, and gave it several rough jerks and pats. These seemed to satisfy it, and it snuggled down contentedly to sleep again. It was a dingy crumpled baby, but riotously healthy.

"Let me see," said Mrs Burdett thoughtfully. "Which of them have you got staying here now?"

"Geoffrey and Susannah and Charles and Rubina—"

Miss Burdett stopped in amazement. Only four? It couldn't be only four. She'd felt as if it had been at least a dozen. She counted again. It *was* only four . . . Once more she opened her lips and drew in her breath ("I have to go tomorrow, Lilia. By the ten-thirty. I'm sorry. I really can't stand any more of it"), but Mrs Burdett was gazing round serenely and saying: "I'm so glad to be able to give you a holiday like this, Hessie. It's lovely for you to be here in all this peace and quiet." And so pleased did Mrs Burdett look at the thought of being able to give Hessie a holiday in all this peace and quiet that again Hessie had not the heart to say the words. Suddenly Mrs Burdett turned and saw Jenifer and Lorna and Mark coming towards her.

"Oh, here's Lorna and Jenifer . . . They'll be staying at the cottage tonight. And so will Mark. And one or two of the others. I'll take the ones that have been here back with me, of course . . . Isn't it a lovely place, children! Now run off and play with the others."

Most of the others had left the stream and were playing a game in the field. They had a wide selection of games, but all of them seemed in practice to resolve themselves into an ordinary football scrum. Lorna and Mark withdrew to the edge of the field and, sitting down, began a desultory and somewhat stilted conversation. His admiration rendered him almost tongue-tied in her presence, and her knowledge of his admiration, though gratifying, made her also self-conscious and embarrassed. She longed to feel haughty and poised and assured, as she had felt when she met him in the village yesterday, but she could only feel like a shy little girl.

Jenifer looked around her. Some of the Burdetts were swinging on a home-made swing, consisting of a long loop of frayed rope hung from the branch of a tree. The rope broke at frequent intervals, precipitating them violently to the ground. They would get up, tie the ends of rope together, and continue the interrupted swing till it broke again. On the whole she thought that the game looked more interesting. It appeared to be the sort of game in which anyone can join at any point. Jenifer joined in and, soon mastering its rudimentary principles, began to push and scuffle with the rest, stopping occasionally to set the howling Michael on his feet. Once or twice she lifted him clear of the scrum, but he immediately returned to the heart of it. The white pique sailor-suit became stained with green where she rolled upon the grass, and several gathers were torn out where a pursuing Burdett caught hold of it. As the excitement of the game grew on her she began to shout as loudly as the others, wrestling, struggling, pushing . . . She even forgot to pick up Michael when she had knocked him over. There was certainly something infectious about the vitality of the young Burdetts. The game was interrupted by cries of "Tea," at which the whole crowd of players ran in a struggling mass to the cottage door. Michael followed at their heels, howling more loudly than ever at being thus left behind by his tormentors.

The baby had been taken into the cottage, and Mrs Burdett and her cousin stood at the door, dealing out enormous chunks of bread and jam. The young Burdetts dispensed with plates and knives.

Mark had secured a slice of bread and jam for Lorna. He was well aware, of course, that this was not the way such things should be done. He had helped to hand round cakes and cups of tea to parents at his school speech-day—dainty cakes on lace-covered plates, elegant china cups . . . It pained him to have to hand to this marvellous creature from a higher world a chunk of bread and jam on a grubby palm (he had tried without success to find a plate, and if he had stopped to wash his hands all the bread and jam would have disappeared), but there was nothing else to be done. He informed his manner as he did it with an almost exaggerated courtliness to make up for the absence of other amenities. Lorna received it with equal politeness and began to eat it with dainty disapproval, as if to prove that she was unaccustomed to such fare. But it was a long time since she had had lunch, and the open air had made her hungry, so, hearing a cry of "Hurry up if you want seconds. The bread's nearly finished," she abandoned further pretence of gentility and set to work on it with gusto. Mark, much relieved, followed her example, then ran to join the throng of claimants for "seconds," forcing his way unceremoniously to the front. He met Jenifer on his way back, and she accompanied him to where Lorna sat waiting for him. Lorna looked with disapproval at Jenifer's dishevelled hair, dirty face, and stained suit.

"Really, Jenifer!" she said. "What a dreadful mess you're in!"

She had an undefined feeling that this haughty, elder sister attitude somehow counteracted the effect of sitting under a hedge, eating thick chunks of bread and jam.

Jenifer looked down at her once white suit.

"Oh well," she said, "it's a picnic. You can't keep clean on a picnic."

"You mean *you* can't," said Lorna crushingly.

Then she turned to Mark and began to ask him about his school, speaking in an affected grown-up voice, and frequently laughing the new laugh. Mark's admiration increased each moment.

"When are you going away?" he said.

"At the end of the month. We've got a house at Westonlea. It's a very good beach for bathing, I believe, and there are some splendid walks along the top of the cliff."

Then she glanced up and caught Jenifer's eye. Jenifer was watching her in a detached impersonal way that Lorna found unspeakably exasperating.

"Go away and play with the others, Jenifer," she said severely. "Don't stand about listening to other people's conversation like that."

"You weren't saying anything private," said Jenifer.

"We don't want a baby like you listening to us *whatever* we say. Do you know, Mark, she's such a baby that once she woke up and screamed because she thought she saw a ghost, and it was only her own dressing-gown hanging over a chair."

She laughed, and Mark joined in. Jenifer's thoughts went back to the dreadful night when she woke up and thought that she saw two horrible eyes gleaming at her through the darkness, and it was only two of the metal buttons of her dressing-gown. Lorna had been very sweet and sympathetic and understanding, letting her come into her bed and comforting her. And now she was laughing at her . . .

Jenifer walked slowly away. The feeling she was chiefly conscious of was that of having made an important discovery. People could change quite suddenly from being nice about a thing to being nasty. The same people. And the same thing. And so you ought to be very careful about what you told people, even when they were being nice, because they might change quite suddenly to being nasty and laugh at you . . .

Chapter Six

Mrs Burdett sat on the wooden bench outside the cottage door, holding Michael on her knee and thrusting pieces of bread and jam into his mouth. His face was smeared with tears and dirt, and his nose was swollen with crying. During the scrimmage known as "tea," every piece of bread and jam he had managed to secure had been promptly taken from him and eaten by someone else. Miss Burdett sat beside them, still trying to screw up her courage to break the news that she was going home by the ten-thirty tomorrow morning.

"I quite envy you, you know, dear," Mrs Burdett was saying. "I'd come to stay here myself if it wasn't for looking after George. I had Cousin Maggie here last year. And the year before I had Charlotte, George's sister-in-law's friend, you know. It happened that none of them could come again, but in any case I think it's nicer to give someone else a chance, because it *is* such a perfect spot for a holiday, and, of course, the children stop you feeling lonely."

Miss Burdett agreed that they did, and added, "I simply *can't* get them to bed in time."

"Oh, that's all right," said Mrs Burdett. "They generally come in when they're tired."

"And the farmer was complaining of them this morning. I don't quite know what it was. Something about gates left open and a pig they'd let out of the farmyard. They said they'd been playing cowboys on it."

"Oh well, leave it to him," said Mrs Burdett imperturbably. "It's his business to keep them out of places he doesn't want them to go into. That's what I always say."

"And they've broken two windows with cricket-balls."

"Yes, of course, they do . . . Cardboard's a good idea, but it doesn't really keep the rain out. Generally I wait till there are enough broken to make it worth while to have someone up to mend them."

There was a short silence, during which Miss Burdett once more opened her mouth to say, "I'm sorry, Lilia. I've simply got to go by the ten-thirty tomorrow," but before she had time to say it Mrs Burdett broke the silence.

"It's so nice to feel that you're here, Hessie, and to know that everything's going on all right."

Miss Burdett closed her mouth again. Again she felt that she could not strip that look of content from Lilia's passive relaxed face. It would be like striking a child. There was something infinitely disarming about Lilia when she wasn't being either magnificent or rushed off her feet. Oh well . . . she supposed she'd just have to go through with it. It would come to an end some time. Things did. You just went on and on and on, and you found that a minute had gone, then five, then an hour, and at last it was the next day. And so on. If it didn't drive her into a lunatic asylum first. After all, she'd feel awful if she went now and left Lilia with no one to look after the cottage. That was the worst of being conscientious. She often envied people who weren't. They seemed to get so much more out of life. But if you were, you were, and it wasn't any use trying to fight against it. You might as well try to alter the shape of your nose. She sat up suddenly, her face tense with horror.

"Lilia," she said, "look at Charles."

Mrs Burdett turned her head and looked at the small figure that could be seen dangling precariously from the highest branch of the elm tree. Suddenly it began to drop from branch to branch. Miss Burdett drew in her breath sharply, but Mrs Burdett's expression of sleepy content did not alter.

"He'll be all right," she said, and added, "It's not Charles. It's Luke."

Miss Burdett watched, still stiff with horror, as the reckless descent continued. But Mrs Burdett's prophecy was fulfilled. He was all right. He landed, apparently, on his head, but immediately picked himself up and ran off shouting to join in the nearest game.

Lorna, looking cool and dainty and immaculate, still sat in the shadow of the hedge with Mark. The zest of the situation was fading somewhat. She was being very sweet to Mark, but he was so obviously and finally infatuated that it seemed rather a waste of sweetness. Some of the elder Burdett boys were holding a wrestling match near her. They were dishevelled and tousled and dirty—the shirt-sleeve of one had been torn right out, another had a black eye, and another a streak of mud all down his face— but despite that Lorna felt interested in them. She wanted to know them. She wanted them to know her . . . An unusually strenuous throw sent one of the wrestlers rolling to her feet. They apologised.

"It's quite all right," she said graciously.

They looked at her, timid and wild and on the defensive like young colts. She tried to think of something grownup to say but could only think of the immortal opening gambit of childhood, "How old are you?"

They answered in turn, evidently impressed by her looks and manner, then the boy with the black eye returned diffidently:

"How old are you?"

"Ten . . . Isn't it jolly here? Do you come here every summer?"

They began to talk, shyly at first, then with increasing vivacity, telling her about the woods on the hill-side and the games they played there, about the stream and the fishes they had caught.

"Honest, I caught ten in about two minutes once. Jolly big ones. Tiddlers."

"I think there's really big fish higher up where it gets deeper. Trout an' things. I shan't be surprised if there's salmon. I've seen big holes there where I bet they hide up."

"An' I think there's wolves in the wood that only come out at night. I bet you anything I saw a wolf's foot-mark there this morning."

Lorna showed a flattering interest and credulity.

"Did you *really*. . .?"

She had a pleasant mental picture of herself surrounded by these young savages. Beauty and the beasts. Mark drew away, vaguely hurt.

A crowd of children rushed past, shouting, "Come on. We're going to play."

Suddenly Lorna felt tired of sitting by the hedge and being grown-up. She leapt to her feet and joined in the game, shouting and pushing . . .

Michael had wandered off to the farm and had fallen into the midden, from which he had been rescued by Eglantine, the eldest girl. He was making his way across the field now, an unsavoury little object, covered with manure. The others ran away from him, holding their noses in exaggerated disgust. He pursued them on short fat legs, howling loudly. He wanted to be in the thick of them, being knocked over and pushed about and trodden on. He couldn't bear being left alone . . .

Miss Burdett led him to his mother, her thin face again transfixed with horror.

"What *shall* we do with him?" she said.

Mrs Burdett glanced down undismayed at her dung-encrusted son.

"It'll brush off when it dries," she said and, gathering him, manure and smell and all, into her large lap, crooned: "There, there, my pet. It's all right. Don't cry."

The neat precise figure of Mr Burdett, who had cycled over to escort his family home, now appeared among the crowd. He met Jenifer, took off his hat politely, and opened his mouth to speak. His face worked convulsively for some moments, but no words came. Suddenly he abandoned the attempt and sang in a clear tenor voice: "How are you, my dear child? And how are your parents?"

"Very well, thank you," said Jenifer, conquering a strong desire to sing back at him.

Mrs Burdett greeted her husband affectionately.

"Oh, there you are, dear. It's about time we were collecting together, isn't it? We've had such a lovely time, haven't we, Hessie?"

Miss Burdett blinked speechlessly behind her glasses.

"I think it's done Hessie good already, don't you?" went on Mrs Burdett. "She's got quite a colour."

Miss Burdett, still hot and breathless from pursuing a small Burdett who had run off with the only remaining pot of jam, again blinked speechlessly behind her glasses.

Noah was harnessing the ancient cart horse to the wagonette, while young Burdetts swarmed over him, climbing from his back on to the horse, from the horse on to the wagonette.

Mrs Burdett fetched the baby, who was still asleep in the cottage, and there was a scene of indescribable chaos as they all prepared to depart. Finally, the loaded wagonette set off with its shouting cargo, leaving Mark, Lorna, Jenifer, Claude, Davida, and Marigold to stay the night at the cottage.

Miss Burdett gazed despairingly in the direction in which it was disappearing. She simply couldn't imagine why she hadn't been firmer. It was terrible to think that she wasn't going home by the ten-thirty tomorrow morning, after all. She went upstairs to her small attic bedroom, sat down on her bed, and had a good cry. Then she looked at her watch and realised that it was supper time. The good cry had made her feel better, and she was now ready to do her duty. She went downstairs to the little kitchen, got out another loaf, and began to cut huge chunks of bread and spread them with jam. She seemed to have been doing that for weeks, months, years. Ever since she was born. She couldn't realise that she'd only been here a few days. You made great saucepanfuls of stew and potatoes and vegetables and suet puddings for dinner in the middle of the day, but for all the other meals you sawed chunks of bread and spread them with jam. And they disappeared as soon as you'd spread them. The first day she'd really thought that her arm was going to drop off. Lilia had said when she arrived that there would be nothing to do beyond just looking after the children. It had sounded so simple . . .

They were pouring in at the open door now, panting, hot,

dishevelled. There weren't many of them, but even two of the little Burdetts could seem a crowd. Even one could . . . The two little girls who had come to stay the night had been so fresh and clean and nicely behaved at first, but now they looked almost as bad as the others. The younger one quite as bad. Mark, too, was beginning to lose his beautiful manners, and to push and scuffle like the rest. Two extra children had turned up, who had been left behind by the wagonette. They'd have to have her bed, and she'd have to sleep in the sitting-room. How on earth was she going to stand a whole month of it? Oh well, she'd made up her mind to it now and she'd just go through with it. Even if it killed her, as it probably would.

She put on water for washing, and went out to fetch some of them in to bed. Getting them to bed was the worst part of the whole day. But tonight they weren't as bad as usual. They were tired and came in about the fifth time she called them.

The bedroom in which Jenifer and Lorna were to sleep contained two small beds, one of which Lorna was to share with Marigold, the other of which Jenifer was to share with Davida. Jenifer got into bed quickly. All her excitement had faded and she was feeling homesick and miserable. Home and Mother seemed so far away as to be in another world. She had a horrible feeling that she might never see them again . . . The others were still scampering up and down stairs, shouting and laughing and throwing pillows at each other. Suddenly they all invaded her bedroom and began to tickle her. It was like a nightmare... . Hot fingers under her arms, on her neck, all over her body. She tried to scream, but she couldn't get her breath.

"Leave her alone," said Lorna suddenly. "She doesn't like it."

The Burdetts stopped, amazed.

"Doesn't like being *tickled?*" they said.

They couldn't believe it.

Jenifer was trying to get her breath. It came in little sobbing gasps.

They looked at her with dispassionate interest.

"What's the matter with her? Is she choking?"

"No," said Lorna. "She doesn't like being tickled, that's all. It always makes her like that. She'll be sick if you go on."

"Isn't she funny?" they said, and lost interest in her.

Gradually silence fell over the house. Davida got into bed with Jenifer, and Marigold with Lorna. Cousin Hessie came upstairs and tucked up the children, then went down to the sitting-room, drinking in the silence as a thirsty man drinks water. Sounds of deep breathing came from the bed where Lorna and Marigold were. Sounds of deep breathing came from Davida. Jenifer stirred and wriggled uneasily. Davida's soft warm body was pressing against her. Jenifer couldn't bear being touched. It was almost as bad as being tickled. People didn't touch you at home except just to kiss you, and they didn't kiss you often. She and Lorna had always had separate beds. The feeling of Davida's warm soft body was horrible. She shrank away from it . . . Davida, sleeping peacefully, followed her, and again the plump warm softness of her was pressed against Jenifer. Again Jenifer shrank from it, finding herself now at the very edge of the bed. Even there it pursued and overtook her. She got out of bed and stood for a moment, gazing at the three sleeping children. Then she went to the window. It was almost dark—a twilit dark that seemed to hold the trees and fields in a tender embrace as they slept. Not the sort of dark that frightened you. The sky was a deep blue, sprinkled with stars. She leant out of the window and let the cool night breeze fan her face. She still felt hot and sticky. She still seemed to feel Davida's warm plump body pressing against hers . . .

She leant out further. The stream was the only thing that was not asleep besides herself. It ran and danced unresting in the starlight. She opened the door carefully and crept down the stairs on her bare feet. The sitting-room door was open, and through it she could see the form of Cousin Hessie outstretched on a bed made from a sofa and two chairs, sleeping the sleep of utter exhaustion.

She tried the cottage door. It was unlocked. She walked down to the stream. The dew-drenched grass was grateful to her hot feet.

When she came to the stream she drew off her nightdress and stood naked for a moment in the half light, then stepped into the stream and lay down in the water, first on her stomach, then on her back. She rubbed with her hand all the places where Davida's plump little body had pressed against her and where the fingers of the ticklers had clutched and mauled. She seemed actually to see the marks being washed off and carried down the stream—dark little swirls like stains. Cold and cleansing, the water flowed over her. She plunged her face into it, wetting her red-gold curls. Then she rose, shivering but happy, put on her nightdress, and returned to the cottage. Inside the door she paused irresolute. She couldn't go back to the bed where Davida awaited her. She peeped into the sitting-room again. Cousin Hessie still snored peacefully. She went into the kitchen. There was a rag hearthrug in front of the fireplace. It was rather dirty, but Jenifer curled up on it and in spite of her general dampness soon went to sleep.

Miss Burdett found her there in the morning and, waking her, informed her with much perturbation that she must have walked from the bedroom in her sleep. Jenifer did not contradict her, and the story caused something of a mild sensation in the cottage, the children shouting the news to each other from room to room.

"I say, Jenifer walked in her sleep. She went down to the kitchen."

But the sensation was overshadowed by the sudden realisation that no arrangements had been made for sending Lorna and Jenifer home.

"Mother's expecting us for lunch," said Lorna firmly. "We *must* be home by lunch time."

"But how are you to get there?" moaned Cousin Hessie. "The others are staying till the end of the week, and there's no station or bus, and you can't possibly walk."

It was Mark who suggested running over to the farm, to find out if anyone was driving into Merrowvale from there, and who came back triumphant with the information that a milk-cart was on the point of setting out. He took leave of Lorna with obvious devotion, but the extreme courtliness of his manners was certainly wearing thin, and Lorna felt that he ought to have been far more

69

apologetic for the general inadequateness of the entertainment than he was.

Jenifer loved the drive down to Merrowvale, standing upright in the little cart among the tall gleaming milk-cans. The man let her drive and told her about the dog at the farm who stole apples and the cow who *would* jump over the hedge.

To Lorna it was an acute humiliation to go bumping along in a milk-cart, wearing a tumbled, soiled, white sailor suit (though it wasn't half as bad as Jenifer's, which was *dreadful)* on the road where she had so often imagined herself driving in her own carriage and pair. The people they passed threw glances of mild interest at them, but Lorna felt that all the countryside was watching her in shocked disapprobation and would never forget it. The whole visit had been dreadful. No, it hadn't, though . . . not altogether. The memory of Mark's admiration was very pleasant. And the other boys, too . . . They'd obviously liked her. She looked at the man who was driving the cart. He was a pleasant, nice-looking young man. Jenifer was chattering to him, and, as Lorna watched, he threw back his head and roared with laughter at something she had said.

Lorna came out of her sulks and began to join in the conversation. Soon she had ousted Jenifer from her place next the driver and was absorbing his whole attention.

Miss Marchant opened the door and gave a scream of horror when she saw them.

"Go *straight* upstairs and wash, and change those clothes at once," she ordered.

Mother came out of the kitchen and laughed as she kissed them.

"You might be little Burdetts," she said. "It's my fault for sending you in your new sailor-suits. It's all right, Miss Marchant," with slight irritation, as Miss Marchant continued to cluck and fuss over the crumpled stained dresses.

"They'll wash, and it's only torn out of the seam . . . Well, what was it like?"

"It wasn't really too bad," said Lorna. "Jenifer walked in her sleep. They found her asleep on the kitchen rug this morning. She must have gone all the way downstairs in her sleep. The stairs are awfully steep, and Miss Burdett said it was a mercy she hadn't broken her neck."

They looked at Jenifer with interest, and Jenifer's eyes slid away guiltily.

"You've never done that before, have you, dear?" said Mother.

"No," said Jennifer.

"Well, run along and get clean now."

They went upstairs. Adrian and Laurence came out of the playroom.

"Oh, there you are," said Laurence. There was a warmly welcoming note in his voice. "Was it awful?"

"It wasn't too bad," said Lorna again. "Jenifer walked in her sleep."

"We came home in the milk-cart," said Jenifer, hastily changing the subject.

Adrian took two humbugs from his pocket and handed one to each of them.

"I bought them yesterday and kept them for you," he said.

They were sticky and slightly hairy from contact with Adrian's pocket, but they tasted all right once you'd got past the fluff.

Lorna and Jenifer sucked contentedly as they went upstairs to the bathroom, where Miss Marchant was already turning on the taps.

It was nice to be home again . . .

Chapter Seven

It was the week before they were to go away to the sea, and there was an air of excitement over everything. On the Thursday Marcia and Miss Marchant went into Leaveston to do some final shopping, leaving the children in Emma's charge. The children always enjoyed being left with Emma. She was good-natured and easy-going and let them do what they liked. The only thing that made her cross was pulling the long streamers of her cap. Otherwise she was imperturbable. She let them ride on her back while she scrubbed the floor, and play shop with the kitchen scales, and make tents of the table cloths, and slide downstairs on tin trays, and do innumerable other things that were forbidden by Miss Marchant.

They had meant to go into the garden to build a fort in the new sand heap and man it with Laurence's toy soldiers, but it had begun to rain soon after breakfast, so Lorna and Adrian and Laurence were sliding downstairs on tin trays, and Jenifer was sitting astride the big banister at the bottom of the stairs, singing her banister song in a shrill tuneless voice.

> "Here I sit on the banisto,
> Laughing at my husband O,
> Who's cross because I will not go
> To church on a Sunday morning."

She didn't know when she'd made it up, but she'd sung it ever since she could remember, and it always gave her a pleasant feeling of exultation and lawlessness to sit on the big banister shouting it out at the top of her voice. She never sang it anywhere else.

Suddenly Emma called from the kitchen.

"Anyone want to make a cookie boy?"

They scrambled downstairs with a rattle of tin trays and swarmed into the kitchen. Jenifer arrived last because it took her some time to get down from her perch. They all thought that the kitchen was the nicest room in the house. It looked so cosy and cheerful, with the firelight gleaming on to the six brightly polished metal dish-covers of graduated size that hung over the dresser. The names of the dish covers were Father, Mother, Lorna, Adrian, Laurence, and Jenifer. Jenifer was the teeny, teeny one, and the real Jenifer always gave it a look of friendly greeting when she went into the kitchen.

Emma was just taking a cloth from the row of baking-tins that stood on the hearth.

The dough had risen in smooth pale balloons over each tin, and on each were the three knife-marks that the children loved to be allowed to make.

"Oh, you've not let us do the jabs," said Laurence.

"Well, you weren't here," said Emma. "Now, make your cookie boys quick, because I'm just going to put them in." She took down a jar from the cupboard. "There are the currants."

The four seized upon the pieces of dough that had been left on the flour-covered table, and began to work them together as Emma did when she made bread, turning up the edges and pressing them down into the middle. They prolonged the fascinating process as much as they could, then made the cookie boys—round head, round body, cylindrical arms and legs, currants for eyes, nose, mouth, and buttons. Emma put them on a tin and slipped them into the oven with the loaves.

"They'll be as hard as nails the way you've been messing them about," she said.

They knew, of course, that it made the cookie boys uneatable to work the dough about so much, but they could never resist doing it.

Emma began to get out materials for making a cake. They crowded round her, begging to be allowed to help.

"*Help!*" jeered Emma sarcastically. "A fine lot of helping you do."

Emma, however, was the eldest of a family of thirteen, and never felt quite in her element unless surrounded by a flock of children.

"All right," she went on, "but don't get under my feet all the time, for goodness' sake."

"Can I scrape the dish when you've finished, Emma?"

"Can I lick the spoon?"

"Get out of my way, *do!*" said Emma, but she let Lorna weigh the flour and Jenifer the butter, and Laurence mix it and Adrian stir it. Then she let them make little balls of the cake mixture and dip them in sugar, and after that gave them liberal handfuls of currants.

"I don't know what that Miss Marchant would say if she saw me."

Emma lived in a state of perpetual feud with the mother's help and always referred to her as "that Miss Marchant." She filled the tins, leaving liberal "scrapings" in the bowl and on the spoon, and after a short scuffle Lorna and Adrian secured the bowl, and Jenifer and Laurence the spoon.

"Isn't it lovely?" said Jenifer, her small nose covered with the mixture. "It's much nicer raw than cake."

"Keep out of my way, do! I never saw such children for getting under my feet," said Emma as she bustled about the kitchen.

"Emma, let me clean a window. *Please.* I did once."

"Yes, and nearly went through it."

"Let me clean silver, then. I promise I'll do it nicely."

"*Clean!*" echoed Emma. "A nice lot of cleaning you'll do."

She lifted the silver teapot from the cupboard, however, and Jenifer, swathed in a large apron, mixed the Goddard powder with water, rubbed it on the shining surface, and then brushed it with a little brush.

"I *am* helping, aren't I?" she said anxiously.

"Of course you are, bless your heart," replied Emma.

"Emma, tell us about your uncle," pleaded Lorna, who was leaning against the table and nibbling currants from the jar that Emma had left there. "The one that saw a ghost."

"Yes," said Emma, wiping down the dresser with sweeping

movements of her large red arms. "That Miss Marchant can say there's no such things till she's black in the face. He seed it plain as I see you now. He was taking a short cut through the churchyard late one night an' all of a sudden it come along, tall an' white, movin' through the tombstones . . ."

They had heard the story dozens of times before, but they never tired of it.

The smell of baking bread was filling the kitchen. Emma opened the oven door, and the children crowded round excitedly, claiming their cookie boys and demanding "run-overs."

"There didn't ought to be no run-overs by rights," said Emma cheerfully, breaking off the crisp brown pieces of newly baked bread that hung down over the tins, and distributing them. "It's bad baking, that's what my mother'd say."

The children crunched the delicious "run-overs" and examined their cookie boys critically. They had, as usual, changed beyond recognition, spreading in all directions, losing the shapely contours that had been so carefully bestowed on them by their makers. They nibbled them tentatively, but they were, as always, hard and unpalatable.

"It's with you messing them about so much," said Emma. "I tell you every time."

She was running a knife along the tins and turning out the fragrant loaves on to a wire tray.

"I've finished the teapot," said Jenifer.

"Finished is as finished does," said Emma.

She took the smeared teapot and polished it up with brisk jerky movements. Then she blew a hearty breath that covered the whole surface with a grey film, which she rubbed away to a dazzling brightness.

"Let me do that," pleaded Jenifer, and blew with all her might, but her breath would only make an inch or two of film. She drew little patterns on it before it faded, then blew another and drew a little face.

"Now, that'll do," said Emma briskly, sweeping the teapot up, giving it a final polish, and putting it back in the cupboard.

"I wish it would stop raining," said Lorna disconsolately.

Jenifer joined her at the window and continued the fascinating process of making a film with her breath and drawing faces in it.

"You are disgusting," said Lorna in her grown-up voice.

Jenifer went on blowing and making little faces.

"I'm going up to the playroom," said Lorna.

Laurence had been leaning over the kitchen table, eating lemon peel and currants, and the front of his suit was covered with flour.

"Just look at you!" said Emma. "I don't know what your Ma would say."

"She'd laugh and tell Miss Marchant to brush it off," said Jenifer.

"Smarty!" said Emma. She began to clear up the table. "Who's upset all these currants?"

"I haven't," said the children in chorus.

"Oh no, you're all lily-white hens," said Emma.

"Let's act," said Jenifer suddenly.

"No, I'm going to the playroom," said Lorna, who considered acting babyish.

"I'll go, too," said Laurence. "I'm going to tidy my shelf."

"Yes, you'd better," said Emma, "or you'll have that Miss Marchant on your track. I never saw such a mess as it's in."

'You act, Adrian," pleaded Jenifer.

"All right," said Adrian, who enjoyed acting almost as much as Jenifer did.

The other two went upstairs, and Jenifer and Adrian began to prepare their scene. They always acted episodes from *The Knights of the Round Table*, and they always wore aprons tied round their necks and hanging over one arm for cloaks, and tea-cosies or saucepans on their heads. This time they were two knights fighting in a tourney, and Jenifer kept running to the back kitchen to plunge her face into water, which she pretended was blood pouring down from a wound in her head.

Emma watched with naïve interest as she worked, every now and then ejaculating, "Well, I never!" or "Fancy that!"

But, as always happened when they acted, Adrian suddenly got over-excited, and began to hit out wildly with the walking stick that was his sword. He was obviously going to do some damage with it, and then, of course, he would burst into tears. At present he was laughing hilariously, but Emma read the signs of over-excitement.

"Now, that's enough," she said briskly. "You'll be laughing the other side of your face next thing we know. Out you get, while I red up the kitchen."

Emma's mother had come from Yorkshire, and Emma always said "red" instead of "tidy."

They went upstairs to the playroom. The long rainy morning was beginning to get on their nerves. Lorna was in her bedroom, ostensibly tidying her drawers, really arranging her hair in different styles, tying her ringlets first on one side of her head, then on the other, then in the nape of her neck, then letting them flow loose over her shoulders. Tiring of that, she went into her mother's room for some hairpins, and did her hair up into a "bun," draping the dressing-table cover over her shoulders for a scarf.

In the playroom, Laurence was putting the last stamp album neatly on the shelf.

"I've tidied it," he said, with an air of conscious virtue as Jenifer entered. "Some things had fallen on to it from your shelf, but only rubbish. I've thrown them away."

"What were they?" said Jenifer.

"Only some old picture post cards. I threw them away with my rubbish. I knew you didn't want them."

Jenifer's small face flamed crimson with anger.

"I *did* want them. You *beast!* I'll throw *your* things away. I'll—"

She snatched an envelope marked "swops" from his shelf and was just going to tear it up when he sprang at her. In a second they were fighting like a couple of small animals, their faces, tense and red with fury, hitting, scratching, biting, punching, wrestling. Jenifer was small, but wiry, and rage gave her strength. Emma heard the sounds of the struggle from the kitchen, but beyond a mildly remonstrative "Now then, you there!" she took no notice of it. In her dealings with children her guiding principle was to "leave them to it"—a method that was generally successful. A crash was followed by a sudden silence. In the course of the fight Jenifer had fallen with her head against the skirting-board.

"I'm awfully sorry, Jen," said Laurence contritely. "Have I hurt you?"

Jenifer sat up and rubbed her head. She was bruised and breathless, but she felt much better than before she had fought Laurence, and suddenly she didn't mind his having thrown away her post cards.

"I saw stars," she said. "I honestly did. Real stars."

"You're going to have an awful lump."

"Well, you've got a scratch all down the side of your face."

"I'm sorry."

"I'm sorry."

He helped her to her feet, and they both laughed.

Adrian, sitting cross-legged on the window seat, had watched the struggle with a mixture of horror and excitement. He felt righteously indignant with Laurence, and was vaguely piqued and disappointed by their reconciliation. He went to Jenifer and put his arm consolingly about her shoulders.

"Poor little Jen!" he said, and to Laurence: "You ought to be ashamed. Hitting a girl like that, and a girl younger than yourself!"

"You shut up and mind your own business," said Laurence with spirit.

Jenifer shook off the consoling arm. "Yes, you shut up and mind your own business," she said.

Adrian turned and went quickly out of the room.

Laurence shrugged.

"Now we've hurt his feelings. I don't care." He went to the window. "It's stopped raining. Let's go out. I say, I've got twopence in my money-box. Let's go out and spend it. A penny for you, and a penny for me."

"Oh, Laurie, how lovely! I'll buy a sugar pig."

Jenifer loved sugar pigs. Their only drawback was that they looked so attractive that she could hardly bear to eat them.

"Well, we've got to get the twopence out first."

Laurence's money-box was in the shape of a pillar-box with a slot for coins at the top, and the only way to get the money out was to shake it up and down or, as a last resort, put in a kitchen knife. They shook it ineffectively for some time, growing excited whenever the pennies appeared in the aperture and seemed to be on the point of coming out.

"It's no good," said Laurence at last. "We'll have to get a knife."

They ran down to the kitchen, where Emma put a knife down the slot and manoeuvred the pennies out.

"Spending all your money!" she said. "I never saw the like. The workhouse is where you'll end."

As they were putting on their hats in the hall, Lorna appeared at the top of the stairs.

"Where are you going?"

"Down to the shop to spend Laurence's twopence."

Lorna waited for a moment in case they were going to ask her to join them but, as they didn't, decided to take the offensive.

"You've been fighting," she said severely, "and you've made Adrian cry. I shall tell Mother."

"Shut up and mind your own business," said Laurence again rudely.

Outside the air was clean and fragrant after the rain. The sun had come out and was shining on the drops that hung on hedges and trees and roadside grass, making them sparkle like tiny jewels.

"I'll race you to the shop," said Laurence, and they ran down the road, splashing through puddles or leaping over them. Jenifer was a good runner and was not far behind Laurence when they reached the shop. He had not run his fastest, of course, because he was still feeling a slight compunction for having hurt her.

They entered the shop, breathless. Old Mrs Cannon, the proprietress, smiled at them over her spectacles.

"Well, lovies?" she said.

"Two sugar pigs, please," panted Jenifer, pushing her penny on to the counter.

"Penny liquorice pipe, please," said Laurence.

"Liquorice pipes is always your favourite, isn't it, sonny?" she said, as she handed the pipe across the counter. "An' sugar pigs is yours, isn't it, missie?"

"What was your favourite when you were a little girl?" demanded Jenifer.

Mrs Cannon shook her head.

"Eh, I've forgotten," she said. "It's so long ago."

A wave of depression swept over Jenifer. How dreadful to be so old that you'd forgotten which had been your favourite sweets when you were a little girl!

They went out into the road again.

"When I'm very old, Laurie," said Jenifer, "will you remind me that I liked sugar pigs best? And I'll remind you that you liked liquorice pipes."

"Um," said Laurence.

He walked on happily, sucking his pipe, occasionally opening his lips with little popping noises in imitation of his father. Then he took it out and handed it to her.

"Have a suck?"

"Thanks," said Jenifer gratefully, taking several sucks at the fast disappearing stem of the pipe before she handed it back. "You don't mind not having any of the sugar pigs just yet, do you?" she went on. "I'm not starting eating them just yet. I'll give you two legs as soon as I do."

It was still fine and sunny. The birds sang blithely, and the raindrops pattered merrily upon the leaves as the breeze swayed the branches, sending little showers down upon the children underneath, who laughed and ducked.

"Oo, it's raining again."

"No, it isn't . . . it's only pretending."

A group of Burdetts were coming along the road, clustered round Marigold, who walked in the middle, looking pale and tense. Her godmother had sent her a shilling that morning, and the others were coming to help her spend it at the shop. They saw Jenifer and Laurence, and halted.

"Hello," they said.

"Hello," replied Jenifer and Laurence, trying to hold the pipe and sugar pigs out of sight. They had suffered before from the young Burdetts' raids on their sweets.

"We've got a shilling to spend," said a young Burdett importantly.

"It's *my* shilling," said Marigold, tightening her clasp on it till her little knuckles looked like bare bones.

"Well, you'll give me some, won't you, Marigold? I've said I'm sorry for pinching you this morning."

"You'll give *me* some, won't you, Marigold? *I* didn't pinch you."

"Marigold, I'll give you that doll's chair of mine from the doll's house. It's only a little broken."

They pressed close to her affectionately, pleadingly.

"Oh, do stop *pushing* me," snapped Marigold, and moved on, a small, pale, anxious figure in the midst of her clamorous bodyguard.

Laurence heaved a sigh of relief.

"I'm glad they've got some money of their own," he said. "There wouldn't have been much left of my pipe by the time they'd all had a suck."

They walked slowly along the road, sometimes jumping over the puddles, sometimes deliberately splashing into them with a pleasant sense of lawlessness, glad that Lorna wasn't there to "boss" them.

At the bend of the road they met Rosa Pickering with her mother. Rosa wasn't allowed to play with other children, because her mother never knew what she might "pick up" from them. Occasionally a few carefully selected children were asked to tea and played quiet games, organised and presided over by Mrs Pickering, but these parties were not popular, and only such guests as had not been able to prevail upon their parents to refuse the invitation attended them. Rosa was a plain uninteresting child with a vacant horselike face, but Mrs Pickering laboured under the delusion that she was both beautiful and gifted. She taught her herself in order that her rare intellect might not be vulgarised by contact with the ordinary teacher and the ordinary teaching methods, and concentrated on what she called the "artistic side" of her. The result was that Rosa was a walking mass of parlour tricks. She danced the hornpipe, the Irish Jig, and the Scotch Reel; she recited innumerable "pieces" and could play "The Maiden's Prayer" and "The Merry Peasant" without music. Moreover, she did all these things on the slightest provocation. Quite simply she accepted her mother's estimate of her and took for granted that her performances gave intense delight to her audiences. She accompanied Mrs Pickering to all the local tea-parties, and the parcel containing Rosa's dancing shoes reposed on the hatstand next to the parcel containing Mrs Pickering's songs. They were the days when guests took their music out to parties with them as a matter of course, left it in the hall, and affected surprise and dismay when asked to perform. Rosa, however, dispensed with the surprise and dismay, and, once started, was impossible to stop. She would go through her entire repertoire, while Mrs Pickering smiled proudly and beat time with her hands.

"Well, dears, how are you?" said Mrs Pickering to Laurence and Jennifer. "Shake hands nicely, Rosa."

Rosa shook hands nicely.

"Rosa can say good afternoon in French," went on Mrs Pickering. "Say it, Rosa."

"*Bong jure,*" said Rosa complacently.

"*There!*" said Mrs Pickering. "And she can say goodbye too. Say it, Rosa."

"*O-revoor*" said Rosa still more complacently.

"*There!*" said Mrs Pickering again to Jenifer. "You can't say that, can you, dear?"

"Yes," said Jenifer simply, and repeated "*O-revoor.*"

Mrs Pickering laughed.

"Funny little girl . . . Come along, Rosa. Say goodbye nicely."

Rosa said goodbye nicely, and they went on down the road.

"Aren't they awful!" said Laurence. "Have another suck?"

"Thanks. I'm going to start the sugar pig now. Have a leg?"

Near the gate of The Chestnuts Miss Frewin overtook them. The Frewins had been at The Firs for several weeks now, but the little girl had not yet appeared. Miss Frewin was a thin, small, worn-looking woman, bowlegged and almost hunchbacked.

Looking at her bowed spindly figure, you saw her as she must have been in her childhood—underfed, overworked, staggering about under the weight of coal buckets or pails of water, carrying a baby almost before she could walk herself. Her face was shrewd and sharp and deeply lined, shining generally from a good wash with kitchen soap. She dressed in rusty black and never seemed to have any new clothes. Yet the dingy stooping little figure radiated vitality. Thin and misshapen though it was, it seemed capable of never-ceasing energy and endurance. Miss Frewin scorned the amenities that her brother's wealth could now give her. She despised "hired help" and labour-saving devices. With her skirts tucked up to her knees, wearing an apron of coarse sacking, she scrubbed and scoured the floors, she polished and dusted, washed the clothes, and cooked the meals. The Leaveston tradesmen had learnt to respect and fear her. She would tramp from shop to shop, pricing what she wanted in each before she bought anything—a process known to the tradesmen as "Ma Frewin's route march." She took for granted that the chief aim of every tradesman in the district was to swindle her, and her energy found periodic outlet in a row of heroic proportions that would leave the erring tradesman speechless and shaken. She carried a laden shopping basket now that drew her figure on to one side, making her walk with an odd, crab-like gait.

"Well, how are you?" she asked the children. "What time are your Ma and Miss Marchant coming back?"

She never seemed to look out of her window or to take her eyes off her work, but she knew everything that went on in the next house.

"Tea-time," answered Jenifer.

"We're expecting Ruby home about that time, too. My niece, you know."

About tea-time, when the children were gathered at the window, watching for the return of Marcia and Miss Marchant, a cab drew up at the next door, and a little girl got down from it. She was a very pretty little girl, with dark silky ringlets and dark eyes. She threw a casual glance at the window of The Chestnuts, and, completely self-assured despite the scrutiny of the four children, walked up the steps to the front door of The Firs.

Chapter Eight

Westonlea was a small village perched on the edge of the cliff, from which a flight of ramshackle wooden steps led down to a little bay, where fishing-boats lay beached on the pebbles and fishermen's wives sat mending the nets.

There was an ancient bathing-machine, attached to a somnolent grey horse, who drew it out into the water so that the bathers might emerge with decency, and a gloomy old woman attendant, who thought all bathing dangerous and unhygienic, and was constantly advising her charges to come out before they caught their deaths.

The children loved the place. Low tide showed firm golden sand, but at high tide there were the pebbles to play with—pebbles of all colours, washed round and shining by the sea, and among them shells, some of them almost too tiny and perfect to be real. Jenifer hunted among them for hours, putting her finds into an old boot-box that Emma had given her.

The little cottage where they were staying was spotlessly clean. Hedges of lavender bordered the path that led down from the front door to the little green gate. There were white muslin curtains at the windows, and from all the rooms you could hear the sound of the sea, sometimes singing softly to itself, sometimes grumbling, sometimes roaring . . .

The sitting-room was full of shells—small shells, large shells, shells of every size and shape and colour. They stood between the pots of geraniums on the window sill and on the little fretwork brackets that hung in all the corners of the room. Photograph frames made of shells, alternating with boxes made of shells, covered mantelpiece and sideboard.

There was a horsehair sofa by the wall, on which Laurence and Adrian sat for meals, but they had to have cushions to sit on, because the little hairs that protruded from the surface of the seat worked their way through even the stoutest knickers.

Miss Marchant was spending her holiday with the invalid aunt, and Emma had come to look after them. Emma regarded all the domestic arrangements of the cottage with fierce contempt, especially the oil-lamps and water-pump.

"If people've got to live like savages, they've got to," she said, as she stood at the bedroom window, combing Jenifer's hair, and watching Frank working the pump handle in his shirt-sleeves just below. "What I can't understand is them doing it for pleasure."

"He's not a savage," laughed Jenifer. "He doesn't look a bit like a savage."

"Now then!" said Emma. "Laugh before breakfast, cry before night."

Frank did most of the rough work of the little cottage when Emma was busy with the children. He hated to see his wife doing manual work of any description. He liked to think of her beautifully dressed, sitting at her ease and waiting for him to return to her from wherever he was. The streak of indolence in her made her accept the role with that faintly ironic amusement with which she accepted most things.

Already Major Pettigrew, who lived in the big house beyond the village, was her slave, bringing fruit and flowers and vegetables from his garden, recklessly offering her the services of his staff for the work of the cottage, sending his carriage to take her for drives, staggering himself down the steps to the beach under the weight of her deck-chair and books and work-box.

"The man's really a nuisance," grumbled Frank.

"No, darling, he isn't," said Marcia. "His peaches are lovely, and it's so nice to have everything taken down to the beach every day."

"I'd take your things down for you."

"Why should you fag more than you need on your holiday? Let him do it!"

Frank was teaching Jenifer and Lorna to swim, though they liked best to be carried out to sea by him, holding on to his shoulder. Laurence was a good swimmer already (he had learnt the year before), but Adrian was nervous, and, after the first few mornings, refused to go into the water at all. He refused to go out in the fishing boats with the others, too, because the sight of the dead and dying fish made him feel sick. Instead, he would bring a sketching block down to the beach and paint his oddly effective little sketches of sky and sea and cliff. Laurence went for long walks alone, absorbed in the study of the cliff wildlife, lying motionless for hours watching the birds. Sometimes, on a promise of implicit obedience and quietness, he let Jenifer go with him, and she would crouch silently on the ground by his side, waiting and watching . . . She wasn't as much interested in birds and insects as Laurence was, but she liked to be with him, and she used to pretend that they were outlaws hiding from their pursuers.

Lorna had quickly become popular with all the inhabitants of the village—the fishermen, the coastguard men, the bathing-van woman, the proprietress of the little shop. She talked to them and always remembered to ask after their relations and ailments. There was a morose old man with one leg, who used to sit on a kitchen chair in the sun in the doorway of his cottage, and his complete ignoring of her overtures hung over her spirit like a cloud. She didn't like the old man—he was, indeed, a very disagreeable old man—but she wanted him to like her, to smile at her, to call her (as she overheard the others calling her) a "sweet little missie."

Gradually they came to know the other people who were living or staying in the village. There was the vicar, a pleasant unaffected young man, and the doctor, a burly middle-aged giant with a beard and twinkling brown eyes, who had three dogs called Buller, Roberts, and Kitchener, after the generals who were conducting the war in South Africa. There was a large fat child of about two, who sat on the beach all day and every day, absorbed in watching the effect of its saliva on the pebbles. Tiring of this pursuit, it would begin to howl on a peculiarly raucous note, its eyes screwed up, its mouth wide open. Whereupon the red-faced country girl in charge of it would say, "Stop that, or I'll give you something to cry for."

"Perhaps he's *got* something to cry for, and that's why he's crying," Jenifer once suggested.

"Now then, sauce-box!" retorted the nurse.

Occasionally she would fulfil her threat and shake the fat child vigorously, a proceeding that generally stopped its tears and sent it back, happy and exhilarated, to its occupation of spitting on the pebbles. One Sunday the mother came down, an elaborately dressed woman, with very golden hair, very red lips, and very pink and white cheeks. People watched her covertly, and talked of her in whispers, changing the subject abruptly when the children approached.

Then there were the Melfords, who lived in a rather dreary bungalow beyond the coastguard cottages and ran wild over the cliffs and beach. Their father was a commercial traveller, who came home occasionally at weekends; their mother, a thin, fragile-looking woman, with a gentle voice and an air of extreme weariness. She did all the work of the bungalow, and, though both it and the children were scrupulously clean, they were obviously very badly off.

It was Derek, the youngest boy, who first made friends with Jenifer, as she scrambled over the rocks at the foot of the cliff in her short blue cotton frock and sunbonnet, her brown legs bare, her feet shod in stout and battered sandals. He approached her shyly and presented her with a piece of seaweed.

"Would you like it?" he said. "It's dry. You can pop the bubbles in it."

He was a tall slender child, with fair curling hair, blue eyes, and an exquisitely shaped mouth.

"Thank you," she said, looking at him with approval. Then she popped the bubbles, and they both laughed.

"There are heaps of different sorts here," he said, "but I like that best. There's a sort that looks like a flower that's rather nice. I'll find you some of it, shall I?"

"Let's look for it together," she suggested.

"Yes. I say, let's see how many different sorts we can find before tea-time."

They hunted together over the rocks. Their conversation was the usual conversation of childhood; they told each other their ages and their names, and the names and ages of their brothers and sisters, and what they wanted to do when they grew up. (He said that he wanted to be a sailor, and Jenifer said that she was going to marry and have ten children.) He told her in a matter-of-fact, unemotional way that he hated his father, and that when he was grown-up and rich he was going to build a beautiful house for his mother with lots of servants and lovely things to eat.

Then Emma came to fetch Jenifer in to bed, and they agreed to meet on the beach the next morning.

The Vicar called at the beginning of the second week. He found only Adrian at home, perched on a cushion on the sofa, painting at the table. The Vicar was young, keen, and intelligent, full of zest for his work and interest in everything around him. He began to draw Adrian out, admiring the painting, asking him questions. His friendliness was so unaffected that Adrian, usually shy and reserved to the point of rudeness with strangers, was soon talking freely and volubly.

"Will you come for a walk with me tomorrow morning?" said the young man when he took his leave.

Adrian's face flamed with pleasure, as he thanked him. He lay awake far into the night, too much excited by the new friendship to sleep.

In the morning he spent half an hour making himself clean and tidy for the walk. He looked pale and nervous as he set off, but he returned glowing with happiness. He was to go to tea to the Vicarage that afternoon, and he and the young Vicar were to go for another walk together the next morning. The friendship deepened. The young man, who was sympathetic and understanding, was strongly attracted by the talented, highly-strung boy.

While Lorna chatted with the fishermen on the beach, and Laurence went for long solitary expeditions, watching birds and insects, and Jenifer played among the rocks with Derek, Adrian would be perched on the Vicar's desk in his study or walking with him over the cliffs. It was a new experience for him. It was, indeed, the first real friendship of his life. He told the Vicar things that he had never before told anyone, that he had thought he never could tell anyone—describing his most secret ambitions, expounding naïve childish theories of life. The Vicar, himself ingenuous enough to enter into the boy's outlook, never struck the false note of grown-up condescension.

Adrian's hero worship was as unbalanced as most of his emotions. Nervously anxious to be worthy of his new friend, he would fuss incessantly over his appearance before meeting him, once sobbing in hysterical fury because Emma would not allow him a clean collar for the occasion. Sometimes as he lay awake at night, thinking over the events of the day, he would break into a cold perspiration at the thought of something he had said or done that might have lowered his friend's opinion of him.

Old Mrs Silver came down to spend a day with them in the last week, accompanied by André and Lena.

Lena was feeling, as usual, slightly aggrieved. Mother and André had talked French all the way down in the train, and she had felt out of it. She knew French, of course, but not when it was spoken as quickly as they spoke it. Sometimes she thought that they talked too quickly for her to understand, on purpose. Moreover, she had a suspicion that they were talking about things that weren't quite proper. One always had when people talked French. And though André was a member of a very aristocratic family and an old friend of Mother's, still, she couldn't help feeling that he wasn't quite the sort of man whom Aunt Letty would have liked her to know. They had laughed a good deal as they talked, and at first she had laughed, too, because she didn't want them to think that she couldn't understand what they were saying, then she had withdrawn from them and sat with her pale-blue eyes fixed unseeingly on the landscape, thinking of the full, rich, interesting life she might be living now if she hadn't sacrificed herself so entirely to Mother. And, of course, one wouldn't mind if only Mother were grateful and depended on one and confided in one and took one's advice . . . That hat, now. She'd begged Mother to get a nice black bonnet with strings to tie under her chin, and Mother had insisted on buying that hat instead. It was black, certainly, but it wasn't a bonnet, and it was trimmed with red roses, and—well, it was ridiculous of anyone as old as Mother to care what she looked like. And again Lena pictured that feeble, gentle, dependent old lady whom she would have looked after so beautifully.

After lunch Lena suggested taking the children for a walk along the cliffs, but it seemed that Adrian was going to tea with the Vicar, and that Laurence wanted to go alone to a certain spot where he had seen several rock-pipits the day before, and Jenifer was going to play with someone called Derek, and Lorna so obviously didn't want to come that the project was dropped. Lena felt hurt again. They were such extraordinary children. Any other children would be clinging to her affectionately as they walked along the cliff, and she would be telling them one of the dear old fairy stories, like Cinderella or Goldilocks, that she had loved so in her own childhood, but that seemed only to bore them. It was so disheartening to be ready and willing to be a perfect daughter and perfect aunt to people who simply didn't seem to know how to respond. She did begin to tell the children the story of Cinderella after lunch, but they edged away, so patently bored that she had to stop. They really weren't at all attractive children . . . And she was worried about Marcia. Marcia, of course, had a wonderful complexion, but surely—surely that bloom wasn't *quite* natural. She didn't want to do Marcia an injustice, even in her thoughts, but she couldn't help suspecting that Marcia had been using powder. Lena had never used powder in her life. Aunt Letty had said, "No man ever respects a woman who paints and powders." She could still hear the gentle precise voice saying the words, and, though

Aunt Letty had been dead for more than ten years, the familiar longing for her swept over her niece.

She had brought her bathing-dress down with her—a voluminous garment of navy-blue that she had had ever since her girlhood—and she bathed after tea from the ancient machine, wearing a cloak to walk down the steps. Though the tunic came down to her knees, and the legs to her ankles, and though her feet were clad in black woollen stockings and shoes, she always felt that there was something slightly indecent about the costume. It was dreadful somehow to see one's legs apart and separate like that in the open air. And the way Marcia let the children run about on the beach in bathing-suits was disgusting. There was no other word for it. One hardly knew where to look. Marcia, of course, never had had the slightest idea how to bring up children . . .

Mother and André hadn't come down to the beach, but Lena could see them up on the cliff, and Mother's laugh rang out at intervals—absurdly clear and silvery. André was always saying things that made her laugh. She, Lena, often made quite good jokes, but Mother never laughed at them. She splashed about disconsolately near the edge, keeping just at the point where the end of her tunic met the water. She didn't want to go right in, because when one's costume got wet it clung to one's figure and looked so awful. After all, in spite of Marcia and everything else, modesty was modesty, and you couldn't get away from it.

They had tea in the little sitting-room. Marcia said, "Why don't you come down and stay, too, Mother? There's a cottage beyond the village that would just suit you and Lena."

The old lady shook her head.

"I'm too old to go away for holidays. I like just to come and look at the sea once a year or so. I've always felt that I've a lot in common with the sea."

Jenifer watched her, feeling that strange impersonal satisfaction that Grandma always made her feel. She was so perfect and so remote—a sort of shining in the distance, a light that you wanted to worship, that never flickered or wavered or came any nearer.

"Do you remember when we were at Rapallo, Mother," said Marcia, "and the fat woman in the purple bathing dress whose wig came off in the water?"

The three of them laughed at the memory, and again Lena had that hateful sense of being shut out in the cold while the others sat in a warm lighted room.

"The cliffs in Devonshire are very beautiful," she said. "The red cliffs, I mean. Aunt Letty and I once stayed a week in Sidmouth. I believe that it's iron in the soil that gives them that colour."

She spoke in her prim stilted voice, sitting upright on her chair, as she always sat, her hands folded in her lap, but in reality she was battering at the closed door and shouting, "Let me in."

There was a moment's constrained silence, then Marcia said vaguely, "Yes, of course," and André turned a polite smile in her direction before saying, "But what I shall never forget is the woman at Nice who dressed her little dog in bathing dresses always to match her own."

They all began to talk about Nice, and again Lena was left outside the warm lighted room of their comradeship. "I've always longed to travel," she said, "but my duties have kept me at home." Then she rose jerkily. "It's time we started home, Mother. We can't have you getting overtired. And I'm afraid this sea air will bring on your rheumatism again."

It was so absurd of Mother to behave—or rather, to let herself be treated—as though she were young, when she was nearly seventy.

"Perhaps you're right, my dear," said Mrs Silver.

Her face wore that look of faintly ironic amusement that it always wore when Lena reminded her that she was an old woman.

Chapter Nine

It was the last day of the holiday. Emma was packing the big leather trunks with the rounded tops that always looked as if they were going to hold so much more than they really did, refusing sternly to pack seaweed or crabs or more than a small proportion of their collection of pebbles.

Adrian was spending his last afternoon at the Vicarage, and Jenifer was going for a picnic with the Melfords. Everyone was slightly irritable because the holiday had come to an end, and no one wanted to say goodbye to the little cottage, with its shells and fretwork and mingled smell of soap and furniture polish and lavender and sea.

Jenifer was sent down to the village shop to buy some more luggage labels, and the pleasant-faced elderly woman who owned it smiled at her with kindly interest.

"Haven't you got brown since you came here!" she said. "We shall miss you all when you've gone. Will you be coming again next year?"

"I hope so," said Jenifer. "It's such a *lovely* beach, isn't it?"

The woman smiled at her.

"I suppose so, missie. I've not been down there for twenty years or so."

Jenifer stared, incredulous, amazed. To live within five minutes' walk of the paradise and not to have gone there for twenty years or so!

"Why haven't you?" she said.

The woman shrugged.

"Can't be bothered, I suppose."

A sudden terror possessed Jenifer, as at the approach of some ruthless, irresistible, hostile force. You grew older and older and older . . . so gradually that you didn't notice it till suddenly you were so old that you'd forgotten what sweets you liked best when you were a little girl, till you couldn't be bothered to go down to the beach, though it was only a few wooden steps away, till you were an old, old woman—like Grandma. Then the terror vanished. People could be old and yet like Grandma—a light shining clear and bright and unwavering in the distance.

Her thoughts went to the afternoon. She was going with the Melfords by train to Dellingham to picnic in Raddock Woods. She felt sad because it was the last time she would see Derek. But, of course, it wasn't really the last time. They would come here next year. Or the Melfords would come to Merrowvale. She had a child's blind unreasoning trust in life. You couldn't love anyone as much as she loved Derek and never see them again . . .

Immediately after lunch Adrian began to fuss about his visit to the Vicarage. He wanted to put on his best suit, which Emma had already packed. He complained that his shoes had not been properly cleaned and that a darn showed in his stocking. His voice was beginning to take on that high-pitched quaver that preluded a storm, when Frank laid a hand on his shoulder and said quietly, "That'll do, old chap." Frank's calm steady voice and touch generally had the effect of quieting Adrian, where expostulation only precipitated the crisis. Gulping, he retired to rub up his shoes and brush his hair with a wet brush till not a vestige of its curl remained. It had been arranged that he was to come and stay with the Vicar next spring, otherwise he would have been inconsolable at the thought of the parting. Even now he had worked himself up into an acute state of nerves.

The Vicar was at the front door to meet him, and put him at his ease at once with that pleasant friendliness that was unaffected enough now but would obviously in time develop into a professional manner.

"Come along, old boy. Let's see if we can find any fruit . . ."

They went into the kitchen garden, and there, among the plums and peaches, Adrian gradually lost his tragic intensity and became a normal boy again.

Tea was laid in the Vicar's study, a room that had always thrilled Adrian. Round the walls hung groups of school and college elevens, in all of which the Vicar's handsome athletic form was prominent. A shield, emblazoned with the arms of his college, hung over the mantelpiece, flanked on either side by pipe-racks. Low bookcases ran round the room, and on the knee-hole desk was an ebony crucifix.

The tea flattered the boy by a display of his favourite cakes and biscuits and a dish of bananas, mixed with strawberry jam, for which he had once admitted a weakness,

"A real beanfeast for the last one," said the Vicar heartily, taking his place at the low tea-table behind the teapot.

"I wish it wasn't the last," said Adrian, his voice suddenly unsteady. "I don't know how I'm going to *live*."

"There, there!" said the Vicar reassuringly. "It's not the last. I don't know what I was thinking of to say the last. You'll be here again in the spring, and we'll have to spend the time between now and then in making plans for it. The weeks will slip by quickly. Only too quickly, you'll find when you get to my age. Spring's wonderful here, you know. You'll love it."

The dangerous moment was tided over. The suggestion of hysteria had left the boy's manner. He was gazing steadily at the young man, his eyes dark and heavy with worship.

"I haven't shown you half the walks about here," went on his host, "and you'll have to set to and help with the garden. That keeps me busy in the spring, I can tell you. And reading . . . I'm going to ram lots more books down your throat."

"I've loved all the ones you've lent me," said Adrian.

"Splendid!" said the Vicar lightly, trying to combat the heavy emotional atmosphere that Adrian's hero-worship brought with it. "Have some more tea? Well, one of these biscuits, then. I got them specially for you. No? You've eaten nothing, old boy . . . Well, what shall we do now? Would you like a game of croquet, or shall we read something?"

"Let's read," said Adrian.

The Vicar selected one or two books, and they went into the garden, where they both lay outstretched on the grass in the orchard.

"Well, what shall it be?" said the Vicar. "Another from *Wild Animals I have Known*, or some Kipling?"

"You choose," said Adrian. "I'd rather you chose today."

"Well, let's have another wild animal," said the Vicar cheerfully, turning to the place in the book.

Settling himself comfortably on the grass, he read the story of "Bingo" in his pleasant, well-modulated voice, but it did little to relieve the tension of the atmosphere.

"Thank you," said Adrian in a stifled voice when he had finished.

"Now let's have something a little more cheerful," said the Vicar hastily, taking up *Songs of the Seven Seas*.

He read "The Merchantmen," "Song of the Banjo," "The Liner she's a Lady," with somewhat exaggerated heartiness, then a silence fell between them.

"I can't bear it," said Adrian at last in a strangled voice.

"Can't bear what, old boy?"

"Knowing that I'm not going to see you again for months and months."

The young man sat up and slowly filled his pipe.

"Look here, Adrian," he said at last, "you've got to take this like a man. Once you're away from me, back among your own home interests, it will all seem quite different, but I know it's no use telling you that now. I'm awfully fond of you—perhaps fonder of you than you are of me— but you can be just as fond of people when they aren't there as when they are. You've got to work hard and—and help people as much as you can"—the young man stumbled slightly (he always found unofficial preaching the hardest part of his job)—"and—and just peg on at things, you know, and the time will pass very quickly. And work hard at your painting. That's a real talent, and it's your duty to cultivate it . . . Well, I suppose it's time you went home now. Just come into the study a minute. There's something I want to give you."

They went together across the lawn into the study.

"I want you to have this, Adrian," said the Vicar, taking a book from a drawer in his desk and handing it to him, "and I want you to read it every day."

Adrian took the book. It was Keble's *Christian Year*, the flyleaf inscribed "With love to my friend, Adrian," with the Vicar's signature. Adrian looked at it in silence, his heart a riot of conflicting emotions. Beneath the devotion and gratitude that the gift aroused was a strange hot resentment.

From the beginning he had felt an uncomprehended jealousy of the Vicar's office. There was an unchildlike possessiveness about his love, and the religion that dominated the man's life challenged that possessiveness, making him sometimes torture himself by questioning the disingenuousness of his friend's affection.

"Thank you," he said, in a choking voice.

The Vicar had opened another drawer and was taking out a paper.

"And I want you to join this, Adrian. I started it about three years ago. It's not only for this parish. All my boy friends belong to it . . . Just read it through . . . You sign here."

Adrian read the paper. It was headed "League of Sir Galahad," and the members undertook to say their prayers regularly morning and evening, to read a certain portion of the Scriptures daily, to

> Speak no scandal, no, nor listen to it,
> To honour his own word as if his God's,
> To live a life of purest chastity.

A thick mist swam before Adrian's eyes, so that he could hardly read the words. All the vague suspicions that had tormented him seemed suddenly justified . . . This, then, was the object of the Vicar's kindness; this was where his pretended friendship had been leading all the time. It had been just part of his work as a clergyman, a tiresome and perhaps even disagreeable duty, adding another name to his League of Sir Galahad.

To the boy's distorted vision the man's friendship became suddenly a piece of the vilest treachery, his every kind word and look an intolerable insult. Bored to death by him, probably . . . thinking what a little fool he was . . . just pretending to be fond of him . . . all for this . . . all for this . . .

The man had turned to the window while the boy read the printed card. Now he turned round, smiling pleasantly.

"Well, what do you——"

He stopped abruptly.

"What on earth's the matter, Adrian?"

With flushed cheeks and blazing eyes, Adrian was tearing the piece of paper into tiny shreds. His breath came in sobbing gasps. His thin childish form was taut and trembling.

"*Adrian!*" said the man, laying a hand on his shoulder.

Adrian shook it off.

"Leave me alone," he sobbed. "I hate you . . . I hope I never see you again . . . all the time . . . all the time . . . when I thought . . ." his voice rose hysterically, "and all the time . . . it was this . . . it was this . . . I *hate* you."

He burst suddenly into a tempest of sobs and plunged blindly from the room, across the lawn, and out of the gate. The young man stared after him, paralysed by amazement, then stooped down and carefully picked up the pieces of torn paper from the carpet.

Chapter Ten

Jenifer and Derek, hot and tired but very happy, came slowly back to the clearing in the wood where they had had tea.

Derek had put into his cap the various treasures he had collected during the afternoon—pine-cones, flowers, ferns, and tiny pebbles—and carried it carefully in both hands.

At first it had seemed strange to Jenifer that the Melfords should want to leave the paradise of the beach and come inland, but, as Derek had explained, "You see, you get tired of *anything* if you have it every day." And certainly the woods were lovely, with little paths that wound in and out among the trees, and a stream that ran between banks studded with moss and ferns, forming here a miniature lake and there a small cascade.

They had come to Dellingham immediately after lunch and walked from the little country station through the lanes to Raddock Woods.

They had held a regatta on the stream, with twigs for boats, before tea, and then Jenifer and Derek had wandered off alone to explore.

Mrs Melford was sitting where they had left her, leaning against a tree, the picnic basket by her side, her sweet lined face wearing its usual expression of patient weariness. She sat motionless, relaxed, as if revelling in the knowledge that just for this moment, at any rate, there was nothing to do, no decisions to make, no claims to meet.

Near her the two little girls were playing house behind a blackberry bush. Occasionally one of them would sally forth to do her shopping, carrying a tiny basket, and would put into it berries and leaves and the heads of grasses, paying imaginary money and holding conversation with imaginary shopkeepers, while the other busied herself with imaginary household tasks behind the blackberry bush. They wore blue cotton frocks faded to a uniform grey, except the hems, which had been let down as far as they would go and which still showed blue. The frocks were tight in the sleeves and across the chest, and had evidently been made for them several years ago. The eldest boy was at the top of a pine tree, surveying the landscape through an imaginary telescope and shouting nautical directions to no one in particular.

"Look, Mummy!" said Derek, dropping on his knees and taking the treasures one by one out of his cap. "Isn't this a darling little pine-cone . . . and this bit of moss, with teeny flowers growing in it . . . and I'm sure this little fern isn't an ordinary one. I've never seen one like it before. I'm sure it's frightfully, frightfully rare . . . Jenifer found it . . . and Jenifer found this little stone, too. Look, isn't it sweet?"

Jenifer watched him as he knelt there, thin, eager, tremulous, his cheeks flushed with excitement, his curls matted damply to his forehead. A slanting ray of sunshine fell upon him through the branches, making him, hot and dirty as he was, look almost startlingly beautiful. An odd pain stirred at her heart, an aching longing to protect him and take care of him. Perhaps she would never see him again after today . . . At that thought the pain sharpened till it was unbearable. If only he were her brother and were coming back to Merrowvale with them! She loved him far more than she loved Laurence or Adrian. Vague daydreams floated through her mind, dreams in which her father and mother adopted Derek, or Mr and Mrs Melford adopted her . . .

In a small breathless voice she said:

"I expect we shall come here again next year."

"I hope you will, dear," said Mrs Melford. "Derek will miss you very much when you've gone."

A lump came into Jenifer's throat, a sudden rush of tears to her eyes. Horrified and ashamed, she bent her head down, pretending to examine the moss, digging her teeth into her lip.

"I'll write to you, Jen," Derek was saying, "and I'll look for those pebbles you like—the blue ones with the red lines—and I'll have heaps and heaps for you when you come next year."

"Thank you," said Jenifer in a small hard voice, her face still bent over the moss.

The notes of the church clock came slowly through the sleepy summer air.

"Six o'clock," said Mrs Melford, seeming to drag herself by a sheer physical effort from her lethargy of weariness. "Time we were going. Help me to pack, children."

They packed up the knives and crockery and the bottle that had held the milk and water. There were no eatables left. It had been a sparse enough meal—barely sufficient for the five children. Jenifer had gathered that the little Melfords often went hungry.

She watched Derek in silence as he bent over the basket, helping to pack the crockery. She wished that she were rich, so that she could give him everything he wanted, so that she could pour out gifts, precious and innumerable, at his feet.

"Come along, children!" called Mrs Melford again.

Derek raised his head from the fastenings of the picnic basket.

"Is father coming home tonight?" he said.

"I don't think so, dear," said his mother. She spoke reassuringly. "If he does, it won't be till after you're in bed."

But they met the squat, thick-set figure when they were a few yards from the bungalow. Jenifer had never seen him before, and from the way the children had spoken of him she had vaguely imagined some towering, ferocious giant. But he was very short and seemed even shorter than he was because of his stoutness. There was an air of flashy smartness about him: his suit looked too tight, his shoes too yellow, and his tie-pin, composed of artificial diamonds, too large. His rubicund face was slightly blue about the jowl, and his eyes, behind gleaming pince-nez, reminded Jenifer of pig's eyes—small and round and set close together. A short black moustache hung on his full moist

The little party stopped motionless at sight of him, alert, on the defensive, like a troop of deer suddenly sighting an enemy. He advanced on them with his rolling, self-important strut, his face set in lines of glowering ill-humour.

"Where have you been?" he said. He had a harsh voice, high-pitched and discordant.

"We've only been for a picnic, dear," said his wife.

She spoke gently, propitiatingly, as if trying to fend off his anger as long as possible.

"Where?" he shot out.

"To Raddock Woods. We didn't know you were coming home tonight, dear. You never wrote."

"To Raddock Woods?" His voice took on a sharper edge. "You mean to say you've been by train?"

"Yes . . . there's no other way of getting there. We couldn't have walked."

"So that's how you waste my money behind my back! Aren't there enough places for you to picnic in here that you must go wasting my money on train fares?"

"Fred, dear," she pleaded, "the children are so tired of all the places here. It was just a treat. It's the first time we've been anywhere by train this year. It was only fourpence each."

"Fourpence each!" he exploded. "If you can afford to throw fourpences away at that rate, let me tell you I can't. Here I am slaving all week while you play ducks and drakes with my money behind my back. Fourpence each, indeed!"

"This is Jenifer Gainsborough, dear," said his wife, in a forlorn attempt to induce him to curb his ill-humour by reminding him of the presence of a stranger.

His gaze flicked Jenifer up and down then returned to his wife. "Haven't you got enough brats of your own," he said, "that you must needs drag other people's about? I suppose you paid for her train fare and gave her tea?"

"Yes . . . I——"

The corners of his little mouth shot up in an ugly sneer.

"Oh well, if you can afford to feed other people's children on the money I allow you, I'll remember to allow you less in future."

"Oh *Fred!*" she expostulated. "You know——"

He turned on Derek, who stood staring up at him, his face set in tense unchildish lines.

"Put your cap on," he shouted angrily.

Derek looked down at his carefully arranged treasures. His hesitation seemed to infuriate the man. He snatched the cap from his hands, struck him across the face, emptied the little collection of flowers and cones and ferns on to the ground, and rammed the cap roughly on his head, at the same time grinding the fallen treasures into the earth with a short broad foot.

"You *rotter!*" said Derek in a slow clear voice.

The man raised his hand to strike him again, then dropped it, suddenly mindful that the scene was overlooked by the cottages on the cliff.

"I'll teach you manners when I get you indoors," he said between his teeth. "Go on." He gave him a push and began to walk on quickly towards the bungalow. His wife accompanied him. His harsh bullying voice beat down her gentle pleading.

"I slave away to keep you here in idleness, and you can't even bring up the children decently. I won't have it, I tell you . . . Oh yes, you're always full of excuses. Only fourpence each! Haven't I forbidden you over and over again to spend a single *penny* that isn't necessary? Well, I'll see to it that you haven't any fourpences to throw away next week. I can promise you *that*. And I'll see those children have a bit of discipline, too. What do you think you do for your keep, I'd like to know. You——"

The doctor appeared round the bend of the road, and Mr Melford's manner changed abruptly. He smiled ingratiatingly and greeted him with ringing heartiness.

"Well, doctor, how's the world treating you? All serene, eh?"

"Yes, thank you," said the doctor. "You just got back?"

"Yes." Mr Melford threw a toothy affectionate smile round the silent little group behind him. "Always glad to get back to home and family. Best tonic for a hard-working man, eh, doctor? Home and family. Nothing like it, eh?" The toothy smile flashed upon his wife now. "How do you think the wife's looking?"

"A little tired," said the doctor.

"Now I'm home I must look after her, mustn't I? These young ruffians wear the life out of her when I'm not here." Again his hearty laugh rang out. "Well, goodbye, doctor."

As he moved on, the amiability vanished from his face like something being wiped off a slate, and it fell again into its familiar lines of vicious ill-humour.

Derek and Jenifer had dropped behind.

"He's always like that when other people are there," said Derek. "Pretending to be kind and jolly and that sort of thing. He's like that to the people he sells things to in the week. They think he's really jolly. He's never like it with us—except, of course, when other people are there, too. He makes people think he's like that, and he can always put it on, but he isn't really . . . He's a *beast* really. I wish we could all run away from him, but of course we can't. We haven't any money."

Jenifer walked along with him without speaking. It never occurred to her to leave him and go home. The others walked some distance behind, silent, wary, clutching their bunches of drooping flowers, all their happiness and animation gone. They went up the little path to the bungalow door. The man stood at the doorway and, as Derek entered, caught him by the shoulder.

"Now I'll teach you manners, you young devil!"

He threw the door to and snatched up a cane from the umbrella-stand. Still holding Derek by the shoulders, he brought it down again and again . . . Suddenly he caught sight of something through the kitchen door and dropped the cane to investigate.

"What's this?" he said to his wife, taking up a new saucepan from the stove. "What do you mean by buying a new saucepan? Wasting my money right and left! What was wrong with the old one?"

"Fred, it only cost a shilling. There was a leak in the old one."

"Why couldn't you have had it mended?"

"It had been mended till it couldn't possibly be mended any more. I did ask——"

"Where is it?"

"I threw it away."

"Get it out and let me see it."

"I think it's in the dustbin."

"Get it out, I tell you."

While Mrs Melford burrowed in the dustbin for the saucepan, her husband went round the kitchen and larder, opening tins and paper bags . . . When she finally appeared with the battered, leaking saucepan in her hand, he had lost interest in it. He asked her how much she had paid for each of the meagre household supplies, rating her soundly the while for extravagance.

"How much did you pay for this tin of baked beans?"

"Sixpence."

"Sixpence! Nothing better to do than throw sixpences about, have you? Sixpence is nothing to you, of course. You don't have to earn it . . . How many beans could you have bought for sixpence and baked yourself? Never think of trying to save my money. I slave away to keep you and all those great louts of children eating your heads off in idleness here, and you can't even run the house decently. Look at that filthy paint. How long is it since you scrubbed it?"

"It was scrubbed this morning, Fred. It isn't dirty. The paint's worn off the wood. It wants re-doing."

"Excuses for everything, of course!"

He was still opening the tins that stood on the larder shelf. "What's this? Cake? Haven't I forbidden you to give the children luxuries?"

"I made it myself, and it cost hardly anything. It's the plainest possible cake."

"I've forbidden you to give them cake, do you hear, and that's enough. Of course," he sneered, "I'm glad that you find the housekeeping money enough to fritter away on luxuries. I shall feel quite justified in cutting it down."

"Fred," she pleaded, "you know I can't possibly manage on less. The children are almost in rags."

The children had crept down to the bottom of the garden, discussing the affair in lowered voices.

"Now he won't give us enough money for next week. He always pays us out that way when he thinks we've been enjoying ourselves. He can't bear to think we've been enjoying ourselves. And Mummy won't eat anything so that we can have it. He's a *beast*."

They could still hear the raucous penetrating voice from the house.

Philip, the eldest boy, crept near to listen.

"He's rowing her because he says she's got nothing fit for him to eat for supper," he reported. "He's saying 'What sort of a housekeeper do you think you are?' and things like that. And he never told her he'd be here tonight."

They began to imitate him, pretending to ransack the hedge, mimicking the harsh discordant voice. "What do you mean by buying baked beans? Why can't you buy beans and bake them? Here I slave away all week keeping you in luxury . . . What d'you mean by eating food at all? Why can't you starve?"

They giggled as they imitated him, but beneath their amusement was an undercurrent of fierce concentrated hatred.

Mrs Melford came out to them, her face white and strained.

"Darlings," she whispered, "go to bed now. Quickly and very quietly. He's in the dining-room having his supper."

"Can't we have any supper, Mummy?"

"I'll get something for you later if I can, but I may not be able to. Try to go to sleep."

"You'll come in and see us, won't you?"

"Yes . . . Darlings, run along now."

"Mummy, he's a——"

"Hush, dear. Run along. Very quietly. Creep upstairs so that he won't hear you. Jenifer, dear, you'd better go home now. We did so enjoy having you this afternoon. Goodbye, dear. Come along, children."

She put her arms about them to draw them with her towards the door, but Derek broke away and ran back to Jenifer.

"Wait for me a minute, Jen," he whispered.

She stood waiting in the shadow of the hedge. Her heart was beating wildly. She felt breathless, as if she had been running for a long time, and, in some strange way that she couldn't understand, bruised and shaken.

Derek came back to her, hurrying down the little path. His face was streaked with dirt and tears, but he was smiling.

"Look!" he said breathlessly, opening his hand and showing her a shell that she knew was one of his greatest treasures. "I want you to have it for a keepsake, to remember me by always. It's a magic shell, you know. When you put it to your ear you can hear the sea."

"Oh, *Derek!*"

She looked down at her dress and saw the silver brooch with J. on that Aunt Lena had given her last Christmas. She tore it off.

"And you have this for a keepsake, Derek."

He put it into his pocket.

"Thank you, Jen. I must go now. Mummy's waiting for me. Goodbye."

"Goodbye."

They kissed—a long passionless kiss—holding each other tightly in thin childish arms. Then Derek ran back to the house, and Jenifer set off quickly homewards.

Grief and anger tore at her heart. It would have been bad enough, in any case, saying goodbye to Derek, but to leave him in the power of the hateful man who was his father . . . Again she saw his treasures trampled in the dust, saw the cane descending on his fragile little body . . . And he'd be going supperless and hungry to bed. She heard the sound of someone sobbing as she ran, and realised with surprise that it was herself . . .

She stopped aghast. She mustn't let them see at home that anything was the matter. They'd talk about it and try to comfort her, and it was dreadful when that happened. It was like people pushing their fingers into a sore place.

She took out her handkerchief and carefully wiped away the tears and grime from her face, moistening the linen with her tongue and rubbing briskly till her cheeks smarted. Then she smoothed back her hair, pulled down her short, crumpled, holland frock, and walked slowly homewards.

*

Emma, rather cross and tired, was still busy with the packing. The others, she told Jenifer curtly, were down on the beach, except Adrian, who had "come over sick" and gone to bed.

Jenifer went slowly down the wooden stairs to the beach. There was a feeling of constriction in her breast, as if something there were so tight that it must burst, but her lips were set firmly. She wouldn't cry again. Her hands stole to her pocket and closed round the shell that Derek had given her.

Marcia was sitting on a deck-chair on the sands at the foot of the steps, her feet upon a foot-rest. She wore a white flounced dress of embroidered muslin and looked very cool and dainty and pink and white and golden as she lay back against her cushion, smiling faintly. A shady leghorn hat, trimmed with black velvet ribbons, threw an alluring shadow over her blue eyes. By her side lay the frilled parasol that she always put up when the sun was too strong. There was no trace of sunburn upon her smooth fair skin. At her feet sat Major Pettigrew, his bronzed face drawn and haggard. He had fallen passionately in love with her in the few weeks of her visit, but with practised adroitness she had kept him at arm's length. At times, in his despair, he had fancied that there was something slightly malicious in the faint smile her lips always wore. He had been allowed to fetch and carry for her, to send fruit and flowers and vegetables daily to the little cottage, to clamber up and down the cliffs with cushions and deck-chairs and footrests, but he had not been allowed to do more than kiss her hand. And she was going away tomorrow . . .

"I don't know how I'm going to get through the days when you've gone," he said.

Her blue eyes smiled at him with their faint hint of mockery.

"You'll have forgotten me in a week."

"I shan't—I——"

The hand he was about to snatch moved upward, as if by chance, to straighten the golden curls beneath the shady hat.

"You'll wake up tomorrow, and you'll find that it will really be something of a relief to think that you won't have to carry chairs and things about all day. You can finish your smoke in peace after breakfast without feeling that I might be wanting to go down to the beach. You can have your afternoon nap in comfort. You'll miss me in a way, but you'll be grateful to me for not having let you do anything foolish."

"You're cruel," he said. "You——"

She turned and saw Jenifer coming down the wooden steps.

"Hello, darling," she said. "Did you have a nice time?"

"Yes, thank you," said Jenifer.

"It's really bed-time, but as it's your last evening you can play with Lorna for half an hour first, if you like. Laurence and Father have gone for a walk and haven't come in yet, and Adrian's in bed with a bilious attack."

Lorna came running up from the rocks. She had been bored and lonely and was glad to see Jenifer. Mother and Major Pettigrew quite obviously hadn't wanted her, and the way in which they hadn't wanted her had made her feel a very small and unimportant little girl.

"Oh, Jen, there you are! Come and play with me. Make up a new game."

Jenifer was rather good at making up new games, though Lorna always pretended to be scornful of them when she was in her grown-up mood.

"It's been awfully dull," went on Lorna. "Laurence and Father went off before tea, and when Adrian came home he was all upset."

"Why?"

"I don't know. He was crying, and then he was sick and went to bed. And then the Vicar came and wanted to see him, and Adrian wouldn't and started crying again. The Vicar didn't know what had upset him, but Mother told him he'd better go or Adrian would be getting hysterical, so he went."

Jenifer listened without much interest. A dull heavy weight of misery still hung at her heart.

"Was the picnic nice, Jen?" Lorna went on.

"Yes, thanks."

Lorna was looking up and down the crumpled holland frock.

"Where's your brooch? I thought you had it on this afternoon."

"Yes . . . I had it on."

"You've lost it, then . . . Oh, *Jen!*" She ran off to Marcia, followed slowly by Jenifer. "Mother, Jen's lost her silver brooch on the picnic."

Marcia turned her smiling blue eyes to Jenifer.

"How careless of you, darling!"

"Miss Marchant would be *awfully* cross," said Lorna, feeling that Marcia's reception of the news was inadequate. "Well, come on and play, Jenifer, anyway."

Jenifer followed her back to the rocks. Turning suddenly, Lorna caught sight of Jenifer's mouth, set in a tight line.

"Jen," she said, "is anything the matter?"

"No," said Jennifer breathlessly. "Why?"

"You looked unhappy. Never mind about the brooch, Jen. Aunt Lena will give you another for your birthday present . . . Was that what you were unhappy about?"

"No—I mean yes."

"Well, never mind. Let's play that game you made up yesterday. Highwaymen, you know."

Some other children joined them, and they raced and splashed among the rocks. Jenifer shouted and laughed more loudly than any of the others. It was as if something right inside her were crying and she had to make a noise to stop people hearing it.

Frank Gainsborough came round the rocks with Laurence. His trousers were rolled up to his knees, and Laurence carried a glass jam-jar filled with water creatures and seaweed. Frank waved to his daughters, then went on to where his wife sat, the handsome, middle-aged soldier at her feet. She smiled up at him from under her shady hat.

"Had a nice walk?" she said.

"Splendid . . . You been all right?"

"Of course . . . Major Pettigrew has looked after me beautifully. Isn't it terrible that it's the last evening? And yet in a way it will be lovely to get home again."

After that deliberate little stab of cruelty she relented. "We're so grateful to you, Major Pettigrew, for making our visit such a pleasant one. We shall always remember you, shan't we, Frank?"

"Mother," broke in Laurence eagerly, "I may take them home, mayn't I? I'll carry them myself. I want to make an aquarium. I don't see why they shouldn't breed. I've got two of each."

"All right, darling. If you won't splash them all over everyone in the train."

Frank was watching the children playing among the rocks.

"Look at little sobersides Jenny," he said. "She's gone quite mad. I've never seen her so excited."

"She had a lovely afternoon with the Melfords. I expect that's it."

"Is Adrian still at the Vicarage?"

"No. He had a nerve-storm and came home soon after tea. I don't know what had upset him; neither did the Vicar. I apologised to him for the child . . . I must get Jenifer and Lorna in to bed now. Oh, thank you so much, Major," as the soldier leapt to his feet to collect her things for her.

"Let me," said Frank, trying to relieve the Major of some of his impedimenta, but he clung to them grimly, so Frank helped his wife up the steps, his hand on her arm, while the devoted Major staggered after them with his burden.

The light had been turned out in the girls' bedroom. Lorna had said good-night and nestled down in bed to sleep. Jenifer lay with wide dry eyes, staring at the ceiling, while the blackness that she had pushed down out of sight at the bottom of her heart spread and spread till it seemed to fill every atom of her being. She felt that after today life could never be the same again. All the safeness and sureness had gone from it. It wasn't only that Derek, whom she loved, was frightened and hurt and hungry. It was that to some people home could mean a place of terror and unhappiness instead of the shining refuge of love and kindness that home had always meant to her; it was that the word Father could mean cruelty and tyranny instead of the tender protectiveness that Father had meant to her. She had known vaguely that there were wicked people and unhappy people, but the words had had no meaning; they had seemed to belong to a world that was as remote from hers as the world of her fairy tales. Now, for the first time, she had caught a glimpse of some hostile force beneath the kindly surface of things. People had often been cross with her, she had often been punished, but behind the crossness and punishment had always been a deep tenderness surrounding her on all sides. She had never in her life before met with deliberate unkindness, and it shook her world to its foundations. She buried her face in her pillow . . .

Lorna sat up in bed.

"Jenifer . . . are you crying?"

Jenifer made a desperate effort to stop crying, but it was too late. Her gasping stifled sobs cut through the darkness.

"Jenifer . . . what is it?"

She got out of her bed and came across the room to Jenifer's.

"Jenifer . . ."

She lifted the bedclothes and slipped in beside her, gathering her into her arms.

"Jenifer . . . don't cry."

Jenifer clung to her, sobbing. The tight clasp of the comforting arms seemed to lighten the black desolation of her misery.

"Jenifer . . . is it because you've lost your brooch? It doesn't matter. There's the one with a little clover leaf on that Mother gave you. You can wear that one." The slow difficult sobs continued. "Jen, is it because it's the end of the holiday? But it'll be nice to be home again." Jenifer still clung to her, her sobs growing gradually less. Lorna's sweetness seemed to be shutting out the ugliness that had frightened her. The whole story of the afternoon was already quivering on her lips. She had thought that she could never tell anyone, but she could tell this Lorna, who was so kind and understanding. Then suddenly she was conscious of some subtle change in the atmosphere. Lorna still held her tightly, still murmured words of comfort, but she wasn't thinking of her any longer. She was thinking of herself, of her own sweetness and sympathy, she was enjoying the feeling of Jenifer's clinging to her for comfort, she was dispassionately curious about what had made Jenifer cry

. . . Her voice hadn't changed, her clasp hadn't relaxed, but that first impulse of pure love and compassion had spent itself . . . Jenifer's clinging to her for comfort now gave her an exhilarating sense of power, made her feel important and grown-up.

"Tell me, darling," she murmured softly.

A terrible feeling of being handled and possessed swept over Jenifer. She drew away from Lorna's arm with a quick movement and spoke in a small jerky voice.

"It's all right, Lorna. Thanks awfully for being so nice to me. I'm all right now. It was just—the brooch."

Lorna gave her a final condescending pat and got back into her own bed. What a silly kid Jenifer was, crying because she'd lost the brooch when no one had been cross with her about it! Just for a moment she'd thought that she had been going to tell her something interesting, something she hadn't known before. But she was just a silly kid, after all. Anyway she, Lorna, had been awfully nice to her. She seemed to hear her own voice again, murmuring reassurance and consolation. She enjoyed being nice to people. There was something thrilling about it . . . She drifted off into a dreamless sleep.

Jenifer lay awake, staring into the darkness.

Occasionally her hand crept under her pillow to make sure that the shell Derek had given her was still there.

PART II

1910

Chapter Eleven

Marcia, Lena, and Miss Marchant sat round the dining-room table. They were having tea before the young people came in, so as to be sure of having it in peace, but there was a sense of incompleteness, of waiting for something . . . The house never really seemed itself except when it was filled with the turmoil and exuberance of young life.

It was ten years since the holiday at Westonlea. During those ten years Marcia's figure had settled into more matronly lines, but her white-and-gold beauty was undimmed. Miss Marchant at thirty-four looked drab and middle-aged, but hardly more drab and middle-aged than she had looked at twenty-four. Miss Marchant even as a baby had never looked young.

Now that she was not needed for the children she was retreating more and more into the background of the family life. Marcia often played with the idea of getting rid of her altogether, but she knew that she could not afford to. Marcia was what is known as a "poor manager." She hated cheap things and makeshifts. Though she went out very little, she spent, she knew, an undue proportion of Frank's salary on her clothes. "Darling," she would say to him, "I know I ought to buy cheap things, but somehow I can't. I shouldn't be myself in them. It would make me horribly disagreeable."

But as long as Miss Marchant was there the household budget was made more or less to balance. Miss Marchant did the housekeeping and often, indeed, the entire work of the house. Sometimes it seemed as if she guessed their desire to get rid of her, and her manner would become almost nauseatingly servile.

The feud between Miss Marchant and Emma still continued, though Emma was now engaged in another and more exciting feud with a baker who had opened a little shop in the village (several new houses were being built on the outskirts of Merrowvale), and who supplied the family with bread on the days when Emma was too busy to bake. Emma was fiercely contemptuous of his wares and would return loaf after loaf to the shop as being too lightly baked or too hard-baked, occasionally calling in person to rate him soundly over the counter. He was a small cheerful man, always covered with flour from head to foot, whom the children called "Floury Charlie."

Lena had altered more than the other two, growing faded and lined and angular. She had aged considerably since Mrs Silver's death three years ago. She now lived alone at Brightmet House with a huge tabby cat (called Peter after his predecessor), several canaries, and a young inexperienced maid generally referred to as "the girl."

"I wonder you don't go away, Lena," Marcia was saying, "and travel for a little. You once said you'd like to travel. I don't know whether you meant it."

"Of course I meant it, Marcia," said Lena with dignity. "I've always wanted to travel. It's nothing but duty that has kept me at Merrowvale all these years. Dear Mother needed me."

"You could go now."

"I can't possibly go now, dear," said Lena still in that slightly affronted tone. "I couldn't leave Peter just now. He's not been at all well lately. I had to have the vet to him only yesterday. And I couldn't trust the girl to look after things properly in my absence. You've no *idea* how careless she is. Why, only yesterday——"

"Then why don't you get a properly trained maid instead of a girl straight from school?" said Marcia impatiently, cutting short the familiar recital.

Lena set her lips.

"I can't afford it, Marcia. I have to be very careful."

"Oh, *Lena!*'

"And anyway," went on Lena hastily, "I couldn't possibly leave my district."

"Lena, *surely* you could find someone to take over your district."

"No one who would understand it as I do. Old Mrs Marsden is practically blind now, and I go every other afternoon to sit with her. She'd *hate* a stranger. And it would be too cruel to leave Mrs Cannon. She only has another month to live . . . There are lots of little pieces of work in the parish I couldn't leave just now. The new Vicar's a very good worker, but he's young and unmethodical. No, Marcia, I want to go away, and, as soon as I can arrange things, I will."

Her thin cheeks flushed, as if she interpreted aright the faint amusement in Marcia's blue eyes, and she added sharply, "I have always wanted to travel, but I can't neglect obvious duties for that or anything else." She seemed so ruffled that Marcia hastily changed the conversation.

"Have you seen André lately?"

The question, however, did not restore Lena's good humour.

"Yes, he called last week. He brings over the most ridiculously expensive flowers for Mother's grave. Orchids! Just fancy! I really haven't any patience with him. I told him that the money he'd spent on those flowers would have kept a poor family for a week, and he said he wasn't interested in poor families." She turned her faded short-sighted eyes upon the flowers that stood massed on mantelpiece and side-table of Marcia's dining-room. "I wonder you can afford flowers like that, Marcia."

"I can't. Mr Frewin sent them in. He sends them in every few days. He did up this room, too. He said that he had lots of wallpaper left over from his own decorating and an odd-job man with nothing to do so he did it. He knew I'd like the wallpaper because I'd chosen it myself."

Lena pursed her lips.

"I wonder Frank allows it."

"Oh, Frank loves it. He says that next to being able to give me nice things himself, he likes other people to give me them . . ."

"Mr Frewin's really *very* kind to us," said Miss Marchant. "We never have to buy any fruit. And his odd-job man does everything that needs doing in the house and garden."

Lena's disapproving eyes went from the flowers to the wallpaper. Taking Presents from Men. It wasn't Nice . . .

"He admires Miss Marchant," put in Marcia, her blue eyes dancing demurely.

"*Really*, Mrs Gainsborough," said Miss Marchant, but she bridled and blushed as she spoke.

"Where are the children?" asked Lena grimly.

"They've gone for a bicycle ride. At least, Adrian and Lorna have gone together, and Jenifer and Laurence. I think they were meeting for tea, but Laurence likes to watch birds and take photographs, and the other two don't. Adrian hates photographs. He says they're inartistic."

"How ridiculous! It depends entirely on what you take, whether they're artistic or not. The other day the Vicar showed me some *beautiful* photographs he'd taken of the Vicarage. One was wonderful. You could see the smallest detail perfectly—even the blisters on the front door."

"I hope they won't be late. It's Ruby's party tonight."

"Ruby?" said Lena, who could never remember anyone's name.

"Ruby Frewin. It's her birthday. Everyone's going. The Burdetts, or rather *some* of the Burdetts. And the Lenhams—the new people at the Hall, you know."

Sir Gerald and Lady Carfax had died the year before. They had grown so feeble with the passing of the years that in the end there had seemed to be nothing left of them. They had become frail painted ghosts, so light that you would think it was only their wigs and make-up, still meticulously adjusted, that weighed them down. One day they failed to take their usual constitutional through the village, and the next day the news went round that Lady Carfax had pneumonia. By the end of the week she was dead. Sir Gerald appeared at her funeral, bewigged, rouged, padded, and laced as usual, a jerky little marionette, moving with short mincing steps, bowing courteously to all his friends, his wizened lips set in a twisted line, his eyes blank with misery. There was something very strange in the sight of the lonely figure, and people realised that not for years had husband and wife been seen apart. They had grown old side by side, keeping up the ridiculous pretence of youth that deceived no one but themselves. Now it didn't even deceive him. He was a grey ghost of old age behind his crumbling facade of youth, lonely, terrified. He had a seizure on the way home from the funeral and never recovered consciousness.

"I didn't know they'd moved in."

"They moved in last week. They're very nice, I believe. There's a boy and girl—twins—about Lorna's age."

"Here's Miss Burdett," said Miss Marchant, who always kept an eye upon the road from her seat at table. "She's coming here."

Almost immediately Emma announced Miss Burdett. The past ten years had altered her more than any of the others. She had grown stout and comfortable-looking, and the anxious hollows of her face had filled in. Ten years ago that holiday at the Burdetts' cottage had seemed to her a waking nightmare whose memory would shadow the rest of her life. Having made up her mind to go through with it, she had literally lived for the end. And yet, as soon as she returned to the peace and comfort of her own home, she began to feel lonely. She missed the children. The days dragged. She hadn't enough to do. Waiting on her invalid mother took up so little of her time. She found herself continually thinking of the Burdetts and wondering how they were going on—how Rubina's cough was and whether anyone was making James change his socks when he got them wet. No one but she seemed to realise how delicate the child was. She wrote to Susannah and Marigold, who were her favourites, and sent them presents and made dresses for them. Then, rather to her surprise, she wrote to Lilia, telling her that she would go over next summer and stay at the cottage again if it would be any help to her. Lilia wrote back, gratefully accepting the offer. It was as dreadful as ever, but somehow she minded it less. The children were delighted to see her, the new baby seemed to take to her at once, and there was no doubt at all that the open-air life did her good. The next year her mother died, and Miss Burdett bought the cottage, had it done up, built two more rooms on to it, furnished it properly, and made it her permanent home. The children came over just as usual every summer, and in the winter Miss Burdett generally went to stay with them in Merrowvale.

As the years went on, things had gradually improved in the Burdett household. It was partly Miss Burdett, of course, but it was chiefly Eglantine, the eldest girl, who, despite her upbringing, was turning out unexpectedly domesticated and efficient. She bullied the younger children into some semblance of neatness and was gradually taking over the housekeeping and management from her mother. In her grand moments Mrs Burdett would prophesy a career of international fame for Eglantine. "The child has the most amazing talent for organisation." In her more private moments she would put the matter more simply. "It's so nice that there's someone in the house at last who knows where things have been put."

Although she was nearly fifty, Mrs Burdett had had another baby last year, to the amazement and delight of herself, her husband, and the other children. It was a boy, christened Benjamin, and the whole family treated him as an amusing pet.

"Tea!" said Miss Burdett, smiling at the table. "How nice!"

"Yes," said Marcia, "we were having it early before the children come in. Do have some. I'll ring for a fresh pot. This is stewed."

"No, don't. I like it stewed. I really oughtn't to have any, because I'm going to have it with the children when I get back."

"I'm sure you won't have time for a *bite* if you're having it with the children. How are they all?"

"Splendid!" Miss Burdett's smiling weather-beaten face glowed with vicarious maternal pride. "Jackie can read quite nicely now. I've been teaching him in the evenings. I've got five of them at the cottage, and I'm taking Petronella back with me as well tonight. She's had a little cold, and I think the change of air will do her good. I make them all put in some work on the garden. The garden's really lovely now. I wish you'd come over and see it."

Miss Burdett had bought the two fields behind the cottage. One had been turned into a garden, and the other was set apart for the children's playground. A stout swing with wooden supports stood at one end and near it a seesaw and a sand-pit.

"I remember that Jenifer and Lorna came over the first year I was there," went on Miss Burdett. She had quite forgotten how unhappy she had been that first year. "We had great fun. They wore white sailor-suits and looked so sweet."

"They came home with them filthy," smiled Marcia.

"And wasn't it there that Jenifer lost the brooch I gave her?" put in Lena.

"No, that was at Westonlea, the same year, at a picnic she went to with some people called Melford."

"You liked the place, didn't you?" asked Miss Burdett idly.

"Yes, but somehow we never went again. The Croombs went there the next year. They met the Melfords. They said that he was very pleasant, but she was a miserable little creature."

Miss Marchant's eye was still fixed restlessly on the road. Her mole seemed to quiver with anxiety.

"I do hope the children won't be late," she said. "It would be just like Jenifer to forget all about the Frewins' party tonight."

"But Lorna wouldn't," put in Marcia.

Lena fancied that there was something faintly derogatory in Marcia's smile and rose indignantly to the defence of her favourite niece.

"I'm sure that Lorna's not at all unduly fond of pleasure," she said stiffly. "I always find her *most* ready to be interested in serious things."

When Lorna had nothing else to do, she amused herself by acting a sort of charade in which she took the character of Ray of Sunshine in Poor Aunt Lena's life.

She always enjoyed acting charades of that sort. Moreover, though she didn't quite know how much money Aunt Lena had to leave, she intended to secure the position of favourite niece in good time. She took flowers to her and admired Peter and the canaries and asked her advice (never for a moment intending to take it) and showed an intelligent interest in her district, remembering who had what diseases and occasionally sending inexpensive delicacies to Mrs Cannon, who for the last two years had only had another month to live. Aunt Lena was deeply touched by these attentions and attempted to be to Lorna in some degree what Aunt Letty had been to her. Lorna, on her side, was an expert at evading these attempts while professing the deepest gratitude for them.

"That's really what I called about," said Miss Burdett. "Davida's going to the Frewins' tonight, and she wanted to know what Lorna and Jenifer were going to wear."

"I think that Lorna's going in her pink silk, and Jenifer in her white muslin."

"That's all right. Davida just wanted to be sure that Lorna wasn't going in her evening dress . . . She can wear her white muslin, too. I put a new blue ribbon sash on it this afternoon and ran some new blue ribbon through her camisole. She's borrowing Marigold's bronze slippers. They take just the same size. Of course sometimes it leads to trouble . . ."

"Here's Jenifer and Laurence," said Miss Marchant.

Jenifer and Laurence wheeled their bicycles past the dining-room window to the bicycle-shed at the back of the house. They looked very hot and untidy and were laughing together over some joke. Jenifer had grown into a tall slender girl; too slender, indeed, at present. Her chestnut hair was tied in the nape of her neck by a large bow of stiff black ribbon, whose ends, in the schoolgirl fashion of the day, were pinned up to her hair to make them stand out. From this descended a plait tied at the bottom by another large black ribbon bow. She wore a small round sailor-hat, tilted over her forehead and secured at the back by a hatpin, a white shirt blouse with a stiff linen collar and tie, and a navy-blue serge skirt that fell from a trim-belted waist almost to her ankles. Her face was still pale and freckled, and there was still something childish and wistful about the small crooked mouth. Jenifer was the only one of the four now at school. Laurence had just left, and Lorna and Adrian had left the year before. Adrian had gone into his father's business, and Lorna had lengthened her skirts, put up her hair, and now accompanied Marcia to such mild festivities as the neighbourhood had to offer.

The two were still laughing as they bumped their bicycles roughly into the shed.

"I shall never forget you and that hen, Laurie," Jenifer was saying. "I expect it's squawking yet."

"Well, I don't care," grinned Laurence. "It was perfectly sound advice, and it's come off every other time I've tried it."

The hens on the country roads outside the farms were a great trial to them on their bicycle rides. They would flutter about and run on in front or suddenly cross the road under their wheels. Jenifer was nervous and would wobble dangerously when she found herself in the middle of them.

"I'm so *terrified* of running over one," she explained.

"Well, it's fatal to wobble about like that and try to avoid them," Laurence had said. "The only thing to do is to ride right through them. They always get out of the way. Watch me when we come to the next lot."

At the next farm the usual group of hens straggled about on the road.

"Now watch me," said Laurence again and rode straight into them. There was a wild fluttering, and Laurence was precipitated headlong on to the ground on top of his bicycle, while a hen, denuded of most of its tail feathers, flew squawking down the road. Jenifer dismounted and stood helpless with laughter watching Laurence pick himself up. Then an angry-looking woman came down to the gate, and they made off as fast as they could.

"*And* the thermos!" went on Jenifer. "I suppose there's nothing left but twigs. Where is it?"

Passing through Leaveston, they had called at a confectioner's and had a fourpenny ice put into their thermos. When they dismounted to eat it on the way home, however, it was found to be firmly wedged at the bottom of the thermos, and all their attempts to extricate it were in vain. They tried twigs and even Jenifer's hat-pin without success. Jenifer now took it from her bicycle basket and inspected it critically.

"It's just a mass of broken twigs," she announced. "Let's get them out and suck them."

"We can't unless we melt the whole thing, and melted ice cream's horrid."

"I say, will you help me develop those plates this evening, Jen?"

"We're going to Ruby's party."

"Oh dash! I'd forgotten. What a bore!"

"Adrian won't think so. He's quite potty on her."

"Oh Lord, and won't he fuss getting ready! He'll change his suit about ten times and try every tie in the house. He's worse than any girl."

"Poor old Adrian!"

"I'm filthy. I'd better go up and wash. I say, I believe that *was* a whitethroat that we saw in the wood."

"I don't. I think it was a——"

"Well, let's look at the book."

"We'd better go into the dining-room first. Aunt Lena's come to tea, you know, and she'll be hurt if we don't speak to her."

"All right."

He followed her into the dining-room.

"Hello, Mother . . . Hello, Aunt Lena . . . Hasn't it been a heavenly day? We're absolutely filthy. We're just going up to wash."

"Haven't you got a kiss for your poor old Auntie, Jenifer?" said Aunt Lena.

She had a habit of referring to herself as "your poor old Auntie" that always irritated Jenifer. Lorna reacted to it automatically, at once staging her charade of Devoted Little Niece. Jenifer, who hated kissing, brushed the wrinkled cheek hastily with her lips, and Aunt Lena withdrew into the state known as Hurt. Jenifer evidently thought her Poor Old Auntie a Nuisance, and frequent references would be made to the fact in the plaintive voice that Aunt Lena kept for such occasions.

"You've not forgotten Ruby's party tonight, have you, Jenifer?" said Miss Marchant.

"No . . . I must go and get clean now. So must Laurie. Come on, Laurie."

126

They went upstairs together.

The old playroom had been turned into a sitting-room. Lorna had made spasmodic attempts to embellish it, painting the woodwork a not very successful blue, dyeing the curtains a somewhat patchy orange, and hanging on the walls coloured prints, cut out from the Christmas numbers of magazines and framed rather unevenly in *passe-partout*. On the cupboard stood an aspidistra that Emma had given them at Christmas. She had ornamented it by a green paper frill, but Miss Marchant had removed the frill, much to Emma's annoyance.

Two old armchairs, turned out of the dining-room, had been added to the furniture (Jenifer still preferred to curl up on the window-seat), and there was a new tablecloth. Otherwise the room was as it had been in their childhood. The carpet was still threadbare, and Marcia was still planning to buy a new one when she could afford it. Jenifer shared a table with Laurence, and Lorna with Adrian. Laurence was still an ardent stamp collector, and his table was generally covered with stamps and stamp catalogues. On Lorna's was a bowl of flowers (she loved feminine touches), a half-made paper hat (hats of thick plaited paper were the rage among her contemporaries), and the diabolo sticks whose use showed off her figure to best advantage. Laurence took his bird-book from the shelves and sat down at his table, turning over the leaves.

"What about the concert, Laurie?" said Jenifer as she swung herself up on to the window-seat.

He continued to read in silence.

"Laurie!"

He made no answer.

Once Laurence became interested in anything it was almost impossible to draw his attention from it. He seemed deaf, dumb, and blind to everything else. She slipped down from the window-seat and stood by him.

"Laurie!"

He appeared to emerge from a deep trance.

"Yes."

"About that concert . . ."

"It *was* a whitethroat, Jen. I felt sure it was. Listen to this. 'Ash-grey head, dusky wings, lower part white.'"

"Laurie, about the concert?"

"'It hops from twig to twig with untiring restlessness.' It was doing that, wasn't it? I believe it was a white-throat's nest we found in the spring. Do you remember? In our walk."

They always called a particular walk—through the woods to a hill with a tuft of trees on the top, known locally as Toothbrush Hill—"our walk," and felt slightly annoyed if ever they met anyone else there. The woods were full of birds and nests in the spring, and they loved the climb to Toothbrush Hill and the sense of exhilaration it gave them to sit there—on the top of the world, as it seemed to them.

She put her hand over the page he was reading.

"Laurie, listen. What—about—the—concert?"

"Concert? Don't, Jen." He drew her hand away. "Look, here's a picture of it. It *was* a whitethroat."

"*Laurie!* We are going to the concert, aren't we?"

With an effort he turned his mind to what she was saying.

"Yes, rather! I thought we'd fixed it all up."

Music was one of the many interests that Jenifer and Laurence shared, and they were in the habit of attending the orchestral concerts that were periodically held in Leaveston. The difficulty was that Adrian generally wanted to accompany them, and they disliked going with him because he was intense and emotional and his rhapsodies made them hotly uncomfortable. Both Laurence and Jenifer were reserved and preferred to keep their emotions well beneath the surface.

"Shall I get the tickets?"

"Yes. I'll settle with you if you will. Get the cheapest."

"Of course. I'll get the one-and-sixpennies. But what about Adrian?"

"Oh, hang Adrian! I won't come if he's coming. I can't stand the way he gasses about it afterwards."

"He'll go by himself and be hurt."

"I can't help that," said Laurence, returning to his book.

"We'd better not tell him we're going," said Jenifer.

But Laurence didn't hear . . . Jenifer swung herself up to the window-seat again.

"Here are Adrian and Lorna," she announced.

"Uh-huh," grunted Laurence.

Adrian and Lorna were now wheeling their bicycles round to the bicycle-shed. Adrian was handsome in a sombre, somewhat effeminate style, with dark brooding eyes, a pale clear skin, and sensitive mobile lips. He let his dark hair grow rather longer than was fashionable and affected a slightly Byronic neckwear. He still produced strikingly original and effective little sketches belonging to the impressionist school, but he shirked the self-discipline that would have developed his talent and was hurt and affronted by any adverse criticism. Although he did not like working in his father's office, he realised that his artistic gifts would not earn him a livelihood, and indeed rather shrank from the idea of putting them to the test.

Lorna was already a beauty, with a firm graceful figure, a dazzlingly fair complexion, and perfect features. Like Jenifer she wore a blouse and skirt and sailor hat, but her blouse was a dainty affair of embroidered voile, with a high wired collar surmounted by a frill, and its transparency showed a glimpse of a lace-trimmed camisole, threaded with pale blue ribbon. Adrian admired Lorna intensely, and she took considerable pains to retain his devotion. This afternoon, as they sat resting in a wood on their way home, he had suddenly confided to her his love for Ruby Frewin.

"I can't tell you what I feel about her, Lorna. I adore her. It's—terrible in a way. I simply can't think of anything else. I lie awake thinking of her. I feel that I—well, I can't go on living if she won't marry me, and yet heaven knows why she should. I'm no good at anything, and I never shall be."

Adrian's moods alternated between extravagant self-confidence and equally extravagant abasement.

Lorna, to whom reassurance and encouragement came very easily, reassured and encouraged him, and he was naïvely grateful to her.

"You're so awfully sweet to me, Lorna. You always make me think that everything will be all right."

"Of *course* it will be all right, Adrian. I'm quite sure that Ruby's fond of you."

They put their bicycles in the shed and went into the dining-room, where Marcia, Lena, and Miss Marchant still sat idly gossiping round the tea-table.

"There you are, darlings," said Marcia. "Had a nice time?"

"Lovely," said Lorna.

"Miss Burdett called to ask what you were going to wear. I said your blue silk. You are, aren't you?"

"Yes. Ruby said it was quite a small party, so I think my blue silk, don't you, Auntie?"

"It doesn't matter what I think," said Lena distantly.

She was still feeling hurt because Jenifer hadn't seemed pleased to see her Poor Old Auntie and hadn't kissed her properly.

"Don't be silly, Lena," said Marcia rather impatiently.

"Of course it matters what you think," said Lorna affectionately, laying her cheek against Lena's faded hair.

"*You're* pleased to see your poor old auntie, aren't you?" said Lena.

"Of course I am," said Lorna. "I always am."

"I think it's time that you and Jenifer began to get ready," said Marcia.

"All right . . . You'll stay and see us before we go, won't you, Auntie?"

"I'm afraid I must get back to Peter, darling," said Lena, now completely restored to good-humour, "but it's very nice to think that you want your poor old auntie to stay."

When she had gone, Adrian and Lorna went upstairs to the playroom, where Laurence still sat at the table, deep in his bird-book, and Jenifer was still curled up on the window-seat, gazing dreamily down at the garden.

"Hello!" said Jenifer, turning her head as they entered. "Wasn't it heavenly out?"

"You might have started getting ready," said Lorna, "then we shouldn't be on top of each other in the bedroom."

Relations between Lorna and Jenifer were variable. Often their common interests drew them together. They were both good tennis-players and were frequently asked out to play. It was, of course, the decorous game of the period. They wore long white pique skirts that showed a swirl of white petticoats as they ran, and considered it rather unsporting deliberately to place a ball out of reach of their opponent. For the rest, Lorna would sometimes put on an elder sister manner, snubbing Jenifer and ordering her about, sometimes exert all her charm in order to add her to the train of her admirers, sometimes drop all her poses and become simple and happy and affectionate, the little-girl Lorna.

At present relations between them were fairly amicable.

"I suppose I'd better," said Jenifer, uncurling from the window-seat.

"Aren't you going to start changing, Laurie?" went on Lorna.

Laurence made no sign that he had heard.

"Well, you'd better," said Lorna rather sharply. "Adrian's gone to change."

Adrian, his face set and tragic, was in fact just tearing off in despair the sixth tie he had tried on.

Chapter Twelve

Lorna brushed her front hair over her face, back-combed it with quick flashes of the comb, pinned into position the sausage-like wire pad that supported her pompadour, swept her hair over it, and twisted it into a shining "bun" on the top of her head. Lorna's hair was thick and firm. Its pompadour did not part, revealing the pad beneath, as did that of many of her contemporaries, nor did untidy strands of her "bun" descend down her back at any exertion.

Jenifer sat on her bed, watching her dreamily. As a little girl she had loved to watch Marcia doing her hair, now she loved to watch Lorna. Lorna, too, had slender white hands that moved swiftly and gracefully among the shining meshes. Next year Jenifer would have to put her own hair up. Sometimes she practised when she was alone, but she could never make the smooth coils that Lorna seemed to make so easily. Her "bun" was lumpy and uneven, with little ends sticking out all over it.

Jenifer was quite ready for the party. Broad white hair ribbons took the place of the broad black hair ribbons of the daytime. Her white muslin dress had a V-shaped opening at the neck and short sleeves just reaching her elbows. She wore open-work stockings and bronze slippers worked with bronze beads, which had been Marcia's birthday present to her last year.

Lorna was putting her blue silk dress over the carefully built-up edifice of her hair.

"Give me a hand, Jen."

Jenifer roused herself from her day-dreams and came to the rescue, holding the opening of the dress wide apart, so that no stray hook could catch in the ordered coils.

"Now do me up, there's a dear."

Jenifer did up the intricate fastenings, the lining first, then the blue silk. Tiny hooks to be run home into tiny loops from the white neck down to the slim waist. Lorna was proud of her nineteen-inch waist and cultivated it assiduously, lacing her corsets as tightly as she could, pulling the leather belt she wore in the daytime to the last hole regardless of discomfort.

"Thanks," she said, and stood for a moment, silent and motionless, looking at herself in the glass.

"You do look nice, Lorna," said Jenifer, giving a final touch to the blue silk bow at the back.

"So do you, Jen," said Lorna.

The consciousness of her own beauty made her feel generously disposed towards Jenifer, anxious that she should have some share in the happiness that possessed her as she gazed at the radiant figure in the mirror.

"Let me lend you my amber beads," she went on. "I can't wear them with blue, of course."

"Oh, Lorna, how sweet of you!"

Lorna fastened the amber beads round Jenifer's neck, straightened the two white hair ribbons, tucked in a few straying tendrils of hair, and pulled the dress into shape about the waist.

"Well," she said, "we're ready, aren't we? Let's go downstairs."

Frank had just come home from business. He looked definitely middle-aged now, but there was about him still that suggestion of simplicity and kindliness that had always made him seem to Jenifer like a bulwark shutting away from them everything that could harm them.

He smiled at Jenifer as she entered and said, "Hello, Baby."

He was intensely proud of his four children and felt a special tenderness for Jenifer because there was still so much of the little girl about her. She was ingenuous and shy and gay with childhood's light-hearted irresponsible gaiety.

Then he caught sight of Lorna and realised that both girls were in gala attire.

"Hello! Hello! Hello! What's all this? You're not going out, are you?"

"Darling, have you forgotten?" said Marcia. "It's Ruby Frewin's party."

"Bother Ruby Frewin!" he said, slipping an arm round each of them.

He always felt disappointed when they went out in the evening. He liked to have his family about him and he still enjoyed "a little music" after dinner. He loved to see the two girls at the piano, Lorna singing while Jenifer played her accompaniment. Lorna's voice, though clear and true, was very small, and Jenifer's touch was fumbling and unsure, but their performance filled him with deep pride and delight.

"Are the boys going, too?"

"Yes, darling," said Marcia. "I'm afraid you'll have to put up with playing Darby to my Joan this evening."

He smiled.

"Aren't they a smart couple? I can't get used to having two grown-up daughters."

"Jen's not grown up," said Marcia. "I don't intend to feel really old till Jen puts up her pig-tail. Then I shall buy a white lace cap and retire to the chimney corner."

As Adrian and Laurence descended the stairs, Miss Marchant came into the hall and began to fuss around with coats and wraps.

"Oh, we don't need coats," said Lorna impatiently. "It's only next door."

She wanted to walk the few yards that separated The Chestnuts from The Firs without a coat. In the character of a passer-by she saw herself doing this and was much impressed.

"You might this evening when you come home," said Miss Marchant. "It turns cold after the sun's gone in."

Lorna wrapped a scarf of filmy blue gauze round her head, less because she needed it than because it gave her loveliness a cloud-like ethereal quality, and Marcia and Frank saw them off, standing arm-in-arm on the front door-step, Miss Marchant peering short-sightedly over their shoulders.

A handful of guests had arrived and stood rather selfconsciously in the middle of the Frewins' drawing-room, making desultory conversation. Mr Frewin's unceasing attempts at jocularity did little to lighten the atmosphere.

Ruby, who had grown from an assured sophisticated little girl into an assured sophisticated young woman, flitted restlessly about the room, glancing at the clock, looking out of the window, asking people questions and not waiting for the answers.

She was beautiful in a Jewish fashion (her mother had been a Jewess), with dark hair, dark eyes, and a complexion as radiant and flawless as Lorna's. The two girls were, indeed, excellent foils to each other, and there was between them a surface friendliness that hid an underlying rivalry. Lorna's universal charm made her the more popular, but Ruby's dress allowance was double that of Lorna's, and her clothes always put Lorna's in the shade. Mr Frewin was an indulgent father. He gave his daughter everything she asked for, never interfered with her, and watched her social manoeuvres with a slightly cynical amusement. He included everything and everyone around him, even himself and his success, in that slightly cynical amusement. Everything and everyone except Marcia. His devotion to Marcia was unchanged, despite the fact, or perhaps because of the fact, that she still kept him at arm's length. His own marriage had not been a happy one. Ruby's mother had proved fickle and unfaithful, and his opinion of women in general was consequently a low one. Marcia alone stood outside it, perfect, incomparable.

He had now opened several fresh branches of his stores and had more money than he knew how to spend even with an extravagant daughter, but Miss Frewin still dressed in rusty black and took her "route march" among the Leaveston shops, pricing everything at every shop before she bought anything, sharing the work of the house with the maid whom Ruby had insisted on her engaging. Between Miss Frewin and her niece there was an armed neutrality.

Miss Frewin realised that friction with Ruby might rob her of her home, while Ruby, on her side, had no wish to take over the responsibility of housekeeping. Miss Frewin had watched silently, grimly, while Ruby turned out all the solid old Victorian furniture of which Miss Frewin had been so proud and filled the house with an assortment of what Miss Frewin called "jimcrack rubbish." She now sat stiffly on an upright chair, her hair scraped back into a small tight bun, her face shining from a vigorous application of the strong yellow kitchen soap that still formed the basis of her toilet, dressed in a shabby black silk dress, whose collar was secured by a brooch made of her mother's hair, watching disapprovingly the group of young people in the middle of the room.

The door opened and Amelia, the general servant, sulkily announced, "The Gainsboroughs." Ruby had insisted that she should announce the guests, and she was still feeling affronted by the idea.

"Makin' a bloomin' fool of me!" she muttered angrily as she retired. "She knows 'oo they are as well as me."

Ruby detached herself from the group and sailed across to greet the new arrivals.

"'The Gainsboroughs!'" she echoed in a high-pitched, amused little voice. "Isn't she a *scream!* She's quite a character, you know. That's why we keep her."

Inwardly she fumed at the maid's mistake. She'd meant to show the Gainsboroughs how things should be done at a party . . .

Lorna's eyes flashed over Ruby's dress—an elaborate affair of white tulle and chiffon with a blue silk sash. It was like Ruby to say "It's quite a small party, just afternoon dresses," and then herself put on a dress like that. As if for comfort Lorna's eyes rested finally on the blue sash. Ruby was inclined to be plump, and, though she always said her waist was a twenty-two, it must be a twenty-six at least.

Adrian had somehow remained in the doorway with Charlie Burdett—a boy of about fourteen—when the others joined the group in the middle of the room. The appearance of Lorna with her easy pleasant charm had helped to break the ice, and they were now laughing and chaffing each other.

Adrian felt agonisingly out of it. He had not the courage to leave the doorway and cross the expanse of floor to the laughing group, yet he felt that everyone in the room must be thinking how unpopular he was—avoided, ostracised, left by himself in the doorway . . . In order to lessen the impression of unpopularity that he was sure he must be making upon innumerable onlookers (though in reality no one had noticed him at all) he began a painfully animated conversation with Charlie Burdett.

Adrian had always suffered acutely at parties. The parties in his middle teens at which such games as "Turn the Trencher" or "Kiss in the Ring" were played had been literally torment to him. He had suffered as much whether he was chosen for the ordeal of kissing or whether he was passed over. His self-consciousness had made all his friendships erratic and insecure. He was anxious to make friends but could never forget himself in any relationship. If ever, in the excitement of a new friendship, he did let down his defences, he did it so suddenly and thoroughly that the memory of his unguarded confidences would afterwards turn him hot and cold with embarrassment, and the friendship would come to an abrupt end. People called him a "queer fish," but he was so obviously well-meaning and ingenuous that no one really disliked him.

Though he had known Ruby since his childhood, he had never thought much about her till this year, when he had fallen in love with her violently and quite suddenly at a tennis party. The emotion was as intense and unbalanced as all his emotions, and he had spent many sleepless nights tormenting himself and, because of his youth and the novelty of his condition, taking a mournful pride in his torment.

Ruby was, of course, well aware of the situation and was making the most of it. To encourage him one minute and ignore him the next gave her a heady sense of power. It was so easy and exciting to plunge him into despair or raise him to ecstasy by a careless word.

He was watching her covertly now as he stood talking to Charlie

Burdett, who felt both flattered and embarrassed by the sudden affability of the usually moody young man, and Ruby, though she never moved her eyes in his direction, was conscious in every nerve of his scrutiny. She kept her profile turned towards him, and once, as she laughed gaily at something someone had said, she laid her hand on Mark Burdett's arm, just because she knew how harrowing the sight would be to the watching Adrian. Mark himself was quite unmoved by the pressure of her dainty hand. His boyhood's admiration of Lorna had developed into a devotion that was now accepted by the neighbourhood as one of the normal features of the landscape. Lorna included him in the kindness with which she treated all her friends, but she intended to marry someone far more exciting than Mark Burdett.

She was sitting next to Miss Frewin, showing herself so pleasant and sympathetic and appreciative of all the trouble that Miss Frewin must have taken over the preparations for the party, that Miss Frewin's grimness had relaxed to something almost approaching cordiality.

The four eldest Burdett girls were there as well as Charlie and Mark. Their white muslin dresses had been frequently let down, but they were fresh and neat and spotlessly clean. Eglantine wore the expression of a general in command of an army. Each of her sisters had had to pass a rigid inspection. One had had to clean her nails again, another to do her hair again, and the third to darn a small hole in her stocking. Mrs Burdett had murmured "Does it matter, dear? They look so nice," but Eglantine was as ruthless as a sergeant-major in charge of a band of raw recruits.

Even Mrs Burdett was slightly in awe of Eglantine, for Eglantine stood no nonsense from anybody, not even her mother.

"You can't wear that, Mother," she would say sternly, when Mrs Burdett appeared in a new hat that she had trimmed elaborately with flowers taken off two or three old ones, and Mrs Burdett would meekly remove the offending trimming.

Bobby and Sylvia Lenham were the last to arrive. Their arrival created something of a stir, for there was a certain glamour attached to the young Lenhams in the eyes of the neighbourhood. Their parents had taken the Hall, the largest house in the district, and they moved in an atmosphere of careless wealth and luxury. They had had the whole house expensively redecorated, the gardens altered, and an artificial lake made in one of the meadows. They engaged more servants than anyone at the Hall had ever been known to engage before, and they kept two cars as well as a carriage. The Gainsboroughs had not met them yet, though they had seen them in church every Sunday since their arrival. Mrs Lenham was an invalid and seldom appeared, but Mr Lenham was a regular churchgoer. He was a strikingly handsome man with a fine head, greying hair, clean-cut features, and a cleft chin. His tall, well-proportioned figure was perfectly tailored, and his man-about-town air made him a conspicuous personage in the little country village. The first time he appeared in church Jenifer had watched with a covert interest that changed gradually to a strange secret excitement. He looked so handsome and kind and good . . . Jenifer was romantic, with the romanticism of an inexperienced schoolgirl. Heroes of impossible charm and nobility jostled each other in her mind, and all seemed to take final shape and form in the person of the new squire.

She still had the unquestioning faith of childhood, and his regular appearance at church, his devout behaviour there, and his many gifts to charity, raised him in her eyes to a pinnacle of perfection at which she worshipped in humble reverence. Whenever she passed the gate of the Hall, she passed it with a beating heart, wondering if she would see him. The mere thought of him had power to send a wave of exultant happiness through her. It was as if his very existence made the whole world a better and more thrilling place than it had been before.

The day when she ran into him at the corner of the lane, and he put out his hand to steady her, apologising with his pleasant kindly smile, always seemed to her, looking back, to have been a day of brilliant sunshine, though really it had not stopped raining once from morning to night.

Bobby Lenham was unlike both father and mother. He was very fair, with blunt features and a long, humorous, impudent mouth.

The girl had her mother's brown eyes and soft brown hair, though her smile was as humorous and impudent as Bobby's. The two carried with them the atmosphere of a smarter and more sophisticated world than the world of Merrowvale, but they were friendly and unaffected, obviously ready to enter into any fun that might be going on.

Ruby swept across the room to greet them, eyeing Sylvia's dress with furtive interest. It was much plainer than hers, but with a plainness that had probably come from London or Paris.

With the arrival of the Lenhams things suddenly began to go with a swing. Their glamour seemed to communicate itself to the whole party. There is a glamour that emphasises the dullness around it, and there is a glamour that banishes the dullness around it, and the glamour of the Lenhams was of the latter kind. Even Clumps and Up Jenkins (the games with which Merrowvale parties always began) became new and original and full of unexpected amusement. It was the "thing" in Merrowvale to show yourself bored and *blasé* at parties in order to prove that you were accustomed to far better and brighter affairs. But the Lenhams, who obviously were accustomed to far better and brighter affairs (they had just come from London, where they had seen Pelissier's Follies, Maud Allan, Galsworthy's new play, *Justice*, and various other things that were only names to Merrowvale), were working as hard to make this party a success as if it had been their own. The result was that everyone else hastily dropped their bored and *blasé* airs, which were evidently not, after all, correct.

The atmosphere was damped slightly by the arrival of Rosa Pickering. Rosa had grown into a plain lanky girl, with an arch assured manner. She attended elocution classes in Leaveston and was vaguely destined for the stage. She frequently referred to "we artists" in her conversation and expected to be asked to recite at every party she attended. So strong and confident indeed was her expectation that it hypnotised people into acquiescing. The heavy depression that was invariably cast by the thought of the recitation spread over the room as soon as she entered, and Ruby, bowing to the inevitable and deciding wisely that it would be best to get it over quickly, stopped the game of Up Jenkins and said:

"Will you recite for us, Rosa?"

Rosa smiled coyly as she replied:

"Are you sure everyone *really* wants me to?"

A faint murmur went round, and Rosa at once leapt into the centre of the room and began to recite Kipling's "The Garden." It would seem to be an undramatic enough poem, but not as recited by Rosa. Her voice and manner plumbed the whole range of the emotional gamut with little or no encouragement from the words themselves. Her arms kept up a series of rhythmic and meaningless revolutions, and at the last line of each verse she flung them both out before her horizontally then dropped them heavily to her side. Faint applause greeted the end. Rosa bowed with every sign of gratification and began her encore. This was supposed to be spoken by a small boy, so she planted her feet sturdily apart and adopted a high, squeaky, childish voice, continuing the rhythmic arm movements. Each verse ended, "If I dare—but I darsent," which was the signal for her arch smile to flash round the room. Ruby felt ashamed of the exhibition and sorry that she had invited it. She glanced furtively at Bobby Lenham and was surprised to see that he was watching the performance with deep interest. She did not know that he was storing every word and tone and movement in his memory, and that later in the evening in his sister's bedroom he would reproduce it with such exquisite fidelity that Sylvia would be helpless with laughter. During that summer, in fact, Bobby cultivated Rosa so assiduously that the matchmaking gossips of the neighbourhood began to put their heads together. He was, however, merely completing his study of her. Bobby collected characters, and Rosa was destined to become the brightest jewel in his crown. For years afterwards his imitation of Rosa's arch smile and coy yet heavy manner was famous among his friends, and no party was complete without Bobby's recital of "The Garden" and "If I dare—but I darsent." Bobby was a light-hearted irresponsible youth, who managed to extract amusement from the most unlikely situations.

Ruby looked round despairingly at the door, hoping that Amelia would appear to announce supper. Amelia was standing in the doorway, all her grimness gone, a smile hovering on her flushed face, her eyes misty with tears. Amelia was the only person in Merrowvale who appreciated Rosa's reciting, and to Amelia it was the most beautiful thing that had ever come into her life.

"Is supper ready, Amelia?" said Ruby, speaking quickly and sharply because she saw Rosa gathering breath for a third recitation.

The sullenness returned to Amelia's face.

"Aye," she muttered, and went abruptly from the room.

Chapter Thirteen

Supper was a stand-up affair of coffee, sandwiches, sausage-rolls, jellies, and trifle. Ruby, who had left all the preparatory work of the party to Miss Frewin, was now flitting about among her guests and playing hostess very prettily, keeping her aunt and father, of whom she was ashamed, in the background. She flushed with anger once to hear him say facetiously to Sylvia Lenham, "May I press you to jelly?" Whatever would she *think!* . . . But she stood too much in awe of him to snub him openly.

Sylvia was sitting on the window-seat by Jenifer. She had taken a fancy to Jenifer as soon as she saw her, and had joined her there when the party drifted into the dining-room. Jenifer felt almost paralysed by shyness. She would have much preferred to watch and admire this paragon from a distance. Glamorous enough on her own account, Sylvia was doubly glamorous from being her father's daughter. She lived in the same house, saw him, heard him, spoke to him every day. Jenifer's imagination staggered at the idea, and a wave of that strange sweet excitement surged over her again. She wanted to lead the conversation round to him, but lacked the courage. When Sylvia said, "Daddy's going to take us to Switzerland for the winter sports," she gave a sharp little intake of breath. To be his daughter . . . The very thought of it made her feel dizzy. She loved her own father, but this, somehow, would be quite different . . .

"We're having a dance next month," Sylvia was saying. "You must come. You and your sister and brothers. And you must stay the night. We want as many people as possible to stay the night because it's so much more fun."

"I'd love to," said Jenifer eagerly. Her eyes were star-like, her usually pale cheeks softly flushed. The white muslin dress and the schoolgirl plait tied with white ribbon emphasised her immaturity, and Sylvia, looking at her, thought: What a darling she is! I hope we're going to be friends.

Lorna was covertly watching them as she laughed dutifully at Mr Frewin's invitation to have a "trifle of trifle." It always gave her a curious feeling of depression to see people making overtures of friendship to Jenifer, and she would generally lose no time in attaching Jenifer's new friend to herself. She looked upon this as a natural and kindly desire to be on good terms with Jenifer's friends, and it was not her fault if the friends came ultimately to prefer her to Jenifer.

Rosa Pickering was standing by the table, absent-mindedly eating sausage-rolls. She was bathed in that hazy glow of happiness that always came to her when she had been reciting. As she ate sausage-rolls (she had a large appetite) she wasn't in the stuffy overcrowded little dining-room. She was on an enormous platform, in an enormous hall, looking over a sea of upturned faces and reciting inspiring poems like "If," and "The Garden," and all the upturned faces went home determined to live better lives. Amelia hovered devoutly near, offering her sausage-rolls at intervals. Miss Frewin came up to her and asked her to have more coffee.

"Which of the two did you like best?" said Rosa, awakening slowly from her dreams.

"The two what, dear?"

"My two recitations."

"I'm a little deaf, dear, so I didn't hear either very well, but"— remembering the arm movements, and not wishing to sound ungracious—"they both looked very pretty."

"A gift like that is a great responsibility," said Rosa with a sigh.

"Of course, dear," said Miss Frewin absently.

"Everyone says I ought to take a Hall and give a recital in London, but it's so expensive."

"Of course," agreed Miss Frewin again absently. She was wondering if she could make any sort of a pudding out of all that bread and butter and fruit salad and trifle that was going to be left. Both Ruby and James were so difficult about "eating up" . . .

"I could go on the stage, of course," went on Rosa, "but Mother thinks the atmosphere's so bad for a young girl."

"Of course," agreed Miss Frewin again.

There were going to be dozens of sausage-rolls and sandwiches left, too. Her gaze fell rather grimly upon Amelia, who was still hanging around Rosa in a bemused state of adoration, offering her jellies and biscuits and cakes. Amelia, at any rate, should have sausage-rolls and sandwiches for breakfast, dinner, tea, and supper, till they were finished. Amelia might sulk (and certainly would), but she couldn't refuse to eat them, as James and Ruby did. She'd never forgotten the time at breakfast when James had thrown a plate of bread and butter into the fire. It had been left over from tea-time the day before, and she'd thought that if she didn't bring in the loaf he'd *have* to eat it . . . Amelia couldn't do that, or, if she did, she'd be Packed Straight Off . . . Miss Frewin's eyes glinted pugnaciously. Her life with Amelia was a protracted struggle that was bound to culminate sooner or later in the Packing Off of Amelia. Miss Frewin did not wish this *grand finale* to occur sooner than was necessary, but she knew that she would thoroughly enjoy it when it did . . . The thought of it was a sort of pleasant background to all her dealings with the girl. Amelia was not the Meek Sort who would be Packed Off without a scene. The occasion, when it arrived, would be a Regular Row of the sort that was necessary at frequent intervals for the health of Miss Frewin's soul.

"I wouldn't have any difficulty in getting on the stage, of course," went on Rosa, "but Mother has a cousin who's met a lot of actors and actresses, and she says they aren't at all nice."

"I expect they aren't, dear," said Miss Frewin. "I've never met any, but I've always understood that they aren't."

"Of course, reciting's *different*," said Rosa, taking a chocolate biscuit from a dish reverently offered to her by Amelia. "I mean, it's so much more refined than acting."

Ruby, seeing that everyone else had finished and knowing by

experience that Rosa would go on eating as long as there was anything left to eat, said brightly:

"Has everyone finished? Shall we go back to the drawing-room?"

They all went back to the drawing-room, Rosa absent-mindedly taking a macaroon from a dish on the sideboard on her way to the door.

"Now what shall we do?" went on Ruby, a note of anxiety invading her brightness, for the moment immediately after supper was notoriously a difficult one. She saw an offer to recite again trembling on Rosa's lips, and hastily went on, "What about a dance? We could have a set of Lancers, anyway."

Lancers could generally be trusted to degenerate into a romp and break the after-supper ice. And with the Lenhams' help it degenerated into a romp almost before it had begun. Bobby Lenham swung his partners off their feet with wild war-whoops, the Grand Chain became a mad riot, and in a few moments the decorous party was a mass of dishevelled shouting young people. Coiled ends of hair appeared on the girls' shoulders, pads of wire or false hair became visible through their coverings, and "buns" drifted precariously from their moorings. Piercing shrieks arose as flounced skirts flew knee-high, revealing the lace edges of cambric drawers.

Miss Frewin watched with a mixture of disapproval and appreciation. The conscious part of her disapproved. They were certainly Getting Rough, which wasn't Nice. But the less conscious part of her that revelled in Rows and Scenes and Packings Off was romping about with the best of them, its hair coming down and its skirts flying up to its knees (Miss Frewin wore red flannel drawers, devoid of lace).

The set was encored and encored again, then the girls fled from the room, still hot and laughing, clutching at torn flounces and dishevelled hair, while Bobby Lenham picked up the hairpins that were scattered all over the floor and followed the girls up to Ruby's bedroom door, offering his help, to an accompaniment of screams of laughter from within. The girls stood in breathless groups before Ruby's mirror, twisting up the coils of the collapsed buns, emptying Ruby's china dish of hairpins as quickly as she filled it. They did not powder or make up. They waited to do that till they were in the lavatory (Lorna always carried a book of *papiers poudrés* concealed in her garter for the purpose). "Make up" of any kind was disapproved of in Merrowvale, and, though most of the girls used it, they used it secretly and wished the results to be looked upon as the work of Nature. Only Sylvia Lenham took out a box of powder and openly powdered her smooth skin, to the surprise and disapproval of the others.

Downstairs the men, under the direction of Bobby, were laying booby traps for the girls at the bottom of the stairs. The stiffness characteristic of Merrowvale parties had completely vanished. Even Adrian had forgotten his usual self-consciousness in the hilarious romping of the Lancers.

"What shall we do now?" cried Ruby, as she came downstairs, tidy but still flushed and excited.

"Charades!" called Bobby, and the others all cheered.

The charades were, of course, as great a success as the Lancers. They rushed up and downstairs, collecting properties; they ransacked Ruby's bedroom, and even Miss Frewin's. Bobby stage-managed his side and made Rosa take all the star parts. As Cleopatra, wearing a Nottingham lace window curtain, with a wicker plant pot on her head, simpering in a coy but equine fashion at Bobby, who knelt at her feet in a panoply of dish-covers and tin trays, Rosa won rapturous applause and almost decided to go on the stage, after all.

In the course of the charades, Adrian managed to get Ruby alone in the conservatory. The atmosphere of carefree merrymaking had lifted him out of himself and given him sudden courage. He was caught up into an exalted region where anything could happen, a region in which diffidence and self-distrust simply did not exist. His dark eyes were brilliant, his pale cheeks flushed, as he caught her hand in his.

"Ruby," he pleaded, "do listen. I must tell you. I love you. I— Ruby, say you'll marry me. I can't go on living if you won't."

Ruby, too, was exalted by the excitement of the evening and by the new atmosphere of irresponsibility that the young Lenhams seemed to have brought with them. She had always meant to marry and to marry early. She found life in her father's house constricted and monotonous, and she wanted to escape from it as soon as possible. But—Adrian? He was good-looking and he adored her, but there was something odd about him. People made fun of him . . . Still, they made fun of him because he was—different. She didn't like his paintings, but she had often heard people say that they were clever. He had talked more than once of giving up his work in his father's office and making painting his career. Suppose he were to break loose from the dull world of Merrowvale and become famous . . . She'd love to be the wife of a famous artist. They'd live in London and have a butler. She'd give parties and wear wonderful dresses with trains and diamonds, and have her portrait in the Royal Academy. Better than marrying a tradesman like her father, however wealthy. And in Merrowvale, or even in Leaveston, one met so few people. She didn't want to miss any really good chance . . .

While she hesitated he caught her to him and pressed his lips upon hers. Passion flared up suddenly between them, and when he released her she was trembling.

"You'll marry me?" he said hoarsely. "You must . . . Ruby, I can't live without you."

"But, Adrian"—she tried to speak calmly, to steady the wild beating of her heart—"you've—I mean, you've no money."

"I'll work," he protested. "I'll never do anything at business, I know, but I'll chuck it. I'll go to an art school and work hard. That's the only thing I ever could be any good at, and I know I could be good at that. I'll work like a donkey . . . Ruby, I love you so . . . Won't you wait for me? Promise."

He kissed her again and she relaxed in his arms, weakening visibly.

"Promise, promise," he urged. "If you knew how I worship you!"

She tried to collect her forces. She mustn't let the chance go, but she mustn't commit herself too definitely.

"Adrian," she said, "if I do, it must be secret. No one else must know."

"But why not? I want everyone else in the world to know."

"No, Adrian"—her voice was steady now and quite firm—"they mustn't. Not yet. Not till I say so. If you won't agree to that I won't be engaged to you."

"But, Ruby "

"Adrian, you must do as I say, or else it's all off."

"But you love me?"

"Of course I love you."

"Ruby, I can't believe it. You're so wonderful, and I—I'm nothing at all. But I'll try all the rest of my life to be worthy of you. I'd never even dared to hope. Ruby . . . darling . . . let me kiss you just once more. I——"

"No, *don't,* Adrian."

There was a sharp edge to her voice, and she pushed away his arm urgently. Already she was wondering if she had been unwise. She'd been rushed into it. There was a lot to consider. He might not become a famous artist, after all. Still—it didn't really bind her to anything. She could always get out of it . . . And—he was nice-looking and terribly in love with her. It was rather thrilling
. . .

"Well, just one more," she conceded, "but for heaven's sake be careful of my hair. You've messed it up enough."

She relaxed in his arms, yielding herself again to his kisses. There was something poignantly clumsy and inexperienced about his love-making, and a faint maternal tenderness stirred at her heart. She held his face between her hands.

"Adrian, darling . . . I believe it's the first time you've ever kissed a girl."

"Of course it is . . . Oh, Ruby . . . I'd never even dared to hope
. . ."

He'd already said that once. As a lover he would probably be rather dull. However, as long as the engagement was secret she needn't see too much of him. And he was rather sweet. Apart from all that, he was a living symbol of her power, the first-fruits of her spear. He had proved to her that she was the sort of woman men fell passionately in love with. And—it came round to it again—she *was* fond of him . . .

"Oh, *Ruby!*"

He'd have to learn not to keep on saying her name like that. It would soon get on one's nerves.

Someone called, "Ruby! Where are you?"

"Let me go . . . Good heavens! What on earth's my hair like? *Don't,* Adrian . . . Here I am. Just coming."

With a few deft touches Ruby tidied her hair, then joined the others, cool, unperturbed.

"Well, have you decided on the word?"

Adrian stayed behind in the conservatory. He felt intoxicated by emotion, uplifted to the very heavens by ecstasy. He wanted to fall on his knees and thank God . . . He wanted to do something noble and heroic to prove himself worthy of the miracle that had happened to him.

"Where's Adrian? Come on, Adrian. We're ready."

Adrian came slowly from the conservatory. He looked pale and bemused. There was a faint tremulous smile on his lips. Ruby threw him a warning glance. She'd never forgive him if he gave the show away. But no one was looking at him. They were all arranging the charade.

"We want a fire-guard," said Bobby. "Have you got one, Miss Frewin?"

"Yes, there's one in the attic. I'll get it."

"I'll come with you," said Bobby quickly, before anyone else could offer. He followed her lightly up the two flights of stairs to the attic.

"I know there's one here," she said, as they entered the dim room piled up with lumber. "Have you got a match?"

He struck a match and held it above his head. Its flickering light showed trunks, packing-cases, cardboard boxes, an old treadle sewing-machine, several broken chairs, and, scattered everywhere, a medley of odds and ends.

"Here it is!" she said.

The match went out as she spoke, and, turning, she suddenly found Bobby's arms about her, his lips against hers. There was none of Adrian's fumbling uncertainty about Bobby's kiss. It was quick and sure, impudent and experienced. He released her almost at once, and, snatching up the fire-guard, plunged downstairs, laughing mischievously. She followed slowly and thoughtfully. It was cheek, of course, but—well, the Lenhams were wealthy, well-connected people. It might, perhaps, be better to become Bobby Lenham's wife than the wife even of a fashionable artist. And he was a dear. One could easily become fond of him. He'd be less trying than Adrian in lots of ways. His kiss, of course, meant nothing. But—it had made her glad that she had insisted on Adrian's keeping their engagement secret, because a secret engagement wasn't really binding. Not like a public one.

He waited for her on the landing, grinning impudently. She gave him a haughty glance and passed on in front of him. He followed, still grinning, in no way deceived by the haughty glance.

The charade proceeded, to an accompaniment of screams of merriment . . . Bobby as Nero, Rosa as Agrippina, various other guests as lions and gladiators . . . Mr Frewin had bought a lot of funny masks in order to make the evening "go," and he duly appeared in them, one after another, but no one took any notice of him.

Miss Frewin had suddenly decided not to risk the Packing Off of Amelia over the question of a diet of sausage-rolls and stale sandwiches. When it came it must come over something a little more worthy of a Regular Row than that. She drew Eglantine Burdett into the dining-room.

"My dear," she said tentatively, "I wonder—you know how it is—my brother and Ruby both have such small appetites. Do you think the children would like some of these sandwiches and the jelly and trifle? It would really be doing us a favour."

But Miss Frewin need not have been tentative. Eglantine's eyes gleamed as the eyes of a general of a starving army might gleam when he finds an abandoned store of the enemy's commissariat.

They roved in a business-like way over table and sideboard, where the dishes still stood.

"Thank you," she said. "Yes, they'll be very useful. I'll send the twins round for them with the handcart first thing in the morning. You'll cover the bread and butter and sandwiches with damp cloths during the night, of course, won't you?"

"Yes," said Miss Frewin, somewhat taken aback by this brisk and matter-of-fact acceptance of her offer.

"They'll be here by nine, then. Will that be all right?"

"Yes, my dear, certainly."

Immediately after breakfast Eglantine was in the habit of giving her family their orders for the morning. Even Mrs Burdett did not escape her eldest daughter's rule, and often had to set herself briskly to her household tasks when she would far rather have sat reading the newspaper or a novel. The twins would be chivvied off with the handcart as soon as they had swallowed their last mouthful, and they would not dare to loiter on the way. It was Eglantine who had sat on the roof on one chimney-pot with her feet upon another, but it would have fared ill now with any young brother or sister who indulged in such an escapade.

Then, quite suddenly, the party came to an end.

Mr Lenham arrived with the car to call for his children. He said that he had spent the day in Town and was on his way home.

He stood in the doorway, watching a charade in which Bobby as a faun in a hearthrug pursued Rosa as a nymph in a sheet through a forest of tables and chairs and stools and plant pots.

Jenifer happened to be standing next to him, and he looked down at her with his pleasant smile.

"I suppose my young people have turned the whole place upside-down as usual?"

Again that strange sweet excitement surged over Jenifer. It seemed hardly credible that this most godlike of creatures should even recognise her existence. She flushed and smiled at him shyly.

"It's been such fun."

Sylvia came up and slipped her arm through his.

"Jenifer's coming to our dance," she said. "She's going to stay the night."

He smiled again at Jenifer—the kind friendly smile that made her wish she were really good, so that she would feel more worthy of it, that made her decide to try to be good harder than she'd ever tried in her life before.

Bobby was helping Ruby to put the things away.

"Let's take the fire-guard back to the attic," he suggested.

"Certainly not," said Ruby, but the glance she threw him was no longer haughty. It was deliberately provocative. He helped her move a footstool, holding his hand over hers as he did so.

Adrian did not notice. He never took his eyes off Ruby, but so intoxicated was he with happiness that he simply did not see anyone else in the room, even Bobby.

Chapter Fourteen

The prospect of the dance at the Hall threw the young people into a ferment of excitement. Ruby, to the secret envy of the others, went up to London to buy a new dress, and Eglantine set to work with grim determination upon a dozen yards of embroidered voile that she had bought cheap at the sales. She intended it to make dresses for Davida, Marigold, Rubina, and herself. They were all quite confident of the results. They felt that not even a dozen yards of embroidered voile would dare to defy Eglantine. Marcia ordered a new dress for Lorna at the Leaveston dressmakers, but decided that Jenifer's white muslin would do if the elbow sleeves were shortened into puff sleeves and the V-neck made a little lower, because, after all, Jenifer was not officially "out" yet. Lena, in fact, was horrified at the thought of her being allowed to go to the dance at all and came to The Chestnuts to remonstrate as soon as she heard of it.

She found Marcia at work on the white muslin dress. She had altered the sleeves and neck and was stitching a new yellow-ribbon sash on to it.

Lena took her seat, as usual, on the edge of an upright chair and fixed her eyes grimly on Marcia's handiwork.

"It isn't right, you know, Marcia," she said earnestly. "Aunt Letty would never have allowed it."

Marcia tactfully changed the subject and asked how Lena's maid was getting on, and Lena, promptly forgetting Jenifer and the Lenhams' dance, began a recital of the maid's misdemeanours that lasted half-way through tea. Then she suddenly remembered the object of her visit and returned to the attack.

"But, my dear Lena," said Marcia impatiently, "times have changed. People don't fuss about that sort of thing any more."

"Times may have changed," said Lena severely, "but that is no reason for the standards of gentlepeople to relax."

"It isn't as if it were a proper dance. It's only a young people's party. It's absurd for her not to go there with Lorna."

"Lorna's a different matter, of course. She's 'out.' I suppose she'll wear her white evening dress?"

"No. Miss Fenwick's making her a new one."

"Why?" said Lena indignantly. "Her other's perfectly good. Really, Marcia, you oughtn't to encourage the children in extravagance."

"It's not extravagance . . . Lena, you're eating no tea."

"I'm not hungry. I've had a good deal of indigestion lately."

"Why don't you see a doctor?"

"I can't afford to go running up doctors' bills."

Marcia shrugged her shoulders, and soon Lena rose to go. Marcia had decided, however, to say something about the coat and hat that Lena had worn regularly ever since Mother died. People were talking about it and saying that she was "getting queer." Nothing, of course, gave such an appearance of queerness as old clothes. And everyone knew how much money Mother had left her. There wasn't any excuse . . .

"It's time you got a new coat, Lena," she said as she helped her on with it. "This is simply not fit to be seen."

Lena's thin cheeks flushed and she compressed her lips. "It's a perfectly good coat, Marcia," she said stiffly. "I can't afford to fritter all my money away on clothes, as some people do. I have to be very careful."

Lorna came in at the front door, called "Hello! Auntie," and ran lightly upstairs. She was in a hurry because the Lenhams were giving an informal party that evening, and she'd promised to be there early to help with the preparations. They were going to play hide-and-seek in the garden with bicycle-lamps—red lights for seekers and green for hiders. The idea had occurred to them suddenly after lunch, and they had flown round the village issuing wholesale invitations.

*

Lena walked slowly back to Brightmet House. The air of graciousness and expansiveness that had lain over the house in the old days had gone. The drawing-room blinds were kept drawn and holland covers hid the furniture. The dining-room, too, was only used by Lena on the rare occasions when she entertained. She lived generally in the rather poky little room next the kitchen, which had been used in Mrs Silver's time as a sewing-room. It enabled her, she said, to keep an eye on the girl and saved money on heating and lighting. Now that Mrs Silver was dead Lena was beginning to give full rein to a latent parsimoniousness. Though she was well off and had no need to economise, she cut down the household expenses to a minimum, scrutinised every penny's expenditure, and rationed her maid's food with a grudging hand. The result was that she was frequently without a maid, and the work of the house was done by a series of odd charwomen or "daily helps."

She exercised a curious sort of cunning with herself, as if trying to conceal from herself the fact that she was living on about quarter of her income. She would hold conversations with herself: "Let's shut up the house and go abroad—France, Italy, Spain. We might even go to Greece." And she would reply, "We can't possibly afford it. You know how careful we have to be." She always managed to outwit and silence the part of her that wanted to spend money and travel and enjoy life.

As she sat in her little sitting-room, dining off two sausage-rolls (sausage-rolls did not really agree with her, but she had found a shop in Leaveston where you could get them for a penny each, and she could not resist them), the tears began to steal down her cheeks. Her mind went over her grievances. Nobody loved her. Marcia had sneered at her coat (which was as good as new), Lorna had run past her without kissing her poor old Auntie, she'd always wanted to travel and see the world and she'd never been able to—first because she'd had to sacrifice her whole life to Mother and now, because she couldn't afford to—she suffered terribly from indigestion, and the girl was careless and extravagant and greedy and unsympathetic and had flatly refused to eat sausage-rolls, though they were delicious. Well, perhaps not delicious, but wonderful value for the money. Gazing into the distance with tear-filled eyes she saw that imaginary self whom no one else had ever seen—radiant, cultured, beloved by everyone, a mixture of Mother's charm and Aunt Letty's solid worth. Then she surrendered to the mingled pangs of self-pity and dyspepsia, and the tears coursed unchecked down her sallow cheeks. If only there'd ever been anyone in the whole world who *understood*.... After a few minutes she pulled herself together, dried her eyes, and went into the kitchen to ask the girl what had happened to that piece of bacon that she *knew* had been left yesterday. The girl was impudent and gave notice, and Lena returned to her little sitting-room and abandoned herself again to the luxury of tears.

Adrian was now working hard at the Leaveston Art School.

He had pleaded earnestly with Frank to be given his chance to make good in art, and Frank, realising that the boy would never settle down to office work till he had had the chance, agreed. He promised, moreover, that, if his work seemed to justify it at the end of the year, he should go to study in London. Inspired and uplifted by his love for Ruby, Adrian was working harder than he had ever worked in his life before. Nothing seemed real to him but his work and Ruby. Ruby, on her side, was finding the secret engagement unexpectedly enjoyable. The fact that Adrian was away from Merrowvale all day simplified the situation, and stolen meetings in the evenings provided her with the furtive excitement and atmosphere of intrigue that she loved. When his clumsy love-making began to bore her, she could always put an end to the meeting by saying that she must go now or her father would suspect. Adrian had stopped objecting to the secrecy of the engagement, because, whenever he did so she told him that if he would not agree to a secret engagement there must be none at all. For the first time in his life he was learning to control his tendency to hysteria.

"Stop it, Adrian," Ruby would say. "I'll go straight indoors if you don't. My nerves won't stand it."

Ruby's nerves, of course, were of iron, but she generally found it convenient to refer to them as if they were the most sensitive of organs.

Once when he cried and begged her to let him announce their engagement she refused to meet him again for a week. When she did meet him again, however, she was radiantly sweet and loving.

During Adrian's absences in Leaveston, she was discreetly pursuing her flirtation with Bobby Lenham. Bobby was a pleasant change from Adrian—Adrian with his unbalanced emotionalism, his cringing adoration, his clumsy and reverent love-making. Bobby's admiration was tempered by an impudence that sometimes took her breath away, and his love-making was neither clumsy nor reverent. Under the combined excitement of that and of Adrian's worship her prettiness was slowly ripening into a dark vivid beauty.

Adrian had decided not to go to the Lenhams' dance. Late nights, he found, left him no energy for his next day's work. Besides, he would see Ruby only among the other guests, which was always torture to him. He pleaded with her for a short meeting before the dance, but Ruby was adamant. He would only claw her about and disarrange her hair, and she was particularly anxious to look her best that evening.

"No, Adrian darling," she said, "we must be careful. And it would be so tantalising—it would only make us want to spend all the evening together . . . I'll be thinking of you all the time, you know. I'd much rather be with you than at the dance, but people would only talk if I stayed away."

And he had to be content with that.

Sylvia had insisted that Jenifer and Lorna, who were both staying the night, should come to the Hall in time for tea.

"Then you can meet everyone," she said. "Several oddments of the family are coming over for it, of course."

They set off for the Hall in the afternoon, carrying their suitcases, feeling excited and secretly a little apprehensive. They were disappointed to find that both Sylvia and Bobby had gone to the station to meet some friends and that only Mrs Lenham and a cousin and aunt were in the drawing-room.

Marion Lenham had been, in her youth, a "stunner" of the Rossetti type. Now, fragile and faded, she reclined all day upon a sofa, round which the entire household was expected to revolve. No one—not even herself—seemed quite sure what was her exact complaint. She was a survival of the type of female Victorian who considered invalidism a merit in itself. Mrs Lenham's mother had spent most of her life on a sofa, and Mrs Lenham even as a child had subconsciously noticed the fact that invalidism if properly manipulated can dominate a household far more thoroughly than can the rudest health. She had drifted naturally into the state of professional invalidism as her beauty faded and she felt the need of other weapons. She found, too, that existence on a sofa solves a good many of life's problems. An invalid wife and mother cannot be expected to wait on her family or perform any of the more arduous tasks connected with housekeeping. An invalid wife and mother must not be "upset." When "upset," Mrs Lenham took to her bed, and her "upsetness" brooded over the whole house like a black cloud. Normally, however, she was sweet and patient and resigned, after the manner of her type. With her faded loveliness, her mellifluous, slightly plaintive voice, the long practised grace of her posture, her vague but frequent references to her "sufferings," she was the unquestioned autocrat of the family circle.

The legend of her beauty and invalidism had won Jenifer's heart even before she met her.

"Your mother is simply wonderful, isn't she?" she said shyly to Sylvia, and Sylvia replied casually, "Oh yes. Mother's all right if you take her the right way."

The young Lenhams were not analytical or introspective. They drifted through life easily, happily, making the most of every pleasure that came their way, avoiding its unpleasantness as best they could. They accepted their parents as one accepts the natural landscape around one. Father was a sport, and Mother was all right when she wasn't upset, so you had to avoid upsetting her, even if it meant a little duplicity. And you had to fuss round her, because she liked it and got upset if you didn't.

Geoffrey Lenham's devotion to his invalid wife was a byword throughout the neighbourhood. It thrilled Jenifer and brought a lump to her throat to watch him bending over her sofa, arranging her shawls (she was essentially the type of woman for shawls), asking solicitously after her health, presenting the gift—book, flowers, or fruit—that he never failed to bring back with him from Town. And Jenifer joined in his devotion, adoring humbly at the invalid's shrine, though Mrs Lenham, who disliked young people, remained unaware of her existence. Once Jenifer had dared to take her some flowers when she was going to tea at the Hall, but shyness overcome her on the way up the drive and she thrust them into a laurel bush.

Mrs Lenham turned her great lustrous eyes upon the Gainsborough girls as they were announced.

"There you are, my dears. The children are sure to be in soon. They've only gone to the station."

She introduced the cousin and aunt as Mrs Grantham and Miss Lenham, then closed her eyes with that air of suffering that she always assumed when she didn't want the trouble of entertaining boring visitors.

Mrs Grantham was much younger than her cousin and strikingly beautiful, with springing waves of bronze hair, deep-set hazel eyes, and exquisitely moulded mouth and chin. She raised her head from her needlework when the girls were introduced to her, greeted them languidly in her slow deep voice, stifled a yawn, glanced at the clock, then returned to her needlework.

The aunt, however, greeted them eagerly and at once began to talk about the Lenhams. She was one of those aunts who exist in every family, who know all the ramifications for generations past and take an impassioned interest in each. She always welcomed an opportunity of talking to strangers. The family itself had heard her stories so often that, except occasionally, when they remembered that she had money to leave, they somewhat cold-shouldered her. She took the two girls over to the fireplace, where a collection of

160

miniatures hung above the mantelpiece, and began to hold forth in the manner of a guide.

"That is my great-great-grandfather. I think Geoffrey's like him, don't you? He married one of the Ingrams of Worcestershire. That's their daughter, my great-grandmother. She married her second cousin, and their third son went out to America, and that line still lives in New Orleans."

She went on and on in her gentle, far-off voice—little scraps of information, little anecdotes, little reminiscences. It was evident that she kept in touch with every member of the family, spending most of her time in writing to more or less distant relations and giving them news of other more or less distant relations. She was like some industrious old spider sitting in the middle of a web, whose threads issued from her in all directions. It was pathetically wasted labour, as the Lenhams were wholly uninterested in each other. Jenifer's interest, however, was sincere enough. Not one of the delicately tinted faces but shared in some degree the glamour that surrounded her hero. His grandfather . . . his great uncle . . . his second cousin once removed . . .

Lorna was making a pretence of listening, but her bright eyes were darting round the room, noticing its every detail. She saw herself moving about, beautifully dressed, the owner of just such another room. She'd have brocade curtains at the windows like that, and panels of white-painted wood, and rose-shaded standard lamps . . .

But she wouldn't lie on a sofa, wrapped in a shawl. She'd sweep about, tall and graceful, in silk dresses with long trains that rustled as she walked.

Suddenly the door flew open, and Bobby and Sylvia entered with the guests they had brought from the station. Among them was Major Lenham, a brother of Mr Lenham's—a tall, handsome, horsy-looking man with a black moustache, an eyeglass, and a check suit. The atmosphere of the room became animated, full of greetings and talk and laughter. Tea was brought in, and two footmen carried trays and cake-stands about the room. Miss Lenham relinquished Jenifer and Lorna, and took possession of Major Lenham, to whom she began at once to retail the latest family news.

"I heard from Rose last week, Harold."

"Rose?" echoed Major Lenham blankly.

"Yes . . . She married George's son, you know. She's going to have Muriel's girls over for the season next year. I think it's so good of her, don't you?"

"Yes," agreed Major Lenham vaguely.

"But—I'm afraid Lucie's bronchitis is no better. Norman's wife, you know."

"Er—really," said Major Lenham, looking round for escape.

Lorna had taken her seat by the sofa and was talking to Mrs Lenham. Mrs Lenham's ignoring of her had been a kind of challenge. Lorna put on her sweetest manner, but she soon found that it was as nothing to the sweetness of Mrs Lenham's manner. And the sweetness of Mrs Lenham opposed a sort of barrier, against which Lorna's sweetness could make no headway. Feeling strangely baffled, she drifted away to where Miss Lenham sat alone. The Major had now made his escape and was talking to Mrs Grantham. Mrs Grantham was silent, unresponsive, her beautiful head still bent over her needlework, but there was about her some compelling quality of charm in which he preened himself, stroking his moustache and exaggerating his recent sporting activities. Miss Lenham brightened when she saw Lorna approaching.

"There you are, dear. I wondered where you were. Your sister's with the young people. You seemed so much interested in what I was showing you. I wonder if you'd care to see some of our old photographs."

Lorna assured her that she'd love to, and Miss Lenham, taking a photograph album from a cupboard, assumed again her air of a priestess expounding a sacred cult.

"My sister and I at eighteen . . . She married one of the Devonshire Marpletons. Oddly enough, another of the Lenhams married a Marpleton in the seventeenth century."

"How lovely you look!" said Lorna, examining the photograph.

"We were going to our first dance. Girls dressed and behaved in those days very differently from the way they do now. I'm afraid I don't altogether approve of the way modern girls behave." She glanced at Lorna's sweet demure profile and added, "Some of them, at any rate." Lorna lifted wistful blue eyes. "Not all of them, of course, dear."

Then Miss Lenham was called away, and Major Lenham came across the room to talk to Lorna.

Major Lenham liked sporting girls, jolly girls, girls with a spice of the devil in them, and Lorna's Early-Victorianism dropped from her as he greeted her. Soon she was talking to him merrily, chaffing him daringly, her head thrown back, her eyes meeting his squarely.

That evening Miss Lenham and the Major agreed that Lorna was one of the most charming girls they had ever met, but, when they came to discuss her, they disagreed quite vehemently.

"So sweet," said Miss Lenham. "Such a perfect lady. So unlike the modern girl."

"Nonsense!" said the Major. "There's nothing wrong with the modern girl. She's a jolly good sport, and that's what I like about Miss Lorna. I like a girl with a bit of the devil in her."

Lorna would have been surprised to hear the conversation. She had not deliberately played a part with each. When Lorna met people, instinctively, almost unconsciously, she presented them with a sheet of blank paper and let them draw upon it just the picture of her that they would most like to see.

Chapter Fifteen

Mr Lenham had entered while Major Lenham was talking to Lorna. Jenifer's heart quickened as she watched him bend over his wife and kiss her tenderly. He was so good, so kind, so infinitely wonderful . . . Her mind drifted off upon a hazy sea of dreams in which she gave her life for him in some romantic fashion without his ever knowing anything about it.

Sylvia broke in upon her day-dream, taking both her hands and swinging her to her feet.

"Come along, lazy-bones. Let's see how they're getting on with the library."

The library was the largest room in the house, with a polished floor that was well suited for dancing. When the furniture was moved out the book-lined walls made a pleasant background to the girls' gay dresses. Sylvia began scattering powder on the floor, and the others slid, danced, or romped on it, rubbing it into the wood, laughing and jostling each other.

Then someone suddenly discovered that it was time to change, and they raced upstairs together.

Lorna and Jenifer shared a large bedroom overlooking the lawn and lake. Next to it was Mrs Grantham's room.

"Cousin Helen's next to you," Sylvia had said. "She's a bit stiff, but quite well meaning. Don't be afraid of asking her to help you."

But not even Lorna would have dared to ask the help of anyone as aloof and cold and flawlessly beautiful as Cousin Helen. Jenifer had noticed that even when *he* came into the room she had merely glanced up from her needle-work, greeted him shortly, then bent her beautiful head over her needlework again as if he were of no importance. As they passed her open door they saw her maid taking filmy lace-trimmed undergarments from a drawer. A chiffon negligée edged with swansdown hung over a chair back, and on the dressing-table was spread an array of crystal and enamel jars. They tiptoed past silently, and Lorna's thoughts flew to the time when she would have married the rich husband whom she vaguely took for granted in all her day-dreams. She would have crystal and enamel toilet jars, lace-trimmed undergarments, chiffon negligées edged with swansdown. She would be cold, aloof, flawlessly beautiful, like Mrs Grantham.

Jenifer put on her white muslin dress, plaited her hair, adjusted the white hair-ribbons, and then helped Lorna into her evening dress. Sylvia had sent up sprays of tea-roses for them to wear. Jenifer pinned hers at her waist, but Lorna couldn't quite make up her mind where to put hers. She tried them at her breast, waist, and shoulder, and even in her hair. She wished she knew where Mrs Grantham was going to wear her flowers. In the end she decided that the left shoulder was the most sophisticated place and carefully pinned them there.

She looked lovely in the new evening dress of palest green, and Jenifer, in the white muslin dress, with short puff sleeves and yellow sash, wearing round her neck the gold cross she had had for her confirmation, her tawny hair plaited neatly back, looked very young and sweet.

The guests were arriving as they went downstairs. There was Ruby Frewin, elegant and assured in the Bond Street model; Eglantine Burdett, walking in front of her flock, with the air of a general marshalling her forces (the embroidered voile dresses looked very well on the whole, if a trifle skimpy); Mark Burdett, his eyes searching for Lorna as soon as he entered the house; and Laurence, looking grim and determined, for Laurence had been taking dancing lessons and regarded this dance solely as a test of his proficiency. The new Vicar arrived next—young, diffident, eager to show that he did not disapprove of Innocent Enjoyment. The wistful anxiety of his expression was due to the fact that he always found it so difficult to judge when Innocent Enjoyment ended and Rowdiness (of which, of course, he must disapprove) began. There was quite a big borderland between the two that always caused him acute discomfort. However, this party wasn't likely to become really rowdy, so he needn't start worrying—except that he always did worry on principle. He felt that he wasn't doing his duty as a Christian if he wasn't worrying about something. He went up to Eglantine Burdett and asked her for a dance. Her decisiveness of manner attracted him. He felt instinctively that she would know what to do in an emergency, and he never did. That was one of the things he worried about.

Mrs Grantham swept into the room, languid, indifferent, exquisitely beautiful, in a dress of gold lame with a long train. Mrs Lenham appeared on her husband's arm, wearing a tea gown of grey lace with a spray of orchids across her breast. As soon as she had arranged herself on a sofa near the fireplace, the small band in the window-recess struck up, and the dance began.

The slight constraint that marked the beginning of the proceedings soon wore off, especially after supper, at which champagne was freely served.

Bobby and Ruby went into the garden to the shrubbery that bordered the big lawn. He tried to kiss her, and she escaped, running lightly between the bushes, her silvery dress shimmering in the dusk. He caught her at last and held her closely, pressing his lips upon hers. The chase had excited him, the champagne had gone slightly to his head, and there was an unexpected thrill in the yielding softness of her lips and the pressure of her firm warm body against his. Her dress was cut low and showed the beginning of the white mounds of her breasts. A faint sweet perfume came from her hair. He crushed her to him so passionately that she could hardly breathe.

"Don't, Bobby, don't!" she said. Her voice was breathless, but there was a little triumphant catch in it. It suddenly wasn't a flirtation any longer. Bobby's face was set and tense, stripped of its laughing impudence.

Her shrewd little mind worked quickly. Tonight's display of easy opulence at the Hall had impressed her. Bobby would be rich . . .

She must go very carefully. He mustn't know about Adrian. She could easily get out of her engagement with Adrian, of course. Well, it was hardly an engagement—-just an understanding. Hardly an understanding even—merely a friendship that he was exaggerating as he exaggerated everything. He'd mistaken her kindness for love. Still—Bobby mightn't understand that. She must go very carefully.

She drew away from him, but slowly, temptingly.

"Don't, Bobby . . ."

"Kiss me again . . ."

"No . . . I'm going indoors."

"You shan't . . . you mustn't . . . Ruby, darling . . . I love you so."

"But—Bobby, you're too young to marry."

Whether or not he had meant marriage before she said that, he meant it now. The evening seemed to have laid a spell upon him. He had never known that she was so beautiful or that he could love anyone so madly.

"What nonsense! Darling, say you love me. Do you love me?"

"Yes."

"Let me go back and tell them we're engaged."

"No, wait a minute . . . Bobby, listen. Father's funny about things." She'd have to think out a more convincing reason for a secret engagement than she'd given Adrian. "I mean, he's terribly fond of me, and I've given him a solemn promise not to get engaged till I'm twenty. He'd never forgive me if I broke it. It's only three months. Let it be a secret till then, Bobby."

Three months would give her time to break it off gradually with Adrian. Adrian was a fool, anyway. She'd just tell him that she'd found she wasn't really fond of him, after all. He'd make a scene, but—oh, she'd be able to manage him.

"Darling, it'll be an awfully long three months."

"It won't. It will soon go. Perhaps you'll have got tired of me by the end of it."

"Don't you *dare* to say that."

He kissed her again on lips and cheeks and closed eyes.

*

In the library Laurence was dancing each dance with frowning concentration. His lips moved silently as he counted to himself. He was wholly unaware of his partners.

Jenifer had been dancing with Mr Lenham. When first he put his arm about her she had felt dizzy and breathless . . . The room swam before her eyes. She could only answer in monosyllables when he spoke to her. Now, sitting alone in the shadow of a group of palms, she was thinking about him, picturing him in some terrible trouble—struck blind, perhaps, or falsely accused and imprisoned. Everyone else would desert him. She only would remain loyal. She would stay with him always, give up the rest of her life to him. She shook herself sharply from the dream. It was dreadful to imagine things like that about him, as if she wanted him to be in trouble just so that she could help him. It showed how wicked she was. So wicked that, if he, who was goodness itself, knew how wicked she was, he probably wouldn't ever want to dance with her again . . . She *would* try to be good. She'd start tomorrow morning. She'd get up the minute she was called, so that she'd have time to say her prayers properly. Sometimes she was so lazy that she stayed in bed till she'd only time just to gabble the Lord's Prayer quickly before she went down to breakfast . . . The room seemed to be growing hotter and hotter.

She rose and went out into the passage and then down to the conservatory, which stood open to the garden. It would be cooler in there. She had entered it before she realised that it was already occupied. A murmur of voices came from behind a palm. The first was a man's voice— the low pleasant voice that always thrilled her.

"Tonight, then?"

A woman's voice answered, deep and slow, unmistakably the voice of Mrs Grantham.

"Geoffrey, we must be careful. If Marion were to suspect——"

"Marion won't suspect."

"You mustn't come if she doesn't take her sleeping draught."

"I'll see she does take it."

Jenifer turned and went slowly back to the library. She couldn't understand why the room was still there, with its band and flowers and dancers and rows of books . . . The world had come to an end, and they ought to have come to an end with it.

Suddenly someone caught her by the hand.

"Come on, Jen. The Lancers! Come in ours?"

She joined the set. Mr Lenham entered and sat by his wife's chair, bending over her solicitously, asking her if she felt tired. Lorna was dancing with Mark Burdett. She looked flushed and happy. Her programme had been filled in the first few minutes, and she had had to turn away innumerable would-be partners. Rosa Pickering, dancing with Charlie Burdett, looked slightly sulky. No one had suggested her reciting, and Bobby had not asked her for a dance. Bobby had now completed his study of her. He had mastered her every movement and expression and had no further need of his model.

Jenifer seemed to herself to be moving in a dream. She wasn't real. No one around her was real. Little doll-like mechanical figures dancing up and down jerkily at the end of wires. She'd stopped living. Everyone had stopped living.

As they passed and repassed each other in the figures of the Lancers, Bobby Lenham and Ruby exchanged furtive hand-squeezes and hot secret glances.

Mrs Lenham went up to bed soon after twelve, and at quarter to one Eglantine collected her flock in her brisk business-like fashion, disregarding its pleas to be allowed to stay a little longer. The Vicar made his excuses at the same time and went away with them. Half-way down the drive he summoned all his courage and asked Eglantine to help in the Sunday-school. The Vicar had beautiful theories about the training of children. "Appeal to a child's better self," he used to say, "and you'll have no more trouble." But the children of Merrowvale had refused to support his theories, and, though he continued to appeal to their better selves, the Sunday-school became more of a pandemonium each week. He was beginning, however, to have a pathetic trust in Eglantine. He couldn't imagine pandemonium existing in her presence. It wasn't that she bossed or nagged or bullied. She certainly didn't appeal to people's better selves. It was just something about her . . .

Carriages and cars began to arrive. A party had left some time ago to catch the last train to London. Mr Frewin called for Ruby. He had had an evening of supreme happiness, sitting with Frank and Marcia in the pleasant, shabby little drawing-room of The Chestnuts. All three had been silent. Frank read his newspaper, Marcia sewed, and Mr Frewin sat basking in the sense of peace that he was always so supremely conscious of in Marcia's presence. Adrian had been upstairs in his room, studying with pathetic absorption a History of Art that he had got out of the Leaveston public library.

"Good evening. I've come for my gel," announced Mr Frewin to Sylvia Lenham, who was standing at the front door of the Hall, saying good-bye to some departing guests.

"Do come in. I'll look for her."

Mr Frewin sat down in the hall, casting speculative glances round him, mentally valuing the decorations and furniture and wondering how much Lenham was worth. Ruby could not be found at once— Bobby was snatching a farewell kiss from her in the conservatory.

"Remember . . ." she whispered. "You promised not to tell a soul."

He buried his face in her hair.

"Not for three months . . . then I'll shout it from the house-tops. I'll send sandwich men round with it. I'll get a special licence. I'll—"

"Hush . . . someone's coming."

"Your father's come for you, Ruby," called Sylvia.

Ruby ran upstairs to get her wrap, then came down to her father, who was still sitting in the hall, a podgy hand on either podgy knee. He was thinking: I bet I cut up for as much as he does. He must spend every halfpenny he makes. The place fairly stinks of money. Shouldn't be surprised if I could buy him out any day.

"Hello, Daddy."

"There you are, my gel."

She looked radiantly lovely, her dark eyes brilliant, her cheeks softly flushed above her white fur wrap. He felt a thrill of pride in her. You never knew what she was up to, you couldn't trust her further than you could see her, but, Gad, she was a looker . . .

They walked away, side by side, down the drive.

"Had a good time?" he said.

"Oh yes, quite," she said. "Nothing terribly exciting, of course."

The last guest had gone, and suddenly everything seemed rather flat.

Sylvia was yawning openly, and Bobby was strangely quiet and pensive.

"Let's go to bed," said Sylvia. "Everything always looks so squalid after a party, doesn't it?"

"Have another drink," said Bobby, pouring himself out a glass of champagne. There was an odd feeling at the pit of his stomach that he had never experienced before. By Jove, he'd gone and been and done it now with a vengeance. But he didn't regret it. She was a peach. He'd never met anyone so utterly lovely and desirable, and he wasn't likely to. He was a lucky chap. And it had been decent of her to insist on keeping her promise to her father. He raised his glass slightly. "Well, here's to us," he said silently.

Mr Lenham came in and began turning out the lights.

"You've had enough to drink for one night, my lad," he said in his pleasant voice. "Off to bed, all of you!"

They ran upstairs. Jenifer was tired, but not unhappy any longer. Whatever it had meant, it couldn't have meant—that. She didn't know now how she could ever have thought it did—even for a moment. It had been horrible of her. Lorna unpinned the drooping roses from her left shoulder. (It had been all right. Mrs Grantham had worn hers on her left shoulder.)

"Hasn't it been *lovely*?" she said in her happy little-girl voice. "Have you enjoyed it, Jennie?"

"Yes, I've loved it," said Jenifer slowly. She remembered his kind smile as he asked her to dance, his gentle skilful piloting of her uncertain steps, and added, "It's been the happiest day of my life."

Lorna laughed.

"You are funny, Jen."

She slipped off her dress and stood in her petticoat and ribbon-threaded camisole, taking the pins from her hair one by one. The gleaming golden coils fell down over her white shoulders.

"I'm too tired to brush it. I'm going to just wash and get straight into bed. I'll say my prayers in bed . . . Goodnight, Jen."

Jenifer went to sleep almost at once. The sound that woke her was so small that she wasn't sure it was a sound at all. She sat up in bed, listening. Everything was quite still. The room was full of moonlight, and she could see by the clock on the mantelpiece that it was half-past five. Then the noise came again, a small cautious creak. She never knew what instinct made her get out of bed and open her door. He was there in the corridor in his dressing-gown, shutting the door of Mrs Grantham's bedroom very slowly and carefully. His back was towards her, and he was just letting the handle slip back into place. Then he turned round and they stood in silence, looking at each other in the moon-flooded corridor. His face seemed to have changed so that she hardly recognised it, the features distorted by sudden guilt and fear and by a lingering furtive sensuality about the mouth and eyes. Jenifer's face was as white as her nightdress, her eyes dilated. Neither spoke or moved for several moments. At last he turned abruptly away and walked down the corridor to his own room. She didn't know how long she stood there motionless after he had left her. Then she went back to her bedroom, washed her face in cold water (she didn't know why she did that), and got into bed again . . . So men were like that. He had dwindled from heroic stature to pigmy size, but all men had dwindled with him. He still towered head and shoulders above his kind. Men were like that . . . She lay dry eyed, staring into the moonlight.

He did not appear at breakfast the next morning, but when Jenifer came out from the dining-room with Lorna he was standing in the hall.

"There you are, Jenifer," he said. "I want to show you those carnations I was telling you about."

He hadn't told her about any carnations. He wanted to say something about last night. Her spirit shrank from him in sick horror, and her heart beat unevenly as she accompanied him across the lawn to the greenhouses.

The gardener had been mowing the lawn, and it lay in long lines like strips of silk ribbon—dark green, then light green, then dark green again. She did not notice the lawn, and she could never understand why for years afterwards the sight of a freshly mown lawn gave her an odd feeling of revulsion.

"Here are the carnations, Jenifer," he said.

She threw him a shrinking glance His face looked lined and haggard in the morning sunshine, and a stab of pity stirred beneath the horror at her heart, a pity more intolerable even than the horror, making her catch her breath in a little shuddering sigh. Panic seized her. She couldn't bear it. I don't know what he's going to say, she cried silently, but, please God, let me die before he says it. Let me die now . . . here . . . I don't want to go on living any more after this . . . He turned and looked at her. Her eyes met his unfalteringly—child's eyes wide with fear. His slid away and he began to speak mechanically, precisely, as if repeating a speech that he had learnt by heart.

"Last night I had a slight heart attack, Jenifer, and didn't want to frighten my wife, so I went to Mrs Grantham's bedroom, because I knew that she suffers from attacks of the same sort and has some tablets to relieve them. I don't want you to mention this to anyone, Jenifer, because I don't want my wife or anyone else to know that I have those attacks."

His expression was furtive and ashamed. He wasn't asking her to believe him. He didn't for a moment expect her to believe him. He was throwing himself on her mercy, begging her not to betray him.

"Yes," she said breathlessly. "I won't tell anyone. I promise."

He looked at her, meeting squarely her honest young gaze, then drew a breath of relief. There was nothing to be afraid of here. The child would keep her word. Something of the constraint vanished from his manner.

"Thank you."

He held out his hand. She hesitated, then, her whole body taut and rigid, placed hers in it for a second. It was horrible touching him. She drew it away with a little gasp.

"I must go now . . . Lorna's waiting for me . . ."

She turned and ran back across the lawn to the house.

"Lorna, oughtn't we to go now? Mother will be expecting us."

"You look a bit green about the gills, kid," said Bobby. "What was it? Too much fizzy and trifle last night?"

"Do you feel sick, darling?" said Lorna.

"Yes . . . a little," said Jenifer truthfully.

She didn't see Mr Lenham again before they went.

Bobby and Sylvia accompanied them to The Chestnuts, Bobby carrying their suitcase. Jenifer listened to their chatter, smiling mechanically at Bobby's jokes. She mustn't think of it. She couldn't bear it if she let herself think of it. Don't think of it . . . don't look at it . . . push it down out of sight. She laughed suddenly and capped one of Bobby's jokes, making them all laugh. Push it down out of sight . . . don't think of it.

As Bobby and Sylvia left them, Bobby glanced up at the next house in hopes of seeing Ruby.

Marcia came into the hall to welcome them.

"There you are, children. I thought you'd be here earlier. It seemed so quiet since Father and Adrian went. Had a good time? Tell me all about it."

They told her about everything, both talking at once. Jenifer's laugh, high-pitched and rather unsteady, rang out frequently. Push it down out of sight . . . don't look at it . . . don't think of it . . .

Chapter Sixteen

Laurence and Jenifer free-wheeled down the hill on their bicycles, laughing from sheer high spirits and joy of life. They wore rucksacks on their shoulders, and Jenifer's carrier and the basket on her handlebars were piled with various oddments that their rucksacks would not hold, as well as their picnic lunch.

A friend of Frank's had offered Laurence a post in his firm, and, as it was a bigger and much more prosperous business than Frank's, Frank had advised Laurence to take it and had resigned himself to having neither of his sons in his own business.

Marcia had suggested that he should have a short holiday before settling down to work, and it was taken as a matter of course that Jenifer should be his companion. Marcia was glad for Jenifer to have a holiday. She had seemed overstrained and nervous lately, and once or twice had looked as if she had been crying. Adolescence, of course, was a trying time . . .

To Jenifer the plan was like a sudden release from prison. There had been a nightmare quality about life since the day of the Hall dance. She had tried to forget what had happened, but, even when she managed to forget it, she was aware all the time of the memory waiting to pounce on her thoughts the moment they were unoccupied. And when she couldn't hold it off any longer, when the memory of it surged over her with wave upon wave of shame and horror, a sort of desperation would seize her, and she would feel that she could not face any longer a life in which everything that had been lovely was spoilt and besmirched. She shrank from going out in case she might meet him, she shrank even from looking out of her bedroom window because the sight of the Hall chimneys over the trees gave her a sudden sick sinking of the heart.

But once she had started on the holiday with Laurence, everything was changed. The nightmare feeling vanished. The holiday was an adventure (it was the first time that she and Laurence had been away without the rest of the family) and her youth rose exultantly to meet it. Her friendship with Laurence was a quiet friendship, independent of words, independent, indeed, of any sort of intercourse. It was not so much that Laurence always understood, as that he did not even need to understand.

Laurence, freed from the trammels of school life, his feet already on the road of manhood, was in higher spirits than she had ever known him. Even the inevitable little contretemps of the journey added to their enjoyment, the fact that the brakes of Laurence's bicycle did not work properly, and that he had to use his foot as an emergency brake when necessary, taking it from the pedal to the tyre with a quick rotatory movement, being one of their staple jokes.

The holiday, of course, had to be as economical as possible, and they stayed in rooms, buying their own food.

Sometimes they would stay one night in a place, sometimes they would stay a day or two, making it their centre and going for long walks. Laurence still loved to watch birds and insects, crouching silent and absorbed in the undergrowth with Jenifer beside him. He had brought his camera with him, and they took photographs, developing the plates in a home-made "dark room" under one of their beds, always with a great deal of laughter, but often with very little success.

The idiosyncrasies of the landladies and the discomfort of the rooms were all part of the fun.

The last day of the holiday turned out wet, but they rode gaily through the rain, their faces glowing with health and good spirits.

That night, over their sitting-room fire, Laurence began to chuckle.

"What are you laughing at?" said Jenifer.

"I keep remembering you riding along with the rain pouring off the end of your nose."

"You looked just as funny, if only you'd seen yourself."

"And tomorrow's the last day," he said, suddenly growing serious. "I'm sorry it's come to an end. It's been great."

"Yes," sighed Jenifer, "it's over. And you're going to be a business man next week . . . You'll be what they call a financial magnate before you've finished, I suppose."

He laughed.

"I dunno about that, but"—the laughter died out of his face, and something grim and determined took its place—"I jolly well mean to make good somehow."

Frank was relieved to see them home again. He had been far more anxious about them than Marcia had been. Marcia, indeed, had not been anxious about them at all and had laughed at him for a fussy mother hen. He had been afraid that they would meet with some accident (Laurence had never had those brakes seen to), or that Laurence would overtire Baby, who had been so strangely pale and listless lately . . .

He met them at the front door and drew them into the drawing-room with him, an arm round each.

"Here they are," he said. "And Baby's got the roses back into her cheeks again."

He liked old-fashioned and sentimental phrases of that sort.

They both talked animatedly, recounting the jokes that had accumulated during the holiday, and that seemed suddenly rather flat and pointless. Marcia and Frank watched them with pleasure, hardly listening to what they said, but thinking how well and handsome Laurence looked and how nice it was to see little Jen so eager and happy again.

Lorna rose rather abruptly from her chair as Laurence was mimicking the landlady who had seen better days.

She felt vaguely irritated by the welcome that was being accorded to the returned travellers, and by the fact that they had so obviously enjoyed the holiday, which she had prophesied would be a complete failure.

"Well, I think you've been holiday-making long enough," she said, somewhat tartly. "There's a nice little pile of mending waiting for you upstairs, Jenifer. And you left your drawers in an awful state. I do wish you could keep them tidier."

"I've seen to Jenifer's mending," said Miss Marchant, coming in. "Had a good time, dear?"

"Yes, it's been lovely," said Jenifer, feeling glad that Miss Marchant had not kissed her, and then, illogically, remorseful that she had not kissed Miss Marchant. After all, one could shut one's eyes and try not to think about the mole . . .

Lorna slipped her arm through Miss Marchant's with an affectionate gesture, as if consoling her for Jenifer's casual greeting and for the way in which Frank, Marcia, Laurence, and Jenifer seemed to stand in a little group that excluded her

"Oh well, we've managed to get on quite all right without you, haven't we, Miss Marchant?"

"Where's Adrian?" said Laurence.

Marcia's face clouded over.

"He's not come in yet. He gets in so late from that wretched art school, and works so hard, poor boy. He's beginning to look awfully overdone."

Things were not running smoothly with Adrian. Ruby had managed her two secret engagements deftly enough at first, but it was not a state of things that could last indefinitely. She was finding it more difficult than she had imagined it would be to break with Adrian. He was so overwrought that the slightest hint of coldness in her manner threw him into one of his old states of hysterical distress, and she was no longer able to control them. Moreover, Bobby was growing more ardent and pursuing her more openly, and rumours of this inevitably reached Adrian. There were passionate quarrels, followed by passionate reconciliations. I'll tell him when he's in a quiet sensible mood, Ruby kept saying to herself, but he never seemed to be in a quiet sensible mood, or, if he was, any discussion of their feelings for each other would quickly disperse it.

The week after Laurence and Jenifer's return it was arranged that Bobby and Sylvia Lenham and Davida and Marigold Burdett should come to tea. It was to be a young people's tea party, and Marcia was going to spend the afternoon with Lena.

Marcia hated visiting Brightmet House now, so different was it from the days when her mother's charm had hovered over it like some gracious spirit. Lena, in her ugly, poky little sitting-room, which she had branded with her own niggardliness and meanness . . . Lena scraping and paring, her balance at the bank growing steadily larger, grumbling at every penny spent, starving herself, weeping in maudlin self-pity, nagging at the "girl" . . . There were no flowers in Lena's rooms. ("I simply can't afford them—the wicked price they are.") On chilly autumn days she would shiver over the empty grate, wrapped in her old coat. ("I'm perfectly warm, Marcia. No, I certainly won't have a fire—not with coals the price they are.") Or Marcia would find her in the dusk, her book upside-down on her knee, waiting drearily till she considered it dark enough to light the gas.

September had come in with an unexpectedly cold spell, and Lena had had a touch of bronchitis and was still in bed recuperating.

She was sitting up when Marcia arrived, a shabby cardigan drawn round her shoulders. The bedroom was clean and well-furnished, yet there was over it that elusive suggestion of cheerlessness that seemed to pervade every room where Lena was. In spite of the coldness of the day there was no fire in the grate, and Peter, moulting and bleary eyed, lay in the only easy-chair, wheezing as he slept. Lena's face wore that sharp strained look that is the mark of chronic dyspepsia. Her long thin nose was red, her greying hair strained back into a wispy plait. Marcia had brought fruit and cakes for tea, as she knew that Lena hated having to provide for a visitor, and Lena's grim visage lightened somewhat when she saw them.

"It's kind of you to think of your poor old sister, dear," she said. "Everyone seems to have forgotten me nowadays. I lead a very lonely life."

"You needn't lead a lonely life," said Marcia rather sharply as she took her seat on the bed. She had meant to be kind and forbearing, but that note of pathos in Lena's voice always irritated her. "You've got heaps of friends living near."

"They never come to see me."

"Because you never ask them. You owe them all hospitality, and you never ask them back. You can't expect to keep friends without a little trouble."

"It isn't a question of trouble, dear," said Lena stiffly. "It's a question of expense. I can't afford to entertain,"

"Oh, Lena!" sighed Marcia, but she knew that Lena really saw herself as a poverty-stricken old woman, and that it was quite useless to suggest to her that she was anything else.

"I'll order tea now, shall I? What did you have for lunch, Lena?"

Lena shut her lips grimly.

"I didn't feel very hungry at lunch."

Marcia shrugged and went into the kitchen to interview the new maid, who had arrived last week. Madam had had some bread and cheese for lunch, said the girl sullenly. The cheese was nearly all rind, but Madam had insisted on eating it. Marcia said that she would send round a chicken for Madam's lunch tomorrow. She felt exasperated at having to provide food for Lena out of her own meagre housekeeping allowance, but she couldn't let the poor old thing starve . . .

She returned to the bedroom, and Lena began the long recital of the girl's delinquencies that now formed her only subject of conversation. As her thin complaining voice went on and on, the familiar depression that she always felt when she was with Lena descended upon Marcia's spirit, and she wished she were at home with the party of noisy young people who were having tea at The Chestnuts.

The young people were certainly noisy. Bobby was in high spirits, and Ruby, exulting in her power over him, lost her usual cautiousness and began to show off to the others. He responded, nothing loth, and even Jenifer was beginning to suspect an understanding between them. They went upstairs to the old nursery after tea, and sang songs from the *Scottish Students' Song Book* and *Songs of a*

Savoyard. Bobby sang "Take a Pair of Sparkling Eyes" to Ruby in burlesque operatic fashion and ended by kissing her on the lips.

"Well, you certainly ought to propose after that," said Marigold.

"Oh, let's tell them, Ruby," said Bobby. "They won't breathe a word to a soul. Besides, it's only your father who hasn't got to know yet. Listen, everyone. Friends, Romans, countrymen, we are engaged. We've been engaged since the dance. Only Ruby promised her father not to get engaged till she was twenty. Anyway, there's only a week or two to run now."

The room was a pandemonium of screams and laughter. Behind Ruby's placid demure smile her shrewd brain was working quickly. Bobby mustn't find out about Adrian. She'd get hold of Adrian as soon as he came home tonight, and she'd make it all right somehow. She'd tell him straight out that she found she loved Bobby and not him. He couldn't say anything. And she'd make him promise never to let Bobby know about her promise to marry him. She'd *make* him be reasonable . . .

"We must drink their healths," Lorna was saying, flinging open the big cupboard in the wall where they kept glasses and a bottle of lemonade. Jenifer got a jug of water from the bathroom and, laughing excitedly, they mixed the lemonade and held up their glasses to Bobby and Ruby, who stood in the centre of the circle.

It was upon this scene that Adrian entered. He had come home early, remembering that Ruby was expected to tea, ardently longing to see her again, if only for a few minutes, and before the others.

He stood in the doorway, looking at them, his face white and strained.

"Come and drink their healths, Adrian," called Davida. "They're engaged."

"Engaged?" he said slowly. "Who are engaged?"

"Ruby and Bobby."

His eyes went to Ruby, bewildered, uncomprehending.

"That's not true," he said at last.

Ruby met his gaze stonily. She must brazen it out now.

"Why shouldn't it be true?"

"Because you're engaged to me."

181

She gave a scornful little laugh.

"You're surely not such a fool that you took that seriously, are you? You made a nuisance of yourself, and I tried to be kind to you, that's all. I evidently made a mistake. I should have told you straight out that I'd no use for you."

"That's not true, either," said Adrian in a tense breathless voice. "You were engaged to me. You promised to marry me—only you said we must keep it secret for the present."

Ruby looked at Bobby. His eyes were fixed on her, as if waiting for her explanation. A sudden hatred of Adrian seized her. The fool! Butting in like this and messing everything up! Her eyes were bright with anger as she answered him.

"Well, suppose I did think I cared for you. It wasn't my fault, was it"—her lips took on an ugly curve as she searched for the words that would hurt him most—"that I found out afterwards I couldn't love you, that you weren't a bit what I had thought you, that you just bored and irritated me, and that it was Bobby I really loved."

She smiled at Bobby—a complacent, confident smile, as she offered him this sacrifice of a defeated and humiliated rival. But Bobby wasn't looking at her now. His eyes were fixed on Adrian's white twisted face.

"Ruby, you can't——" stammered Adrian. "You do love me . . . you've told me so . . . I can't bear it . . . I can't give you up . . . Ruby, I love you ... I love you . . . There's nothing left . . . Say it's a joke . . . say you don't mean it . . . Ruby! . . ."

His voice cringed and grovelled. It increased her contempt for him, rousing still further her latent cruelty.

"You little fool!" she said scornfully. "You surely don't think I ever meant to marry a cissie like you?"

Suddenly and without any warning, he burst into tears.

Shame enveloped Jenifer like a sheet of fire from head to foot. She closed her eyes so that she should not see him. He turned and stumbled blindly from the room followed by Lorna, who threw a glance of fury at Ruby as she went. Lorna's affection for Adrian went right down to the honest loving little girl who lived somewhere beneath the veneer of meaningless universal sweetness.

With their departure a spell seemed to be lifted from the room. Ruby laughed.

"Well," she said, "that's that."

She was excited and stimulated by the little scene. It made her feel vaguely like Helen of Troy or Cleopatra—a woman men loved to distraction, fought for, wept for. She was, on the whole, glad that Bobby had witnessed it. He would realise—if he hadn't realised already—the sort of woman she was.

"We'd better tell people now, Bobby," she said. "I'll manage Father, somehow."

"Tell people what?" he said slowly.

"That we're engaged."

He looked at her. His eyes were hard and narrowed, his lips tight.

"Do you think I'd have you now at any price?" he said.

She gave a little gasp of amazement. Then quickly she recovered her poise and laughed harshly.

"Don't, then," she said. "I'm sure you're no great loss."

She regretted the vulgarity of the words as soon as they were uttered, and wished she could have thought of some more dignified retort. Oh, well—she'd lost Adrian, and she'd lost Bobby, but there were other fish in the sea as good or better than both. She'd received a letter that morning from a school friend who lived in Yorkshire asking her to stay there for a few weeks. There were several unmarried brothers, and the family seemed fairly well-off.

She shrugged her shoulders, said: "Well, good-afternoon all" in a pert shrill voice, and went out of the room, swinging her hips.

PART THREE

1919

Chapter Seventeen

The "children" had gathered together at The Chestnuts for Marcia's birthday. The strain of the war—just over—had aged both Marcia and Frank more than the past ten years warranted. Marcia looked worn and fragile, her soft wavy hair was almost grey, and the black dress she wore for Lena, who had died last month, accentuated her pallor.

None of them could pretend much sorrow over Lena's death. The war had given justification to her passion for economy, which towards the end of her life had bordered on mania. She had dismissed her maid, and lived alone in the old house—a scarecrow object in ancient clothes that latterly she had not even troubled to mend, her thin wizened face looking repellently witchlike. Marcia had done what she could for her, but Lena had grown increasingly difficult with the years, sometimes flying into grotesque rages and accusing Marcia of having prevented her from travelling and living her own life, sometimes sobbing for hours in futile self-pity, insisting always that she was too poor to buy new clothes or proper food. The house was neglected and dirty, and Marcia often tried to clean it, but Lena would follow her about suspiciously, accusing her of "poking and prying," though she always ate without comment the food that Marcia left in the empty larder. Going to see her one morning, Marcia had found her lying dead in bed, her emaciated figure covered by a patched sheet and tattered blanket.

She had left her money to be divided equally between her nephews and nieces, and, though Lorna felt slightly piqued at not having the foremost place in the will as Aunt Lena's favourite niece, the largeness of the legacy consoled her, for it turned out that, in spite of the fact that Lena had practically starved herself to death, she had been a very rich woman.

There was a faint undercurrent of sadness in the gathering today. The old home life seemed definitely to have come to an end. During the war they had marked time—Adrian and Laurence at the front, Lorna and Jenifer working as V.A.D.s at the Hall, which had been turned into a hospital. Now they were separating from the home and from each other . . .

Lorna was marrying Mark in a month's time. She had been the most popular of the V.A.D.s at the hospital, and Mark, coming home on leave, had found her always surrounded by a host of admirers, her free time completely occupied by her patients or ex-patients or adoring little V.A.D.s, for Lorna was quite a cult among the younger nurses. For several leaves he hung about disconsolately in the background while Lorna received his occasional reproaches with her unfailing sweetness. ("Mark, dear, it's my *duty* to cheer up these people . . . Well, I mean, they're my particular job. I'd love to have more time for you, but I simply haven't got it.") Then came a leave when Mark in his turn ignored Lorna and began to go about with a shy little nurse who had just joined the staff of the hospital. There was no subtlety in it. He still loved Lorna, but he was tired of hanging round in the background with a crowd of other admirers. Lorna became rather thoughtful. She missed Mark from the background more than she had thought possible. His absence from it, in fact, made the admiration of the others somewhat savourless. The next time he came home on leave she had plenty of time to spare for him, and when he returned to the Front (it was his last leave before the end of the war) they became engaged. Rather to her own surprise she found that she was passionately in love with him. For the first time in her life other people ceased to matter to her. She cared only for Mark . . .

They were expecting Mark for tea this afternoon, and Lorna sat by the window watching the gate, her blue eyes soft and dreamy.

Mark had got a post with a wholesale leather firm in London

and had taken a small house in Dulwich. Lorna and Marcia had been down several times to prepare it and buy the furniture.

"Lorna, darling," Marcia was saying, "did you remember to write about those sheets?"

Lorna still gazed dreamily out of the window without answering.

"*Mark!*" said Laurence suddenly.

Lorna turned round with a start, and they all laughed.

"That's the only way to get you to listen to anything anyone says nowadays," explained Laurence.

"Don't be an idiot," she said. "I wasn't thinking of Mark at all . . . Not *really* thinking of him."

Miss Marchant entered with an armful of curtains and, sitting upright on the corner of the sofa, began to sew rings on to them with quick jerky movements. She still looked as they remembered her in their childhood. Her lank greasy hair was untouched by grey; not a line or feature of the sallow face, with the large disfiguring mole, seemed to have altered. She still worked indefatigably in the background, keeping the house running smoothly, even through the days when every domestic servant in England seemed to have left "service" and entered a munition factory. Emma had married "Floury Charlie" just before the war, and, large, cheerful, and almost as floury as Charlie himself had been, carried on the business alone through the four years of it. She made "cookie boys" for her own children now . . .

"Miss Marchant's worked like a Trojan over your curtains, Lorna," said Marcia.

"Angel, isn't she?" said Lorna absently.

"It's going to be the sweetest little house," said Miss Marchant brightly. "And I'm going to be one of its first visitors, aren't I, darling?"

"Of *course*," said Lorna with rather overdone heartiness.

"And you'll *never* get rid of me, once I'm there," went on Miss Marchant with her high-pitched laugh.

"I shan't try to," responded Lorna. "I'll keep you till Mother drags you from me by force."

It was dreadful, thought Jenifer despairingly, the way, ever since she could remember, they always overdid it when they were trying to be nice to Miss Marchant. It set one's teeth on edge. *Surely* she must see . . . But she didn't. There was a complacent little smile on her face as she bent industriously over her sewing. She was pleased because Lorna wanted her to stay with her in her new house . . .

"Darling, why don't you go a little more modern here?" said Adrian. "I mean, clear out all this old stuff and start fresh?"

He waved his hand round the room that had seemed so pretty and up to date in their childhood, but that now looked shabby and old-fashioned.

Marcia smiled.

"I like it," she said, "and your father likes it. We shouldn't feel at home in a modern room. We arranged it when we got married. It's full of happy memories."

"Darby and Joan!" jeered Adrian. "But it's terribly hideous, sweetheart, all the same. One must face facts."

"It isn't hideous to us," said Marcia, "and it doesn't matter to you children. You'll all be leaving home soon."

Adrian's eyes grew dreamy . . . The last four years had changed him more than the others, giving to his girlish good looks a new quality of sternness and gravity. The war had seared his very soul, but it had purified it of the passion for Ruby that he had cherished even after her marriage. He had felt a sick revulsion from his art when she threw him over, and had returned to Frank's office, where he worked industriously enough, but with a secret smouldering resentment against Fate. Then came the war —four years of torment that had yet somehow made him see Ruby as she really was and given him back his love for his art, deepened and enriched.

He had formed his plans as soon as he heard of Aunt Lena's legacy. He would go to live in London, and take up his art training again seriously at the Slade School. Already the bitterness of his memories of the war was fading, and he was filled with an eager zest for work, an intoxicating confidence of success. He had finished with women, he told himself. That poison was washed out of his soul for ever . . .

"It's the sale at Brightmet House today," said Marcia suddenly. "I'd meant to go, but I really feel too tired."

"Shall I go?" said Jenifer. "Will you come with me if I do, Laurie?"

"Right," said Laurence, rising.

"We won't be long, darling," said Jenifer to Marcia. "We'll just look in and come back."

"I'm glad you're going," replied Marcia. "I feel that someone in the family ought to be there."

"Here's Mark," murmured Lorna and slipped from the room like a shadow.

Jenifer and Laurence, following her a few moments later, saw the lovers pass down the hall and out by the side door into the garden.

"Lorna's terribly in love," said Jenifer, as they set off down the road. "It's made her quite different . . . Are you ever going to marry, Laurie?"

Laurence laughed.

"Me? Good Lord, no! I haven't any time for that sort of thing. I'm going to work."

"Surely you could work *and* get married?"

"I can't. I couldn't be bothered with marriage and a wife . . . You know that Franklin's asked me to be junior partner, don't you?"

"Mother told me."

"I feel terribly bucked about it, though, of course, I'm sorry about young Franklin. If he'd come through the war I'd never have got this chance. Aunt Lena, too . . . If I hadn't had her money to put into the business . . ."

"You've deserved it, Laurie. You worked awfully hard those years before the war."

"I found it all so frightfully interesting. Business *is* thrilling, you know, Jennie. It's an adventure—just as much an adventure as sailing out to undiscovered lands must have been."

She looked at his handsome boyish face and laughed a little breathlessly.

"Oh, Laurie, don't let it make you forget all the other adventures."

"What other adventures?"

"The adventures we used to have together in the old days. Music and books and the country. You remember, don't you?"

He smiled, tolerant and indulgent.

"Oh, those! They weren't adventures. They were amusements—recreations."

"They *were* adventures," she protested. "You *used* to think of them as adventures. You see—they were adventures that I could share with you. I can't share your business adventures with you, but I can share those, I'd hate us to drift apart. We were doing, you know, before the war, because you were always so busy. And then the war brought us together again. Do you remember that cycling holiday we had years ago, just before you went into business?"

He looked at her, his face softened.

"Yes. It was great, wasn't it?"

"Let's do it again some time."

"Of course we must, Jennie," he said affectionately. "No, we won't drift apart. We couldn't . . . You'll be coming up to London often, I suppose, won't you?"

"Sylvia wants me to share her flat."

Sylvia Lenham had taken a small flat in Chelsea. She had worked in the Ministry of Information during the war, and Jenifer had spent occasional week-ends with her. The friendship between the two girls had mellowed and deepened. It was a friendship without intimacy, a friendship in which each respected the reserves and integrity of the other, the only kind of friendship in which Jenifer could have found happiness. Beneath its light and casual surface there was a deep sympathy and understanding, but there was no exchange of confidences, none of the easy endearments that generally mark women's friendships.

Jenifer had written several sketches and short stories that had been accepted by not very important papers, and, now that the war was over, Sylvia was anxious for her to come to London and take up literary work seriously.

"You could, of course," said Laurence. "Aunt Lena's money's made us all so gloriously independent. It's helped me to get a junior partnership, it'll help old Adrian to take up art again, it'll set up Lorna and Mark in housekeeping, and it'll give you a chance to make good. I'm sure you will, Jennie . . . What did you say to Sylvia?"

"I told her I couldn't decide in a hurry . . . but I think I will. I don't think I could just hang about at home after working hard for four years. You get out of the way of just pottering—shopping and arranging flowers and that sort of thing. You see, Father's retiring this year, and Mother doesn't need me. They've never needed us really when they had each other, have they? And Miss Marchant's so horribly capable that there'd be nothing for me to do in the house."

"Come to London, then . . . You can drag me to concerts and make me read and keep me human."

"Don't sound so horribly middle-aged, Laurie. You're a young man."

"I don't feel young," he said seriously. "I don't think that anyone who's been through the war feels young. One began by being so terribly keen, and then—oh well, don't let's talk about that. Poor old Adrian! He hated it more than I did."

They had reached Brightmet House now. A policeman stood at the gate directing the traffic, and groups of people were scattered about the drive. Several women and girls, who had obviously come not to buy but in a spirit of curiosity, were wandering about the garden and looking in the summer-house and the outhouses.

Laurence and Jenifer passed into the house. The sale was going on in the drawing-room. The auctioneer sat at a desk, his clerk beside him, in front of him a cup of tea from which he took surreptitious sips. His eyes were slightly prominent, as if from the unceasing strain of collecting bids. They darted about the room, collecting them from an almost imperceptible movement of the head here, a flicker of an eyelid there. His voice was encouraging, but weary, with a faint undertone of cynicism, as if the bitterness of seeing goods go for less than their worth had eaten into his soul. Occasionally he turned to a group of women who were talking loudly in a window recess, and said, "Ladies, ladies!" in a tone of resigned expostulation.

To Jenifer, Brightmet House had always been full of Grandma's gracious presence—it had from the first disowned Aunt Lena's drabness—and it seemed an outrage that these people should be fingering her possessions and tramping through the rooms where she had queened it so royally. She frowned angrily at a man who was throwing a cigarette-end upon the parquet floor that had once shone like glass, but was now thick with dust, scattered with orange peel, 'bus tickets, cigarette-ends, and bits of waste paper.

The auctioneer was holding up the red-and-white chessmen, and a vivid memory came to Jenifer of the day when she had played with them on the floor, wearing the clean frilled pinafore that tickled her neck, the day she had had toothache . . .

She began to bid for them stammeringly, with flushed cheeks . . . Laurence glanced at her in amused surprise. They were knocked down to her at three pounds.

The next lot was a collection of oddments, in which was the blue satin cushion, embroidered with red, that Aunt Lena had made for Grandma's birthday. It was crumpled and faded, as hideous as ever, but now infinitely pathetic . . . Jenifer turned away, her eyes brimming suddenly with tears, and made her way through the crowd, followed by Laurence.

"It's dreadful, isn't it?" she said unsteadily when they reached the front door.

He smiled at her.

"I thought it was rather fun. Still, it was pretty stuffy. It's nice to get out into the open air again."

She drew a deep breath.

"It was full of ghosts," she said. "I'm sorry I was so silly. Let's go for our walk before we go home. *Our* walk. Do you remember? Through the woods to Toothbrush Hill."

He took out his watch.

"Right you are. I needn't start back till the six-ten." They set off with long swinging strides up the road and out of the village. It was late May. In the gardens laburnum, lilac, and red hawthorn made splashes of colour against the clear sky. Beyond the village the fields were golden with buttercups, the hedgerows white with the feathery tufts of cow chervil. In the woods the wild hyacinth stretched away into the distance like a blue sea, made bluer by the black tree-trunks that rose from them. Overhead was a delicate tracery of vivid green beech leaves.

Jenifer caught her breath.

"Isn't it lovely, Laurie?"

He stood looking at it absently and said:

"Franklin's used to have a large connection in the north. I don't know how they lost it. I'm going to try to get it back again."

"Do you remember how we used to come here to watch the birds?"

Again he smiled vaguely.

"Yes. How keen we were on that sort of thing!"

"But it's still quite interesting, isn't it?"

Jenifer spoke eagerly, breathlessly. She felt as if she were fighting for the old Laurence, struggling to rescue him from captivity.

"Oh yes," he said easily, "if one's time for it."

She was peeping into a hole in a tree-trunk.

"A robin used to build here, didn't it? . . . *Laurie* . . . there's a nest there now . .. and some tiny robins . . . Do took."

He peeped over the hole, and his lips curved into a smile that brought back the old Laurence.

"I say, let's stay and watch them for a bit," he said.

They watched for a few moments in silence, then he said:

"Where was it that blackbird used to build, the one with the white face? I expect he's dead now, but there may be another there."

They made their way to the thicker part of the wood, where thrushes and blackbirds built among the undergrowth. He found a nest full of young thrushes and another of young blackbirds, and they stayed watching them in silence. A tremulous gladness seized

195

Jenifer. The years of the war and the new interests that were claiming him seemed to fade away.

"Do you remember that swallow we found with a broken wing?" he said as they walked homewards.

"Yes. And we kept it in the play-room and fed it with insects."

He chuckled.

"You spent the whole day catching them."

"I went round spiders' webs taking them out. They must have been the wrong sort because the poor thing died."

He turned at the end of the wood and looked back.

"I shall be sorry to go away from all this," he said. "I shall often think of it."

"Yes, do, Laurie," said Jenifer earnestly.

"Do what?"

"Often think of it."

He laughed, looking down at her.

"What a funny kid you are, Jennie!"

They quickened their pace as they approached the village.

The Burdetts still lived in their old house, but it had lost the air of spick-and-spanness that it had worn during Eglantine's reign. It was as if it had heaved a sigh of relief when she married the Vicar, and had relaxed into its old shiftlessness. Eglantine kept Miss Burdett busy in the parish, and what time she could spare from that was given to her garden at the cottage, for she had become an enthusiastic gardener. The youngest child, now ten years old, was making mud pies in the middle of a flower-bed, and Mrs Burdett stood at the window nursing a neighbour's baby. Eglantine had several babies, but they were very scientifically brought up, and Mrs Burdett was not allowed to nurse them. So that, when her longing to nurse a baby became irresistible, as it frequently did, she had to borrow a neighbour's.

The baby had pulled her hair down and was now tugging at her nose, but she still wore her old air of bland magnificence.

Mr Lenham was coming out of the post-office as they passed it. Mrs Lenham had died two years ago, but her husband had not married again. He had become rather stout during the last ten years, and the garrulity that so often marks later middle-age was growing upon him. He was an interesting talker and a charming man, but people were beginning to notice that he grew restive whenever he was not holding the floor. He raised his hat, greeted them pleasantly, and went on without stopping. Sometimes Jenifer fancied that he still felt slightly uncomfortable in her presence. She had learnt with some surprise that Bobby and Sylvia had known all about his intrigue with Mrs. Grantham.

Swinging round the corner came a band of Boy Scouts, walking two and two. At the back marched Eglantine, her eye ready to note and quell the slightest attempt at insubordination.

They dived into a lane to avoid Rosa Pickering and crept out furtively when she had passed. During the war Rosa had instituted herself entertainer-in-chief of the local hospitals. She had engaged an accompanist and now recited her poems to soft music. She had written several child poems to an almost incredible banality, and these she recited continually, her child-voice increasing in archness and shrillness on each occasion.

"Ye gods!" murmured Laurence as they crept out. "Why doesn't someone murder her?"

They looked after her. She walked with a mincing dancing step, slightly reminiscent of the hornpipe of her childhood, and, though they could not see her face, they could picture all too well the complacent smile it wore.

"Don't worry," said Jenifer with conviction. "Someone will some day. Let's call at Emma's."

They went into Emma's shop and sat on the counter, eating her halfpenny buns.

"Just fancy!" sighed Emma. "All you children going out into the world and leaving your poor Ma and Pa alone . . . Well, well, well . . . And that Miss Marchant staying on, I suppose?"

"Of course."

"*She's* a deep one, she is," said Emma grimly.

"Get along with you!" laughed Laurence. "You're still annoyed because she took the frill off your aspidistra."

Emma smiled and shook her head.

"She's a deep one. Mark my words."

She kissed them both heartily when they went, and gave them one of her home-made cakes to take to Marcia, whom she still called "the mistress."

André was at The Chestnuts when they reached home. He had arrived after tea with a large bouquet of flowers, just as he used to arrive on Grandma's birthday. His carefully trimmed beard was quite grey, but he was as upright and elegant as ever. He made his home permanently in England now, in a quaint little house at the back of Knightsbridge, looked after by an old woman who had been his mother's maid. His manner as he talked to Marcia was deferential, but reserved. He discussed only impersonal matters, never mentioning her mother or the days when he had known her as a child, but he often watched her narrowly when she was not looking at him, as if waiting for the likeness to her mother that flashed out every now and then in smile or movement.

Frank arrived home just before supper and asked at once after Marcia's cough. He was very much worried by her thinness and by the cough that had troubled her all the year. Marcia, as usual, laughed at his solicitude, but Jenifer, catching something of his anxiety, suddenly saw how frail and worn she looked. After supper André departed and Mr Frewin came in. He had sent some flowers to Marcia in the morning, but he brought with him now an enormous box of chocolates tied up with a great bow of satin ribbon, the lid depicting a blonde beauty with enormous eyelashes and protruding teeth.

"Ruby's coming over next week," he said, as he lowered his short stout figure into the chair in which he always sat.

Adrian's lips curved into a faint smile. It gave him a thrill of sardonic triumph to think of Ruby as she really was—a stout common-looking woman (for Ruby's looks had gone off since her marriage), with prominent features and over-frizzed hair. He exulted silently, cruelly, in the mental picture of her and rejoiced at his escape.

"She's bringing two of her children."

"How nice!" murmured Marcia vaguely.

Marcia was not fond of other people's children, and Ruby's were spoilt and stupid.

"She'll be surprised to see the changes at Merrowvale," said Laurence. "She's not been over since they started building, has she?"

They began to discuss the large new housing estate—forerunner of the post-war riot of building—that was being erected between Merrowvale and Leaveston.

Marcia watched them dreamily. They were grown up now. They didn't need her any longer. She and Frank were alone, as they had been before the children were born. That was what happened to most parents, of course. Her eyes brooded lovingly on the four children. It seemed such a short time since they were little. She had a sudden vision of them in sailor-suits and pinafores, clustering round the piano, scuffling for the possession of the piano stool.

"What are you smiling at?" said Adrian.

"I was just remembering things . . ."

Jenifer was sitting on the piano stool and swinging herself idly round and round.

"I've been remembering things all day," she said. "It's made me feel terribly old. I expect that that's what makes old age—memories. Perhaps if one could forget everything as soon as it happened, one would never grow old."

"Idiot!" said Laurence.

"What were you remembering, dear?" said Marcia. "You know, that piano stool must have been a really good one. You children have played with it like that ever since I can remember."

"It's hideous," said Adrian. "No one has them like that nowadays."

"I was remembering that Laurence always bought a liquorice pipe with his Saturday penny."

"And you always bought sugar pigs," said Laurence. "Once you asked me to remind you of it when you were old . . ."

"Well, don't forget . . . I'm glad the war came too late to spoil my childhood. I've got a sort of feeling that things are never going to be as nice again . . . I'm glad I had my childhood in the days when you could buy a sugar pig for a halfpenny and spin piano stools round and round. You can't do either now."

Frank got up to knock out his pipe against the hearth.

"Will you sing tonight, dear, or are you too tired?"

Marcia's voice had lost its youthful mellowness and clarity, but to Frank it was still as beautiful as ever. To him her singing was still the culminating-point of the evening's peace and happiness.

She took out a pile of tattered songs from the music-rack and turned them over. Then she struck the chords, and her voice, sweet as ever, but a little thin, rose in the strains of "Cherry Ripe."

They sat motionless and silent, listening . . . It was dusk outside, and the light of the room lit up the pale green tendrils of climbing honeysuckle that still curled in through the open window. Jenifer remembered how, in her childhood, she used to imagine that it was the fairy Metaphelia protecting them from the wizard's spells . . .

A wave of almost unbearable homesickness swept over her. They would come back here to stay, of course, but it would never be quite the same again. And she saw suddenly that what they were leaving now, for ever, what it was inevitable that they should leave for ever, was not only something very lovely, but something that was woven into the very tissue of their beings.

Lorna and Mark sat side by side on the sofa, Lorna's hand in Mark's. Adrian's lips smiled tremulously as his mind floated vaguely on the sentimental strains. Laurence sat gazing before him, deaf to the music, planning, scheming for the future.

Frank's eyes were fixed tenderly on his wife.

Chapter Eighteen

Adrian had taken two furnished rooms in Gray's Inn Road. They were clean and on the whole comfortable, despite a superabundance of china ornaments, plush upholstery, and little mats. He had discovered them with relief after a wearisome round of inspection of frowsy rooms presided over by frowsy landladies. So terrified had he been of the landladies that he had nearly engaged the frowsiest of the lot out of sheer cowardice.

Marcia had meant to come up to London to help him choose the rooms, but the work and excitement of Lorna's wedding had been too much for her, and the doctor had ordered her to bed.

Mrs Holroyd, Adrian's landlady, was a large middle-aged woman with a surprisingly small face and sparse grey hair that was generally done up in gigantic curling-pins. She wore old-fashioned corsets that must have been several sizes too big even for her, as the top of them stuck out under her bodice like a broad shelf all the way round. Adrian found her terrifying. Her thin lips never relaxed, her voice was sharp and aggressive, and she had a way of emphasising phrases every now and then that seemed to give them some sinister significance.

"I'm sure you aren't one to Give Trouble, sir. Mind you, I'm willing to Do my Duty by you as such, but Fair's Fair and Consideration's Consideration. Visitors in moderation I don't object to, so long as you realise that they Make Work and are willing to Act According."

At first Adrian was nervously apologetic for everything she had to do for him, but she had obviously taken a fancy to him (his shyness and boyish good looks always appealed to women) and used to come up to his room occasionally to talk to him in the evening. She belonged to a strict religious sect called the Brethren of the Election, whose tenets she expounded at great length to Adrian. Its members were Saved, and Saved so securely that nothing they did could possibly affect their salvation. Adrian was afraid that she might try to convert him to it, but he soon realised that she would have resented any intrusion into the ranks of the Elect. She liked Adrian, but she quite definitely enjoyed watching him smoke his pipe or drink a glass of wine or beer in the confidence that his doing so included him securely in the numbers of the Damned.

She lived in hourly expectation of the Second Advent, having once had a dream in which a man with a beard and a white robe, whom she identified as Elijah, had told her that she was one of the Chosen, and that she would live to see the end of the world. She was continually finding portents of this in the most everyday happenings. A thunderstorm would send her up to the attic window to watch for the angel who would come to sound the Trump of Doom, and even the sight of a piebald horse or a bird-dropping on her window-sill or the accidental inclusion of a blood orange among the half-dozen bought at the grocer's would seem to her omens of the event. Adrian always knew when she was expecting the end of the world because on those days and on those days only she took her hair out of curling-pins. She once confided to Adrian that her husband had gone off with a hussy sixteen years ago, and Adrian gathered that the expectation of witnessing his and the hussy's punishment in the after-life added considerable zest to her religion.

Her only relaxation from this religious tension was a rivalry with her next-door neighbour in the matter of clean doorsteps, artificial flowers in the window, and coloured bows on the lace curtains. Adrian soon learnt that he was expected to step across the front doorstep, not on it, and that the window in his sitting-room that gave on to the next-door back garden was merely a sort of show case for artificial flowers and be-ribboned curtains, and must not in any circumstances be opened. Fortunately there was another window that could not be seen from next door and that was not included in the competition.

He spent most of his time attending classes at the Slade School. His teachers recognised the streak of ill-disciplined genius in him, but found him supersensitive and touchy, plunged often into extravagant depression about his work, but resenting any criticism of it. The years—and the years of the war particularly—had brought to him a veneer of normality and self-control, but beneath it he was as emotionally unbalanced as ever. He longed for friends, but he was still self-conscious in his friendships, alienating even those who were attracted to him, by his sudden changes of mood, over-confidential one minute and over-brusque the next, quick to imagine slights and rebuffs.

He spent his leisure time wandering about the streets. The beauty of London, its colour and romance and history, intoxicated him with delight. He loved to hang over the parapet of the embankment watching the seagulls skim over the surface of the river, watching the dusk blaze into the sudden glory of sunset, then fade slowly into the silver hush of night.

But he was lonely, and the streets, crowded with people who seemed all intent on their own business, made him feel lonelier still. He sometimes visited Jenifer and Sylvia in their flat in Chelsea. The experiment of sharing the flat had turned out a great success. Each of the two girls went her own way and had her own interests, but beneath their casual surface intercourse was still that deep understanding and loyalty. They did not go about much together. Sylvia was restless and sophisticated and high-spirited, and seemed to spend her time flying from one party to another with a crowd of the bright young people of the period.

Jenifer often thought that her restlessness hid a deep unhappiness, and one night, in a mood of unusual expansiveness Sylvia told her that she had been in love for years with a man who had no feeling for her beyond that of the merest friendship. His name, she said, was Peter Headingly, and Jenifer remembered having met him at the Hall in the old days—a middle-aged rather silent man, with a pleasant heavy-featured face and hair turning grey at the temples

—the last man in the world she would have expected Sylvia to fall in love with. He came to the flat occasionally and occasionally took Sylvia out to a show.

"He does it in the spirit in which he used to take us to a pantomime," said Sylvia. "He still thinks of me as a child." A good many bright young males were in love with Sylvia. There was a young man with tired eyes and white hair called Monty, who danced like a professional and kept a collection of snakes, who proposed to her regularly. So did a handsome young man of the matinee idol type, who owned an estate in Yorkshire that he had not once visited since inheriting it six years ago and whose chief accomplishments were yodelling and imitating farmyard noises . . . Sylvia was the life and leader of her set, the originator of its most daring escapades, its maddest parties. Often she did not get back to the flat till six or seven in the morning, when she would change quickly and go out again to ride or start on a break-neck motor ride into the country with members of her "crowd." She seemed to dread an unoccupied moment more than anything else in the world, and, despite her loveliness, was growing thin and haggard.

"Darling, I've got to," she said to Jenifer, when Jenifer, breaking down the wall of reserve between them, once remonstrated with her. "I can't just sit at home and think about Peter. I've got to try to forget somehow. I wish he hadn't come again last week. It's made it worse ever since. Do you know, Jenifer, I'm thinking of giving him a hint and asking him not to come. I might have a chance of getting over it then, though I don't believe I ever shall . . . I think I'll marry Monty."

"*Sylvia!* Why Monty?"

"Well, any of them. It doesn't matter which. One might as well marry as not, don't you think?"

Adrian didn't get on well with the young people who filled Sylvia's flat. They chaffed and teased him as they chaffed and teased each other, and his self-esteem found perpetual sneers and slights in their careless raillery. He would sometimes take his leave in the middle of a party, obviously offended.

"I'm sorry," Sylvia would apologise to Jenifer, "but he's too terribly thin-skinned for ordinary life. And he thinks such a terrific lot of himself."

"He doesn't really," Jenifer would say. "It's what people call an inferiority complex. He thinks such a little of himself that he's afraid of other people thinking a little, too, and he's always taking for granted that they're trying to show him how little they do think of him."

"Anyway it's all too absurd," said Sylvia impatiently, "and one simply hasn't time for it."

Adrian gradually stopped coming to the flat and began to go out to Dulwich to visit Lorna and Mark, but Lorna and Mark were so wrapped up in each other that it only increased his loneliness. He took to wandering about the streets again, enjoying their pageant of light and colour and movement, but carrying always that heavy burden of loneliness at his heart, sometimes only restrained by his shyness from replying to the unspoken invitation he read in girls' eyes.

When he had been in his rooms for about a month Mrs Holroyd fell from a step-ladder and sprained her ankle. A niece was sent for from Islington, and Mrs Holroyd, lying on the kitchen sofa, explained the situation to Adrian.

"Evie will cook for you, sir, and wait on you and suchlike, but, of course, she won't do your bedroom or anything that might Look Funny. Mrs Coggins from over the way will run in and see to all that."

Her face wore a strained and harassed expression. She was terrified lest the Second Advent should come while she was incapacitated.

That evening, as Adrian sat reading by the window, the door was opened rather noisily, and a girl entered carrying his supper tray.

Feeling suddenly nervous, Adrian murmured "Good-evening" and kept his head bent over his book. But he watched her surreptitiously as she moved about the room, shaking out the cloth over his table, putting oh it the china and cutlery. She was plump and fair and rather untidy. Her wavy golden hair was gathered into a knot at the back of her neck, from which a good many strands escaped and hung about her face. She wore a soiled white apron over a sleeveless dress of cheap yellow silk. He took this in with a few hurried glances. He did not dare look at her face in case he met her eyes. He tried to concentrate on his book, but her presence (she was taking a long time laying his table) vaguely disturbed him, and he kept losing the thread of the sentences. His eyes, despite all his endeavours to control them, strayed continually to her bare elbows. He could look at them without the fear of meeting her eye. They were white and round and dimpled. They fascinated him. In the end he gave up the effort to keep his eyes away from them. He could imagine a man longing to kiss the dimples in them. Perhaps men had kissed them . . .

"Is that all right?" she said suddenly.

Her voice was slightly husky with an undercurrent of laughter. He raised his eyes slowly to her face. Her skin was thick and white, but not unhealthy-looking, her eyes vividly blue, her mouth large and generous. She pushed a strand of fair hair away from her eyes and said again:

"Is it all right?"

His eyes left her face with something of an effort and went to the table.

"Yes, thank you," he said stiffly.

She laughed suddenly. It was more a giggle than a laugh. A soft rich giggle.

"She's in a proper state," she said. "Afraid I'll put the things in the wrong place. 'Well,' I said, 'if I do, he's got hands, hasn't he? He can move them, can't he?'"

"Of course," he said, still more stiffly, as he sat down at the table and shook out his napkin.

She walked over to the window and took up the vase of paper chrysanthemums, which Mrs Holroyd had put there last week as an answering gesture to her neighbour's vase of paper poppies.

"Aren't they silly?" she said and giggled again, that soft rich giggle. He did not answer. He felt suddenly furious with her for hanging about the room like that. She was going to be a nuisance.

He opened his book ostentatiously and began to read. She went to the door and stood there, leaning against the door-post, looking at him. He stole a glance at her elbows, but he couldn't see the dimples now.

"You aren't a bit what I thought artists looked like," she said. "I thought you'd have a beard and a funny tie."

She began to giggle again, and a sudden unreasoning fury seized him.

"I've got everything I want, thank you," he said with dignity. "You needn't wait."

She turned and went out, laughing. He heard her singing to herself as she went down the stairs. He still felt furious. He felt furious all night. What a nuisance the girl was going to be, hanging about his room like that and giggling! He couldn't sleep because he felt so furious—and because he couldn't stop thinking of the dimples in her elbows. He hoped that she would not bring his breakfast up the next morning, and when Mrs Coggins from over the way brought it up he felt unreasonably disappointed.

Chapter Nineteen

Towards the end of the summer Jenifer went to Dulwich to spend a week with Lorna and Mark. The little house was still shiningly new, with wedding presents conspicuously displayed in every room, but Jenifer noticed a slight change in Lorna. She was lovelier than ever, but, whereas before she had been a young bride deeply and selflessly in love with her husband, wholly absorbed in keeping house for him, now an element of self-consciousness had crept into her attitude. It was as if she had suddenly realised what an attractive picture she made and were deliberately retaining the pose for that reason. She was still the happy, busy little bride, still deeply in love with Mark, but part of her now stood aloof, forming, as it were, an appreciative spectator of the picture.

It was indeed quite an attractive picture. The little house was well run (for Lorna was capable enough), and she was immensely popular with the neighbours, tradespeople, her own little maid, and the charwoman. She moved, in fact, in the atmosphere of admiration that was meat and drink to her. When she and Jenifer went out shopping together Lorna was met on all sides by smiles and greetings. The grimmest tradesman seemed to unbend to her, and she had, with each, one of those pleasant little "chats" at which she was an expert. Lorna never forgot whose wife had been ill or what people's children's names were. She was still the little girl who had remembered to ask after old Jarvis's rheumatism, and had loitered near the coastguards at Westonlea to hear them call her a "sweet little missie."

Jenifer waited rather self-consciously one morning while Lorna talked to an old woman who sold matches in the street.

"She's quite a friend of mine," explained Lorna, as she rejoined her. "She has an invalid daughter. I take her things sometimes."

And Jenifer felt a sudden compunction, because, right down at the bottom, mixed up with all the play-acting and posing and craving for admiration, there was a foundation of real kindness and goodness. Lorna would have hated people not to know that she was kind to the old woman and her invalid daughter, but she wasn't kind just for the sake of that and nothing else . . .

When first she married, Lorna had been content to spend her evenings alone with Mark, had indeed resented any intrusions upon their privacy, but now she was growing slightly restive (very, very sweetly restive) and impatient of Mark's desire to monopolise her.

"Darling, we *must* be friendly with our neighbours. It's a social duty."

So she and Mark joined the local tennis club. Lorna was a good player, and her looks and charm had the usual effect of making her immediately the most popular member of the club. Mark was proud of her popularity and of the numerous invitations that she received as a consequence, but he was beginning to resent her habit of cultivating friendships with everyone she met.

On the last day of Jenifer's visit she and Lorna went to the West End to do some shopping and see a matinée. Lorna was in an excellent humour. The shop assistants, the waitress at lunch, the cloak-room attendant at the theatre, had responded to her overtures with obvious admiration. It always spoilt the whole day for Lorna when that didn't happen. The feeling that there was anyone near her in any capacity whatsoever who did not admire her was like the pea beneath the mattress of the princess in the fairy tale.

When they reached home Mark was already there. It had been an oppressively close day, and he looked tired and limp.

"We're not going out tonight, are we?" he said.

"Yes, dear," said Lorna brightly. "To the Mertons'."

He groaned.

"Why on *earth*——?" he said. "They're the dullest couple in the length and breadth of England."

"That's the reason, partly," said Lorna with her sweet deprecating little laugh. "People aren't a bit nice to them, and they're so grateful for any kindness."

From the dull and second-rate, of course, Lorna won an admiration so uncritical and whole-hearted that she could seldom resist making the little effort necessary to win it, but Mark found their company intolerably boring.

"Well, I hope there's *one* evening this week when you haven't fixed anything up."

"No, there isn't. Nor next. Darling, I keep telling you, we *must* be friendly with our neighbours. It's our duty."

She handed him her engagement calendar, and he examined it, his face darkening. Then suddenly he became angry.

"Look here, Lorna," he exploded, "this is the limit. I wish you wouldn't make all these engagements without consulting me. I come home from business tired out, and I simply can't stand night after night of people like the Mertons. You've no right to ask me to."

Lorna went out of the room without answering, and Mark sat frowning in silence. Then he looked at Jenifer and said, "I'm sorry I was such a bear to her, Jen. I'm just tired out. I'll go and apologise."

At that moment Lorna came back.

"I'm so sorry, darling," she said sweetly. "I was hateful. Do forgive me."

"It was my fault," he muttered ungraciously.

His figure had gone rigid, and Jenifer could see that the forgiving sweetness of Lorna's manner irritated him almost beyond endurance.

He made a great effort to be pleasant at the Mertons', however, and when they came home he apologised to Lorna for his bad temper, and Lorna offered to cancel all their engagements, and he indignantly refused, and they seemed more in love with each other than ever.

When Jenifer returned to the flat, she was surprised to find Sylvia there alone, sitting in the dusk, gazing out of the window. When she turned Jenifer saw that her cheeks were flushed, her eyes bright.

"Oh, Jen," she said, "I'm so glad you've come. I wanted you to be the first to know. Peter's been . . . I was just trying to get up courage to—tell him and ask him to keep away, when he said that he'd better not go on seeing me, because he couldn't stand it any longer. The funniest part of it is that he took for granted he hadn't any chance. Aren't we funny? People, I mean. Living in little watertight compartments, shut away from each other and not even understanding each other's language . . . Oh, Jen, I've often imagined this happening, but I could never imagine anything as wonderful as it really is."

"Darling, I'm so glad," said Jenifer. The sight of Sylvia with her defences down, eager, young, tremulous, brought a sudden catch to her throat. "I do hope you'll be happy."

"I know I shall be happy," said Sylvia in a tone of deep conviction. "I've loved him ever since I was old enough to love anyone at all. I'm so happy even now that I can hardly bear it. It doesn't seem possible, somehow, to be as happy as this and go on living. He's coming tomorrow to talk over arrangements. We want to be married quite soon at Merrowvale—a very quiet wedding, because we both hate fuss. You do like him, don't you, Jennie?"

"Yes, I do."

"I know that he seems rather—stupid when he comes here. He *is* rather stupid. I mean, he's not clever and witty like some of the other men who come here. But he's so good and kind."

"He reminds me a little of Father," said Jenifer. "Men like that make their wives awfully happy."

"My father wasn't like that," said Sylvia slowly. "He didn't make Mother happy. It used to be a sort of joke with us that she was always imagining she was ill, but since she died I've often wished that I'd tried to—understand, and been kinder to her. She must have gone through a bad time with him in the beginning, when they were both young and she still cared. There were so many others before Cousin Helen. Bobby's like Father in that way, you know. I'm sorry, because he's so nice in others . . . Oh well"—she shook her head—"nothing in the world seems to matter now, not even Bobby. Being in love makes you terribly selfish, doesn't it?"

"Does it?" smiled Jenifer. "I don't know."

Sylvia was not married at Merrowvale, as Mr Lenham had decided to sell the Hall and go to live in the South of France. Sylvia shrugged her shoulders when she heard it.

"One never knows what he's up to. Poor old Dad! But he's still rather charming, isn't he? . . . I'm glad that Peter isn't charming."

Jenifer stayed on at the flat alone after Sylvia married. She thought that she would miss Sylvia, but she found that, on the contrary, she preferred being alone. There seemed to be a part of her that hungered for solitude and savoured it with deliberate enjoyment. A deep peace seemed to possess her spirit when she was alone. It was as if something that grew taut and curled up when anyone else was with her relaxed and spread itself out luxuriously in solitude. She had plenty of friends, but she liked to know that her solitude was there, waiting for her, a refuge in the rear . . . Her friends were chiefly women. She did not get on very well with men, and the men who had visited the flat while Sylvia lived there gradually stopped coming. She was vaguely worried by this and tried hard to overcome the secret shrinking that prevented her making men friends. It worried her because it made her feel that she was growing like Aunt Lena—Aunt Lena, who had been so afraid of the very idea of sex that she could hardly bring herself to speak to a man except when it was necessary. She fought against it, but her whole being seemed to go tense and rigid when any man showed a special interest in her, while an attempt at love-making, however mild, would throw her into a blind unreasoning panic. Sometimes she suspected that it was connected with Geoffrey Lenham. She knew now that she had been in love with him without realising it, and that her discovery of his intrigue with Mrs Grantham had warped some vital part of her.

Her only two real men friends were André and Bobby Lenham. With them alone she felt no restraint. André visited her at regular intervals, always bringing flowers or a box of chocolates. He liked to talk of abstract subjects and would lend her books on philosophy, which she tried hard to understand. Sometimes he would insist on her talking to him in French, so that he might correct what he called her "atrocious English schoolgirl accent."

She became very fond of the old man. There was in him an innate fastidiousness and reserve that responded to something in herself.

Bobby was just like another brother, and the fact that his sex interests lay definitely elsewhere made their friendship unselfconscious and straightforward. He was a charming scapegrace who roused all her maternal tenderness. She would sometimes scold him affectionately.

"Bobby, I wish you'd settle down to some work."

"I would, my pet," he would reply, "but my social conscience won't let me take a job out of an honest man's mouth. I'm unselfish enough to stand aside."

He was a delightful companion. He always had a fund of entertaining stories to tell her, and his powers of mimicry were undiminished. He and Jenifer would "collect" people on their frequent walks through London, and, when they came home, would bring out the "collection" one by one till they were both helpless with laughter. She had expected to see more of Adrian now that she was alone in the flat, but Adrian had suddenly become very elusive, full of mysterious "engagements," of which he told her no details; nervy, furtive, oddly excited.

"He's probably carrying on with someone," suggested Bobby.

"Oh, not Adrian," said Jenifer. "He's too shy even to speak to a girl."

"Ah, those are the ones!" grinned Bobby.

Laurence came to see her on Sundays occasionally, or they would go into the country together, but it was becoming more and more difficult to get down to what she still thought of as the "real Laurence." He was deeply absorbed in his business, thinking out ways and means, planning, scheming, even when he was out with her.

"Laurie, where *are* you?" she would say, when she had asked him the same question several times without receiving an answer.

"Sorry," he would reply, smiling. "I suppose I was in the office."

"Well, come out of the office . . . It's such a heavenly day. Don't spoil it by going about in your office like a snail in its shell."

He used to take work home with him to his rooms, and was sometimes busy with it during the whole week-end.

"I can't manage anything next week-end, Jennie, I'm afraid."

"But you won't be working all the time, will you? I don't mind your not doing anything with me—I'd love you to have a change from me—but I just want you to do *something*. Go out and forget the office. Pick up a girl and take her on the river or to the pictures."

He laughed. He was tall and good-looking, in the classic Greek style, with fair hair and regular features, and girls often made overtures of friendship to him. He ignored them, not from shyness or self-consciousness, like Adrian, but simply because he had no time for them.

"I'm surprised at you, Jennie," he teased, "trying to lead me down the broad path to destruction. What would Aunt Lena have said if she'd heard you?"

"Well, it's hateful for anyone to be such a slave to their work as you are."

"I'm not a slave to it. I love it. It's all so thrilling and interesting. We're completely reorganising the office work. It was my idea. I thought . . ."

She let him talk about his work for some minutes, watching his eager face with a sort of motherly tenderness, then she said:

"And can't you take even Sunday off?"

"No, I can't. I'm doing all this reorganising out of office hours, and it's going to save the firm hundreds of pounds. You see, Jennie—-"

She slipped her hand over his mouth.

"Don't," she said.

"Don't what?" he asked, surprised.

She laughed.

"I had a horrible feeling that in another moment you were going to say 'Time is Money.' "

"Well, it is, isn't it?"

"No," she said vehemently. "It isn't. It's blasphemy to say it is."

"You are a funny kid. Look here, we'll go out together the Sunday after. You know I love going out with you."

"You love it next to your work, don't you?"

"I love you more than my work. You know I do." Always when he went out with her he grew more and more human as the day wore on, till generally by evening he had regained something of the care-free zest of his boyhood. However deeply he was absorbed in his work, she was conscious of the bond that united them, but often she had the impression of fighting some ruthless intangible force that was trying to take possession of him.

He had begun not only to subordinate everything in his life to his work, but also to measure the success of his work solely by money.

"Penny for your thoughts," she said the next Sunday, as they sat in a Surrey wood beneath a roof of luminous beach leaves.

He threw her his disarming smile.

"Next quarter's turnover," he confessed. "It's going to break the record."

She pulled a face.

"Did you work all last Sunday?"

"Like a donkey"

"You'll never keep fit if you don't get out more."

"Yes, I will. I do exercises. They only take about ten minutes, and they keep me fit without my walking at all."

"Oh, Laurie," she laughed.

Each time she went out with him it took a little longer to bring back the boy she knew. His face in repose was beginning to have a hard, set look.

Sometimes on Sundays, when he was working, she would go to his rooms in Kensington and make tea for him. They were correct, dull, impersonal rooms, devoid of all evidence of leisure occupations. There were no flowers there unless she brought them.

"Haven't you any books, Laurie?" she asked once, looking round.

"My dear girl, I've no time for reading," he had replied impatiently.

That note of impatience was beginning to creep into his voice frequently, but at the slightest hint that she was tired or depressed, he forgot everything else in his solicitude, and still anything small and weak roused that womanlike tenderness that he had shown as a boy. He delighted in a Siamese kitten that Bobby had given her, and would play with it for hours when he visited her.

"It would be the saving of Laurie to marry and have children," she said to Bobby, "but I suppose he'd say he's no time."

"He's too much sense," said Bobby with a short laugh.

She had felt rather uneasy after her visit to Lorna and Mark, and made an excuse for going over again soon afterwards. To her relief she found them happy and cheerful and obviously still deeply in love with each other. Mark had begun to take an interest in the little garden, and worked there every evening when he and Lorna were not going out or having people in. Two young married couples came to dinner the evening of Jenifer's visit, and Mark was patently delighted by their admiration of Lorna's housekeeping, for she had managed to cook an excellent dinner and yet to be ready to receive her guests, cool and dainty and exquisitely dressed. The sisters did not get a chance to speak to each other alone till Jenifer was putting on her coat to go home. Then Lorna said, "What's happened to Adrian nowadays?"

"I don't know," said Jenifer. "I've not seen him lately. Hasn't he been here?"

"No. He used to come nearly every week, but we've not seen him for months."

"I'll ring him up . . ."

When she got back she found Bobby waiting for her in the flat.

"Well," he said, "how's the scalp-hunter?"

"Whom do you mean by that?"

"You know quite well whom I mean by that."

"She isn't a scalp-hunter, Bobby. You don't like her, but everyone else does."

"I know. She leaves a treacly trail of popularity wherever she goes."

She laughed. It was impossible to be cross with Bobby.

"I suppose you're peeved because she's always refused to fall for you."

"Think that if you like . . . Do you know, Jen, I've got a theory about Lorna. I believe that when she's quite alone she vanishes. You see, she's always just what the person she's with wants her to be, and so, when there's no one there to want her to be anything, there's nothing for her to be, and she just goes out like a candle. I mean to prove it one day. I shall hide in a room where she's alone, and I shall see her in the act of vanishing."

"What an *idiot* you are, Bobby!"

"Now you, on the contrary," he went on, warming to his theme, half serious, but using a mock oratorical manner, "only exist when you're alone. I mean, just as Lorna isn't a real person at all when she's alone, so you are only a real person when you're alone. You curl up into yourself when other people are there. Right down at the bottom you're unsociable, self-sufficient, and *very* nearly smug."

"Oh no," she protested. "Not smug. I'd rather be anything than that."

"Perhaps not smug," he conceded, "but priggish. Yes, darling, you *are* priggish. When I tell you a low tale you purse your lips and change the subject. I always think that's such an odd verb—to purse. And you never find it about anything but lips. Why shouldn't one purse other things besides lips? Isn't the English language adorable?"

Jenifer laughed, but the old fear had caught her by the throat again. She *was* growing like Aunt Lena—prudish, priggish, old-maidish. Suppose she grew more and more like Aunt Lena as time went on till she actually became Aunt Lena . . . Things like that happened so gradually that you never realised they were happening till they'd happened. You didn't realise even then. That was what was so terrible. Aunt Lena had never known that she was Aunt Lena. . .

"Why so pensive all of a sudden?" said Bobby.

"I'm thinking that life's—frightening," said Jenifer. "It gets hold of you, and turns you into something you don't want to be in the least, before you know what it's doing."

"Don't be morbid, my child," he said. "The great point is——"

The telephone rang, and Jenifer went to answer it. It was Laurence's voice.

"Jen, Father's just rung me up. Mother's very ill, and they want us all to go down there at once. I'll call for you. I'm starting now. You can be ready in a few minutes, can't you?"

Chapter Twenty

Marcia died of pneumonia the day after the children were summoned home. She was unconscious most of the time, but when she was conscious her old gaiety seemed to shine through her weariness, and there was the ghost of the old laughter in her eyes up to the end.

Throughout her illness Miss Marchant carried the weight of the entire household on her shoulders, doing most of the cooking, taking her turn with the nursing, looking after them all in the background with quiet efficiency. She seemed to understand what Marcia wanted better than anyone, and Frank turned to her like a child for everything.

The others returned to London immediately after the funeral, but Jenifer stayed with Frank for a few days longer. She had offered to come to live at home permanently, but Frank refused even to consider the idea. He was pathetically proud of her and of the work she had had published.

"You've got your career, Baby, and it would worry me more than I can say to think that I'd interfered with it. No, I'm all right. You come down here whenever you can, and I'll trot up to London now and then to see you all. I don't want any of you to live here with me. I shall be all right. I'm not really an old man yet, you know."

He looked old, old and broken by this sudden stroke of fate. He seemed bewildered, too, as if he did not realise yet what had happened to him. It was strange to see him sitting alone in the evenings, he who had never spent an evening away from Marcia since their marriage. He had always been fond of his children, but they had never meant very much to him. No one had ever meant very much to him except Marcia. She had filled his whole life, and, now that she had left him, his life seemed to have come to an end. To himself he seemed in some strange way to have died with Marcia and yet to have to go on living.

Jenifer began to suspect that her presence worried him and that he would rather be alone, so she went back to London at the end of a week.

It was Adrian who seemed to feel Marcia's death the most. Always emotional and easily upset, he broke down and cried hysterically both when she died and after the funeral. He was worn-out and nerve-racked when he returned to his rooms. He had been seeing a good deal of Evie lately. Mrs Holroyd's ankle had developed complications, and Evie, in her shiftless good-natured way, did most of the work of the house. She insisted, however, on an "afternoon out," and Adrian had slipped into the habit of spending it with her. Her imperturbability soothed his frayed nerves, and her uncritical admiration his constantly ruffled self-esteem. Even her undeniable commonness satisfied him in some obscure way, so far removed was it from the world where he was always acutely suspicious of slights or criticism. Marcia's death drew them nearer together, for unconsciously he now turned to her for the motherliness that underlay her casual cheerful manner. He had not yet kissed the dimple in her elbow, but the longing to do so had lately become almost irresistible.

Meantime Mrs Holroyd's lameness, together with the persistent delay of the Second Advent, was having a souring effect upon her temper, and she resented the fact that Evie's presence in the house was still necessary. She nagged at the girl incessantly, but her scoldings slid off Evie's placidity like the proverbial water from a duck's back. She shrugged her plump shoulders and laughed her soft rich gurgle of laughter and went about her work in her happy-go-lucky slovenly way. For not even Adrian could deny that Evie was slovenly. Her soft fair hair was generally falling about her face. Her shoes were down-at-heel, her apron stained, her blouse or jumper in holes. Mrs Holroyd was, of course, unaware of the growing friendship between Evie and her lodger. On Evie's afternoons out she ostensibly went to see another aunt, who lived in Peckham, and with whom Mrs Holroyd had not been on speaking terms for several years. Adrian would meet her at some distance from the house, and they would take a 'bus or train into the country. Evie would get herself up gallantly for these expeditions, in a pink silk lace-trimmed blouse, a black silk skirt, and a black straw hat trimmed with red roses. They went out together the week after Marcia's death, and Adrian, telling her about it, broke down again, and she held him in her arms and comforted him. He could feel her soft warm breasts through the thin silk of her blouse, and her rich consoling womanhood was like a protective haze about him.

After that their friendship became more intimate. They went into the country regularly on her free afternoons. He told her how he had always longed to kiss the dimple in her white elbow, and, with her deep rich gurgle, she rolled up the sleeve of the pink silk blouse and offered it to him. He kissed it shyly, and even then did not try to kiss her lips.

"You're just a baby," she laughed, and, drawing his head on to her lap, began to stroke his hair back from his brow. He closed his eyes and lay there in a state between sleeping and waking, feeling himself again a child in his mother's arms.

During the winter they frequently went for long country walks. Adrian bought her a warm coat and a pair of comfortable shoes, which she told Mrs Holroyd her aunt in Peckham had given her. She would have preferred to go to picture palaces, but Adrian liked to get right away from everyone. Alone with her, he seemed to be enclosed in that world of warm uncritical mother-love in which alone he felt really happy and at his ease. She was pliant and accommodating, falling in with all his suggestions, never sulky or put out by anything.

Mrs Holroyd's ankle gradually improved, but, as she had obstinately refused to go into hospital or carry out any of the treatment prescribed by the doctor (she didn't Believe in Doctors), recovery was naturally slow. She could manage the flight of stairs up to her own bedroom but not the steep one up to Adrian's rooms. Moreover, a neglected tooth (she didn't Believe in Dentists either) was causing her a great deal of pain, and she vented her irritation upon Evie, only allowing her the one free afternoon a week, though she could easily have spared her on Saturday or Sunday as well.

As the spring came round Adrian became restless and irritable, blaming Evie because she could not come out with him oftener, objecting to all her suggestions, changing his plans for the expeditions at the last moment.

On the first warm day in May they went to a wood in Kent, where the air was sweet with the wild hyacinths that stretched like a blue haze on all sides. There they sat down beneath an oak tree, and Adrian took out his sketching things. He had often tried to draw Evie and was always tormented because he could not infuse into his portraits anything of the warm rich womanhood that pervaded her. Her mouth especially tantalised him, and today he went over it again and again, rubbing it out as soon as he had finished it and starting afresh just for the sake of tracing its full sensuous curves with his pencil.

She sat among the bracken near him, softly pulling off the tiny fronds and stripping them.

"I wish to heaven you'd keep still," he snapped irritably.

She stared at him.

"What's been the matter with you lately, kid?" she said.

He did not answer, so she repeated her question.

"I don't know," he muttered.

She laughed—that deep chuckling laugh that he never thought of now as a giggle.

"Don't you?" she said.

He bent over his sketch again. It was maddeningly difficult to get on paper any real impression of her, to reproduce the smooth heavy opaqueness of her skin, the pallor that nevertheless suggested abounding health and vitality. She had taken off her hat, and her fair hair fell untidily about her face as usual. He could see the outlines of her unconfined breasts beneath the flimsy silk of her cheap blouse. Her blue eyes mocked him.

"Do you know you've never kissed me?" she said.

He looked at her, and the lazy invitation of eyes and mouth sent the blood flaming into his cheeks.

"Once you begin that sort of thing," he said unsteadily, "you never know where it'll end."

"Don't you?" she said again.

He began to pack up his things.

"It's time we went back," he said shortly.

For answer she lay down among the bracken and looked up at him, laughing. The green curling fronds almost hid her. Her laughter seemed part of the warm spring evening, part of the hum of the insects and song of the birds and the faint sweet smell of the bluebells. She caught his hand and laid it on her breast, so that he could feel the slow strong pulse of her heart.

"Kiss me," she said.

He swayed towards her. She drew his head down and they lay there motionless, his lips against hers. He felt as though the sweetness of her lips were sapping all the strength from his body and all the will from his mind. He surrendered to it, clinging to her like a drowning man.

It was dusk when they rose from the bed of bracken and long fragrant grass. He watched her in silence as she pushed back her tumbled hair and straightened her disordered dress. His face was white and set.

"We must get married now," he said.

She laughed.

"Why?" she mocked. "Do you want to do the right thing by me?"

"No, no!" he said hastily. "It's that—oh, you *must* see it. Of *course* we must get married."

She looked at him with a faint smile, tender, motherly.

"You needn't worry about me, kid, if that's what you're thinking," she said. "I can look after myself."

"Oh, it isn't only—that. It's—Evie, *I want* you. I want you to belong to me now."

"Well, don't I? We can go on meeting like this. And Aunt can't manage the steps yet. I can come to your room."

He shuddered.

"No, that's horrible. I couldn't bear that. Even this"— he pointed to the tumbled bed of bracken—"it's—beastly. I never meant—I wish I hadn't—Evie, you *must* marry me."

She shook her head, still smiling that faint tender smile.

"It wouldn't do," she said. "You know it wouldn't do. We're—different."

"How do you mean—different?"

She shrugged.

"Every way. Class and all that."

"*Class!*" he echoed in fierce disgust. "What does class matter?"

"It does matter. And it isn't only class. We're different every way."

He sat among the bracken looking at her, his chin resting on his hands, his eyes dark and unhappy in his pale face.

She bent down and kissed him on the forehead. Then, moving nearer, she gathered his head to her breast and held it, stroking his hair, kissing his closed eyes.

"There, there!" she said. "Don't you worry, kid. There's nothing to worry about."

He lay against her breast, relaxed, his passion spent, a child in its mother's arms. There was silence all around them. The dusk deepened slowly to night. He stirred at last, dragging himself from his drowsy contentment.

"We must go . . . it's awfully late."

"I suppose it is . . ."

In the train he said suddenly:

"What about your aunt? We've never been as late as this before."

She shrugged.

"She'll have gone to bed. I told her that Aunt Annie might be having some people in and I'd be late."

"I'd better wait and go in about half an hour after you."

"Oh, don't be silly. You can't moon about the streets for half an hour this time of night. You're tired out as it is. I tell you, she'll be asleep. We'll just go in quietly, and it'll be all right. She sleeps like a log."

The house was in darkness when they reached it. Adrian opened the door silently with his latch-key, and, closing it without a sound, they crept across the kitchen and up the stairs. Giggling noiselessly, Evie pointed out the stair that creaked, and they both stepped over it cautiously. It wasn't till they reached the top that they saw Mrs Holroyd. She was standing, arms akimbo, just outside her bedroom door. Her hair was in curl-papers, and she wore a dingy white shawl over a grey flannelette nightgown.

Her face was set in grim angry lines.

Mrs Holroyd had had a trying day. The night before she had dreamed of twelve cows in a field, and this had led her to expect the Second Advent at noon. Its failure to eventuate coincided with a specially bad attack of toothache and with the appearance of a cactus in a highly ornamental pot in the next door window. She had sat all afternoon, holding hot flannels to her aching tooth and brooding over the delayed Second Advent and the cactus. As the toothache grew worse her irritation began to seek fresh fields.

Her ankle was not aching at present, but she knew it would ache if she walked about on it, so she got up and walked about on it till she had made it ache in order deliberately to add it to her list of grievances. The ankle led naturally to that slut Evie whom it compelled her to keep in the house. A great lazy giggling girl. Here she was—tied by the leg and couldn't even get up to Mr Gainsborough's rooms to see what sort of a mess they were in. Hadn't been dusted, as like as not, since she fell from the step-ladder. You'd only got to look at that slut Evie to know that she'd never do corners properly. Corners thick with dust. Crumbs on the carpet. Cigarette ash everywhere. And gentlemen were so helpless. That nice Mr Gainsborough would never dream of turning a hand to it himself as a woman might. He'd be giving notice next, and then where would they be? That slut Evie eating her out of house and home, leaving corners and crumbs and cigarette ash everywhere, losing her best lodger, bringing her to the work-house . . . Self-pity swept over her in an irresistible flood, and she took out her handkerchief for a Good Cry. Generally she felt better after a Good Cry, but this one seemed to aggravate the tooth, sending a jagged pain shooting up into her head. As if in sympathy, her ankle began to ache more violently. The next proceeding to a Good Cry was normally a Nice Cup of Tea, but today Mrs Holroyd felt too much depressed even to make the effort to put the kettle on. And all her irritation and depression centred itself upon Evie. Going off and leaving her to answer the door and get her own tea like this. Didn't care what happened to her as long as she got her afternoon out. Cared for nothing but pleasure, like all modern girls. Gallivanting off to that Annie's every week—or worse. Yes, worse probably. Picking up men and going to the pictures with them, as like as not. This avenue of speculation was so attractive that Mrs Holroyd sat up erect in her chair, forgetting both tooth and ankle in her excitement. Sly. You could see it in the way she looked at you and the way she laughed. *She* wasn't one to be going off to visit an old aunt every week. Not she. After some man she was, more like. These suspicions stimulated her so much that she put on the kettle and made the Nice Cup of Tea. She gave a triumphant snort as she drank it. You wait, my lady. I'll catch you out before you're finished. Just you wait. Her mind went busily back over the past few weeks, unearthing details that had meant nothing to her at the time. There was that new coat and those new shoes. Annie had never given her those, not she! What a fool she'd been to believe the slut! She'd keep a look-out from her bedroom window and see if anyone came to the door with her tonight. She'd—the thought struck her like a blow in the face.

Regularly for weeks Mr Gainsborough had been coming home just about half an hour after Evie on her afternoons out. She dismissed the idea as preposterous, but somehow she couldn't quite get rid of it. It stayed there at the back of her mind. It was preposterous, but—sluts were sluts and men were men, and even a gentleman like Mr Gainsborough, who was as Meek as Milk and Gave no Trouble—well, you couldn't be sure. Not with Sluts and Men. Heaven only knew what Goings On there'd been in his rooms while she'd been laid up with her knee. Righteous anger blazed in her, blazed so high that she was still aflame with it when she went to bed at half-past ten. It needed no great effort to keep awake. Sleep would have been impossible in any case.

Soon after midnight she heard the stealthy opening of the front door. She opened her own door as stealthily and stood just outside where she could watch the stairs. The furtive progress of the couple up the stairs, the way in which Evie pointed out the one that creaked, told her all she wanted to know. She stepped forward and confronted them threateningly as they reached the top.

"And where have you been, my lady?" she demanded in a rasping voice.

"I've been for a walk," said Evie nonchalantly.

"With my lord, I suppose?" said Mrs Holroyd through venomously compressed lips.

"With Adrian," said Evie, still maddeningly unconcerned.

"Oh," said Mrs Holroyd with ominous distinctness, "so he's Adrian to us nowadays, is he? And how long has this been going on, I'd like to know?"

There was a pugnacious gleam behind the laughter in Evie's eyes.

"How long has what been going on?"

"None of your impudence, you slut," shrilled her aunt. "How long have you been carrying on with your fancy man in my house?"

She turned to Adrian, who was watching the scene, sick with horror.

"Oh yes, butter wouldn't melt in your mouth, would it, my lord? And all the time you were"—Mrs Holroyd paused, while memories of the novelettes she had lately read passed through her mind—"you were sedoocing this unprotected child."

She realised as she spoke the incongruity of making Evie both villainess and victim of the piece and stopped rather lamely.

There was a silence, and in the silence Evie laughed—her low rich gurgle of pure amusement. Mrs Holroyd stepped forward and dealt her a stinging blow across each cheek.

"Stop that, you little bitch," she said. "Aren't you *ashamed*, bringing your goings-on into a respectable woman's house? Out you go tomorrow, bag and baggage!" She turned to Adrian, as if to order him out too, but remembered in time that he paid two pounds a week for rooms that were only worth fifteen shillings, and Gave no Trouble.

She swung round upon Evie again, her anger doubled by the fact that Adrian would probably go now whether she turned him out or not.

"You dirty little street tart, you!"

Evie opened her lips, and a stream of pure Billingsgate issued from them. To Adrian the scene was grotesque, incredible. He was trembling, his face ashen.

"*Don't*," he said in a high unsteady voice. Mrs Holroyd turned to him. "I tell you we're going to be married. We're going to be married as soon as we can."

"Not before it's time, I'll be bound," said Mrs Holroyd grimly, and with that she returned to her bedroom, slamming the door.

Adrian and Evie went in silence up the further flight of stairs.

"Evie, you will marry me, won't you?" pleaded Adrian, when they reached the top. "You must."

She smiled at him.

"Because of this?" she said. "You needn't worry, kid. I was going, anyway, and she'll be all right with you. She knows which side her bread's buttered."

"No . . . because I want you. Because I can't live without you. I love you. Say you will, Evie. Promise."

She looked at him, and her smile died away.

"All right," she said. "I will if you really want me to."

Chapter Twenty-One

Jenifer had settled down to a jog-trot routine of work and play. She enjoyed London, she enjoyed her work, and she enjoyed the friendships that it was bringing her, chiefly those of professional women, living on their own like herself and deeply absorbed by their work. The novel she was writing seemed to be going well, and for the first time she was beginning to feel hopeful of success. She was jerked rudely out of this rut by the news of her father's marriage to Miss Marchant. At first she couldn't believe it. She read his letter over and over again, and still it seemed incredible.

> DEAR JENIFER [he had written],
>
> This is just to tell you that Miss Marchant and I are to be married tomorrow. We shall be married probably by the time you receive this letter. We shall, of course, be very glad to see you whenever you care to come down.
>
> Your loving FATHER.

She rang up Lorna. Lorna had received a note with exactly the same wording. Lorna, however, was not greatly perturbed.

"I think it's most suitable," she said. "He's getting old, and he'll need someone to look after him. I certainly haven't time to go down there and nurse him if he's taken ill. I don't know whether you have."

"But, Lorna, it's *dreadful*," protested Jenifer. "*Flossie!* Think of it!"

"Well, my dear, we needn't see anything of her. She's an excellent nurse, and she runs the house quite well. I don't know what you're fussing about."

There was a faint note of irritation in the dulcet tones.

"It really isn't our business," she ended rather sharply.

Jenifer tried to get into touch with Adrian, but his landlady answered the telephone and said that he was away.

Laurence was vaguely sympathetic and concerned.

"I know," he said. "I had a line from the old man, too. I'm sorry. I'm afraid it won't be a success."

"I wish we'd gone down to see him oftener."

"My dear, we couldn't have stopped it. She'd probably made up her mind as soon as Mother died."

"Still—I wish we'd gone. Laurie, will you come down with me and see him?"

"You can hardly barge in on them now. They were only married yesterday."

"Well, at the end of the week, or at the end of the month. Will you come with me?"

"I don't see how I can. I'm terribly busy just now. Franklin's ill, and I don't know when he'll be back at the office. It's all I can do to get through the work. In any case it can't do any good. I shouldn't go there, Jennie, if I were you. He won't expect it. He'll know how we must feel."

At the end of a fortnight Jenifer went down to Merrowvale alone.

Her heart quickened as she approached the house that was so full of memories of her childhood, and a sudden feeling of revulsion possessed her at the thought of Miss Marchant's being its mistress, so that it was all she could do not to turn and run back to the station.

A maid she had never seen before opened the front door to her, showed her into the empty drawing-room, and left her there. She looked about her. Nothing had been altered, and yet the whole atmosphere was different. That elusive something of serenity and graciousness that Marcia had imparted to it had gone. It was now merely a shabby old-fashioned room. Then her stepmother entered, and Jenifer saw at once that she, too, was different, so different that for a moment it took her breath away. The dark greasy hair was hennaed and tightly crimped. Where the mole had been was an angry scar. The sallow cheeks were rouged. Gone were the plain dark clothes that Jenifer had associated with her from babyhood. She wore a dress of saxe blue, elaborately made and trimmed with innumerable buttons and little rows of ruching.

"Well, Jenifer," she said.

Her eyes were hard and bright, and there was a thinly veiled hostility in them as they met Jenifer's. Jenifer had taken for granted that Miss Marchant herself would be unaltered, had indeed expected to find her conciliatory, deprecating. The undercurrent of insolence in voice and manner had the effect of a blow in the face. She had meant to keep herself well in hand, to be studiously courteous, but now, her pulses pounding in her ears, she could only say unsteadily: "I've come to see my father, please."

"He's in the morning room," said the new Mrs Gainsborough, and added tartly, "I'll thank you not to go upsetting him and making a scene."

Jenifer did not answer.

In the old days there had been something noticeably ladylike about Miss Marchant, with her subdued respectful manner and dark clothes, but about the new Mrs Gainsborough, with her bright dress and aggressive voice, there was a distinct air of commonness.

Jenifer went to the morning room. Her father was reading in an armchair by the open window.

As he turned to her she saw with a pang how much the last few months had aged him.

"Hello, Baby," he said cheerfully. "How nice to see you! I thought you'd come."

She flung herself into his arms and clung to him, fighting back her tears. Her love and self-reproach were almost more than she could bear.

"Don't cry, Baby," he said, holding her closely to him and stroking her hair. "There's nothing to cry for."

She lifted her head and smiled at him through her tears.

"I'm not really crying," she said in a strangled voice. "It's just— oh, I don't know."

He drew her on to his knee.

"There's nothing for you to worry about at all, Baby," he said tenderly. "I'm very happy. As happy as I could be, that is, without your mother. Flora was quite right. People were talking, and it couldn't have gone on. And—well, she was the last link with your mother. She'd helped to bring up you children. She seemed—all that was left of the old days. It's just a convenient arrangement. Of course, she couldn't have stayed here if we hadn't married."

Jenifer's eyes hardened, and her lips curled contemptuously. So she'd caught him by that old trick . . . Then she looked up at his drawn face and forgot everything in her concern for him.

"Father, you aren't well," she said unhappily.

"I'm perfectly all right," he assured her. "The last year's been rather a strain, of course. Now stop looking worried, Baby, or I really shall be unhappy."

She smiled unsteadily, then clung to him again in a sudden passionate rush of gratitude for the tenderness that had surrounded her from childhood.

They heard the sound of a step outside the door and separated abruptly, Jenifer going over to the window to hide the trembling of her lips and the tears that still brimmed her eyes.

"Nice to see Baby again, isn't it?" said Frank in his pleasant voice as his wife entered.

"You ought to be resting, Frank," said Mrs Gainsborough.

She addressed Jenifer with that new asperity of voice and manner.

"Your father's not been at all well lately, Jenifer, and the doctor says that he ought to rest in the afternoons."

"I'm certainly not going to rest while Baby's here," said Frank. "She'll do me more good than any amount of resting."

Jenifer turned from the window.

"It's so nice to be back again," she said.

Her voice was pacific, almost propitiating. Her first impulse to accept the woman's challenge had faded. She wouldn't quarrel with her, wouldn't let herself be driven away from her father. That would be simply playing into the enemy's hands. She sat down on the arm of his chair, as she spoke, leaning affectionately against his shoulder. Mrs Gainsborough watched them. A high colour burnt in each cheek beneath her rouge.

"Do you mind not leaning against that shoulder, Jenifer?" she said sharply. "Your father has rheumatism in it." Jenifer withdrew to the window again and sat on the broad cushioned seat, watching them thoughtfully. Mrs Gainsborough fussed about her husband, fetching him a footstool, drawing the curtains to shade his face from the sun. He rose with a quick jerky movement.

"I am not yet a hopeless invalid, my dear Flora," he said. "Don't try to make me out one."

He spoke with schooled patience, but his whole manner betrayed an irritation that was something entirely new in him. He came across to the window, obviously meaning to sit by Jenifer, but his wife quickly took her seat between them, making some casual remark about the garden as she did so. Her breast was rising and falling unevenly, and her voice was not quite steady. Jenifer realised, with surprise and a vague feeling of foreboding, that she was passionately in love with her husband, had probably been in love with him for years, hiding the knowledge even from herself because to admit it would mean that she must conquer it, and she could not bear to do that. It had been the secret solace of her long barren servitude, the reason for her unremitting uncomplaining drudgery. Now it was triumphantly vindicated, but it brought her more pain than joy. She was bitterly, agonisingly jealous of his children, of his first wife, of his memories. His affectionate welcome to Jenifer had been torture to her.

"We haven't really had our honeymoon yet," she was saying. "We think of going to Switzerland."

She spoke with a heavy archness of manner, but in her eyes was something that pleaded desperately for some sign of affection from him, something so cringing and abject that Jenifer turned away, ashamed of having seen it. When Frank took Jenifer into the garden she accompanied them, walking between them, keeping up a ceaseless monologue in her hard bright voice, giving accounts of trivial local and domestic happenings, designed to show herself and her husband enclosed in a happy world of their own from which Jenifer was excluded.

The other two were silent, and her voice grew shriller and more unsteady as she talked. Pity for both of them tore at Jenifer's heart . . .

She made an excuse for going immediately after tea.

"I only just ran over to see you. I'm really frightfully busy now. I'll stay longer next time . . ."

"You must come and stay here properly as soon as you can take a holiday," said Frank, "mustn't she, Flora?"

His wife did not answer.

He insisted on taking her to the station, and his wife insisted on going with them. Before they started she fussed about him, getting his hat and stick, helping him on with his coat, in an ostentatiously proprietary manner that was obviously intended as a challenge to Jenifer. Again Jenifer looked away, less to avoid the sight of her attentions than his obvious though controlled irritation with them. They were very silent on the way to the station. When he had gone to see about the train, Mrs Gainsborough turned to Jenifer and said:

"We shan't be staying long in this house, you know, Jenifer."

"Surely Father wouldn't want to leave it," said Jenifer.

"Why not?" asked Mrs Gainsborough. "It's an old-fashioned inconvenient house and far too big for the two of us. It's shabby, as well. I'd like to move to one of those modern houses they're building nowadays and get some new furniture."

Jenifer trembled with sudden unreasoning anger.

"Father won't want to move," she said again.

Mrs Gainsborough set her lips.

"I think he will . . ."

As she spoke she gave Jenifer a basilisk stare from her cold grey-green eyes.

She's hated us all since we were children, thought Jenifer despairingly. It will only make things worse for him if I try to help him . . .

*

234

She went over to see Lorna the next week-end but found her unsympathetic and distrait.

"I really don't know what you're fussing about, Jenifer . . . It's a most sensible arrangement in every way. Well, naturally he's still upset by Mother's death. It was a great shock, but Miss Marchant will make him an excellent wife, and, as I said before, he needs somebody to look after him. It would worry me terribly to think of his living alone. I feel *quite* happy about the marriage."

Of course you do, thought Jenifer rather bitterly. You've made up your mind to feel happy about it because it's less trouble.

The whole atmosphere of Lorna's house seemed to have altered. It was still neat and trim and pretty and excellently run, but all her zest and interest in it had gone. She was as nearly sulky as Jenifer had ever seen her. There had been, Jenifer gathered, a little "unpleasantness" at the local tennis club. Two of the members had quarrelled, and Lorna had sympathised with each of them, assuring each that the other was in the wrong. They happened to compare notes, and then the fat was in the fire. Lorna, asked to reconcile her statements, had explained, very sweetly and without losing any of her poise, that she could not help seeing an affair of that sort from every possible angle. The explanation did not satisfy them, and several of Lorna's friends had taken sides against her in the dispute.

"It's so ridiculous, Jenifer," she said petulantly. "I simply *am* like that. I can't *help* seeing a question from every point of view. I'm broad-minded and tolerant. People here are so terribly narrow-minded."

The affair did not seriously trouble her, however. It was, indeed, not the first time that such a situation had arisen, and she knew that she could easily win back the friendships she had temporarily lost. Her popularity was now so well founded that even those who did not subscribe to it pretended to do so in order not to be out of the picture.

It was not really this incident that had made her discontented. It was that the whole situation was beginning to pall on her. She was tired of being the happy busy little bride. Everyone liked her, but everyone was beginning to take her for granted. She was no longer a novelty to herself or to those around her. The admiring attentiveness of the tradesmen and her neighbours was in no way diminished, but it had lost all the thrill of conquest. She felt bored by the people whom at first she had found so charming. Like Alexander, she longed for fresh worlds to conquer . . .

Mark went out to work in the garden as soon as he came back from the office and stayed working in it till dinnertime. He was becoming an enthusiastic gardener and had won a "Highly Commended" at the local flower-show for his sweet peas.

"I'm trying to persuade Mark to give up this house," said Lorna as she poured out coffee after dinner. "I think we'd both find a flat much more convenient."

Jenifer glanced at Mark. He seemed somewhat bewildered by Lorna's sudden restlessness and discontent.

"I dunno," he said slowly, looking round the room that they had furnished with such care and pride only a year ago. "I'm awfully fond of this house. We've been so happy here."

"But, darling," said Lorna with a little laugh that barely concealed her irritation, "it's such a poky little place."

"I wouldn't call it 'poky,' " he said. "I think it's charming, don't you, Jenifer?"

"Yes," said Jenifer.

She was watching Lorna and noticing the rather tight lines of her lovely mouth. Lorna was as beautiful as Mother had been— feature for feature, indeed, they were almost exactly alike—but something was missing in Lorna that had been in Mother, some intangible quality that had animated her beauty, making it rare and exquisite. People never turned in the streets to look at Lorna as they had turned to look at Mother.

"But, darling," Lorna was saying again with that exasperated little laugh, "it's so far out of London. A flat in London would be so much more convenient for us both. It's you I'm thinking of chiefly. The journey out here's so tiring for you."

"No, it isn't," he protested. "I love coming out here from London." He glanced through the window at the garden, small, neat, rectangular, where he now spent his happiest hours. "And I'm fond of the garden."

Lorna shrugged.

"Oh, the *garden*!" she said.

"You've made such a lot of friends here, Lorna," he went on. "I should have thought that you'd have hated the idea of leaving it."

"Mark dear, they aren't the type of people I've anything in common with. They're typically suburban."

He stared at her, his bewilderment increasing as he remembered the enthusiasm with which she had pursued her friendships with these people only a short time ago. A thoughtful look came into his face.

"You aren't worried about that fuss at the tennis club, are you, darling? Everyone who knows you understands."

Lorna coloured. Though she felt completely justified, she didn't like being reminded of the fuss at the tennis club. It seemed to put her in the wrong, and she hated to be put in the wrong.

"Of course not," she said rather shortly.

Mark threw her a look that was almost an appeal.

"Honestly, Lorna, I never knew what a home could be till I came here. Don't let's think of giving it up."

Lorna was silent for a second, then suddenly the old loving little-girl radiance shone in her face, and she came over to him, sitting on the arm of his chair and laying her cheek against his head.

"We won't," she said. "I'm so glad you're happy, darling. I am, too, really. It was just a silly fad. Let's forget it."

For the rest of the evening she was the happy eager little bride, sitting on a footstool on the hearthrug, her head resting against Mark's knees, relating little anecdotes about the neighbours and tradesmen that made them all laugh. The tension had gone from the atmosphere, the lines of worry from Mark's face.

"I've seen nothing of the boys for ages," said Lorna, as she helped Jenifer on with her coat. "It must mean that Adrian's beginning to make friends on his own. I'm glad. He was a bit of a nuisance, coming here. Laurence is terribly busy nowadays, of course."

"I think he's too busy."

"Why? He looks quite fit."

"I mean, he's losing all his other interests."

"Well, my dear, he's no time for them. He's doing awfully well. Someone in the City told Mark that they didn't know what Franklin's would do without him."

"But it leaves him no time for anything else."

"Why should it? If a man wants to get on nowadays he's got to put his back into it. There's no room for slackers."

"I suppose not."

The next week Jenifer received a note from her stepmother, saying that they were setting out for Switzerland the next day. It was a note so obviously hostile in tone that it roused Jenifer's fighting instinct, making her again determine not to allow herself to be ousted from her father's life. When he came home she would ignore his wife's dislike and visit him regularly. But his affairs and Lorna's and her uneasiness about Adrian, with whom she could not get into touch, threw a depression over her spirit that she found it impossible to shake off, and she was glad to receive an invitation to stay the next week-end with Sylvia and Peter in Somerset.

She had visited them several times and had been struck by the atmosphere of peace and happiness that surrounded their home. They seemed the ideally happy married couple. Sylvia's radiant serenity and her husband's quiet devotion to her reminded Jenifer of her own parents, though there was not that hampering lack of money that had marred slightly the harmony of her own home life. They lived in a fifteenth-century farmhouse, which had been carefully modernised. Diamond-pane windows gave on to smooth green lawns, with old-fashioned herbaceous borders, and a rose garden. Beyond the garden was an orchard—long straight lines of apple trees, their gnarled trunks whitened, their branches forming a roof overhead. The peace and beauty of it seemed to enclose Sylvia in a warm happy world, outside which she never wanted to stray. She tended her garden and her home and had now no interests that were not her husband's. In the little Chelsea flat she had seemed a townswoman to her finger-tips, smart, restless, sophisticated, always superlatively good company. She dressed now in shabby tweeds and was learning to shoot and fish with her husband. She looked back on the old days as a dim uneasy dream. She was even growing rather plump.

"Isn't it dreadful?" she said to Jenifer. "I find that I'm horribly early Victorian, though I never even suspected it till I married Peter. I never want to do anything that he doesn't want to do. He hates the town. He only stayed in it because I was there. And I find that I hate the town now, too. I know I've grown terribly dull, and I don't even care. The old gang have stopped coming down to see me. They say I'm past hope. I *am* dull, you know. Happiness does make you dull. I never want to see a play or read a latest book again. And all the old jokes seem so childish and pointless. Bobby's terribly fed up about it. He says I might just as well have died. He was staying here last month. He came for a week, but he left after three days. He said he couldn't stand any more of it. He said he'd never stayed in a house before where you couldn't even get a cocktail. And he said there was nothing to do in the evenings. There isn't, of course. I suppose we could get up dances and parties and have people in, but we just can't be bothered. When he went he said, 'My poor girl! What a mess you've made of your life!'"

Jenifer laughed, then, suddenly becoming serious, told her how worried she was about her father. They were in Sylvia's bedroom, sitting on the broad window-seat and looking out over the garden.

"It may not be so bad," Sylvia reassured her. "If she really loves him, that may teach her how not to irritate him. He may even come to love her. In any case, Jenifer, don't let her drive you away from him."

In the light of Sylvia's gentle sympathy the nightmare quality that had informed all Jenifer's thoughts since her visit home and that Lorna's casual reassurances had only deepened, vanished.

"Yes," she agreed, "it might be all right, after all." Sylvia drew a work-basket towards her and took up some knitting.

239

"Did Bobby tell you I was going to have a baby?"

"No. I haven't seen him since he was here. Are you glad, Sylvia?"

Sylvia smiled.

"So terribly glad. Sometimes I can hardly believe it. I feel almost frightened, as if I'd no right to be so happy. . ."

Jenifer found Peter difficult to talk to, but somehow that did not matter, because one did not feel that there was any necessity to talk to him. Sylvia and he would sit silent for long stretches, which seemed strange when one remembered the old Sylvia with her restlessness and clever superficial chatter. So different were the two men that Jenifer could well understand Bobby's dislike of his brother-in-law. She felt that it would take a long time to get to know Peter, but she was conscious always of his rock-like dependability and integrity, and of that gentleness and kindliness that underlay his brusqueness of manner.

After dinner they sat in the library, and Peter read aloud, while Sylvia knitted.

"You don't mind, do you, darling?" said Sylvia apologetically to Jenifer. "We always do it when we're alone. It's horribly Victorian, and we simply daren't do it when Bobby's here, but we both like it."

Peter had a pleasant voice, and Jenifer listened idly, without hearing the words, watching Sylvia's brown head bent so placidly over her work. The atmosphere of enclosed peace, of deep calm happiness, was so potent that it filled her with a sudden envy. It was what at the bottom of her heart she had always wanted, probably what every woman wanted. Sylvia's old friends sneered at her, but there was envy in their sneers.

When she went Sylvia clung to her in sudden affection.

"Jennie, I know I'm losing touch with all the old crowd, and I don't care. I'd rather lose touch with them than not, but I don't want to lose touch with you. Do come here often, though it's so dull."

A sudden lump rose in Jenifer's throat. The untroubled days of their girlhood friendship seemed so far away.

"Of course I will. It will be lovely to come here when I feel I want peace. One gets so little ordinarily. I think that peace—the sort that you and Peter have got—is the rarest thing in the world."

They both saw her off at the station, and Jenifer's last glimpse was of the two of them standing together, Peter's bulk towering protectively over Sylvia's slight frame.

Chapter Twenty-Two

That evening, just as Jenifer was going to ring up Laurence to ask if he had heard anything of Adrian, Adrian himself walked into the flat. He looked flushed and excited.

"*Adrian!*" said Jenifer, putting back the receiver. "Where *have* you been all this time?"

"I've been on my honeymoon," he said. "I was married a month ago."

"You——" she stopped in amazement. "Why on *earth* didn't you tell us?"

He smiled. She noticed that he looked older, more poised, even a little stouter.

"Evie didn't want me to. She had an idea that it would spoil things if people knew. She wanted us to have our honeymoon before we told anyone."

"Evie? . . . Who is she, Adrian?"

"Mrs Holroyd's niece."

"Oh."

Consternation showed in voice and expression. He started forward eagerly.

"Jenifer, she's—she's lovely. You've no idea how sweet she is. I've never been so happy in all my life. She's—wonderful."

She smiled at him, touched by his eager boyish happiness, trying to hide from him the sinking of her heart.

"Why didn't you bring her with you?"

"I did. She's outside. She said she wouldn't come in till I'd told you."

Jenifer went to the door and flung it open. A girl stood at the end of the passage, looking out of the window . . . Well, at any rate, she wasn't listening at the keyhole . . .

She turned as the door opened, and Jenifer recognised the slovenly girl whom she had seen once or twice at Adrian's rooms. Only she didn't look slovenly now. She had obviously taken great pains with her appearance, though the results were not wholly successful. Her clothes were expensive, but just wrong somehow—the stockings the wrong shade for the shoes, a flimsy garden party hat worn with a tailored costume, too many necklaces, flashy earrings, elaborate but badly fitting gloves. She was certainly pretty enough, in a plump pallid fashion that held a peculiar charm of its own, with thick white flawless skin, full red lips, firm rounded body. . . Ugly ankles, and ugly hands, probably, beneath the badly fitting gloves, but no one could deny her sensual appeal.

For a few moments the two women stood looking at each other in silence, then Jenifer held out her hands.

"Oh, my dear," she said, "I'd no idea you were outside till Adrian told me. Do come in."

The girl entered the little sitting-room and glanced around her, perfectly at her ease.

"I told him he'd better get it over by himself," she said. "I thought he'd be able to tell you better if I wasn't there, like."

Then she smiled at Adrian, a reassuring protective smile that raised Jenifer's drooping spirits. There was no mistaking Adrian's happiness or the girl's love for him. She looked stupid, but there was beneath her stupidity a suggestion of placidity and motherliness. Jenifer remembered Adrian's lack of balance, his old tendency to hysteria and nerves, and it occurred to her that he might be happier with a woman like this—placid, motherly, uncritical—than with a woman of his own class or type. Anyway, the thing was done. She could only hope for the best.

She kissed the girl impulsively. "I do so hope you'll be happy," she said.

The girl laughed—a deep, good-humoured laugh.

"I reckon we shall," she said. "I'm not his class, of course, but

I love him all right. I've told him he mustn't expect too much of me, or start trying to change me."

"She's perfect as she is," burst out Adrian. "I wouldn't have her an atom different. She's—wonderful."

Evie laughed again, and her eyes rested on him again with that deep brooding tenderness.

"He's just like a little boy, isn't he?" she said to Jenifer. "But, then, most men are."

She went over to the window and stood there, looking down at the busy street below.

"My!" she said. "It's ever so high up, isn't it? Don't those gentlemen down there look tiny!"

"It's cheaper up here," said Jenifer, "and I like the view."

"That's right," agreed Evie. "Adrian's ever so fond of views, too. I like them all right myself. There was a lovely view in a place that I once went to on a charabanc. I've forgotten its name, but it was a waterfall, and it was all lit up with coloured lights. It looked a treat."

Jenifer glanced at Adrian, but it was obvious that he hardly heard the words. His eyes were fixed on the full red lips and soft white skin. She could have talked the most utter drivel in the vilest Cockney, and she would still have been perfect in his eyes. He was bemused, intoxicated, by love for her.

"You'll stay and have some tea, won't you?"

"I don't mind," said Evie.

"What about you, Adrian?"

"Yes, of course. We'd love to, thanks, Jenifer," said Adrian. "Let me help you off with your coat, dear."

He drew off her coat, straightening the collar of her lace blouse with little lover-like touches. Jenifer's heart contracted as she watched him. There was something so defenceless about anyone as deeply in love, as rapturously happy, as that. It wasn't the calm deep happiness that encompassed Sylvia and Peter. It was tumultuous, ecstatic, unbalanced, like all Adrian's emotions.

During tea Evie was silent, while Adrian and Jenifer discussed family news.

"Poor old boy!" said Adrian. "What on earth made him do it? Do you remember how she used to pull and push us about and shout 'Silence!' at us? . . . *Silence!*" He imitated Miss Marchant's thin harsh voice, and they all laughed. "I'm glad Lorna and Mark are happy, anyway," he went on, smiling across at his wife. "Two happy marriages in a family isn't a bad average for these days."

André arrived soon after they had gone. He wore, as ever, a look of old-fashioned elegance—tall, thin, erect, perfectly tailored, meticulously groomed, his beard trimmed to an exact point, his trousers precisely creased. One felt that he should be wearing lavender kid gloves instead of the chamois ones that modern fashion prescribed. He had grown much thinner lately, and there was something waxlike in the texture of his colourless face.

"Well, my little Jenifer," he said, taking his seat on the upright chair that he always preferred to her easy ones, "and how are you feeling?"

"Depressed," she said. "All the family's marrying the wrong people. Adrian's married his landlady's niece, and Father's married Miss Marchant."

"Miss Marchant? . . . Ah, of course, the mother's help. Why has he married her?"

"Because she wanted him to."

"They may be very happy."

"They can't be. Miracles don't happen."

"But they do, my child. They happen all round us every day. I always smile when I hear people say 'The age of miracles is past.' Growth itself is a miracle." He had forgotten Miss Marchant and her husband, and was off on one of the abstract dissertations that he loved. "The growth of the acorn into the oak tree, the growth of a microscopic cell into a human being, is a miracle. Electricity, magnetism, wireless—they are all miracles. We give them names and think that we have explained them, but they are still miracles—stupendous, unexplained, inexplicable. We swagger about among the forces of nature, thinking that we understand them simply because we have given names to them. We should walk more humbly than we do, surrounded by miracles on all sides."

Jenifer gazed into the distance, her chin cupped in her hand.

"Sometimes I wonder whether Mother knows what's happening to us . . . Do you believe in a life after death, André?"

"I believe in the survival of the soul," he said slowly, "I am not a religious man, but I know that there is no such thing as annihilation in the scheme of the universe. It is impossible to destroy anything. You can reduce it to its component parts, but you cannot destroy it. Therefore the soul, too, must be indestructible."

"Yes, I believe that . . . but I hope the dead don't know what's happening to us. I should hate Mother to know about Father's marriage and Adrian's . . . Do you remember Sylvia Lenham? I've just been staying with her. She married last year. She really is happy."

He smiled at her affectionately.

"And you, Jennie . . . when will you be getting married?"

She looked away. The thought of sex in relation to herself still filled her with a strange revulsion. And still she fought against the revulsion, looking upon it as a heritage of prudery from Aunt Lena, seeing herself sometimes growing more and more like Aunt Lena, even in manner and appearance.

"I don't think I ever shall," she said slowly. "Don't you think that there are women who have a sort of vocation to be unmarried, who *can't* share themselves with anyone, who're only really themselves when they're alone?"

He shrugged.

"I have never met such women, my dear."

She went on earnestly, as if speaking to herself.

"People talk such nonsense about sex inhibition and the sex-starved woman. Sex isn't as important as people pretend it is. Lots and lots of women are happy and whole without it. After all, there are hundreds of instincts as strong as sex that the unmarried woman can satisfy and the married woman can't. The unmarried woman has her freedom and the chance of self-development. I believe that nowadays the average married woman is far more

246

nerve-ridden and starved of self-expression than the average unmarried woman. Friendship is a much more real and lasting thing than love—than sexual love, I mean. I know that there *are* happy marriages—my mother's was one, and Sylvia's is another— but they're not very common."

He smiled at her.

"I've never heard you as an orator before, my little Jennie. They would have called you a New Woman when I was young. But wait till you fall in love."

"I don't think I ever shall fall in love," she replied. "I think I'm cold-blooded. What people call undersexed, nowadays."

"Have you never been in love?"

"Yes, twice. Once with a little boy when I was a little girl. Is that horrid? But I didn't know I was in love at the time. I met him at Westonlea, and I broke my heart when we didn't go back the next year."

She was silent for a few moments, and in the silence the memory of Derek suddenly became clear. She saw again the slim childish figure, the tender nape where small shining curls clustered, the sensitive beautiful lips . . . He would be grown up now, only a year younger than she was. She wondered where he was and what he was doing . . .

"Then again with a man who was old enough to be my father, but I didn't know that I was in love with him at the time, either."

Again memories surged back over her, and she saw Geoffrey Lenham standing in the moon-flooded corridor, furtively closing a bedroom door.

She rose from her seat, and went on rather unsteadily. "I don't think I ever shall be in love again. I hope I shan't, anyway. I think I'm rather like Aunt Lena. She never had any use for men, you know."

He looked at her in silence for a moment, then said:

"These affairs of your father and Adrian have upset you. Why not go away for a little change?"

"Oh, don't be like ordinary people. They always tell you to go away for a little change when anything worries you, as if that were a cure for the worry. If you're really worried, if doesn't matter where you go. The worry goes with you."

"I know.

> 'Coelum non animum mutant
> Qui trans mare currunt.'

But your generation wasn't brought up on the classics, was it? Still—you know the 'black horseman' as well as any generation before you."

In the days that followed she tried to forget her worries in her work, but the story that she was writing seemed to have lost all its vitality. It crept along laboriously like something wounded. She received several post-cards from her father from various addresses in Switzerland, telling her nothing but where they were staying and what sort of weather they were having. Then came a letter from her stepmother, written on a note of hysterical triumph, informing her that she was going to have a child.

Laurence happened to come to see her the day she received it. She told him the news, but he did not seem particularly concerned by it or even interested in it. He was in unusually good spirits, and straddled on the hearthrug, rubbing his hands (a new gesture that he had just acquired), and describing to her in detail the "deals" that he had recently brought off. She had never before seen him so excited. Sums of money tripped lightly and continuously off his tongue. Suddenly she could bear it no longer.

"Can't you talk about *anything* but money, Laurence?" she snapped.

He stared at her in amazement. She was usually so quiet and sympathetic and self-contained. He had never before heard that note of exasperation in her voice.

His good-humour was not dispersed, however. He put his hands into his pockets and laughed.

"Well, is there anything more interesting to talk about? I rather think you're going to have a very rich man for a brother, Jennie, before I've finished. How will you like that?"

"Not at all," she said curtly. "I hate rich people. I once read somewhere—I've forgotten where—that if you look very closely at a rich man you see the little hole where his soul should be . . . I'm sorry, Laurie. I didn't mean that."

But he was hurt now, and refused to be mollified. He took his leave almost at once, very stiffly.

This episode increased her depression so much that she found it impossible to go on with her work at all. She put the unfinished manuscript away in a drawer and began to take long aimless walks, tramping for miles over the hard London pavements, coming home tired out but no more cheerful.

The family tie had always been a particularly strong one in her case. She had loved her family devotedly, and now she seemed to be losing touch with them all. Her father and Adrian were cut off from her by marriages in which she could see no chance of happiness, Lorna was becoming more and more enclosed by her own complacency, Laurence growing so alien to her that she could not restrain her exasperation with him . . . She was glad when Bobby came in to see her, as usual unheralded and unexpected. She had not heard of him for some weeks and had thought that he was abroad.

"Cheer me up, Bobby," she said. "I'm completely down."

"Why, my child?" he said, sitting on her window-seat and drawing his feet up on to the cushion. "You're very snug and cosy in here. What's gone wrong with you?"

"I don't know . . . All the family seems to be breaking up."

"That's what families are made for, my sweet. I think there's no more revolting sight than an adult family clinging together and going about in a sort of gang. The very animals have more sense. They kick the young ones out as soon as they can fend for themselves, and either cut them dead or have a good old scrap with them whenever they happen to meet them afterwards. Far better than humans with their sob stuff about 'family duty' and 'family devotion'—parents hanging like a dead-weight round their children's necks, children swarming round dear Aunt Emily for the sake of the bit of money they think she's got put away."

"Bobby, I'm sure you don't *really* feel like that . . ."

"I do, Honestly. I've not seen the old man for two years, and I don't care if I never see him again. As for Sylvia, I've paid her my last visit. I'm sorry for the poor girl, mind you, but I've finished with her. She can stew in her own juice now."

"I don't know why you should be sorry for Sylvia. She's the only happy person I know."

"My dear girl, that's just why I *am* sorry for her. That's the tragedy of it. She *oughtn't* to be happy. You might say a jellyfish is happy, but it's no credit to it. It's just what's wrong with it. It oughtn't to be happy. The fact that it's happy is the reason why it remains a jellyfish. Sylvia is growing more and more like a jellyfish every time I see her. Enclosed in a sort of jelly of smugness——"

"Bobby, she *isn't* smug."

"Perhaps that's the wrong word. Contentment, shall we say? Contentment's a horrible state, you know. Contentment and self-satisfaction and complacency and—yes, smugness. They all mean the same thing. She just sits about, thinking how lovely it all is and how wonderful that he-ass Peter is and how wonderful the brat's going to be, and pitying all the rest of the world. It's a revolting state. It makes me long to hear that something awful's happened to her—that Peter's robbed a bank or gone off with the housemaid, or that she's been raped by the under-gardener or—anything to smash up the jelly."

"You're jealous."

"I suppose I am, in a way. It's the sort of romantic dream of one's future that one used to have in one's early teens, but it belongs definitely to the world of adolescent dreams and ought to stay there . . . It's almost obscene to find it knocking about in real life."

"Aren't you happy, Bobby?"

"I don't think so. I hope not. I'd hate to think I was . . . I suppose that it rather depends what you mean by happiness. If it's anything static, then I don't want it. I hate anything static—like contentment. I have a good time and I enjoy life, but I don't think that's what most people mean by happiness. I think that most people mean sitting down and feeling smug about oneself and everything around one. I don't want that."

She looked at his face. Despite the perennial boyishness of the blunt nose and impudent mouth, he looked older than his years. There were lines round his mouth and faint pouches beneath his eyes.

"Let's stop being metaphysical, Bobby," she said. "Tell me what you've been doing with yourself while you've been away."

He had been staying in Mentone, and he launched into a high-spirited description of some of the people he had met there. He had, as usual, "collected" a number of oddities, and he brought them out one by one with his old inimitable mimicry. As she listened, something of his carefree light-heartedness communicated itself to her. After all, there was nothing really to worry about. Her father's marriage might turn out well, so might Adrian's. Lorna . . . Laurence . . . She couldn't expect them to stay just as she wanted them. Probably she was just as disappointing to them as they were to her.

Bobby was describing an elderly spinster whose room was just opposite his at his hotel, enacting her cautious opening of her bedroom door, her nervous, rabbit-like dash for the bathroom. He pursed his mouth and screwed up his eyes to represent her short-sighted peering.

"Oh, don't, Bobby," laughed Jenifer. "It's so exactly what I'm going to be like in fifteen years time. I don't believe you really meet these people, anyway. You just make them up."

"On my honour, I don't. I just keep my eyes open. I study human nature. Oh, and I met another specimen. A Frenchman who'd got all the English he knew out of Scott's novels, and he scattered all his remarks with 'Be-shrew me,' or 'By my faith,' and addressed me as 'sirrah,' or 'fair sir.' He told me that the concierge of his apartments was 'a malapert knave,' and when he met an English girl at a dance he always asked her to 'tread a measure' with him."

"Bobby, how priceless! I don't believe it for a moment, but it makes a lovely tale."

He came over to her suddenly and sat on the arm of her chair.

"I like you, Jennie," he said, looking down at her. "I like your funny crooked mouth and the way your hair curls and the way you still look just like a little girl, somehow. Everyone else one knew when one was a child seems to have grown up except you."

She smiled at him.

"I like you too, Bobby . . ."

He went across to the window and stood there, looking out.

"Enough to come away for a week-end with me?" he said, without turning round.

She was silent for some moments: After all, why not? she thought. It would break down the exaggerated fear of sex that had become an obsession with her, making her shrink even from casual friendship with men, that was like a black river surrounding her. She'd swim through it and start fresh on the other side. It would mean nothing to Bobby, so it need mean nothing to her.

"Very well . . . When?"

"Next week-end?"

"All right."

Chapter Twenty-Three

To Jenifer there was a curious quality of unreality about the next week. She seemed to be living in a dream, or, rather, to be taking part in a play, performing mechanical actions, repeating words she had learnt by heart.

She did not deliberate at all about her promise to Bobby. It had ceased to be something over which she had control. It had become fated, inevitable.

Laurence rang her up on the Tuesday and asked her to go to a concert with him. He had been worried by their disagreement, and the concert was an overture of peace.

When he took her out to supper afterwards, he did not once mention his business, but talked chiefly of old times and their childhood. He asked her if she ever saw anything of Bobby Lenham nowadays, and she wondered what he would say if she told him that she was going to spend the next week-end with him. He was old-fashioned and would probably consider that Bobby was "seducing" her, and want to go for him with a horsewhip in the approved fashion of melodrama.

"Let's try and go away together again some time—shall we?—" he said, "if I can manage to get off. The old bicycle tour again, but with a car instead of the bicycles."

His obvious desire to win back her friendship, to keep in abeyance the side of him that had irritated her, would have moved her deeply at any other time, but in her new dream-like state of detachment she hardly noticed it. She seemed to be separated from him and everything around her by an immeasurable gulf.

Before he left her he insisted on giving her five pounds.

"Take a holiday on it or get yourself something nice," he said. "I know I forgot your birthday. I simply can't remember them."

The next afternoon Lorna arrived at the flat. She wore a new and obviously expensive costume with an elaborate set of dark furs, and looked radiantly lovely—a groomed and polished loveliness with a hint now of artificiality in it.

"I've only popped in for a second, darling," she said, as she sank down into an armchair and drew off her gloves. "I'm dying for a cup of tea."

"Are you up shopping?" said Jenifer, putting the kettle on the little gas-ring.

"Shopping and looking for a flat," said Lorna serenely.

"A flat?" said Jenifer in surprise.

"Yes, darling. Didn't you know? We're moving into a flat. Somewhere quite central in London. We shall move as soon as we find it."

"But, Lorna, I thought you'd decided to stay in Dulwich. You had when I was over there last."

Lorna wrinkled her smooth white brows.

"Had we? I quite forget. I know that I stood it as long as I could."

"But it's such a dear little house," protested Jenifer.

"Darling, I'm not strong enough to go on with housekeeping. I've been terribly nervy lately, and the doctor told Mark that I simply must give it up and go into a service flat."

Jenifer looked at her in silence. Her white and golden beauty radiated health.

"Of course," she went on somewhat hastily, "as far as I'm concerned, I'd have stuck it till I dropped. It's really for Mark's sake that I want to move. He finds the journey out from Town too much."

"He didn't seem to," said Jenifer, dryly.

"My dear Jenifer, what's the matter with you today?" said Lorna with calm superiority. "The doctor told me that a journey out to the suburbs was far too much for any man at the end of a long day's work, and I see no reason for disbelieving him. I'm awfully fond of the little house, but I'm not quite selfish enough to insist on living here when a doctor tells me that it's bad for my husband's health."

Jenifer thought that Lorna seemed rather confused as to whether the move was to be made on her own account or on Mark's. But it didn't really matter. She'd made up her mind, and that was all there was to it. She had only to find an accommodating doctor, and women as lovely as Lorna can always find accommodating doctors.

"Oh, well . . ." said Jenifer with a shrug. "I suppose it's all settled."

"*Quite* settled," said Lorna, "except, of course, for finding the flat, and I don't think I shall have much difficulty in that. Mark's had a rise, so we needn't consider expense quite so much . . . And what have you been doing with yourself, my dear? Seen anything of the family lately?"

"I saw Laurence on Tuesday. And I heard from Flora. She's going to have a baby."

"Poor thing! Well, I suppose she knows what she's about . . . Adrian brought his wife round the other evening."

"What did you think of her?"

"*Hopeless*, my dear, isn't she? What on earth was he thinking of? I felt simply *furious*, Jenifer. They came without writing or ringing up just the night we'd got the Kelways in. Did you meet the Kelways when you were over? Well, they're the only people I've met in Dulwich whom I want to keep up with. They're rolling and know everyone and have just taken a marvellous flat in Sloane Street. I explained to Mrs Kelway afterwards, and said that, of course, I wasn't going to have anything to do with the woman socially. I don't want her to think that she's liable to run into the creature whenever she comes to see me . . . And I gave Adrian a hint not to come again without letting me know. I don't want to be unkind, and, of course, I'm quite willing to let them visit me if they want to, but Adrian must understand that I can't introduce her to my friends."

Jenifer thought rather sorrowfully of the old childish friendship between the two.

"Poor Adrian!" she said.

Lorna spread out white manicured hands.

"My dear, he's been a fool, and he's got to pay for it. He's brought it on his own head. I've no patience with men who do that sort of thing. I suppose he got the girl into trouble, and then she and that dreadful aunt of hers between them made him marry her. He was a fool to do it. He could easily have got out of it. In any case the baby—I presume there *is* a baby—probably isn't his. You know what girls of that class are." She made a little gesture as if dismissing a distasteful subject, and went on: "How do you like my hat, Jennie? I got it from a little French milliner in—well, I won't tell you, because I want to keep her to myself. She's so marvellously cheap. It's a copy of a model, but you'd never dream it was only a copy, would you? I *am* so looking forward to living in London and being in the middle of things. The Kelways are going to introduce me to lots of their friends as soon as we're settled." She glowed with energy and enthusiasm, as if a whole new world were opening out before her. She was a general arranging her forces for a new and inevitably successful campaign. "Oh, I'm so sick of that wretched little suburb. It will be heavenly to get out of it . . . Jennie, darling, I'll introduce you to Mrs Kelway if you like." She looked at Jenifer, eyes narrowed and head on one side. "I think I'll take you in hand first and dress you properly. There's nothing really wrong with you, darling, but you do dress rather as if you still lived in the country. Tweeds and shirt blouses and that sort of thing. However, I'll change all that when I'm living in Town, and I'll introduce you to some really nice people."

"I haven't time for really nice people," objected Jenifer. "And I'm not awfully good at them, either. I'd much rather just jog along with my work and the friends I've got."

Lorna laughed gaily.

"Those ghastly frumps one runs into here? Oh, wait till I come to London and take you in hand."

Already she was the sophisticated London lady patronising the country cousin . . .

*

Jenifer had heard nothing from Bobby since the day when she had so impulsively accepted his invitation. She knew that he was quite capable of forgetting the whole affair. He might even have changed his mind. At that thought she felt first relief, then disappointment. She'd strung herself up to go through with it, and she wanted to go through with it. She still had the conviction that she would emerge from the experience saner, less self-conscious, and with a more normal outlook upon sex. It would have lost its mystery and therefore its importance.

But on Friday morning he rang her up.

"You've not forgotten about the week-end, Jennie?"

"No."

"Can you be ready at three o'clock?"

"Yes."

"Right. I'll come and fetch you, then. Goodbye."

"Goodbye."

He arrived punctually at three, and they set off by the Thames valley, Bobby driving at his usual break-neck pace. It was a perfect midsummer day. The hedges were bright with dog-roses, the roadside with meadowsweet, the cottage gardens with roses and Canterbury bells, sweet-william and madonna lilies. The climbing roses seemed weighed down by their weight of bloom. In the fields cows stood in the lush green grass beneath the thick foliage of trees whose topmost branches stirred faintly in an imperceptible breeze. Above was a cloudless blue sky.

Bobby's manner was so casual that Jenifer could hardly believe the expedition to be anything more than one of the country drives they occasionally took together during the spring and summer.

"Isn't it a heavenly day?" she said.

He laughed.

"Of course it is. What did you expect?"

"I hate the end of June, really," she went on. "It's lovely, but somehow it's the beginning of the end. The birds have stopped singing, and you know that soon everything will be looking dusty and tired, and winter will be in sight."

"And why not?" he laughed. "Don't be so morbid, my child.

257

What's wrong with the winter? Think of toasted muffins and roasted chestnuts and Father Christmas and all the rest of it. Don't just think of the fog."

"Oh, but I like the fog. It seems a sort of magic spell over the world. I always have the feeling that *anything* might happen in a fog. I'd never be surprised to see a witch step out of it and give me three wishes."

They were entering the Cotswold district now, and she was rather sorry for that. The Cotswolds always reminded her of that cycling holiday with Laurence that seemed in her memories to mark the end of the carefree days of her childhood.

He pulled up at a cottage gate, where a notice, "Teas," was painted askew on a wooden board.

"You get a most delicious tea in the orchard here," he said. "Everything home-made. Come on."

There were battered wooden tables and rickety chairs in the orchard under the reddening apples, and a rosy-faced young woman in a blue print dress spread a spotless check cloth and brought out home-made bread and butter, fresh crisp lettuce, a dish of newly gathered raspberries, and a jug of yellow cream.

"There!" said Bobby. "Isn't that a feast for the gods? I knew you hated little blue-and-orange wayside cafes, full of stale cakes and arts and crafts."

"It's perfect," she said, drawing a deep breath.

Sunshine fell in shafts through the leaves, dappling the grass. At the further end of the orchard a litter of small white pigs nozzled about under the trees.

Bobby had made no attempt at love-making on the way down. His manner was still so ordinary that only the memory of her suitcase on the back seat proved to her that she was really going away with him.

She thrust the thought from her and gave herself up to the enjoyment of the moment, the peace and quiet of the sun-chequered orchard, and the delicious country tea. A white duck came waddling across the grass . . . then a hen, anxious and fussy, followed by a train of yellow chicks. A cock crowed in the distance, and a chaffinch, perched on a branch just above their heads, broke suddenly into belated song. A slumbrous content stole over Jenifer's spirit, her senses drowsed in the midsummer heat. Everything in life worth having seemed to be crystallised into this perfect moment. Bobby was silent. He had always had an uncanny power of sensing her moods.

At last he rose. "Well . . . how about getting on?"

He paid the woman, and they went slowly through the little garden, sweet with stocks and mignonette and pansies. The pansies seemed to Jenifer to look after her with sad reproachful faces as she went through the gate.

She could tell that Bobby was in excellent spirits from the way he drove, taking hair-breadth risks, laughing aloud as he avoided disaster by a fraction of an inch. The road led through a wood, and at a point where the trees met overhead, making a sort of tunnel, he stopped the car, and helped her out.

"Let's stay here for a bit," he said. "Just round the bend of that path you'd think you were thousands of miles from anywhere."

He took a rug from the car, and they went down a path that wound through the trees.

"Here it is!" he said.

The moss-covered roots of a huge beech tree formed a natural seat, and by it ran a little stream bordered with ferns. Overhead the beech leaves were like brimming cups from which the light spilled down upon the ground. On all sides, as far as they could see, rose the smooth grey-green trunks. Between them were the little ghost-like stalks of seeded bluebells.

Jenifer drew in her breath.

"How heavenly it must be in bluebell time!" she said.

He spread out the rug for her to sit on, then lay outstretched at her feet, his hands behind his head, gazing up at the luminous roof above them.

"Well," he said, "mightn't one be in the heart of a primeval forest? I'm sure this hasn't changed for thousands of years. One could almost expect to see a dinosaurus come loping round the corner any minute."

"Dinosauruses didn't lope."

"How do you know?"

He sat up, took a book out of his pocket, and opened it at random.

"I found this yesterday," he said, "so I brought it along. I knew you'd love it . . ."

He began to read aloud in his clear pleasant voice. It was a parody of a popular author whom they both disliked. The pretentiousness of the style, the inanity of the dialogue, was ludicrously parodied, and Jenifer forgot everything else in her amusement.

Suddenly Bobby shut it up and put it back into his pocket.

"Isn't it priceless?" he said. "But a little of a parody goes a long way, doesn't it? . . . I'm thinking of going abroad again next month, Jennie."

"Where?"

"Dunno. Just here and there. A little flutter at a casino or two, probably, just to break the monotony of life."

"Bobby, I wish you'd get some sort of work. I'm sure you'd be happier."

"Your knowledge of human nature is rudimentary, my dear. Despite the moralists, work does not necessarily entail happiness. There can even be, I believe, such a thing as an unhappy bank clerk."

"I know, but, Bobby, you're so restless, so unanchored. You just—drift along. I wish you would settle down to something . . ." She stopped short and flushed. "I'm sorry. I've no business to preach to you."

He moved his position and laid his head on her lap.

"Yes, go on," he said dreamily. "I like it. You're essentially the type of woman whom one likes to preach to one. Have you read *Oblomov*?"

"No."

"It's quite worth reading. Someone in it says that there are two types of women whom men love. They want the one type to ruin them and the other type to save them. You're the sort one wants to save one."

"I'm not doing much to save you now."

He laughed his mischievous, slightly malicious laugh.

"How do you know? The workings of Providence are supposed to be inscrutable . . . Come along." He got up and swung her to her feet. "We must be wending. It's getting dark."

They returned to the car, and he drove on through the gathering dusk. Suddenly he slowed down, and, taking something from his pocket, handed it to her.

"Put that on," he said. "We're nearly there."

It was a wedding ring.

She took it and looked at it in silence, and, as she looked, there came to her a sudden vision of other women who must have worn it—flashy women, overdressed and meretricious. Despite his charm and understanding, there was nothing fastidious about Bobby. She remembered Sylvia's once saying, "There's a low streak in Bobby that there never was in Father. He has the most appalling women." She saw coarse, over-vermilioned nails. She seemed to catch a breath of cheap perfume.

"I suppose—lots of other people have worn it?" she said slowly.

"Well . . ." He shrugged, and left the sentence unfinished.

She said nothing, and after a bit he turned to her.

"What's the matter?"

"I'm sorry," she said breathlessly. "I—I can't put it on."

He stopped the car and looked at her in bewilderment.

"Why not?" he said. "Surely it's not too small, or anything?"

He took it in his hand and made as if to put it on for her. She drew back with a sharp movement of recoil. She was taut and trembling, and her face was colourless.

"No!"

"What on earth's the matter, Jenifer?"

"I can't wear it. I'm sorry."

Her voice was still breathless and unsteady.

"But, my dear girl," he said patiently, "you surely realised you'd have to wear a wedding ring. The place where I've booked the room wouldn't take us in without it. What's your objection?"

"I can't explain. I just hadn't realised . . . I'd thought . . . I wouldn't have minded, somehow, if it had been a new one." '

He controlled his irritation with some difficulty.

"I simply can't see how it matters whether it's new or not. It's too late to get a new one in any case. We're miles away from a town, and you can't get a wedding ring at a village post office. All the shops are shut now, anyway." She looked at him unhappily. Her pallor gave her an oddly appealing air of childishness.

"I'm sorry, Bobby. I've been a fool. Let me just get out of the car and go back home by train."

"You can't do that. We're miles from a station . . . Is it just the ring?"

"Yes."

He looked at her helplessly.

"I simply can't make head or tail of it. It's not like you to back out of a thing at the last minute like this."

She was very near tears.

"I'm not backing out," she said in a choking voice. "It's just that I can't put that ring on. I'll go anywhere with you where I don't have to wear it."

"There isn't anywhere we can go unless you wear it. Not in this part of the world, anyway . . . Are you serious, Jennie?"

"Yes."

"You mean, you want to go back home?"

"Yes."

He turned the car, and they drove back to London in silence. There was a sort of paralysis over Jenifer's spirit. She felt neither relief nor disappointment—only a dull heavy indifference. She had, indeed, the same almost fated feeling that she had had over the whole affair. It had been inevitable that she should agree to go with him. Equally inevitable that she should not be able to wear the ring. She had had no choice from the beginning.

Bobby carried her suitcase up to her room. Then he spoke for the first time since they had set off homeward.

"Shall I stay here?"

She shook her head.

"No, not here."

"I suppose not . . . Well, will you come out with me? There are plenty of places in London where one needn't have a ring."

"No . . . it's over, Bobby. The whole thing. I couldn't—now. Ever. I'm terribly sorry about it. I can't explain."

"I'd better go, then." He looked down at her, noticing how white and drawn her face was. "And you'd better get to bed. You look fagged out."

"Good-night, Bobby. Do believe I'm sorry."

"I'm sorry, too." He stooped on an impulse and kissed her cheeks. "Good-night."

Then he went. She leant out of the window, listening, till the sound of the car had died away in the distance.

He had taken it well, but she knew that he would never forgive her.

Chapter Twenty-Four

At the sound of Adrian's key in the lock, Evie came out of the little sitting-room into the hall. He was just hanging up his hat on the hat-stand. She noticed that he looked tired and on edge, his mouth compressed, the lines from nose to mouth intensified.

His face did not lighten as his gaze fell on her coronet of steel wavers, her soiled cotton dress, and down-at-heel shoes. When preparing for any special occasion, Evie would go to unnecessary lengths in self-adornment, but the idea of being tidy, or even clean, in the house when visitors were not expected struck her as merely ludicrous.

"One of Adrian's little fads," she called it to herself, and indulged it good-humouredly when he was at home, but today she had not expected him back till later.

She lifted up her face to be kissed, and he kissed her quickly, without relaxing any of his nervous tension, then followed her into the sitting-room, where he sank into a chair and sat looking at her with a frown.

"Need your hair be in curlers at this time of the day, Evie?" he said. He spoke in a jerky, unnatural voice, as if holding his exasperation in check with an effort.

She was unperturbed by his criticism.

"Well, as Mr Blackburn was coming to dinner, I didn't see any sense in taking them out till I started getting ready, like."

"And why *do* you keep wearing that dress?" he went on. "You've got plenty of decent clothes."

"Well, Adrian, it's all right for indoors. I wouldn't go shopping in it, or anything like that. I'm only dirtying it out."

"Dirtying it out!" he repeated, with a short laugh. "My God!"

"But, Adrian," she persisted, "what's the use of putting on good things when I'm alone in the flat? It only messes them up."

She still spoke in a tone of half-amused tolerance, as if reasoning with a fractious child. She was wholly without vanity, and never took offence at his frequent criticisms of her appearance, but beneath her imperturbable good-humour was a streak of obstinacy, and, while giving a surface deference to his wishes, she clung with half-unconscious tenacity to the habits and outlook of her class.

He closed his eyes with a sigh of exasperation. She came over to him and sat on the arm of his chair, drawing her fingers across his forehead.

"Poor kid!" she said. "You're so hot and tired."

In her deep voice was the brooding tenderness that he never could resist, that made him again a child in its mother's arms. His tense figure relaxed, and he leant his head against her breast, then raised his lips to hers, abandoning himself to the warm voluptuousness of her kiss. The impact of a metal curler expelled him abruptly from his paradise.

He opened his eyes and looked at her, remembering with a pang his mother's exquisite personal daintiness, a daintiness whose standards she never relaxed, in no matter what domestic stress or crisis.

"Evie," he said. He spoke gently now, all his irritation gone. "Honestly, I *do* wish you'd try to be tidier. Even when you're by yourself. I mean"—he tried to find a reason that might appeal to her—"after all, *anyone* might call."

She laughed—her low sweet gurgle of laughter—and drew his head down on to her breast again.

"All right, kid, I will. Don't you fuss and worry any more."

He knew that she was promising him as she would have promised a peevish child anything it asked, laughing at him to herself for his "fads," loving him for them as one loves a child for its little foolishnesses. But he was too tired to argue any more. Her tenderness was banishing all his weariness and irritation. He lay in her arms, his lips pressed to hers, silent, motionless. Suddenly she sat up, smiling down at him from the arm of his chair.

"I'd better go now," she said, "and see how Mrs Mangle's getting on. And then I must have a good clean up against Mr Blackburn coming."

Evie cooked their meals generally, but a Mrs Mangle, who "did" some of the other flats, would always come in to "oblige" when necessary, and Adrian had insisted that she should cook the dinner tonight. He had not wanted Evie to appear at the table red-cheeked and with her hair coming down, as she probably would have done if she had cooked the meal. Any effect of grooming in Evie's appearance was hard to achieve and still harder to maintain. The slightest effort seemed to flush her cheeks, dishevel her dress, and bring her hair about her face.

He lay relaxed in his chair when she had left him, gazing into space.

He had been married to her now for six months. The first few months had been a dream, still blurred and hazy with rapture in his memory, so entirely had he surrendered himself to the rich passionate tenderness of her love. Her naïvety had delighted him; her Cockney speech and accent and habits had only made her more adorable in his eyes. Then very, very gradually they had begun to jar on him. It wasn't only that the impulse of his physical passion for her was waning. It was that his work was bringing him into contact with other artists, and for the first time in his life he was forming congenial friendships. His marriage, unsuitable though it was, had given him a new poise and maturity. He was now a man, able to meet other men on equal terms.

At first he brought them proudly to the flat, blind and deaf to everything about Evie but her beauty and the deep sensual notes of her voice.

His sensitiveness in regard to her once aroused, however, he suffered acutely. He was still in love with her, and her tenderness could still soothe away his irritation, but, besides the humilation she caused him before his friends, his eyes were becoming opened to the slovenliness and extravagance of her housekeeping.

He moved his head now with a jerky movement, wrinkling up his nose. He had noticed an unsavoury smell in the room ever since he had entered. He got up and began to wander about the room, trying to trace it to its source. He found it at last—a vase of dead flowers, the water sour and yellow. He took it up and, carrying it into the little kitchen, flung the flowers into the rubbish tin and emptied the water down the sink. Then he went back to the sitting-room and began to walk to and fro with quick nervous steps, stopping every now and then to tidy or straighten something, emptying an ash-tray that was full to overflowing of cigarette-ends and ash, taking out his handkerchief to wipe away a film of dust from the top of a bookcase, moving a cup and saucer from the mantelpiece, picking up toffee papers from the carpet, and putting out of sight a pair of soiled stockings of Evie's, which hung over a chair, and a paper-backed novelette, whose cover depicted in lurid colours a wedding dramatically interrupted by, presumably, someone who had a prior claim on the bridegroom's affections.

He was anxious that Horace Blackburn's visit should be a success. He had been introduced to him by an artist friend and had formed with him one of those swift nervous friendships—composed, on his side, chiefly of hero worship—which he so often formed with new acquaintances. Horace Blackburn had written several novels that had hit the taste of public and critics alike, and Adrian had been an admirer of his works long before he met him. He now considered Blackburn's opinions as the only possible opinions on any subject, his most trivial statements as charged with subtle intelligence and wit.

Horace Blackburn was, on his side, attracted by Adrian's youthful eagerness, his ardent hero-worship, and his whole highly-strung personality. He admired, too, the streak of genius that underlay his erratic, ill-disciplined talent. He had asked Adrian several times to his house, and Adrian had entertained him at his club, but this was the first time he had visited Adrian's flat. He had never met Evie before.

Adrian turned sharply as Evie entered the room. She had taken her hair out of curlers, and it stood in a frizzed halo around her head. He had persuaded her once or twice to go to a good hairdresser to have her hair set, but she had not cared for the result. She said that it was too flat. She liked the standing-out frizz that her own curlers effected, and in a way it suited her plump pale face, with the heavy skin, red mouth, and wide blue eyes. His eyes travelled down to her dress. It was a well-cut, well-fitting dress of black satin. He had chosen it himself, and it suited her, but she had "brightened it up" by a strip of tarnished silver embroidery that she had bought half-price at "the Sales," and had pinned a large posy of battered artificial flowers (also a trophy of "the Sales") on her shoulder. He had a suspicion that the highly decorative shoes she wore were wrong but did not know why. Her look of pleased expectancy, however, was so disarming that again his irritation faded.

"Well," she said, "I look a bit of all right now, don't I?"

"I shouldn't wear the flowers," he suggested gently.

She looked as disappointed as a child deprived of some treasured bit of finery.

"Oh, why?" she said. "I thought they set it off a treat. They were marked ten shillings and I got them for two and six-three."

Reluctantly she unpinned the flowers and took them into her bedroom.

"Now will I do?" she said when she returned, and this time there was a faint amusement in her voice. She was no longer a child deprived of a piece of finery. She was a mother smiling at her child's funny little ways. Fancy him not liking those flowers! Why, the dress had looked awful before she started "brightening it up." She'd never fancied black. It gave her the creeps. She couldn't think why anyone ever wore it that hadn't lost someone and needn't. But if he wanted her to, bless him, she would. The tenderness of her smile deepened. Just a little boy, he was—a funny sweet fussy little boy!

There was a ring at the front door, and Adrian went to admit the visitor.

Horace Blackburn was a tall handsome man with genial

unaffected manners and a good-humoured expression, behind which there was a hint of keenness, as if, while one part of him led on his friends to disclose their weaknesses, the other noted and analysed.

He entered, shook hands heartily with Adrian (who was feeling rather like a fourth-form boy receiving a home visit from a prefect), hung up his hat and coat, and followed his host into the little sitting-room.

"This is my wife," said Adrian.

Evie came forward with her wide friendly smile. Common she undeniably was, but there was no affectation about her. Instead, there was something of generosity, of warm rich motherliness, that showed in every movement of her graceful rounded figure.

The guest greeted her with a suggestion of respectful admiration that was his mechanical tribute to any hostess, but that nevertheless had the effect of breaking the ice and establishing at once cordial relations between the three of them.

"What a charming room!" he said, looking around as he took a glass of sherry from Adrian. "I think these new flats solve nearly all the problems of existence."

Evie smiled her all-embracing smile.

"That's right," she said.

Adrian threw her a quick glance of approval as she took her seat at the head of the table. Yes, despite the strip of tarnished embroidery and the over-frizzed hair, she looked beautiful and dignified. Her guest was treating her with graceful deference, turning to her frequently to include her in the conversation and ask her opinion. She spoke little, and when she did speak it seemed to Adrian that the commonness of her accent was redeemed by the deep musical tones of her voice. A mood of excited optimism had seized him. There was no reason why she should not become the sort of wife he could introduce to his friends without shame. So far he had had to keep his love for her and his friendships separate. He had loved her, and yet, when anyone else had been present, he had been ashamed of her . . .

Under the influence of the wine and his guest's appreciative friendliness, his volatile spirits soared up to a familiar exaltation.

This friendship was only the first of many. He seemed to have been admitted by it into the glorious freemasonry of artists. He saw his own work justified, acclaimed, saw himself taking his place by right in the world that seemed now to be opening to him. His mood of exaltation included Evie. She was beautiful and kind and good. Surely only a little training was necessary to eradicate the accent and mannerisms and outlook of her class. He had often heard of women who had raised themselves from Evie's class and who could now take their place in any society. He felt a sudden compunction. He had failed in his duty to her. He had hidden her away here, feeling ashamed of her commonness, but doing nothing to remedy it. In his new mood of optimism it seemed the simplest thing in the world to change Evie from what she was to the sort of girl one might meet at Lorna's or Jenifer's. There were, after all, only surface differences . . . Lorna or Jenifer would help. On the whole, perhaps, it would be advisable to ask Jenifer. Lorna's taste in clothes was better, but Jenifer was more patient. Lorna had been rather abrupt in her manner when he took Evie to see her. He had felt hurt and annoyed till he received a gracious little note from her, saying how sorry she was (she explained that she had had a bad headache that day), and hoping that he would come again to see her soon. He had handed the note to Evie triumphantly, for Evie had called Lorna "stuck-up" and "stand-offish."

"You see, Evie, she *is* awfully sweet, really," he had said.

Evie read it and smiled.

"She doesn't mention me," she had said.

"But it's naturally meant to include you. You'll come with me and see her again, won't you?"

Evie laughed.

"Oh no, I won't, and she knows I won't. She doesn't mean me to. But you go, Adrian. Honestly, I'd like you to."

He had been to see Lorna several times since then. She had been very sweet to him but had not mentioned Evie. However, as he pointed out to Evie, she was probably hurt because Evie had not accompanied him. Lorna, he explained, was very sensitive and affectionate . . .

He jerked himself out of his vague glamorous daydreams of an Evie perfect in manner and deportment to listen to what Blackburn and she were saying. They seemed to be getting on quite well together now.

"When they removed," Blackburn was saying, "they cleared a lot of old stuff from the attics and sent it to a sale-room, and it turned out that amongst it was a table two hundred years old and a chair three hundred years old."

"My!" said Evie. "They'd be lucky to get anything at all for old stuff like that, wouldn't they?"

He laughed as if she had said something witty, and she laughed because he did.

"I never did fancy second-hand things," she went on. "A friend of mine used to buy her clothes at a second-hand clothes place, but I used to say 'You never know who's had them.' Even her gentleman friend didn't like it. He used to say it made him feel there was someone watching them, like, wherever they went."

Again the guest's hearty laugh rang out. Evie was warming to his evident appreciation of her.

"I was once proper done over a second-hand mangle I tried to get for Auntie. It had a top and turned into a sort of table. Ever so nice, it was. The gentleman that sold it said it had only been used once or twice. Then, when they sent it, it wouldn't work at all. Between you and I, I don't think it was the one he'd showed me in the shop. Anyway, I went back and told him off proper, but it wasn't no good. Then Auntie, she went back and boxed his ears for him, an' he called a cop, an' she nearly got run in. It was one of the days the end of the world hadn't come an' she was feeling mad to start with. So she came back home an' boxed my ears an' we had a good set-to an' the mangle got broke an' we used it up as firewood."

Again the guest laughed heartily. Then he turned to Adrian. Adrian's mood of exaltation still hung about him. A strange sense of power possessed him. He was going to do wonderful things, to paint pictures that would make him famous throughout the world, to transform Evie from a guttersnipe into a *grande dame* . . . The sense of power seemed to sweep him up into a world where nothing was impossible. The author noted his bright eyes and flushed cheeks, and his curiosity about the menage increased. He began to talk books and pictures with Adrian, drawing out his opinions, showing flattering interest in them, talking with easy knowledge, but never laying down the law, showing always a becoming modesty about his own achievements in the world of letters. But, as he kept Adrian enthralled by his easy flow of conversation, seeming to give his whole attention to it, that other critical self that he carried about with him was noting, analysing, drawing deductions, tentatively working up the situation.

The woman was common, but there was something warm and generous about her. The man had been wise to leave her as she was. A superimposed gentility would have ruined her. The relations between the two puzzled him. The man was fastidious and highly strung, and one would imagine that the woman would be intolerably on his nerves, yet she didn't seem to be. Probably she was sometimes. He was all nerves, you could see, up one moment, down the next, knowing no mean between exaltation and the most abject depression.

It was an interesting situation. The woman was interesting. The man was interesting. Good material for comedy or tragedy. Full of almost farcical possibilities, but might quite possibly end in murder. When he took his leave, he left a hearty invitation for the two of them to dine with him the next week.

"He's a nice gentleman, isn't he?" said Evie when he had gone.

With the departure of the guest Adrian's spirits suffered their usual reaction, dropping from excitement to dejection. All Evie's little mannerisms that had not jarred on him during the evening seemed to return now to his memory with doubly irritating force.

"Evie," he said, "when you talk about men I wish you wouldn't always call them gentlemen."

"But he *is* a gentleman, isn't he?" said Evie in surprise.

"That's not the point," Adrian said. "When you talk about gentlemen you call them men, not gentlemen."

"Why?" said Evie simply.

"I don't know," said Adrian irritably. "It doesn't matter why."

"My mother used to teach me quite different," said Evie. "She used to say it was better manners, like, to say gentleman."

"And why on earth do you keep saying 'like?' You're always saying 'like' with no point at all."

A sulky expression came into her face.

"I don't see that it matters."

He sat down in the easy-chair, moving slightly to one side so that she could sit on the arm of it, as she liked to do. His face looked strained and tired after the excitement of the evening.

"Evie," he said, "I want you to try to change just in one or two little ways. They aren't really important, but they just make a difference. I mean—Evie, you do love me, don't you?"

Her sulky look vanished, and her fingers moved, tenderly caressing, over his hair. He was a little boy "in a state" (that was how she always thought of his moods of excitement), and she was soothing and reassuring him. She didn't know or care what had upset him, but her whole being responded instinctively to his need of comfort.

"You know I do, ducks," she said in her deep tender voice.

He winced at the "ducks," then relaxed to the gentle motion of her hand. Her soft cool fingers were moving now across his forehead. They had an indescribably soothing effect. He realised suddenly how tired he was. His exaltation and depression always left him exhausted.

"Go on doing that," he said dreamily. She stroked in silence for a few moments. There was something vital, magnetic, in the touch of her finger-tips. All the virtue of her rich tenderness seemed to be concentrated there.

"Darling," he said at last, "I want you to do something for me. Will you?"

"If it's anything I can do," she said.

"It is . . . I want you to——" He stopped. He was finding it harder than he had thought it would be to put the thing into words. "I want you—well, for one thing I want you to have some elocution lessons."

273

"What's that, ducks?"

"To teach you to speak properly."

"Like you?"

"Yes."

She smiled again as one might smile at the vagaries of a child.

"You once said you wouldn't try to make a lady of me."

"Evie, don't you understand? I have to meet people, make friends and that sort of thing. And I want to be able to ask them here and not——" He stopped.

"Feel ashamed of me?" she supplied, still smiling in tender amusement.

"*No.*" He jerked his head away from her hand. "Won't you try to understand? I'd never feel ashamed of you. You know how much I love you. Only, I want them to know you as you really are. It's just a few unimportant surface things—a way of speaking, and behaving and——"

He was getting "in a state" again, sitting up, tense and rigid, gesticulating, his eyes bright, his cheeks flushed. She drew his head back against her breast.

"Yes, I'll do anything you like, ducks," she said soothingly.

Chapter Twenty-Five

Lorna and Mark moved into their new flat the next month. It was in a not too unfashionable part of Westminster, and, though it was small and inconvenient (for the same rent they could have had a much better flat overlooking Battersea Park), Lorna, who had decided at all costs to be "on the right side of the river," was delighted with it. It transformed her again into the eager happy little bride of two years ago. Everything about the new flat was perfect. She could think and talk of nothing else.

Jenifer had gone over to see them at Dulwich the Sunday before they moved and had found Lorna radiant with excitement at the prospect of the removal.

"Just to think that we're leaving all this behind!" she said. "Doesn't it seem almost too good to be true?"

After tea Mark went into the garden and began to hoe and tidy up the beds as usual.

"Mark, why on *earth* are you doing that when we shan't be here this time next week?" called Lorna from the open window.

"I dunno," he replied. "I've sort of got used to it, I suppose."

He stayed out till it was almost dark, and they saw how he went slowly round the borders, gazing at each plant as if taking a long and tender farewell of it. A faint impatience invaded Lorna's serenity at the sight.

"I think I'm getting Mark out of here just in time," she said. "He's turning into the most appalling specimen of suburban householder. Going straight out to the garden the minute he gets home from work and pottering about till it's dark. Pottering about in it all Sundays, too, wearing the most awful clothes. It's terribly bad for him to let himself go like this."

"He'll miss the garden," ventured Jenifer.

"He can get lots of other interests," said Lorna. "He can take up golf. He'll meet much more useful people playing golf. He's made no friends at all here except those ghastly creatures who talk about sweet peas and tomatoes over the garden fence. And bridge . . . bridge is a useful sort of game, too. He'd simply run to seed if we stayed here."

Jenifer went to Sylvia's for the next fortnight (the baby was just beginning to walk), and when she returned Lorna was settled in the Westminster flat, still radiantly happy, engaged in establishing those personal contacts with everyone around her that were one of her chief excitements of life. The lift boy already watched for her coming and counted her smile as one of his greatest treasures. The hall porter was another of her admirers. He was a grim unbending man, but he unbent to Lorna. He even showed her photographs of his wife and children, and sometimes Lorna would give him toys to take home to his baby.

He used to tell his wife about her.

"Different from some," he said, "what never have a civil word for you from day's end to day's end."

Then there were the other tenants of the flats. They were barely on speaking terms with each other, but Lorna soon knew them all well. She became, as it were, the focusing point of the little community.

On Sundays Lorna now insisted on Mark's putting on a morning suit and top-hat and accompanying her to church. She loved to join the church parade in the park afterwards, sauntering to and fro among the fashionable throng, serenely aware that she was as beautiful and as well dressed as anyone there. Mark often thought wistfully of the days when he had pottered about the garden in his oldest clothes, but Lorna's happiness compensated for everything.

"It's made all the difference to her, hasn't it?" he said to Jenifer one evening, as he was seeing her to the 'bus after a visit. "She was getting so nervy down at Dulwich. The doctor was quite right.

Housekeeping was too much for her. She's as different as possible now . . . There's only one thing I regret."

"What's that?"

"Well, I wanted children. Lorna did, too, but she said—quite rightly—that she didn't want them till she'd had a year or two to settle down to married life. Now, of course, she says we can't have them in a flat. She's quite right. People shouldn't have children in a flat. But I'm afraid of leaving it too late. Once people adjust themselves to a childless life—get into the rut of it, as it were—then they don't like starting a family. I've often noticed it. However, just at present the main thing is Lorna's health, and I shan't suggest taking a house again till she's absolutely strong and fit. Don't tell her anything of what I've said, will you? It might worry her."

It was a long speech for Mark, and somehow it depressed Jenifer unaccountably. He shouldn't have married Lorna, of course, and yet he wouldn't have been happy with anyone else.

When next André called she asked him if he had seen Lorna since she had moved into the flat. It turned out that he had been to see her the evening before.

"It all seems to be a great success," said Jenifer, more to assure herself than him.

He leant back in his chair, joining the tips of his fingers together.

"It has been interesting but sad to me, little Jenifer, to watch the gradual deterioration of the charm that was so perfect in your grandmother. It was slightly blurred in your mother——"

"Mother was perfect," put in Jenifer hotly.

"She was conscious of her charm, and that blurred it very very slightly. She used it deliberately to get what she wanted from people. Your grandmother was as unconscious of it as she was of the air she breathed. It was so much part of her that she never even knew she had it. While in Lorna," he threw out his long narrow hands in an eloquent gesture, "it has deteriorated into sheer vanity. She craves admiration as a drug fiend craves his drug, and she will stoop to any trick to get it. It is so degraded that now when any turn of her head or note in her voice reminds me of her grandmother I feel as indignant as if she had insulted her."

277

"But there's something awfully sweet deep down in her," protested Jenifer.

André shrugged.

"I think there is very little left that has not been choked by the weeds of her vanity," he said.

Of Bobby, Jenifer had heard nothing. She knew that he had gone abroad, but he had not come to say goodbye or even written to her. Probably she would never see him again. When she thought of her abortive affair with him she felt now an odd secret exultation, as if that something in her that could not endure to share itself, that must at all costs retain its integrity and independence, had triumphed in having won its ends even by a trick. The experience had strengthened her conviction that some women have a vocation for the unmated state, that they can only find their fulfilment in that state, and that she was one of them. She threw herself with renewed energy into her work. Her novel was progressing rather erratically, the characters seeming sometimes so real that the people around her were like shadows, sometimes so dead that she felt inclined to throw the whole thing into the fire.

She had met Laurence several times lately, but there was now a curious constraint between them. He no longer talked to her about his work, and there seemed nothing else to talk about. She felt as though she were making conversation with an uncongenial stranger, searching vainly for points of contact, trying subject after subject . . . He took her to the theatre once or twice but always to the lighter type of revue. "One can't concentrate on anything else after a hard day's work," he said.

He was losing his elasticity, both of body and mind. Despite his good looks there was a suggestion of premature middle age about him. He was growing bald, and his fine physique showed signs of degenerating into corpulency. He had a finger, Jenifer gathered, in innumerable financial pies and was now a man of considerable means, but he lived austerely enough, and there was about him still the old boyish generosity. Jenifer had only to mention a case of hardship or sickness that she had come across for him immediately to offer help.

She did not see very much of Adrian nowadays. He called on her one evening in a state of excitement, talking quickly, gesticulating freely, as he used to when he was excited. She gathered from his somewhat incoherent statements that he was asking her to undertake Evie's social education.

"But, Adrian," she said, horrified, "I couldn't possibly——"

"I only mean clothes and the way she talks and that sort of thing. If you'd just give her a hint now and then . . ."

"But I couldn't. I could go with her to help her choose clothes, of course, if she asked me to. I couldn't do anything else."

"Couldn't you just tell her when she's wearing the wrong things and doing the wrong things?"

Jenifer shook her head.

"It would only make her loathe me, and it would do no good."

"But, Jenifer," he urged, "it *is* honestly rather important. I mean, if my work gets known, and I meet people, and I—well, I can't ask them to the flat with Evie as she is. It isn't that I'm ashamed of her," he added quickly. "It's just that—it doesn't seem fair to her."

"I'll do anything I can, Adrian," she said, "but one of the lessons life has taught me is never to give my advice unasked."

He smiled.

"You may be right," he said, and added, "She's an awfully good sort, you know, Jennie."

"I know. I'm very fond of her. Don't think I'm being beastly about it, Adrian. It's just that it's the sort of thing I couldn't do. I'm not tactful enough."

"All right. I do understand. By the way, I suppose you heard from Father this morning?"

"No. Did you?"

"Yes. He said he was writing to us all. They're giving up The Chestnuts and moving to a smaller house. He said that they were getting rid of most of the furniture, and if there was anything we'd like would we go down and get it. It was all awful Victorian junk, of course. I don't want any of it."

"Have you been down lately?"

"No, and I don't ever mean to. When I think of that woman in Mother's place, I—well, I'll never forgive Father for marrying her as long as I live."

Jenifer remembered Adrian's childish adoration of their mother.

"He couldn't help it, Adrian. She'd have got him whatever he'd done. She'd made up her mind to get him. Did he say anything else?"

"He said that the kid was quite well. If ever I see it I'll wring its blasted little neck. He must have been mad. The woman was bad enough, but the kid finishes it."

His indignation seemed to do him good. He was quite cheerful when he took his leave.

"Give my love to Evie," said Jenifer, "and honestly I'll do all I can."

The letter from her father arrived by that evening's post. He told her shortly that they were giving up The Chestnuts and asked her if she would care to go down to look through her things.

He said that there were still several drawers in the old nursery full of odds and ends belonging to their childhood and that he did not like to throw them away till she, or one of the others, had seen them.

Jenifer rang up Lorna—not very hopefully—to ask if she would go down with her.

"Yes, darling," came in Lorna's sweet voice, "I would if I could possibly manage it, but I find travelling in the heat so tiring. I'm fit for nothing in the evening when Mark comes home, and I do feel that my first duty is to keep fresh for Mark."

Lorna found her wifely duty to Mark a very convenient reason for not doing things she didn't want to do and doing things she wanted to do. She displayed considerable ingenuity in adjusting the various and sometimes rather conflicting standpoints. "And besides," she added as she thought of another reason, "I suppose it's that I'm too loyal. I can't help it. It's just the way I'm made. Loyal to old memories. I don't suppose you understand."

Jenifer went down to Merrowvale alone the next day.

Rather to her surprise her stepmother received her cordially, coming to the front door to welcome her and kissing her affectionately. She looked older and plainer than before the birth of her child, and the over-youthful style of dress she still affected emphasised her appearance of middle age. The scar where the mole had been still showed conspicuously beneath her rouge. Jenifer glanced at it, feeling the old sinister fascination. She couldn't believe that the mole had really gone. The scar seemed like a little door inside which it was hiding and from which it might emerge at any minute to take its old place.

"It's so nice to see you again," said her stepmother, as they entered the drawing-room together. "We all had such happy times here—didn't we?—in the dear old days."

She spoke with the strained arch brightness that used to make them all so hotly uncomfortable in the "dear old days."

"Hardly any changes, you see," she went on. "Full of precious memories, isn't it?"

Jenifer glanced round the room, feeling it again to be the empty shell of something lovely that had gone for ever. She noticed, too, that there were changes. For one thing, the photographs that had stood on the mantelpiece, piano, and occasional-tables—photographs of them all as children, of Marcia in her girlhood, her young motherhood, her beautiful maturity—had gone. That, of course, had been part of her stepmother's first plan of cutting her husband off from his old life. It hadn't succeeded, and Jenifer guessed that that was why she was being welcomed so effusively. Her stepmother was changing her tactics. If her husband's heart could not be weaned from his old life, then she would identify herself with it so completely that the love he bore it should include her too.

Jenifer's eyes were still roving about the room. New curtains of a crude pink at the windows, a few new pieces of furniture, all undistinguished and cheap looking . . .

"I suppose your father told you we were going to remove?"

"Yes."

"This house is really much too big for us. Now that I've got Violet to look after,"—a coyness invaded the brightness of her manner, and she blushed and simpered like a self-conscious young matron—"she keeps me busy, I can tell you."

"Of course," said Jenifer.

She tried to say something nice about the baby, but the old paralysis held her and she couldn't.

"And it's a very old-fashioned and inconvenient house," went on her stepmother.

"Of course," said Jenifer again, feeling a sudden unreasonable anger at the criticism. It seemed disloyal even to agree to it. There was an uncomfortable silence, then her stepmother rose and said—still brightly and affectionately—"Well, you'd like to see your little sister, wouldn't you, dear?"

"Where's Father?" said Jenifer, as they went upstairs together.

"He's gone out for his walk. He generally goes out for a walk in the afternoon. He didn't expect you till after tea."

She opened the door of the old nursery. Curtains of the same crude pink as were in the drawing-room hung at all the windows. On the mantelpiece was a highly ornamental vase full of artificial flowers.

A nursemaid, who looked too young to have left school, stood by the window, holding a baby in her arms.

"Here's Violet," said Mrs Gainsborough proudly. "Isn't she splendid? Come to Mummy, darling."

The baby had a fat pale face, an ugly mouth, small eyes, and a petulant expression.

"Isn't she sweet?" said Flora. "Kiss Auntie Jenifer, darling. I thought she'd better call you Auntie Jenifer when she——"

There came the sound of the opening of the front door, and Jenifer flew downstairs into her father's arms. She drew a long deep breath of relief as they closed about her. There was something sultry and oppressive about Flora's atmosphere. There always had been, she remembered.

282

"Splendid to see you again, Baby," said her father.

She scanned his face anxiously. He looked much older and more worn than when last she had seen him. His hair was quite grey now, and his thin figure (how terribly thin he was growing!) stooped as it never used to. But his smile was the old smile, cheerful, tender.

"Come upstairs and look at Violet, darling," called his wife over the balusters.

The brightness of her voice had a shrill edge to it.

They went slowly upstairs to the nursery.

Flora stood at the door with the child in her arms.

"Here's Daddy," she said as he entered. "Go to Daddy."

She held the child out to him. He touched its cheek gently with his fingers, but his arm remained tightly clasped round Jenifer.

"Nice to have our little Jennie back, isn't it?" she said. "We have missed you so much, darling."

Yes, that was it, of course. She couldn't wean him from the old life, so she wanted to persuade herself and him that she had been an integral part of it. "Our little Jennie."

"Come down to my room, Baby," he said in a low steady voice. "I've turned the old morning room into a den, where I can keep my things and smoke and read."

Mrs Gainsborough thrust the child into the arms of its nursemaid, and, as they turned to go, Jenifer heard her reprove the girl for some slight carelessness in a tone of vicious anger that she had never heard from her before. He could not hide his indifference to the child, of course, and she could not help torturing herself by memories of the tenderness he had always shown to his first wife's children.

In the little "den" downstairs his wife still pursued doggedly her tactics of forcing herself into the intimacy between father and daughter, still kept up that intolerable parody of gaiety. She sat on the arm of his chair, stroking his hair (Jenifer saw his whole figure go tense and rigid), and chattering gaily about the child.

"She's such a pet, isn't she, Daddy? Auntie Jenifer must come to her first birthday party, mustn't she? She reminds me a little of Jennie when she was a baby, doesn't she you, dear?"

There was a strained silence, and it was as if in that silence she recognised failure, complete, irrevocable. She could never force her way into the magic circle that enclosed them, however hard she tried. The fixed bright smile vanished from her face, and it fell into lines of shrewish ill-humour.

Frank broke the silence.

"We're moving next week, you know, Baby. We shan't take long settling in. Come and stay with us at the beginning of next month."

"We can't possibly have Jenifer to stay with us," said his wife shortly. "There won't be a spare room."

He looked at her in surprise.

"My dear, there are four bedrooms."

"I know that, but I must have a night nursery and a day nursery for Violet."

"The child manages all right here with one nursery," expostulated her husband.

She set her thin lips in a tight line.

"It's not healthy. She ought to have two rooms. I really must insist on the child being considered first, Frank."

She'd only had the child in order to bind him to her, of course. If it failed to do that she could still use it to harass and inconvenience him, to oppose him at every turn, to force herself on his notice somehow, anyhow. What she could not endure was to be ignored by him.

He shrugged wearily, indifferently.

"As you wish, of course."

Jenifer rose.

"I'll go upstairs and look through the things."

"It was absurd to bring you over to look through that old rubbish," snapped her stepmother. "If I'd had my way I'd have put the whole lot on the fire. I've no patience with such sentimentality. Your father's made himself perfectly ridiculous about this house and everything in it. I shall be glad to get away from it."

Jenifer went upstairs, her heart beating unevenly. The woman's false gaiety had been bad enough, but this vicious ill-temper was worse. Yet she could not help pitying her. She had hoped so much from this marriage. Her distorted passion must be making life a hell for herself as well as for him.

The little nursemaid was carrying the baby downstairs to its pram. Jenifer stopped and said, "Hello, Baby," but it puckered up its face and began to whimper.

In the nursery she went quickly through the drawers—some unfinished needlework of Lorna's, a tin of "swop" stamps that had belonged to Laurence, an old paint-box of Adrian's, some ribbons from chocolate-boxes smoothed and wrapped in tissue paper, several strings of beads entangled in embroidery silks, a cricket-cap of Laurence's, some ancient photographic plates, a diary of Lorna's for 1909, a Times Book Club Christmas Catalogue for 1912, and a box of her own childish treasures—two celluloid dolls, a "charm" in the shape of a tiny silver pig, a gun-metal pencil-case, a new halfpenny, and—the shell that Derek had given her on the last night of the holiday at Westonlea. She took it in her hand and stood gazing at it, and again the old poignant tenderness stirred at her heart. She remembered their solemn goodbye kiss and how she had sobbed herself to sleep both on that night and on the night when she knew that they were not going to Westonlea the next year. That love was something unique, unforgettable, in her life. She slipped the shell into her pocket and went slowly downstairs.

"There's nothing there that can't be thrown away," she said.

"I'm quite aware of that," said her stepmother contemptuously.

But she had recovered her good-humour by the time Jenifer went. She did not resume the forced brightness that had jarred so on them. Instead there was a furtive excitement in her voice and manner. She wouldn't face failure. This house, with its ghosts and memories, had defeated her, but it was only a temporary defeat. It would be all right once they'd left the house.

"How do you think your father's looking?" she said to Jenifer.

"Not very well," replied Jenifer.

"It's the house," said her stepmother. "It doesn't suit him. It doesn't suit either of us. We'll be all right when we get away from the house."

Chapter Twenty-Six

Jenifer looked at the clock, then laid down her pen reluctantly.

It was odd that parties always seemed to happen on evenings when she was in good writing vein. Or more probably, she corrected herself ruefully, the very fact that she had to stop writing made her imagine, quite erroneously, that if she could have gone on she would at last have written something really good.

She slipped the foolscap into a drawer of her desk and went into her bedroom, where the green evening dress that she usually wore at parties lay across a chair. She had put it out ready in the afternoon so that she could go on working till the last possible minute. She stood looking down at it without enthusiasm. To wear green with her colouring—hazel eyes, red gold hair, and pale freckled skin—was, she knew, obvious and unoriginal, but she hated choosing clothes and always played for safety, buying the kind of thing in which one could not possibly go wrong.

"I never knew anyone so old-fashioned," Lorna had said the last time she went shopping with her. "You'll end by dressing exactly like Aunt Lena."

This remark had roused Jenifer's old fears, and, stung by it to a sort of defiance, she went out alone the next day and bought a model evening dress of a pale dull blue, cut on slender graceful lines with a subtle suggestion of expensive simplicity. She had paid more for it than she had ever paid for a dress before, and she had regretted the purchase as soon as it was made. She had never yet worn it.

"I simply can't," she kept saying to herself in excuse. "It just isn't me."

She took it down from the wardrobe now and looked at it, feeling awed and embarrassed, as one does in the presence of some assured magnificent stranger to whom one has just been introduced and to whom one knows that one will never find anything to say.

"I couldn't possibly wear it tonight in any case," she said. "Everyone will be sitting on the floor, and it would ruin it."

She felt relieved by finding this legitimate excuse for not wearing it, and, hanging it up again in the wardrobe, slipped her green dress over her head. As she fastened it, her thoughts went to the other four. Her father and stepmother had moved into the new house now, but she had not seen it. She had realised that, though her father loved her to visit him, her presence intensified his growing irritation with his wife. She would give Flora her chance with her baby and the new house. She had had one letter from her, an exuberant excited letter describing the furniture they had bought and the various labour-saving devices they had installed. "Violet is sweet," the letter ended, "and her daddy adores her." There was something pitiful in the bravado of it.

Lorna was still darting about like an eager little dragonfly, making new friends, establishing new contacts. The sitting-room of her flat was nearly always full of visitors, busily engaged in exchanging flattery and gossip. Mark was not very much at home now. He said that his work kept him late at the office.

Adrian had persuaded Jenifer to help Evie choose a dress and Jenifer had had a terrible afternoon—Evie growing sulkier and sulkier because Jenifer advised navy blue and Evie had promised Adrian to buy whatever Jenifer advised. She looked lovely in dark colours, but she hankered passionately after pinks and yellows and bright sky blues.

And Laurence . . . working, working, working incessantly, living in a world of figures and big business, moving among bustling hurrying crowds, but always pathetically alone.

Her thoughts flitted round them in a sort of circle, trying to form a barrier through which evil could not come to them. Father, Lorna, Adrian, Laurence . . .

Their photographs stood in a row on her mantelpiece, and in

the middle was the shell that she had brought from the nursery drawer at The Chestnuts. She took it up in her hand now and looked at it . . . The very touch of it seemed to waft her away into a land of glamour. Odd how that holiday belonged to a world of its own, set apart from all the rest of her life. Sometimes she wondered if it had ever really happened or if it had been a dream. Derek . . . again the vivid picture of him returned to her, and suddenly that far-off childish friendship seemed to her to have been the most beautiful thing in her life. She wondered where he was now . . .

The clock struck eight, and, rousing herself from her dreams, she turned to the mirror to put the finishing touches to her hair. But the glamour of her memories still clung about her, making the green dress look unbearably dull and spinsterish. On an impulse she took it off and put on the blue one. It was frivolous and feminine and beautifully cut, unlike any dress she had ever had before. It, too, belonged to a world of glamour, and not to everyday life. In it she could believe that she had run over the golden sands hand in hand with Derek in that sunlit dreamland where nothing ever changed. She slipped on her evening cloak, an odd feeling of excitement at her heart.

"Jenifer darling," called someone as she entered the studio, "how perfectly sweet you look in that dress!"

The dream was continuing. In ordinary life people didn't notice what she wore or what she looked like. She gave a little breathless laugh and, cheeks flushed, eyes bright with excitement, walked into the room.

He was standing near the fireplace at the further end. There was no mistaking the tall slender figure, the sensitive boyish lips, the golden hair with its irrepressible curl. She went straight across the room to him.

"You're Derek Melford, aren't you?"

He looked at her, and the colour flamed into his face. "Yes," he said, "and you're Jenifer."

*

288

They sat in a window-seat, shut away from the noisy room by the folds of an aggressively modern blue and gold curtain.

"I've thought about you such a lot all these years," he was saying. "I've kept wondering where you were and what you were doing."

"I've thought of you, too."

"I went to the cottage once to try to get your address, but they'd lost it. I hoped you'd come again, but you never did."

"I know . . . I hoped we'd go again, too."

"Tell me about all the rest of you."

"Lorna and Adrian are married. Laurence is terribly busy in the city. One hardly see anything of him. Mother's dead."

"I'm sorry. She was so lovely."

"And Father's married Miss Marchant. Do you remember her? Oh no, she wasn't with us, was she?"

"No, but you told me about her. None of you liked her."

"They've got a little girl . . . Now tell me about your family."

"Oh . . . we've all scattered, more or less. My mother's dead, too."

"And your father?"

The old look of bitterness came into his boyish face. "He left us before Mother died. Do you remember how mean he used to be about money?"

"Yes."

"And all the time he was keeping another woman. Giving her everything she wanted." He clenched his fists. "Even now when I think of Mother scraping and screwing and counting every halfpenny, while that woman——"

His voice trembled with anger, and again the old longing came to her to comfort and protect him.

"Don't think of it," she said gently, laying her hand on his sleeve. "Tell me what's happened to the others."

"Philip and Neil have gone abroad. Nita married. We don't see terribly much of each other. Oh," his ingenuous smile flashed out, "I know one thing that'll amuse you. Do you remember that awful fat baby who used to sit on the beach and spit on the stones?"

"Yes."

"It's Donald Masters."

"Not *the* Donald Masters?"

"Yes, the matinee idol. Isn't it priceless? He's the lead in *Red Harvest* now, you know. I went the other day just to enjoy the memory of him spitting on to the stones."

They both laughed.

"And what are you doing?" said Jenifer.

"Oh, I'm jogging along in a stockbroker's office. Times aren't too easy, of course."

She felt a sudden hot indignation because times weren't too easy. She yearned desperately to make them easy.

"Isn't it fun meeting like this?" he went on. "Somehow I've always known at the bottom of my heart that we should . . ."

"I think I have, too."

"Where do you live?" he said.

"I've got a flat in Chelsea. Quite a small one. Will you come and see it?"

"I'd love it. Why not now? Let's slip away. They've started that ghastly gramophone. There are at least ten too many couples for dancing, so it would be a charity to go. I hate parties really, don't you?"

They slipped away, took a 'bus to Chelsea, and then walked slowly along the quiet streets to her flat, A wild sweet happiness possessed her. She was still moving and speaking in a glamorous dream.

Inside the flat he helped her off with her cloak.

"What a darling you look in that dress, Jenifer!"

She laughed.

"I put it on because I was going to meet you."

"But you didn't know."

"I know I didn't."

They both laughed.

"It's so lovely to find you the same," he said. "I sometimes thought how dreadful it would be to meet you again and find you different. But you aren't. You're still just the same."

"And so are you. The minute I saw you tonight I saw you as a little boy in that blue shirt you used to wear and your knickers rolled up as far as they would go and all wet at the edges and bare legs. Do you remember the shell you gave me?"

"Yes."

"I've still got it. I put it away with my treasures and found it last month when I went to clear out my things at home."

She took him into her bedroom to see it, and they both put it to their ears, laughing to hear again the faint roaring that had once held all the thrill of magic for them. Then they went back to the sitting-room and sat on the window-seat, watching the river that gleamed silver in the dark.

"I used to think of you often in the war," she said, "and wonder where you were."

"I was in France most of the time, then I got wounded in 1917, and that finished me off as far as the war was concerned."

"Was it a bad wound?"

"Not really, but it was some time before they found me and it had got into a bit of a mess, of course."

She gathered him to her as he lay wounded on the battlefield and held him to her breast in passionate tenderness.

"I was in hospital in Hampshire," he went on. "When any new nurses were expected I used to think how jolly it would be if one of them turned out to be you, but they never did."

"We were nursing at home at the Hall. It's a lovely house, but it wasn't really suitable for a hospital, though Mr Lenham was awfully generous and had a lot of alterations made."

Mr Lenham . . . Bobby . . . A chill crept over her spirit and she withdrew into the corner of the window seat as if retreating again into the aloneness that was her refuge.

"Did your brothers come through it all right?" said Derek.

"Adrian was wounded. He limps a little, but you'd hardly notice it. Laurie came through all right. I don't think he hated it quite as much as Adrian did. Adrian loathed it."

"So did I. Don't let's talk about it. I hate even to think about it. Let's talk about ourselves. What do you do with yourself now?"

"I try to write. I haven't done anything really worth doing, but I enjoy trying. I couldn't keep myself on it, of course. Aunt Lena—do you remember her? She came down to Westonlea for a day that summer—left us all just enough to live on."

"Do let me see something you've written. I'd love to see what sort of things you write."

She didn't know why that jarred ever so slightly—as though he were trying to invade her privacies, to force his way into her secret self. She always hated the thought of people she knew reading her books. It seemed like exposing to their curiosity the part of her that instinctively she had always tried to keep hidden.

"No, don't," she said. "It sounds silly, but I hate people reading my books—people who know me, I mean . . . When did you last go back to Westonlea?"

"I was there last summer. The cottage is just the same, shells and little mats everywhere. There were some children staying there. Awful children. I hated them. I felt simply furious with them for staying where you'd stayed. I always hated people who stayed at the cottage after you. There was a perfectly loathsome little girl there the summer after your summer, and it made it worse that I'd hoped you'd be coming back that year. I pushed her into one of those pools in the rocks, and her mother came round to complain to Mother."

She laughed.

"We were always getting soaked in those pools, weren't we? Do you remember the day you wore your knickers right through with sliding down the rocks?"

"Rather! And the time we thought we'd got cut off by the tide."

"And the time that crab bit your toe—the one you were keeping for a pet."

"And you tore up your handkerchief for a bandage."

"And old Major Pettigrew . . ."

"He's still alive. He goes about in a bath-chair. It was fun, wasn't it? I've thought about it so often. Somehow the whole place was different the summer you were there. It's never been just like that before or since. Jennie, let's go down and see it again, shall we? We could easily manage it some Sunday."

"Yes, let's. I'd love to."

"And let's go together to see the fat baby in *Red Harvest*."

"Oh yes."

"Why not tomorrow night? Could you?"

"Yes. Come here for dinner first. A picnic dinner. We can grill some chops on the gas-ring."

"I can make omelettes. Let me make you an omelette, Jennie."

"Oh yes. What fun!"

Chapter Twenty-Seven

Adrian opened the front door of the flat with his latch-key and went into the little sitting-room. Evie did not run into the hall to greet him now when he came home, but she looked up from her book with a pleasant smile of welcome as he entered. She wore the navy blue dress that Jenifer had helped her to choose, and her fair hair was waved flat to her head and done in a neat knot at the nape of her neck. There was about her none of the old blowsiness and down-at-heelness.

"How nice you look!" he said, as he closed the door. "I *do* like that dress."

She shrugged.

"That's all right, then. After all, it's you that has to look at it, isn't it?"

She spoke with a new careful gentility of accent.

He sat down by her.

"And your hair looks simply lovely."

She patted the sleek waves.

"They squash it down no end, don't they?" she said, "but I must say they've done it rather nice this time."

"Nicely, darling," he corrected gently.

She repeated the word obediently.

He had thrown himself heart and soul into the task of civilising her, of making her a fit wife for a famous artist. So far his plan had succeeded beyond his most sanguine expectations. Her docility, in fact, amazed him, and he was too much pleased and excited by his success to notice the rather peculiar look that was in her eyes now when they rested on him.

At first she had agreed to his plans for her with a sort of good-natured, amused indulgence, as one would have fallen in with the whims of a child, but that stage was over. He was ceasing to be a child, and becoming, not a lover, but a schoolmaster. More and more often a faint sulkiness invaded her manner to him, but he did not notice it, so elated was he by the success of his scheme. She spoke better, walked better, behaved better, than he had ever hoped she would. He did not shirk his part in the programme. He took her to concerts and for walks in London, during which he discoursed on architecture and history, and they visited antique shops, where he held forth on the various periods of furniture. She would listen to him with that strange new look in her eyes, and he would not know that she was thinking of the days when they used to go out into the country, and all he wanted to do was to lie with his head in her lap. In the evenings she read aloud to him from some good biography, chosen, of course, by him. This served the double purpose of improving her accent (for he corrected her pronunciation as she read) and helping to give her the requisite cultural background.

His enthusiasm made him go to extremes in this as he did over everything, and her docility deceived him into believing that she was as eager to be educated as he was to educate her.

He had made several new friends lately, but had asked none of them to the flat yet. He wanted to wait till he could introduce them to Eve (for he called her Eve now, not Evie) with pride and confidence. Horace Blackburn visited them frequently, but Adrian did not mind his coming. He got on so well with Eve that his presence seemed to transform her most glaring gaucheries into wit, and they all enjoyed the evenings he spent with them.

Adrian was secretly very proud of his friend's admiration of her. If she were a success with a man like that even now, how much greater a success would she be when she had attained the poise and dignity with which his training was to endow her?

He glanced down at the book in her lap. He was supervising her reading, and it was a novel that had been well reviewed and recommended by the Book Society.

"Do you like it, darling?" he said.

"Yes, it's ever so nice," she replied.

She had taken it up and opened it at random when she heard the sound of his key in the lock, slipping behind the book-shelves the paper-backed novelette she had been reading all afternoon.

He put his arm round her and drew her to him so that her head rested on his shoulder.

"Adrian . . ." she said dreamily.

"Yes?"

"I tell you straight, the next dress I get I'm going to get pink, and I'm going to choose it myself. I saw one in Oxford Street today that would suit me a treat."

He laid his cheek affectionately against her hair.

"Not 'a treat,' darling," he remonstrated gently.

"Suit me lovely," she corrected herself.

"Why not 'suit me beautifully?'" he suggested.

She pouted. Such a fuss about nothing! "Lovely" . . . "beautifully" . . . what on earth was the difference? She wished she'd never told him about the pink dress, but she was so sick of wearing these blasted funeral colours. His lips found hers and pressed down upon them hungrily. She took his head and held it between her hands, smiling at him with sudden tenderness. It was silly to get cross with him. He *was* only a little boy, after all, trying to make her play the game he wanted. It was a stupid game, but she'd play it—or pretend to play it—just to please him.

"Would you like to go to the theatre tomorrow?" he said.

She made a little grimace.

"Not if it's like the one we went to last week!"

"I thought it was very interesting," he said. "Didn't you like it?"

"It was that *dull*" she said, "and there wasn't no plot."

"So dull," he corrected patiently, "and *any* plot."

Her face hardened. No, he wasn't a little boy . . . The little boy had gone for ever, leaving in his place this priggish pedant and schoolmaster. She had loved the little boy. She hated this superior stranger . . .

He glanced with satisfaction round the room, from which he

had removed Evie's more blatant attempts at embellishment. It was now a pleasant, dignified little room, and Evie—or rather, Eve—looked a pleasant, dignified mistress of it, in her graceful dark dress, with her fair hair waved and knotted low on her neck like that. He was conscious of a thrill of achievement. How glad he was that he had taken her in hand, instead of either drifting away from her or sinking to her level, as some men would have done! The experiment was proving a glorious success.

"How did you like the concert this afternoon?" he said.

He had a pathetic belief in the civilising powers of classical music, and frequently bought her tickets for concerts.

"I liked it ever so," she said.

"Which piece did you like best?"

"The one they played first," she answered promptly.

"Oh yes. That was Beethoven's Fifth Symphony, wasn't it?"

"I suppose so."

"It's a wonderful thing."

Again the thrill of achievement seized him. The very fact that she liked one piece better than another showed that she was developing a critical faculty, but the piece she had liked the best was the loveliest piece on the programme.

She gazed at him, beyond him, a dreamy look in her eyes. She hadn't been to the concert at all. She was sick of going to concerts and picture galleries and elocution classes and all the rest of it. She had been to an elocution class the day before, and she was so fed-up with the whole thing—doing daft exercises like oo-ah-ey and spitting out words like a parson instead of talking natural—that she'd played truant today. She'd been into the country with Horace Blackburn, and they had sat in a wood, and he had put his head in her lap as Adrian used to, and, when she tried to talk to him in the new way Adrian was teaching her, he'd said, "Oh, stop it, for God's sake," and they'd both laughed, and she'd begun to make fun of the elocution classes and of the way Adrian was trying to make her talk and even of Adrian, and they'd laughed still more hilariously, and suddenly everything became simple and natural and happy, just as it used to before Adrian had turned

297

schoolmaster. She'd promised to play truant from her elocution class tomorrow and go out with him again. Adrian was so unsuspicious that it was quite easy to deceive him. It would never even occur to him that she hadn't gone to her class.

"Well," said Adrian, rising, "I suppose I ought to go and wash. What time are Jenifer and Derek coming?"

"Jenifer rang up this afternoon. She said they couldn't be here before half-past eight, so I said I'd put dinner later."

Evie liked Jenifer better than Lorna, but she didn't really like either of them. She always felt that Adrian was measuring her against them and testing her progress by them.

"They've got engaged pretty quick, haven't they?" she went on. "She doesn't seem to have known him long."

He resisted the temptation to correct the "quick." At least she had not tacked on the once inevitable "like" to the sentence.

"She knew him as a child, you know. We once stayed for a holiday at the place where he lived. They met again by chance and went down to see the place and got engaged there. That's really all I know about it. I've only seen him once since they were engaged . . . Hadn't you better go and make sure that the maid's got everything ready, dear?"

Evie trailed into the little dining-room, the new sulky look on her face. The maid was part of the civilising process. Evie had enjoyed looking after the flat in her slovenly way, but now lessons and walks and concerts were supposed to take up so much of her time that there was none left for house-work. Besides, she must learn how to preside over a household and manage maids.

At first, as Adrian gently pointed out, she fraternised too much with her maid. The two of them would giggle together for hours in the kitchen, exchange confidences, chaff each other, discuss clothes and love affairs, lend each other the novelettes of the *From Mill to Mansion* type that they both loved, and go to the pictures together on the maid's afternoon out. Adrian had just come to the conclusion that he must get rid of the girl, when the two of them had a Homeric row over some trifle. Evie poured out the stream of pure Billingsgate that Adrian had heard from her once before, and the maid responded by slapping her face and walking out of the house. Adrian had a long talk with Evie before the next maid was engaged, telling her gently that a lady is always considerate but distant in her manner to her maids. Evie listened in silence, and dutifully kept the next maid at arm's length, behaving with unnatural hauteur to please Adrian. Beneath the hauteur lurked a sulky resentment, for she was aware that the maid knew she was of her own class, and made fun of her to the tradesmen, mimicking the refined accent that she spasmodically adopted. Her manner to Evie generally bordered on what Evie called "sauce."

She went into the dining-room and glanced vaguely round the table. It looked all right. She couldn't understand why people made such a fuss about knives and forks and glasses and that sort of thing. Finicky little courses of this, that, and the other. Never what she called a real good tuck-in at anything.

Derek would sit there, and Jenifer there. The thought of their visit made her feel depressed and resentful. It was going to be an awful evening . . .

But it wasn't an awful evening. Jenifer was radiant. Her usually pale cheeks were flushed, her eyes bright, and the something of uncertainty and shyness that generally hung about her, even with her own family, had vanished. She was gay and high-spirited, triumphantly aware of her new good looks and charm, exultantly happy in her love. She and Derek chattered and laughed and teased each other, unconsciously drawing the other two into the circle of their own happiness. They told Evie about their childhood friendship at Westonlea, and of their recent visit to it. The visit had not killed the enchantment that had hung over the place in Jenifer's memories. It had deepened it, rather, so that now the little fishing village seemed to be the kernel of her love for Derek. Evie did not talk much during the evening, but, when she took Jenifer into her bedroom at the end, she said curiously:

"And you hadn't seen each other all those years?"

"No," said Jenifer, with an excited little laugh. "It was so funny. We recognised each other at once. Derek was standing by the fireplace in an ordinary dinner jacket, and I suddenly saw a little boy in a blue shirt and knickers rolled up as far as they would go and bare legs."

Evie looked at her.

"You still think of him as a little boy, don't you?" she said.

"I don't know," said Jenifer, surprised. "Yes, I suppose I do."

"I did that with Adrian . . . It's wrong, you know."

"What do you mean? How wrong?"

"I don't know. I only know it is. You—you feel as if you was his mother, like, don't you? I know. But it's wrong to love a man like that. Or, rather, it's wrong to marry him because you love him like that. It's not fair to him nor to you." She searched for words to explain her meaning. "It's not really a mother he wants—nor a son you want. It shouldn't be, anyway. You get married, and then you find out that he isn't a little boy like you thought he was, and it doesn't leave you nothing."

Jenifer was silent. She knew that this marriage of Adrian's and Evie's was not turning out well, despite Adrian's air of elation. It hadn't had a chance from the beginning. It was natural that Evie should look at every other marriage with jaundiced eyes, seeing in them what had wrecked her own, whether it was there or not. And it wasn't her mothering of Adrian that had been the trouble. It was the fact that they belonged to different worlds . . . She tried to see Derek as a dispassionate observer would see him, to think of him as if she had met him for the first time at Sheila's party—a tall, slender, boyish-looking youth (he looked much younger than he was) with a suggestion of delicacy and sensitiveness about him, and—no, she couldn't do it. The picture kept fading, and in its place would come the picture of a little boy in a blue shirt, screwing up his eyes, against the sun.

She laughed rather breathlessly.

"Oh no, Evie, I don't think you're right. I don't think a woman can really love any man unless she loves the little boy in him too. It's always part of a woman's love for a man."

Evie shrugged.

"Oh well . . ." she said, and led the way back to the sitting-room.

"When are you going to be married?" asked Adrian, as she entered.

Derek slipped his arm round her. "In two months' time, we thought. There's really nothing to wait for. Jenifer wants to keep on her work, of course."

"Where shall you live?"

"We'll probably start in Jennie's flat—it's more convenient than my rooms—and look round for something else, perhaps, later."

"It'll be a very quiet wedding," put in Jenifer.

Her eyes were bright with happiness, as she stood there with Derek's arm round her. How absurd Evie had been! Poor Evie!

"Jennie looked quite pretty, didn't she?" said Adrian when they had gone.

"That's right," agreed Evie, and added, "That blue dress suits her a treat." She paused and corrected herself. "I mean, it suits her beautiful."

Chapter Twenty-Eight

"So you are to be married next month?" said André. "I hope you will be very happy."

Jenifer, curled up on her window-seat, turned her head to him with a faint smile.

"Now it's near, it's rather frightening," she said. "So many married people aren't happy, and they must have been so sure once that they were going to be. You're a philosopher. Tell me how to be happy."

He shrugged.

"Ah, I cannot tell you that. I only know that it is one of the things you do not get by going out for it, as you say, and fighting for it. Like everything else in the world worth having, it comes, if it comes at all, by the way, unexpectedly. Liberty is another thing like that. One does not win it by throwing off one's shackles, but by learning to be independent of one's shackles."

"It all sounds so much more simple than it really is, doesn't it?" she sighed. "By the way, I suppose liberty and marriage don't really agree . . ."

"They do not agree at all. One of your own writers says, 'Hate is not the opposite of love. The real opposite of love is individuality.' He says also that, as sure as you begin with a case of true love, you end with a terrific struggle and conflict of two opposing egos or individualities. In the days when it was considered the duty of the woman to sink her individuality in that of her husband, it was more or less straightforward. But nowadays it is not straightforward any longer."

She was silent, then said: "And is there no solution, André?"

He crossed his knees and spread out his hands.

"It is a question of adjustment. Neither should yield entirely. There should be balance, and some sacrifice on both sides."

"I should imagine that's pretty difficult."

"It is, I believe; very difficult. I myself have never tried it."

She gazed thoughtfully into the distance.

"I suppose that really there are no rules for happiness in marriage," she said at last slowly. "I suppose the fact is that every two people in the world are different from any other two, and so every marriage is a unique problem."

"But, you know," he said gently, "on the eve of your marriage you should not be considering recipes for married happiness in this way. You should be taking your happiness for granted."

She flushed.

"Ought I? I wish life were simpler. I love Derek terribly, you know . . . Oh well, it's all too complicated. Let's talk of something else. Tell me what you've been doing this week . . ."

He took his leave of her, when he went, rather sadly. Beneath his detached ironic exterior he was fonder of Jenifer than of anyone else now living. She had inherited none of her grandmother's charm—the charm that had cast a spell over his young manhood—but he loved her for her wistfulness, her sudden moods of gaiety, for the shyness and uncertainty that made her seem poignantly young despite her twenty-seven years.

When he had gone she still sat on the window-seat, gazing dreamily into space. She did love Derek . . . The discovery of a strain of weakness beneath his amiability had not lessened her love, but had rather increased it. Her chief feeling for him was still one of protective tenderness. She wanted to take care of him, to keep from him everything that might harm or trouble him, to make up to him for the unhappiness of his boyhood, his hunger and poverty, his father's unkindness. They talked about those times incessantly.

"Often after that holiday I used to have awful dreams that your father was bullying you."

"Well, he probably was. He didn't do much else but bully us

when he was at home. I used to plan to kill him when I was old enough. It was the way he treated Mother, of course, that made me feel blind with rage. Often he's kept her so short of money that she's gone without food so that we could have it. I still can't bear to think of it."

"And she was such a darling . . ."

"He killed her, you know, in a way. And all the time he was giving that other woman everything she wanted . . . buying her jewels and fur coats while Mother had to wear that old grey cotton dress even in the winter . . . Do you remember that blue dress and sunbonnet of yours, Jennie? I used to remember you best in that."

"Yes . . . Lorna had a pink one just like it."

"I hardly remember Lorna or the others. Only you . . . Do you remember the time when we thought we saw a sea-serpent at the end of the bay, and, when we got to it, it was a net spread out over the rocks to dry?"

So strong was the protective love she bore him, the yearning to defend and comfort him, that sometimes to her horror she found herself imagining him ill or maimed or in some desperate trouble, so that it could find fuller expression, so that he should belong to her entirely . . .

Lorna approved of him. He was good-looking, well turned out, and had charming manners, and, though there was little maternal instinct in Lorna, his ingenuous boyishness appealed to her. She asked them both to her parties (she entertained a good deal nowadays) and told Jenifer that she thought marriage would improve her.

"You're sweet, darling, but you're—what one might call unfinished. It will put a sort of polish on you to be mistress of a house and entertain. You just live anyhow now—cooking messes over your gas ring and only having friends who're bachelor women like yourself. It's high time you got married before you turn into a regular old maid."

"I suppose it is," said Jenifer.

"And Derek's charming."

"I know."

Derek was certainly charming—sweet-tempered, reasonable, falling in with all her plans, agreeing to all her decisions. Jenifer loved going out with him, or sitting in her pleasant little room, talking to him. They arranged their meetings beforehand, and she managed to leave herself plenty of time for writing and reading and for the solitude that had now become a necessity to her. Despite her love for him, she still kept a large part of her life inviolate from him.

"I wish we could go on being engaged for ever," she said once. "It seems such an ideal arrangement."

He laughed.

"I think marriage is a still more ideal arrangement," he retorted.

Something in her still shrank from the thought of marriage—less from the actual fact of marriage than from the loss of the independence that had always been so precious to her. There were times when she longed for Derek, when she was made almost unbearably happy by his very presence, but there were times when she wanted to be alone, when his presence irked and irritated her, giving her a strange feeling of physical constriction. Then she could always make the excuse of her work, even if she really did not want to work, and he would respect it and leave her. The thought occasionally came to her that she would not be able to dismiss him so easily when they were married, and then she would remember her old conviction that she was one of those women who ought not to marry at all.

Sometimes the little boy in Derek would disappear, and with him all the glamour of her love. Then quite ordinary things about him—the way his hair grew on his neck, the way he straddled on the hearthrug or sat with his legs stretched out—would fill her with sudden inexplicable revulsion. But always before long some proof of his dependence on her, some suggestion of wistfulness in him, would fill her again with yearning love for him.

She was still feeling worried about her father. She had been down to see him a few months after they had moved into the new house. Flora had abandoned her policy of conciliation, and her manner to Jenifer was once more definitely hostile. The little house was a small, newly built one on the outskirts of Sydenham—undistinguished both inside and out. Flora had taken a good deal of trouble over the house, choosing a colour scheme for each room, the effects of which were achieved by cheap ornaments and remnants from bargain basements. The little dining-room screamed jade green from every nook and corner. There was a jade-green china cat on the mantelpiece, a jade-green cover on the sideboard, jade-green curtains at the windows, a jade-green bowl in the middle of the table, and a jade-green mat at the hearth. A crude hot pink dominated the drawing-room. Their bedroom was an inharmonious medley of blues of innumerable conflicting shades, blended with a muddy grey. The only room into which she had not been allowed to introduce a "colour scheme" was the small room upstairs that her husband had reserved for his own use. In it were his shabby leather armchair, an old table, a bookcase, and Marcia's piano. In the centre of the mantelpiece was his favourite photograph of Marcia. Here he would sit and read and dream for hours together. It was his refuge from his wife's shrill tyranny. Flora hated the room. At first she had made determined efforts to introduce into it some little touches of her own— a vase of artificial flowers, a bright cretonne pouffe, a newspaper-rack ornamented in poker work, a comic china pig. He turned them all out, silently refusing to have anything in the room that had not been in his old home. Once when she sat down at the piano and with her short stubby fingers began to strum out "Cherry Ripe," he wheeled round on her with such a look that she fled from the room, trembling. But she could not leave him alone. The memory of his adoration of Marcia, his devotion to his other children, still tormented her. His manner to her child was kind and gentle, but he obviously felt no affection for it. It was a peevish, whining little creature, already spoilt by Flora's alternate petting and ill-humour. Flora tried ceaselessly to force the child and herself on his notice. She abandoned the gaiety of manner that had been so unsuccessful, and became bitter and shrewish, using every means in her power to make him uncomfortable. She insisted on his tiptoeing about the house when the child was resting, scolding him if he made a sound. She raised objections to all his plans, and seized the slightest excuse—a pipe left out of place, a finger-mark on the furniture, a piece of mud from his shoes on the carpet—to nag at him. He ignored her for the most part, but sometimes he would be roused to snap back at her in a tone that Jenifer, remembering his unfailing gentleness and good-humour in the old days, could hardly endure to hear.

There was an ugly scene between them the day of Jenifer's visit. Jenifer was sitting in his room with him, and they were talking in a desultory manner of Adrian, Laurence, Lorna, Jenifer's work, the news of the day, of anything but the subject that was in both their minds, when Flora burst in. She had heard the sound of their voices and had been tormented by the suspicion that they were talking about her. She had listened at the keyhole but could hear nothing beyond a low murmur. Two bright spots blazed in her sallow cheeks, and she was trembling with anger as she flung open the door.

"I suppose it doesn't matter to you that you're keeping Violet awake by all this noise."

Her husband looked at her, and his worn face hardened, as it always did when he spoke to her.

"Noise?" he said.

"*Talking* like this!" she went on. "Why can't you come downstairs if you want to talk? Too good for me, I suppose, the two of you!"

"My dear Flora, we'd no idea that you'd any desire for our company. You haven't exactly given us that impression."

He had begun to take refuge from her shrewishness in a somewhat heavy sarcasm.

"Oh yes," she went on, her voice rising shrilly. "I know what you were talking about all right. I don't wonder you were ashamed to come downstairs and look me in the face." She turned on him viciously. "Don't think I don't know the sort of things you say about me behind my back."

"We've said nothing you couldn't have heard, Flora," put in Jenifer unwisely.

Flora wheeled round on her.

"Hold your tongue, you little cat!"

Jenifer shrank back instinctively, and Frank slipped an arm reassuringly round her waist.

"There's no need to be offensive, my dear Flora," he said quietly, "and there seems no reason that I can see for this scene at all. We'll certainly come downstairs, if you want us to."

The sight of them standing there together, facing her, Frank's arm round Jenifer's waist, and the suggestion the picture gave once more of a bond from which she was ever excluded, broke down the last remnant of her self-control.

"Oh, *she* can do nothing wrong, of course. None of them can but me. I slave for you all day and every day—keep your house and cook for you, and what thanks do I get? Tell me that. Never so much as a civil word. Why did you marry me if that's all you care for me? All you wanted was a general servant. Haven't I borne you a child? And you never look at me without thinking of *her* . . .' She snatched the photograph of Marcia from the mantelpiece and held it up as if to fling it on to the floor.

Frank stepped forward, his face white.

"If you harm that," he said steadily, "I shall go away, and I shall never see you or speak to you again as long as I live."

She laid the photograph on the table, sank into a chair, and burst into a hysterical torrent of sobs.

The child in the next room, awakened by the sound, began to whine drearily.

Jenifer was glad to get back to the quiet of her own flat. Derek came to tea the day she returned and was very understanding and sympathetic.

"I wish I knew whether it really makes things better or worse for me to go to see him," she said. "He keeps asking me to go, but she hates it and always takes it out of him . . ."

Lorna drifted in before they had finished tea, looking very beautiful and poised and *soignée,* each hair of her fashionable coiffure in place, her toilet immaculate to the last detail. She was beginning to take endless trouble over her appearance.

"When one gets about thirty," she said to Jenifer earnestly, "it's time to keep a look-out for wrinkles."

She went to a "beauty parlour" every week for treatment. Her flawless skin was massaged and stimulated and tightened and toned up, buried in masks of oil or mud, subjected to electricity, patting, strapping, and countless other processes designed to keep at bay the slightest suspicion of a wrinkle. Her dressing-table held a bewildering array of lotions and creams and toilet waters and special preparations. There was something slightly mask-like about her loveliness now, as indeed there was about the suave charm of her manner. She was still a priestess officiating at the shrine of her own beauty. She certainly did not take these endless pains over her appearance to attract men. Her manner of distant sweetness did attract them, but it also kept them at arm's length. Her careful embellishing of herself seemed, indeed, to be an end in itself. She would spend a whole morning making an exhaustive toilet for no other purpose than to stroll through one of the large stores, and with no other reward than the admiration of the shop-girls from whom she made purchases, and the appreciative glances of strangers.

"Have some tea, Lorna?" said Jenifer. "There's lots left."

Lorna sank gracefully into an easy-chair and drew off her gloves.

"Just a cup, then . . ."

"And have one of those little cakes. They're lovely. Pass her one, Derek."

"No, thanks. I've given up eating at tea-time. I was putting on weight."

Jenifer considered the elegant sveltness of Lorna's figure.

"But, darling, you're thin."

Lorna glanced down critically.

"Oh, one has to be careful . . . Did you go to see Father, Jenifer?"

"Yes."

"What was it like?"

"It was terrible. I've just been telling Derek. She's *hateful*, Lorna."

"Darling, she always was," said Lorna, unperturbed. "He'd known her long enough, too, before he married her. I don't want to be hard, but, honestly, he's no one to blame but himself. We all foresaw how it would turn out."

"He asked when you were going to see him."

"My dear, I shouldn't *dream* of exposing myself to that woman's insolence."

"He'd love to see you. He always asks about you."

"He must come up to Town, then, and put up at an hotel, and we can go about together. I'm not going down there. It's all right for you, Jenifer, but I'm too sensitive for that sort of thing. Insolence really upsets me. Besides, I shall be terribly busy for the next few weeks."

"What doing?"

"Flat-hunting."

"Flat-hunting? I thought you were quite settled where you were."

"It's so very inconvenient." Lorna's voice was plaintive. "There isn't even running water in the bedrooms and it's not central and the rooms are too tiny for words and the people there are *dreadful*. So unspeakably dull."

Lorna had, as usual, surrounded herself with a court of the second rate, from whom alone she could be certain of the unstinted uncritical admiration she craved, and was beginning to discover their limitations as companions.

"Mark isn't keen on moving," she went on, "but he's away from home on business so much nowadays that it really doesn't matter to him one way or the other. It's I who have to put up with the inconveniences, and, honestly, it'll affect my nerves soon if I don't move. After all, I gave up my dear little house in Dulwich for his sake, just because he found the journey from Town too tiring, so I think he ought to consider me now."

"I've no doubt he will," said Jenifer rather dryly, remembering the wearing-down process that Lorna's persistence could achieve so sweetly and so successfully.

The telephone bell rang, and Jenifer went to answer it. "Yes? . . . Oh, is it Adrian?"

"Yes." His voice sounded breathless and high-pitched. "I've just been trying to get on to Lorna, but I couldn't."

"Lorna's here . . . What's the matter, Adrian?"

"It's Evie. She's gone."

"Gone?"

"Yes. I've just got back and found a note. She's gone off with that swine Blackburn."

Chapter Twenty-Nine

Adrian's divorce was put through as quickly as possible. Evie and Horace Blackburn did not defend the action nor did they marry when the decree was made absolute. Blackburn vanished from his usual haunts for several months, then returned alone, and nothing more was heard of Evie.

Lorna moved into an up-to-date flat in Kensington and made innumerable new friends who cultivated her assiduously and pronounced her "charming." None of the three saw much of Laurence. He was often abroad, looking after his interests in various parts of the world, and when he was in Town he was too busy for social engagements. He still paid occasional visits to Jenifer's flat, but he was now more than ever a rather heavy stranger, whom she had to entertain, and who was generally thinking about something else all the time, keeping his eye on the clock, so as not to be late for his next appointment. She tried to interest him in pretty girls, and often invited the more attractive of her friends to meet him, but, though laboriously polite, he was completely immune to their attractions. He visited his father at Sydenham, ignoring his stepmother's insolence till it became too obvious to be ignored any longer, then he ceased his visits, but compromised with his conscience by sending expensive presents at regular intervals to his father, stepmother, and the child. He had met Derek, but the two had nothing in common, as indeed Jenifer had foreseen.

"He's all right," was Derek's verdict, "but, Gosh, aren't these financial magnates heavy on hand!"

And Laurence had said:

"He's all right, Jennie, but he's not what I'd have chosen for you."

"What would you have chosen for me?" said Jenifer.

He considered a moment then said:

"I don't know."

Jenifer had put off the date of her marriage several times. She didn't want to be married till Adrian's affairs were more settled, till Lorna had moved into her new flat, till she had finished the book she was working on.

"Just wait till I've finished it, Derek," she pleaded, "then I can marry you with a clear mind. It would break my heart to have to leave it now—I'm just in sight of the end—even to get married."

"All right," he said sulkily.

Their engagement was not running quite so smoothly as it had done at first. Derek seemed to be realising how large a part of Jenifer's life was independent of him and to be resenting it.

"What's this book you're writing about?" he said once. "Oh, I don't know," she said vaguely.

"You must know," he persisted.

"It's about a girl who—oh, I can't go into all the plot, Derek."

"Why not?"

"I hate talking about the plots of my books."

"One would think you wouldn't mind talking about it to me. I tell you about my work . . ."

"That's different."

"How is it different?"

"It is just different. I can't explain."

"But I'm really interested in your work. When we're married I want to know all about it. I want to share everything with you, Jenifer. We could talk over your plots together. Two heads are better than one, you know, and I should enjoy it."

Her heart sank.

"Derek, I couldn't possibly do that."

"Why? Don't you love me enough?"

"It's not a question of love. I couldn't do that with anyone."

He was hurt and sulky for the rest of the evening. Sometimes he was difficult, too, about their plans, as if he suspected her of trying to "manage" him.

"Shall we go on the river tomorrow, Derek?"

"Why the river?"

"I don't know, but we've been there several times lately and enjoyed it."

"I don't want to go on the river."

"What would you like to do then?"

"I don't know."

"Would you like to go out into the country?"

"No, not particularly."

"A theatre then?"

"Good Lord, no! Not in this heat."

He objected to every proposal she made but had no suggestion to offer in its place. Finally they spent the afternoon wandering about in the park, simply because he was determined to do none of the things she suggested. The next day he apologised to her. But he had become "touchy," easily offended, always ready to suspect her of ignoring or slighting him.

"The truth is," he said, "you don't love me as much as I love you."

"Derek, I *do*."

"You don't. I share everything in my life with you. You won't share anything with me."

"Darling, I do share everything. It's just that—Derek, you know I love you . . . don't you?"

She could always coax him back into a good humour again, but it was beginning to take longer than it had taken at first.

He called for her one evening earlier than they had arranged and found her still writing.

"I won't be a minute, Derek," she said. "Find something to read."

He picked up a book of philosophy that André had lent her the day before.

"Oh, darling, you'll hate that," she went on, knowing that he only cared for light reading. "There are some novels on the bottom shelf."

He flushed.

"I don't know why you should take for granted that I have no intelligence at all," he said stiffly, and was distant and dignified for the rest of the evening.

He would cross-examine her relentlessly sometimes on how she spent her time when he was at work.

"What did you do this morning?"

"I worked. Then I met a friend for lunch."

"Who?"

"Freda Harcomb."

"Do I know her?"

"I don't think so."

"You've met every friend I've got, Jenifer. I think it rather strange that you don't introduce me to yours. Sometimes you almost give the impression that you're ashamed of being engaged to me."

"Oh, Derek, don't be so silly. You know that's not true. I've introduced you to every single friend of mine who could possibly interest you. You'd find Freda terribly dull."

"Too intellectual for me, I suppose."

"No. She isn't intellectual at all," said Jenifer patiently. "She's dull but a very good sort. She's the plainest woman I've ever met, by the way, and she writes beauty hints for one of the women's weeklies."

But he refused to be charmed back into good-humour. It was as if there were two people in him—one the little boy she had loved for so many years, the other a stranger who resented the little boy's dependence on her and her love for him.

At first his love-making had been tentative and respectful, but it was now becoming daring and even sometimes, as it seemed to her, deliberately offensive. He appeared to take a perverse pleasure in beating down her defences of fastidiousness. She broke away from him one evening, hot with anger.

"Derek, I do hate being *mauled* like that. Can't you leave me alone?"

He was suddenly as angry as she was.

"My dear girl, you are engaged to me, I believe."

"I know. I've tried not to be stupid and priggish about it, but there are limits."

"You needn't talk as if I were trying to seduce you."

"I'm sorry. It's just that I hate being mauled. I always have done. You've only just begun to do it. I *loathe* it."

He stared at her, coldly hostile.

"I suppose you know what marriage means," he said. To her surprise she realised that she was on the verge of tears.

"Of course I do."

"Well, all I can say is that I hope you'll have got over a few of your spinsterish scruples before then. I'm not particularly struck by the modern girl who offers to sleep with you the minute she's met you, but on the whole I think I prefer it to the other extreme. There's less hypocrisy about it."

She was silent for some moments then said quietly:

"I think we're both being rather silly, don't you? I dare say it's my fault. I'm tired and irritable. I've been working late trying to finish my book."

His lips curled into a sneer.

"Oh . . . your book!"

"Yes. I'm sorry if I made myself a nuisance over it. I've tried not to."

His sneer grew uglier.

"I suppose that after we've married everything will still have to come second to the book of the moment. I must make up my mind to that, of course."

"Derek, *don't!* . . . It's all so childish."

"Very well. I won't waste any more of your valuable time with my childishness. You can get on with your 'book.'"

He turned to the door, but she laid a hand upon his arm.

"Do stop quarrelling with me, Derek. They say it takes two to make a quarrel, but it doesn't. You're making this one all by yourself."

He was silent, and in the silence the stranger who hated her seemed to go away, leaving the little boy who loved her, hurt and resentful.

"It's because I love you so, Jennie," he said sulkily, "and I sometimes feel that you don't love me at all."

Now that the stranger had gone, she could safely draw his head to hers and kiss him tenderly, murmuring reassurance: "I do love you . . . you know I do . . . Derek."

"Yes?"

"Let's not meet for a week."

"Jennie!"

"Now listen. We're both on edge. We've been quarrelling horribly lately. In a week I'll have finished the wretched book, and it won't stand between us any longer. If I just let it go it'll be worrying me all the time. I won't be able to put it out of my mind and forget it. In a week we'll both be feeling better. I think we're rather on each other's nerves just now."

He was still hurt and resentful.

"But we'd get tickets for that theatre tomorrow night."

"Take someone else."

"I don't want to take anyone else."

"Take Lily Frean."

"Lily Frean!" he echoed in contemptuous indignation. Lily Frean was a girl with whom he had been rather friendly before he met Jenifer. Jenifer had never seen her, but Derek had described her as a "silly little thing without a hap'oth of character or brains."

"I'd rather go alone," he went on.

She had a vision of him going alone, brooding over his imaginary grievances, working himself up into a state of sulky anger with her for not accompanying him.

"No, take Lily," she said.

"I've not seen her for months."

"Well, see her then. Ask her to go with you. You'll enjoy it much better than if you were alone,"

"All right," he agreed at last.

He rang her up late the next night.

"You haven't gone to bed yet, have you, darling?"

"No, I'm still working. Had a nice time?"

"No, it was awful. Lily's such a little ass. You aren't really going into retreat for a whole week, are you?"

"I must, Derek. Then I'll have got the wretched thing off my chest and can play with you properly. I'll be much nicer next week."

"You couldn't be, darling. I hoped you'd rescue me tomorrow night. Lily's roped me in to go to a ghastly party at her sister's."

"Her sister might be nice."

"She couldn't be. I hoped you'd let me say you needed me to come and hold your hand and inspire you. I can't bear not seeing you."

"It's only for a week, darling. A week soon goes."

"That depends entirely on the week. Some last for years."

"Idiot!" she laughed.

"Anyway give me a nice kiss. Louder, I could hardly hear that . . . Good-night, darling."

He rang up the next night.

"Was the party dreadful?" she asked.

"Not too bad. The sister was an awful fool. Lily's got me to promise to take her to the pictures tomorrow night."

"Darling, if she's boring you too dreadfully, can't you get out of it?"

He hesitated, then said:

"Oh, it's not as bad as all that."

The week slipped by quickly. Jenifer finished her novel on Friday evening. She rang Derek up, but he was not in his rooms. She remembered that he said he was going to see a certain film and decided to walk to the cinema and meet him.

She reached it just as the people were coming out. Neither Derek nor Lily saw her. Lily—small and fair with large blue eyes and a rosebud mouth—was clinging to Derek's arm, looking up at him adoringly. He was smiling down at her, masculine, proprietary, arrogant. He swaggered slightly as he walked. He was the Dominant Male incarnate. Jenifer had never seen him look like that before. And it came to her in a blinding flash of knowledge that she knew nothing of him, had never known anything of him. She went back to her rooms and sat there in the darkness curled up on the window-seat, looking down at the shimmering river, thinking of herself and Derek. Each had carried a dream of the other from childhood into maturity. There was a glamour about the dream, but it wasn't love, though each of them had mistaken it for love. He saw her as the grave little girl who had comforted him in his unhappy boyhood. She saw him as the little boy who had come to her for comfort. But he wasn't really that any longer, though the memories she revived had transformed him into it again just for a time. Beyond their memories of childhood they had nothing in common. Already the glamour of the dream was fading. She faced now the fact, which she had tried to hide from herself for months, that, when she could not see him as weak and dependent on her, everything about him irritated her, that she found him stupid and prejudiced, and that he, on his side, found her, she knew, priggish and unresponsive.

And he loved Lily, loved her in the way he wanted to love his wife, with a love that was protective, slightly condescending, that had in it an element of amused tolerance, that responded with superior male magnanimity to her feminine adoration.

She wasted no words when he came the next evening.

"Derek," she said, "I think we've both made a mistake."

He looked at her, surprised, on his guard.

"What do you mean?"

"We don't really love each other."

He began to bluster.

"What right have you to say that? You put your work before me and refuse to have anything to do with me and then turn on me like this."

"I'm not turning on you. You love Lily, don't you?"

He looked sheepish, glancing up at her from beneath his thick lashes, like a little boy detected in some fault.

"I don't know."

"That means that you do."

"I didn't—I mean, honestly, at the beginning of the week I thought I hated her."

"But you know you don't now . . . We'd never have been happy together, Derek."

He was silent, then said:

"You've been awfully sweet to me, Jenifer."

She drew her engagement ring from her finger.

"Let's break it off now before it's too late."

He took the ring, still looking at her sheepishly.

"Perhaps you're right. Somehow lately it hasn't been . . ."

"No, it hasn't, has it? I hope you'll be awfully happy, Derek."

"Honestly, Jenifer, I'm only taking it back because you—it's you who're breaking it off, you know. Tell me if you ever change your mind."

She smiled at him.

"I shan't change my mind . . . Goodbye, Derek."

When he had gone she steeled herself to face a heavy depression, an utter blankness, a bitter regret, but all she was conscious of was a wild relief, as though some horrible menace had been removed from her life, as though she had been released from prison.

PART FOUR

1929

Chapter Thirty

Jenifer was sitting on the lawn at Sylvia's in a deck chair, reading a novel. It had been a hot day, but the sun was verging westwards now and the first dewy freshness of the evening hung in the air.

She had had a letter that morning from Derek, who was staying at Westonlea with Lily and their two children.

"This place always makes me think of you," he wrote. "It's not really altered much yet, but I think it's going to. They're selling the land on the top of the cliff for building, and they're going to run a train service from London. We shan't come down here again, of course, when they've done that. So we're making the most of this year and having a splendid time. The children are enjoying the sea, and Jennie can nearly swim. Love from us all."

Derek, she knew, was happy in his marriage. Lily was a capable housekeeper, a devoted wife and mother. She had no interests outside her own home, and she still adored Derek as whole-heartedly as she had done when she married him.

Her mind went back over the years since her engagement to him had been broken off. Her father's death and Lorna's divorce were the outstanding events. She had been glad when her father died. His ill-health seemed to have broken down his self-control, and ugly scenes between him and Flora took place with increasing frequency towards the end of his life.

After his death Jenifer still paid occasional visits to the little house at Sydenham. She had an uncomfortable feeling of responsibility towards his child, unattractive and wholly Flora's as she seemed to be. She tried hard to establish friendly relations with her, but found her inculcated with Flora's own dislike of her husband's first family. She had been carefully trained by Flora, too, as spy and tale-bearer among the neighbours and was always rewarded when she brought home any particularly spicy bit of gossip, gleaned from maids or tradesmen. Flora was generally in a state of feud with one or other of her neighbours, in which Violet participated with unchildlike zest. In moments of exasperation she would pull and push the child about as she used to pull and push the little Gainsboroughs, shouting "*Silence!*" as the child whined and complained. The stigma of the second-rate that had showed only faintly in Flora in the old days became more and more pronounced as the years went on, and the little house was depressing in its laboured gentility.

Lorna had divorced Mark the year before. She had discovered that he was supporting a second establishment, consisting of a "wife" and three children, in one of the new garden estates just outside London. It was an establishment on a very small scale. The woman did the housework and cooking, and Mark kept up the little garden at the back. He spent many nights there when he was supposed to be away on business, and had won prizes for his roses and sweet peas at the local flower-shows. He went by the name of Mr Jones and was considered by the neighbours as an exemplary husband and father.

The "vulgarity" of the whole affair shocked Lorna inexpressibly. "The commonest woman, my dear," she said to Jenifer. "I've not seen her, of course, but I've heard about her. The type of woman who goes about in an overall all day and talks to the neighbours over the fence. Quite plain, too. And a semi-detached villa without even a *garage*."

If Mark had kept an expensive courtesan in a fashionable part of London, she would have found it much easier to forgive him.

Her friends rallied round her with frenzied loyalty.

"Three children!" they said. "How *disgusting!*"

"How he *could!* And Lorna always so *sweet*."

Mark did not defend the suit, and the divorce was put through as quickly as possible. Lorna made a picturesque figure in the courts, dressed in black, a short veil shading her lovely eyes, her pale oval face looking exquisitely beautiful against her dark furs. Everyone who saw her—even complete strangers—felt a fierce indignation against her husband.

Mark married the woman as soon as the divorce was put through and, except for the regularly paid alimony, passed out of Lorna's life.

Lorna moved into a yet newer and more modern flat. She had lately taken up Bridge and now spent her afternoons and evenings at Bridge parties or Bridge clubs. Her mornings were devoted wholly to the cult of her beauty. Her pale lovely face seemed as youthful as ever, her flawless skin unlined, her wide blue eyes unshadowed. "Over forty?" people said. "My dear, she *can't* be!"

She still drew within the circle of her charm everyone with whom she made the slightest contact, holding a court of admirers wherever she went. Her path through life was still strewn with adoring shop-girls, taxi-men, waiters, and waitresses. To Jenifer, watching her, it seemed that all the old zest had gone out of these conquests, that she was now compelled to make them by some mysterious force that she must obey no matter what trouble it cost her. She had not remarried and showed no signs of doing so. She shrank from emotion of any sort, living lightly and placidly on the surface of things. When Jenifer, who worked at an East End Settlement one day a week, told her some harrowing story of want and unemployment, she would frown quickly, say, "How *terrible!*" then, with a clearing of her white brow, add serenely, "But, darling, those people don't feel things as you or I would."

Adrian, too, had not remarried. After divorcing Evie, he had wandered about Europe, studying art in a desultory fashion, and had then returned to London and tried to take up his work again, but the failure of his marriage seemed to have increased his sensitiveness, and the first set-back in progress made him throw up the attempt in despair. He had settled down to a pernickety, prematurely middle-aged bachelor existence, and he was now living in a boarding-house in Bath. He had a private sitting-room, furnished with the best pieces of furniture from his flat, which he always dusted himself as he did not trust the housemaids, and he gave decorous little tea-parties to the elderly ladies who comprised the rest of the clientéle and who all adored him.

Jenifer had received a visit from Evie the year before. She looked stout and happy and undisguisedly common. She explained that she had not stayed long with Horace Blackburn.

"I knew he wouldn't want me for long and I didn't want him. I only went with him because it was the best way of setting Adrian free. I saw that we'd both made a mistake marrying."

She went on to say that she had now married a greengrocer in Islington, that they had a flourishing business and two children.

"I came to see you," she ended, "because I want you to tell Adrian I'm all right. I've often thought he might be worrying and blaming hisself, like."

She ended by giving Jenifer an invitation to go and see them. Jenifer went there the next week and found a stout kindly little greengrocer, a gay little fruit-shop, a spotless kitchen living-room and a baby asleep in a pram in the back yard. Evie was serving in the shop in an overall, with her sleeves rolled up to her elbows, laughing and chatting with her customers. Jenifer stayed to tea, for which Evie fried sausages and produced an enormous home-made cake. A little girl, ridiculously like Evie, came home from school just before they sat down, and in the middle the baby woke up and began to cry. Evie fed him unashamedly in her seat at the table, opening her blouse and showing her firm white breast. The stout kindly greengrocer was obviously devoted to her. Adrian made no comment when Jenifer told him of the visit.

For Jenifer the years had passed quickly and placidly. She was absorbed in her work (she had had several novels published) but not particularly ambitious, satisfied if each book maintained the reputation for readability that the first had won for her. Her life, with its friendships, reading, occasional country expeditions or visits to concerts and theatres, seemed to have settled down again into the rut into which it had been sinking before she met Derek.

"I'm a *real* old maid now," she said to herself with something of satisfaction. "I needn't try not to be any longer, because it's just come of its own accord, and I enjoy it. I always knew I should."

Each spring she went abroad, generally by herself, because she liked to wander about alone, exploring and watching the people. Every summer she came to stay with Sylvia. Sylvia's father had died in Paris last year. Bobby still appeared at intervals. His once slim figure had grown rather flabby, and he had now the look of a man too fond of the good things of life. He was always very friendly to Jenifer, but she knew that he had never forgiven her for the episode of the ring. She had made him look a fool in his own eyes, and he would never quite forget that.

There was something peculiarly restful about this old house and garden of Sylvia's. It was like entering a world that was cut off from all the stress and strain of modern life. Sylvia was frankly uninterested in everything outside it. Her husband and children and house and garden made up her entire existence. She was still beautiful, with the beauty of one of the old goddesses of Plenty, firm, rounded, deep-bosomed, with calm brown eyes and a tender happy mouth. While Jenifer was there her ordinary life seemed to vanish completely, and nothing in the whole world seemed to matter except that Billy should win his cricket colours this summer or that Pamela should get the double remove she hoped for.

Billy and Pamela came slowly up the drive arm-in-arm, conversing amicably. They were both going back to school the next day. On the day after they came home from school and on the day before they returned, they were always on terms of deep affection. For the rest of the holidays, between those two days, they carried on a fierce and unremitting warfare.

Bunty, the youngest boy, came out of the house and sat on the grass by Jenifer.

"Let's have a meeting, shall we?" he said.

"Yes, let's," she smiled.

Bunty's elder brothers and their friends had a secret society from which Bunty, on account of his tender age, was excluded. So Bunty had formed a secret society with Jenifer, and the two of them held "meetings," which consisted chiefly of desultory conversation about witches, a subject in which Bunty was passionately interested.

Soon the nurse appeared and carried Bunty off to bed, and after that Sylvia came out, wearing a rose-coloured tea-gown that enhanced her sun-flushed beauty.

"I've been bathing baby," she said, sitting down in the chair next Jenifer, "and she splashed me all over, so I thought I might as well change. By the way, I told you that Martin Barrow was coming to dinner, didn't I?"

"Yes . . . I needn't change just yet, need I? Have I met him before?"

"I don't think so. He's staying with his mother. She lives at Fallows, you know. He's rather nice. Peter likes him." She opened her work basket she was carrying and, taking out a pile of socks, began to stitch name-tapes on them.

"Let me help," said Jenifer. "Are they for Micky?"

Micky was going to his prep. school the next term.

"Yes," sighed Sylvia. "Isn't it terrible the way they all grow up? I simply hate the thought of Micky's going away."

"He'll be all right."

"Yes, but he'll be different. They always are. They're never quite the same after they've been to school."

"You'd hate them to stay the same really."

"Yes, I suppose I should . . . But I simply broke my heart when Billy went to school. I couldn't believe that anyone else could look after him or that he could look after himself. I don't really believe it now . . . Darling, let me break it gently. Pam's made the most hideous pincushion you ever saw for your birthday. It's a most ghastly purple covered with lace."

Jenifer laughed.

"I shall adore it. It will comfort me for being thirty-five. Getting on for forty."

"I shall never think of you as forty."

"Forty isn't really an age," said Jenifer. "It's a state of mind. Everyone feels forty at times, but ordinarily people of all ages just feel twenty or eighty according as things happen to be going with them."

"How ridiculous!" laughed Sylvia. "Did I tell you that Bobby

328

and I went down to Merrowvale last week to see about selling the Hall?"

"No. What was it like?"

"Terribly built round. We passed your old house. A woman with an Eton crop was looking out of the drawing-room window, smoking a cigarette in a holder about seven inches long. Old Mr Frewin's still living at The Firs. He looks very frail. We saw him out in his bath-chair, but he didn't know us. Ruby says he's getting senile."

"Was she there?"

"Yes, she'd come over on a visit, bringing four of her children. She's a walking mountain of fat, my dear, and her face shrieks 'Jewess' at you for miles. How she could ever have been pretty!"

"She was, though, wasn't she? Adrian adored her."

"So did Bobby."

"Was there anyone else there we knew?"

"Oh, Rosa's still going strong. Organising the Women's Institute and Girl Guides. We saw her in the village in her girl guide uniform. She looked more like a horse than ever. She told us that she was going to recite at the Women's Institute party that evening."

Peter came out and sat on the grass at Sylvia's feet. Like Sylvia he had grown somewhat stout with the years. Jenifer found him irritatingly slow and limited in outlook, and his Victorian attitude to his wife irked her feminist soul. Sylvia had surrendered her individuality and independence to him completely. She deferred to him and subjected all her plans to his wishes, yet she lived care-free and happy within the magic circle of his tenderness and devotion. Often Jenifer had difficulty in stifling a half-angry protest when he laid down the law with that touch of dogmatism that she found so exasperating. But she always did choke it down. Sylvia needed no champion.

He smiled proudly at his wife, then turned to Jenifer.

"She's looking well, isn't she?"

"She's looking beautiful," said Jenifer.

Sylvia laughed—her low sweet happy laugh.

"I'm getting horribly fat," she said. "I've even stopped trying not to."

"I hate scraggy women," said Peter.

They sat in silence, while the shadows of the cedar tree lengthened over the lawn.

"It is lovely here," said Jenifer dreamily. "When I'm away from it, I can't believe that it's really as lovely as it is."

"Why don't you come and live with us?" said Sylvia. "We're always asking you to. You could have a study of your own to write in. It can't be healthy living in London with all those motor cars."

Jenifer smiled and shook her head.

"No, it's just the contrast that makes it so perfect. I couldn't live in it. It's too peaceful to be lived in by ordinary people."

"Peaceful!" echoed Sylvia. "With Bunty falling from the tops of trees every other minute, and Pam riding her tricycle down the back stairs, and Billy nearly blowing up the house making fireworks!"

"Somehow that's part of the peace," said Jenifer.

Peter smiled. He liked Jenifer, but he always felt glad when her visits came to an end, so that he could be alone with Sylvia and the children again.

"Let me fetch you a wrap, sweetheart," he said to his wife. "It gets chilly when the shadows reach this end of the lawn."

"Thanks, darling," said Sylvia.

He rose and went indoors.

"How can you endure a wrap, Sylvia?" expostulated Jenifer. "It's boiling."

"I know," said Sylvia, "but he does so love fetching me wraps. He always looks so disappointed if I refuse. I think his father used to fetch his mother wraps."

Micky and Billy and Pam came tearing round the side of the house and flung themselves on the grass at Sylvia's feet, panting and scuffling, pouring out a breathless incoherent account of their adventures as Red Indians in the shrubbery.

"Bed-time, children," said Sylvia at last. "Go indoors quickly.

I'll come up and see you when you're in bed." They pleaded for another five minutes, but she shoo-ed them indoors relentlessly.

"Turning us away like dogs!" shouted Billy dramatically over his shoulder as they went. "Your own children!" The noise of their chattering and laughter died away in the distance. Peter came back with the wrap and put it over Sylvia's shoulders, and again they sat in silence, while the peace of the summer evening dropped like dew into Jenifer's soul. She roused herself with an effort.

"I ought to be going in to change," she said. "Who did you say was coming to dinner?"

"Martin Barrows," said Sylvia.

Chapter Thirty-One

The garden was gay with the light-coloured frocks of the women, who were moving to and fro over the lawn, among the formal beds of geraniums, calceolarias, and lobelias. Peter always liked to have formal beds of geraniums, calceolarias, and lobelias on the lawn, because they had been on the lawn of his old home and reminded him of his childhood. A nurse sat in a deck chair under the cedar tree sewing, while at her feet the baby crawled erratically on a striped rug, and Bunty, in a blue linen suit, was filling a little red bucket with grass.

It was the last day of Jenifer's visit (she was going back to London in the evening), and Sylvia had made it the occasion of the annual garden party to which all the neighbourhood was invited.

Jenifer sat on the terrace with a small group of Sylvia's friends. Her regular visits had made her almost one of them, as every year they had met her there and talked to her about their gardens and maids and little domestic happenings, and she had known their children from babyhood. They were comparing their young days with present days.

"I'm glad I'm pre-war," Jenifer was saying. "Nothing's as much fun as it used to be. Look at games. We played rottenly, but we enjoyed them. Nowadays the standard's so grimly professional that there isn't any room for the rabbit. It's the same with music and everything. I suppose it's partly the wireless."

"Our youth was certainly the heyday of the amateur performer," sighed one of Jenifer's contemporaries. "It had its drawbacks."

"Think of Rosa," said Sylvia, who had joined the group.

"I know," said Jenifer. "Some of them were awful, of course.

But at least people *did* something. They painted or sang or played or recited, and, even if they did it rottenly, they worked their little bit of creative instinct out of their systems. I'm sure that half the neurasthenia nowadays is due to the fact that people just don't do things because they know they can't do them professionally, and so they never get them off their chests. And they don't even make their own fun. They have to have it made for them. They go to the cinemas and listen to the wireless or prance about at night clubs. And it isn't really *fun*, even so. Do you remember what fun we used to have acting charades, Sylvia? People simply turn up their noses at that sort of thing nowadays. But we *did* something. We didn't just sit round like lumps, waiting for someone or something to entertain us."

"But think of refrigerators and electric light and motor cars and telephones," protested someone.

"They don't make you any *happier*," said Jenifer. "There's a certain thrill of novelty about them when you first get them, then they take their place in the background of your life and become just habits and leave you no more happy or unhappy than they found you. Some of them are definitely nuisances. People next door used to sing and play the piano, but they didn't go on all day and every day like the wireless. And your own home used to be a sort of refuge against the world, but it isn't any longer since the telephone came in. And, as for motor cars . . . look at the trail of ribbon roads and petrol pumps and week-end bungalows that they've left all over the country."

Sylvia laughed and made her way through her guests to the further end of the lawn, where tea was being prepared. The others began to discuss some new bungalows that were being built just outside the village. Jenifer leant back in her chair, and her eyes roved idly about the lawn in search of Martin Barrows. She had seen him every day for the past week. The children adored him, and he had joined in all their games and picnics. He had dined with them most evenings, and he and Peter and Sylvia and Jenifer had sat talking sometimes till almost midnight. For the first time in her life Jenifer had not been conscious of shyness on meeting a stranger. He didn't seem to be a stranger. Every note in his voice, every feature and movement, seemed familiar. Yet she did not want to talk to him, only to sit there with Sylvia and Peter—watching and listening. There was no excitement about the friendship, only a calm deep happiness that she had never known before Her eyes found him at last. He was talking to a girl in a pale pink dress and shady leghorn hat. He looked younger than his forty-five years, tall and well-built, his face rather thin, his hair turning grey at the temples. He was smiling now at something the girl in pink was saying. Jenifer watched him . . . and again thought how impossible it was to believe that she had only known him for a week. Perhaps that was just because he was so easy to talk to. He had the same gift of talking nonsense, of seeing the funny side of things, that had always attracted her in Bobby, but there was in him none of that irresponsibility that had been like a canker at the heart of Bobby's charm. There was, instead, a rock-like dependability and kindliness that reminded her of Peter. And yet he wasn't just a mixture of Bobby and Peter. He was himself . . . He was laughing again at something the girl in pink was saying, and a sharp unexpected pang shot through Jenifer's heart. It dismayed and frightened her, making her suddenly take stock of her position. She had drifted on from day to day, living in a sort of lazy dream, not realising what was happening to her, but that sharp pang showed her suddenly where she was drifting, and she took herself severely to task. It was a good thing she was going home today and would never see him again. You've no use for nonsense of that sort, she said to herself sternly. It's a waste of time and energy. A man like that would never look at you, and, anyway, you don't want him to. Your life's settled and full and happy. You'll only be miserable if you let this sort of thing come into it. You ought to have more sense at your age . . . She forced herself to watch him and the girl, with a friendly impersonal interest. They made a strikingly good-looking couple. The girl was about twenty-one, ravishingly pretty and exquisitely dressed. He looked as if he admired her. Jenifer tried to hope that he did. She would make a charming wife . . . Suddenly an overpowering longing came to her to get back to the old safe life she had known before this visit. She rose with an abrupt movement and went across the lawn towards Sylvia.

The man saw her leave the group, and, with a hasty word of excuse to the girl in pink, strode forward to intercept her. As he approached, the old shyness overwhelmed her, and with it a strange unreasoning terror. Her heart beating wildly, she turned from him just as he was on the point of speaking to her and began to talk to a large woman in green who stood near. The action must have seemed a deliberate insult to him. It had been, indeed, almost incredibly rude. And she didn't know why she'd done it . . . She had acted at the bidding of some inexplicable, irresistible instinct.

His coming to her like that might have had some vital significance, or it might have been a vague meaningless gesture of friendliness. Her response to it had been so decisive that she would never know. It was over. The whole thing was over. All she wanted to do now was to escape, to forget, to drown the whole memory in work.

The man had hesitated a moment, then returned to the girl in pink. Jenifer continued her journey across the lawn to Sylvia.

"Sylvia," she said, in a voice that was not quite steady, "do you mind if I go now? I can catch the earlier train if I do, and the other would make me so awfully late. It only means ordering the car now instead of later."

"Oh, darling, I'm sorry," said Sylvia. "I can't bear to lose even a few hours of you, but I do understand. I hate getting home late, too. Will you have to go now, this minute?"

"I'm afraid so . . . Goodbye, darling. Don't come. And say goodbye to people for me."

When she got home she tried to settle down to her work, but a strange restlessness possessed her, and she felt glad when Laurence rang up the next morning to say that he was coming to see her in the evening. He had been to Vienna on business and had only returned the day before. He glanced at her clock as usual immediately on entering the room.

"Can't stay very long, old girl," he said. "I've got to see a man on business at ten."

335

"What an hour to see anyone on business!"

"He's coming down from Manchester, and he can't get off early in the day."

"Do you ever sleep, Laurence?"

He smiled.

"Like a top. Every night."

She looked at him thoughtfully.

"I wish you'd get married."

He smiled again.

"Poor old Adrian's example isn't very encouraging, is it? Neither is Lorna's. I think we're best out of it, you and I."

"All the same, I wish you'd marry. I wish you'd marry a very frivolous and exacting wife, who'd make you waste lots of time and money taking her about to places."

"Thanks," he grinned.

"Have a cigarette . . . Well, how did you like Vienna?"

"I did several good strokes of business there."

"I didn't ask you that. I asked you how you liked it."

"I hardly saw it. I just dashed out there and back. I was doing business every minute of the time."

"*Laurie!* But it's the most marvellous country, isn't it?"

"It may be or not, for all I know. I hadn't time to look at it."

"Oh, Laurie!" she sighed.

He glanced again at the clock.

"You're clock's right, isn't it? I don't want to miss this fellow. How are the others? Seen them lately?"

"Not since I came back. I saw Lorna just before I went away."

"How was she?"

"Splendid."

"It's a wonder to me that she hasn't married again. I should think she could marry anyone she liked with her looks . . . I suppose she still cares for Mark. What a swine the fellow was! I'd like to have wrung his neck."

"And I went down to Bath and stayed a night at Adrian's boarding-house," went on Jenifer. "We pottered about together—Adrian loves pottering—and he had a little tea party for me, and we washed up his china afterwards. Adrian never allows anyone but himself to wash his china."

Laurence laughed.

"Poor old Adrian! When did you get back from Sylvia's?"

"Yesterday."

"Had a good time?"

"Yes . . ."

The depression deepened to a dull pain that became sharper and sharper . . . till it was almost unbearable. Her whole life seemed suddenly empty, her friendships unreal, her work meaningless. She remembered the old alliance with Laurence that had been the stay of her childhood and youth. It seemed the only possible refuge against this new danger that was threatening her. She caught her breath in a little frightened gasp.

"Laurence," she said, "are you going to be terribly busy just now?"

"I should think I am, my dear girl. I've got four weeks' headway to make up. Why?"

"Couldn't you leave everything and come away with me?"

He stared at her in amazement.

"What on earth——?"

"Do you remember that holiday we once had together years and years ago? I've always remembered it. Let's go away again like that. Just you and I. Let's get away from everything . . . Do, Laurie."

"But, my dear child"—he was still bewildered—"you must see that I can't."

"What do you mean by 'can't'? Do you mean that you'd lose some money?"

"I suppose so."

"But, Laurie, you're a rich man. You can afford to lose a lot of money."

"It's not exactly that——" he began slowly, but she interrupted him.

"Why do you go on slaving away just for money like this? The best part of your life's going, and you've got nothing to show for it but money. Laurie"—she was pleading earnestly, desperately, for him as well as for herself—"it isn't as if you cared for the things

337

money can buy. You don't. You hate luxury and ostentation and that sort of thing. You love simplicity. And yet you slave and slave away just for money that you don't need and don't want . . . You used to love the country. You never go near it now."

"One changes as one grows older, Jennie."

"But one oughtn't to. Not in that way. One ought to keep in touch with the country. It's terribly bad for one's soul not to. It sounds silly, but it's true. I *know* it's true. That's what that verse in the Psalms means: 'The mountains also shall bring peace, and the little hills righteousness unto the people . . .' Laurie, let everything else go and come away with me. We'll go to the Lake District and walk. Someone gave me the address of a farmhouse there miles away from anywhere. We could make it our headquarters and—and get sane again, both of us. *Do*, Laurie."

He glanced at the clock, then rose and stood looking down at her, bewildered, kindly, unconvinced.

"Sorry, old girl. I simply couldn't manage it. Some day"—vaguely—"we must try to fix up something, but just at present I can't possibly find the time . . . Well, I've got to be off now. Goodbye. See you again soon."

When he had gone Jenifer stood, gazing in front of her, a hard desperate brightness in her eyes. Nothing was left, not even Laurie. The things that had seemed to fill her life so completely before her visit to Sylvia had all deserted her, betrayed her . . . She was left with nothing but this strange heart-sick regret and longing. She set her teeth and squared her shoulders. She wouldn't be beaten, she'd conquer the alien force that was laying waste the purposed orderliness of her life. She wouldn't think of Martin. Determinedly she kept her thoughts away from him, but still she was, in some way she couldn't understand, conscious of him. He seemed to pervade her whole being, to be part of the air she breathed, to lie behind everything to which she turned her mind.

She took out her novel and tried to go on with it, but all her interest in it had vanished. She could hardly remember either characters or plot.

It was a relief when André called to see her the next day after tea. André was an old man now. His beard was silver, his face a network of wrinkles, but about his frail bent figure was still that air of elegance suggestive of a bygone age.

He greeted her with his pleasant smile, then stood looking at her critically.

"You do not look as if you had just come home from a holiday in the country, my child," he said.

She returned his smile unsteadily.

"I don't feel as if I had," she said. "Come and sit down and let me talk to you. I've been thinking hard all day and I want to talk about it . . ."

He sat down by the window.

"About what?" he said.

She took up her favourite position on the window seat, her hands clasped round her knees, gazing down at the river.

"Do you remember our talking about liberty once? I've been thinking about it, and, do you know, I've come to the conclusion that there isn't any such thing as liberty in the whole world. Look at us four. We're all in prison. And we've made our own prisons. We can't blame our parents, as so many people can. We've no one to blame but ourselves. We're barred and locked into our prisons, so that we can't get out however hard we try. There's Lorna. She's forced to work like a galley-slave, charming people she doesn't care two pins for and whose admiration she doesn't really want. She can't even go and have a meal in peace by herself in a restaurant, because she's got to be charming the waitress who waits on her or the woman who's come to sit at the same table. It means nothing to her now—all the thrill's gone—but she's got to go on doing it. She'll go on till she dies—in prison. Then there's Laurence. He might just as well be chained to a treadmill. He's missing everything in life worth having, he's killing himself, to make money that he doesn't want. And Adrian . . . all hedged in by his touchiness so that he can't do anything he really wants to do, his talents rusting because he can't get out of his prison to use them . . ."

"And you?" he said gently.

She answered in a low voice, her head turned away from him.

"I'm the worst of all. I've wanted liberty, and I've clung to it through thick and thin, and now it's become my prison, and I'm so fast in it that even if someone tries to open the door to free me I won't let them. I shut it in their faces."

There was a silence, and in the silence she saw Martin coming across the lawn to speak to her, saw herself turn away from him abruptly.

"You are right in saying that we make our own prisons," said André at last, "but you are wrong in saying that we cannot get out of them. That is what makes life so interesting, my child, that everyone can get out of their prisons if they want to."

"But they don't want to."

"They want to once they realise they are in them." He smiled again. "People are getting out of their prisons every day all around you, little Jenifer. There is no greater mistake than to take a too gloomy view of life. Life has its prisons, yes, but it has also its releases from prisons." He rose and patted her shoulder. "I, too, used to take a gloomy view of life and of my fellow-creatures. It is one of the privileges of youth to do so. As one grows older one becomes more optimistic. One still sees the prisons that people make for themselves, yes, but one also sees people forcing their way out of them, destroying them. The great thing to remember about life, little Jenifer, is that it is wholly unexpected. Unexpected always and at every turn. One cannot—thank God—lay down rules for it. One can never say what this man or that man will do or how this thing or that thing will turn out. One may say of a man 'He is in prison.' Yes. But one can never say 'He will be in prison tomorrow,' for tomorrow one may see him out of his prison dancing in the sunshine."

She laughed unsteadily, and they talked of impersonal topics till he took his leave.

As soon as he had gone, the telephone bell rang. Laurence's voice answered her.

"Is that you, Jennie? I say, I've been thinking over what you said. There's a lot in it. I feel I'd like to let everything go for a time and take that holiday with you."

"Oh, *Laurie!*"

"I'll need about a week to fix things up, and then I'll be able to come. Will you book rooms for us at that farmhouse you mentioned?"

"Oh, Laurie, how lovely! How long will you be able to stay?"

"I promise I'll manage a fortnight, no matter what crops up . . . Oh, by the way, I've just heard from Adrian."

"How is he?"

"He seems to have suddenly got tired of pottering about in boarding-houses. He's going to Paris to take up art again. He says he's really going to get down to it seriously this time."

"I'm glad."

"Well, you'll fix up about the rooms, won't you?"

"Rather! Goodbye."

"Goodbye."

As she put the receiver back a letter dropped through her letter-box. It was from Sylvia.

DARLING JENIFER,

I hope you got back safely. We do miss you so terribly. The enclosed daisy is from Bunty. He says you like them with pink edges, and he's spent all morning finding one with really pink edges for you.

Martin goes tomorrow to stay with some people in Scotland. He'll be in Town at the end of the month, and he's asked me for your address because he wants to look you up. He asked me if I thought you'd go to a show or something with him. I told him you probably would, if you weren't too busy. Well, I must stop now. I've promised Micky to have a game of Halma with him before he goes to bed.

All our love, darling,

SYLVIA

Jenifer stood, the letter in her hand, gazing into the distance.

THE END